THE MATE GAMES BOOK TWO

REJECTION

K. LORAINE

USA Today BESTSELLING AUTHOR

MEG ANNE

Cover Design by CReya-tive Book Cover Design

Edited by Mo Sytsma of Comma Sutra Editorial

For RuLove, our hashtag queen.
The #KingoftheDickSwingers is waiting for you.
Hold onto your panties, or don't.
We won't judge.

"It hurts, but it's okay...I'm used to it."

—— ANONYMOUS

REJECTION

AUTHOR'S NOTE

Rejection contains sexually explicit scenes, as well as mature and graphic content that is not suitable for all audiences. **Reader discretion is advised.**

Welcome to The Mate Games, a detailed list of content and trigger warnings is available on our website. For those of you who prefer to go in blind, keep reading.

ONE

KINGSTON

Seven years ago

Tonight my fate would be sealed forever with Sunday Fallon. I'd never met the girl, but my father had assured me she'd be the perfect mate, that she was meant for me. It had been agreed by our packs from the time she was born that she was destined to be mine, and now that we were nearly of age, we'd solidify our betrothal with this ritual run.

My nerves sang with anticipation as I caught her tantalizing scent on the air. It had to be her. Nothing had ever smelled so good. My wolf howled happily inside of me, eager to be free and to chase his mate through the meadow.

"What do I do?" I asked, staring at my father, who stood next to me at the base of the hill beyond.

He placed his large palm on my shoulder, and I knew it was the Alpha and not my father who answered. "Now you

1

go and claim what's yours. But go slow. She might be skittish."

I didn't want to scare her. I never wanted to do anything but care for her and make her feel safe. As her future Alpha, it was my job to protect her and the family we'd make together. I wouldn't let her down.

My hands shook as I readied myself to climb the hill and meet her at the top. Nervous energy burned through me at all the possibilities that lay ahead. What would she look like? How would her skin feel on mine? Would she be proud to call me hers?

I had no reason to believe she wouldn't. Girls had been coming around trying to get me to go for midnight runs with them since I'd hit my growth spurt a few years back. But knowing I had a mate, that she was waiting for me, I'd turned them all down, saving myself for her. Why give my attention to anyone else when the one fated for me was waiting?

My parents were fated mates, destined for each other, twin halves of the same soul. They told me the same was true for Sunday and me. The Seer had prophesied it.

Releasing a deep breath, I took the first step that would lead me to her. My heart raced with each stride until it felt like it had crawled up into my throat. I'd never been so nervous in my entire life.

She was already waiting for me when I reached the top, her chocolate hair falling in big loose waves down to shoulders bared by the thin straps of her white sundress. She must have caught my scent because her body stiffened and then she slowly turned her head toward me, her ocean-blue eyes widening as they met mine. My entire being called to her, the pull between us already intense and untameable. I'd never wanted anyone the way I wanted this creature.

"Sunday?" I asked stupidly because I had no other word left in my brain.

She nodded, her tongue darting out to wet her lips. "And you must be Kingston."

Her tone was sweet, innocent, and it caught me totally by surprise. I rubbed a hand over the back of my neck. "My parents weren't exactly subtle, were they?"

Her smile damn near knocked me on my ass. "I like it. Not just any guy could pull off a name like that, but it suits you."

Was it wrong of me to want to pull her into my arms right now and kiss her? That was exactly what I wanted. Not just to feel her soft body pressed against mine, but to taste those berry-colored lips. She was so fucking beautiful. More perfect than I'd even dared imagine . . . and I'd imagined a lot over the last seventeen years.

"You're so pretty," I whispered.

She blinked up at me, her cheeks turning a soft pink. Ducking her head, she tucked a piece of hair behind her ear. "So are you."

I couldn't stop my smile. "I promise I'll take care of you. Always. You don't have to be scared."

I wasn't sure if I imagined it or not, but her breaths sounded shaky. Like she was fighting against some intense emotion and struggling to regain control. Then she looked me in the eye, and the sweetness turned hard. "I'm not scared."

It was my turn to blink. This little wolf had bark. I liked it, but I didn't know what to do with it. My mother had always been so soft-spoken. How was I going to tame her?

"We'll have a good life together, Sunshine. I swear it. I'll do everything I can to make you happy."

I glanced down at my pack, all of them now in their

wolf forms as they watched and waited for me to shift and make my claim known. All she had to do was accept me.

They howled in unison as I undressed, closing my eyes and turning my face to the moon. "Accept me, Sunday. Be mine?" My voice was a harsh whisper, but I knew in my heart she was meant to be mine. We were fated. There was no way she'd say anything other than yes.

Then my entire world shattered as a single soul-crushing word left her lips.

"No."

~

Present Day

I ROLLED the blunt between my fingers, staring at the smoke as it curled up into the night and the paper burned away. Fuck, I hadn't even brought the thing to my lips. I was too wrapped up in the uneasy feeling balled up in my gut. Something was happening. Something strange. It had me tight and tense, on alert so high my jaw hurt from the pressure of my clenched teeth.

I took a deep drag, needing help to dull the blade of whatever disruption in the air was raising the hair on the back of my neck. Closing my eyes, I let my lungs fill, willing the drug to act fast as I exhaled. My head lightened as the smoke left me through my nose. Everything already blurred at the edges, taking on the hazy quality I'd been searching for. Dull. Empty. Lifeless. I didn't want to feel *her* anymore.

It had been hours since she and that vampire piece of

shit had gone downstairs to do God knows what. The pain of her choosing him over me yet again was enough to send me spiraling back into my old, familiar, self-destructive cycle.

Want her.

Crave her.

Touch her.

Crash and burn.

Repeat.

Over and over, one endless fucking loop of rejection. Good thing I was a masochist, because I couldn't seem to get enough of Sunday's brand of torture. No matter how much I willed myself to hate her, I couldn't stop my wolf, that fucking traitor, from wanting her.

I flicked the butt of my smoke to the ground and crushed it under the sole of my boot before heading back inside *Iniquity's* walls. I needed a distraction. If she was going to move on, so was I.

A fae warrior made eye contact as I stormed down the alleyway but wisely stepped aside as I stalked past and into the club. Bodies writhed on the dance floor, but I ignored everyone, intent only on getting downstairs and losing myself. If the drugs couldn't take the edge off, maybe a woman would.

"Kingston." A sexy as sin voice brushed over me, stopping me in my pursuit of oblivion. I turned around to find Lilith Duval standing mere inches from me. "You don't want to go down there, young wolf. She's not—"

"This isn't about her."

"Oh, but it is. Deny it all you want, but you forget, I can see what your deepest desire is. Darling, it's what I do. Trust me when I tell you, the last thing you need is to be near them right now."

"She's not mine." Even as I said it, my wolf raged within me. He screamed that I was wrong. That she *was* ours.

Lilith pursed her lips, eyeing me thoughtfully. "Lying to yourself will never get you what you want."

I snarled, my wolf too close to the surface to contain the reaction. "Just send two of your girls down to me. I'll be at my table."

"Something different this time, perhaps? I have a lovely blonde who just joined us. And you've never given a ginger the time of night. Or would you prefer the usual?"

"You know I'm only interested in brunettes."

That was the only way I could get it up. By pretending it was Sunday grinding her ass on me, rubbing her tits in my face. Anything else disrupted my fantasy and made it impossible for my body to relax enough to respond to a woman it didn't want.

"Make sure they smell like—"

"Lilacs. Of course." She smirked.

Something twisted deep inside my chest, the weakness of wanting the girls to look like *her* nagging at me. I couldn't live my life like this, always wanting someone I couldn't have, but there was nothing to be done about it. At least, not until I could work her out of my system. Right now, this was what I needed. A Sunday Fallon detox.

Even as the thought sparked in my brain, it didn't ring true. But I'd gotten this far on willful ignorance and stubborn perseverance. Why change now?

I slid into the corner booth I had frequented before Sunday disrupted my whole life again and waited for my companions for the night to join me. My gaze kept drifting to the darkened hallway that led to the private rooms.

She was in one of those with *him*. What were they doing? What was *he* doing to her? I clenched my fists until

6

my knuckles popped as I tried to drive away memories of her dominating me as we worked to find her wolf.

Fuck, but I'd loved that. I'd fucked my fist to the memory more times than I cared to admit. No one had ever bested me or my wolf, but I'd bared my throat and practically begged for more.

And now I was rock-hard and aching. Goddammit.

I'd never been turned on by the thought of a woman taking control of me or my pleasure, but when I pictured Sunday having her way with me, my cock started to weep. I was so fucking broken.

Two brunettes scented heavily with lilac approached me, momentarily distracting me from my torture session. They were all wrong. The perfume was cloying, leaving a bitter taste in my mouth even from a distance. Their rail-thin bodies lacked Sunday's lush curves, and their hair was fucking fake. I sighed as they slid in on either side of the booth. It would be the only way to get some kind of relief. Pretending they were her.

"What do you want, baby?" one of them asked.

"Don't fucking talk. Are you new here?"

The other slid her palm over my already flagging erection. I gritted my teeth, fighting the impulse to fling her hand away. She moved to kiss me, and I jerked my chin away from her. "Not on the mouth," I growled.

This wasn't working.

I closed my eyes and let the fantasy of Sunday take over like the addict I was. The hands touching me became hers, the scent filling my nose, her cunt, and just like that, my dick thickened, and desire came roaring back. If I let myself, I could almost feel her wolf calling for mine. I could pretend she'd bared her throat and given in, letting me mark her and mate her.

Something inside me went taut, not with need but with an agonizing pain so intense I gasped. My eyes flew open, and I shoved both women off me, not caring that I'd practically thrown them onto the ground.

Something was very fucking wrong with Sunday.

I struggled for breath, my mouth filling with fangs as my wolf clawed its way to the surface. The brittle feeling in my chest intensified to the point I knew something irreplaceable was about to snap.

And then it did.

She was gone.

Sunday was gone, and the pull I'd always felt between us was severed. The only way that could be possible was if she'd left this plane of existence. She was my fated mate. Even if she never accepted me, I'd be able to sense her. Nothing but death could come between us.

I fucking broke.

With a roar, I stood and sent the table flying.

No.

No!

I refused to accept it. She couldn't be dead. But if she wasn't, that meant she'd severed the thread tying us together. No matter how many times she'd rejected me, I couldn't stand the thought that she'd found a way to permanently break the bond between us.

I didn't know which was harder to accept. But either way, I needed to know for sure.

With a precarious grip on my self-control, I stalked toward the hallway. I'd get to her. I'd see the truth with my own eyes.

And if it was her corpse I found, I would burn this entire fucking world to the ground.

TWO

"Ready to go home, dove?" Noah asked, smiling at me as I finished stepping into my heels. He held out his hand for me as I stood.

"As long as I'm going with you, I don't care where we end up."

He tugged me close and kissed me hard. "Careful. When you say things like that, it makes me want to chain you to my bed and never let you out of my sight."

"Sounds like fun."

His eyes darkened with hunger, and he shook his head. "Not an ounce of self-preservation in you."

"Why bother when you offer exactly what I want?"

Noah closed his eyes and exhaled heavily. "I have to get you back. I promised the good priest we'd stop breaking curfew."

"We wouldn't want to get in trouble," I murmured, but my thoughts drifted to being punished by Caleb and what that might look like. Even after the several rounds I'd just gone with Noah, my body was already tingling with arousal once more.

As we approached the now open door, Noah's entire demeanor changed. He tensed, his body going statue still. "Stop where you are, Sunday. Something's not right."

My blood ran cold. "What?"

"They've come for me. The Council."

"Why?"

"Callista Donoghue." He turned, his eyes wild. "Stay here. Whatever you do, do not leave this room. Do not come looking for me. I'll return to you when I can."

"Noah, you're scaring me."

He took my face in his hands, sealing his lips over mine in a kiss that felt entirely too final.

Like it was goodbye.

"Noah—"

"I love you, Sunday. No matter what happens, never doubt it for a second. I have to go. Stay here."

"What? No! I'm not letting you leave me again."

His gaze turned hard and serious. "I'll never willingly leave you. Remember that. But you have to stay here. You can't be with me for what's about to happen. I need you to understand that. Trust me, please?"

After everything we'd just shared, how could I not? He was my mate. He'd marked me. I could feel the depth of his love for me even now.

"Okay," I said, confusion and fear making my voice small. I didn't like anything about this, but the least I could do was try and understand.

He gave me one more bruising kiss, then dropped his head to press his lips over the place he'd marked me. "Mine," he whispered. "Always."

Then he pushed me back into the room and left, the door sealing shut and completely disappearing into the wall. Immediate anxiety shot through my veins as the unnerving feeling of being trapped—caged—unfurled in my gut. He didn't say anything about not being able to leave ever.

Instinct took over, and I clawed at the wall where the door used to be.

"Let me out! Somebody, please, let me out!"

I spun around, my eyes scanning every corner of the room in search of an exit. Even the window was gone.

Fuck.

My heart was racing, panic taking hold of me. I knew I was safe in here, but all I could think about was being trapped, unable to help Noah with whatever fight he was about to be in. Because the only reason he'd do this to me had to involve a risk of death.

I reached out with my mind, trying to sense him, to use our bond so I could at least communicate with him. All I got was a wall of nothing. He'd blocked me out. I made him a promise that I'd never hide my thoughts from him, and then he went and raised a shield between us? Dread pushed away the panic I felt from being locked in this room. I couldn't lose him, but that seemed like exactly what was happening.

My heart felt like it was breaking. Was I assuming the worst, or were things really as dire as they seemed? No. I wasn't imagining this. Noah wouldn't leave me, not after we'd just completed our bond, unless it was life-threatening.

I closed my eyes, freeing the tears I'd been working to keep at bay. *Stop crying, Sunday. You're not going to get out of here by doing that.* I needed to seek control over my emotions because freaking out wouldn't help me right now. I needed to try and calm down. I needed to think.

The bed loomed in the space, a reminder of everything

we'd shared tonight, but now it didn't resemble the one where Noah had so freely given his love and devotion. Where the canopy of gauzy fabric had been was nothing more than a plain wall, and the romantic setting in the room had changed as well.

Noah was gone. So was the love nest we'd created.

I wanted it all back.

The air shifted behind me, and I spun to find the door returned to its place and slowly opening.

"Noah—"

But it wasn't my vampire prince.

Standing in the doorway, amber eyes glowing, chest heaving, looking as if he was a breath away from losing control was . . . Kingston.

His gaze snagged on mine and he sucked in a huge breath, relief replacing all other emotion in his eyes. Then he dropped to knees, his hands gripping my hips, dragging me toward him as he buried his face against my stomach, breathing me in.

He trembled against me. Shaking like a child who'd just lost his dearest possession.

I stared down at him, confusion swirling in my mind. "Kingston? What are you doing?"

"You're not dead," he whispered, voice low and tight. "I saw Thorne's bloody shirt, and I thought—" Rising to his full height, he never stopped touching me. "Fuck, Sunday. You're not dead."

I frowned. "No. I'm not."

Then his gaze hardened, all traces of softness leaving him. "You're. Not. Dead."

The air in the room crackled with tension as those three words filled the space with menace rather than relief.

"Kingston, what—"

Fingers digging into my shoulders, he pulled me to him before taking a long inhale of my scent. "Ruined."

Anger shot through my confusion, and I shoved him away. "Fuck you."

"You smell like *him*."

I was starting to understand his reaction now. His wolf was *pissed*. Well, so was I, and I wasn't going to let him bully me over my choice.

"I hear that happens when you have a fuckfest. You'd know."

"No. This isn't something you can wash away. He's *inside* you. You ruined yourself for a leech."

The bond. He could smell my bond with Noah. I didn't back down. Not for one second. "He's my mate."

"*I* am your mate! Me. Not him."

"This is ridiculous. I'm not having this fight with you again, Kingston. Get out of my way." But as I pushed past the six-foot-something snarling alpha male beside me to get to the door, it was gone.

Again.

"Motherfucker!" I screamed, slamming my fist into the concrete wall and crying out when pain shot through me.

"Looks like this room wants us to stay together a little longer, Sunshine. At least *it* knows you're my mate."

I rounded on him. "Yeah? Well, you and this room can go fuck yourselves because I've already chosen my mate. Newsflash? It wasn't you."

Even as I spoke the words, I knew they weren't entirely true. I was *trying* to hurt him now. Just like he hurt me by saying I was ruined.

"Fuck you, Sunday."

"Back at you, asshole. How much more obvious can I make this for you?" Grabbing my hair in my fist, I lifted it off my neck, exposing the still healing bite wound from Noah. "It's him. Not you."

His big body began shaking, eyes flaring a searing yellow rather than the warm hazel I was used to. The energy in the room sizzled with wild, feral magic I'd only felt when in the presence of an Alpha about to shift. Fur sprouted down his arms, and his teeth lengthened into fangs.

God, he would tear me apart if he couldn't get control of himself. Way to go, Sunday. Poke the angry wolf.

A door appeared. Not the one leading to the hallway, but a new one. Right where my shadow man's window should be. As I watched, it slid open, revealing a dark, misty forest.

A deep growl rumbled in Kingston's throat, pulling my focus back to him.

Frantic eyes met mine, and he let out one terrifying word.

"Run."

CHAPTER
THREE
KINGSTON

Everything in me screamed with the need to chase her as I stood in the doorway, palms braced on either side of the frame, both to keep me in and hold me back from my instincts.

To mark her.

To mate her.

To make her mine.

Just like that fucking bloodsucker had. Tremors rocked my body as I worked to stave off the shift a bit longer. Otherwise, this would be over before it began, and now that the time was upon me, I wanted to draw it out. After all, the first time only happened once.

"Run fast, Sunday. Because when I catch you, I don't know what I'll be."

I'd seen the moment she realized what was happening, that flicker of fear burning away to be immediately replaced by desire. She may not want me, but her wolf sure did. I could smell it all over her.

My Sunshine wasn't afraid of me, but she knew that

standing around when an Alpha was about to lose control was a surefire way to be backed into a corner and claimed. Either for the night, or in her case, forever.

I watched her disappear into the moonlit woods, her hair streaming behind her like a banner. She had to know I'd find her and catch her no matter how far she ran, but maybe if I gave her more time, she'd come to this willingly. As much as I wanted her, I also needed her to say yes.

I managed to wait a dozen more heartbeats before I lost control. Fur rippled down my limbs as my bones bent and snapped, rearranging themselves into my beast. A pain I welcomed like an old friend shot through me as I shifted. The world changed, coming to life in a way only wild creatures born from magic and moonlight could appreciate.

All I knew was her scent. She was my target. I would find her.

I let out a howl as a warning her time was up.

Run as fast as you can, Sunshine. The big bad wolf is coming for you. But I promise I'll make it good.

Coherent thoughts were lost to me then, as instinct overrode reason and my wolf broke through.

Mate her.

Mount her.

Fuck her.

Breed her.

I shook my head, trying to keep my mind clear, to cling to the human side of myself for Sunday. Because if he took control, I'd be trapped until he got what he wanted. But it was a lost cause because my body launched forward as the animal pushed away all that was left of the man. It was always a fight to hold onto my consciousness, but the wolf won every single time.

Mine.

Run.

Chase.

Claim.

Branches turned into dark blurs as my beast surged forward toward the scent of lilacs and honey and the earthy aroma of moss. Under all that, the stench of vampire.

Erase him.

Leave my mark.

Fill her with me.

My hackles rose, and a deep growl came from my chest. I had to get to her; there was no other option. I wouldn't lose her again. Claws dug into the earth with every stride that brought me closer to her.

Even with the extra time, I caught up to her easily, her two legs no match for my four. A human—even part shifter—would never outrun a wolf.

My prey glanced over her shoulder, her glowing amber eyes wide, not with terror, but excitement. Her wolf was as in control of her as mine was of me, even if she couldn't shift into her true form.

"Who's a pretty puppy?" she teased as she began to run faster, her voice flowing through my mind, sending a wave of need and devotion through me. This was my mate, loud and clear. She wanted me. *"Come get me, my king. I've been waiting for you to free me from this prison."*

Yes.

Finally.

My queen.

My mate.

Mine.

My hind legs tensed, then released, springing me forward in a leap that ate up the distance between us with little effort. I was on her before she knew what had happened, my front paws hitting the back of her shoulders and sending us both tumbling to the ground. She twisted in the air and landed on her back with me on top of her, pinning her with my body.

Instead of resisting, she arched into me, burying her hands into my fur, letting out a feral purr, the wolf inside her desperate for me.

I rubbed my face across her shoulders and throat, marking her with my scent, soothing her and promising I'd release her. Promising her everything without saying a word.

She was heady, intoxicating, completely addictive as I breathed her in. It was the closest our beasts had ever been, and the knowledge brought with it a tidal wave of rightness. We were meant to be together. Made for each other. Nothing would ever get between us again.

Especially not a dirty leech.

Sunday. Was. Mine.

She whimpered as I brought my teeth to her neck, something in the sound stopping me. A flicker of my annoying human side sparked to life, demanding attention. As he came to the forefront of our mind, Sunday's eyes bled from amber to blue, her wolf also losing the battle for control.

No.

I let out a snarl, fighting against my human.

I would not lose her again. She was so close. Right here. Within my reach. My body shifted from wolf to man, but I wouldn't let him ruin this for us. I held onto what little I could.

We needed her.

She needed us.

Nothing else mattered.

She rolled her head to the side, baring her throat to me, showing me what she needed the most. I clamped my fangs over the spot I should've marked years ago and took what was mine.

She would never be free of me now.

FOUR

W hite-hot pain mixed with pleasure raced through me, setting my nerves alight and dragging a wild moan from my throat. I was coming. Oh, my God, he wasn't anywhere near my clit, and I was coming so hard stars flashed behind my eyes.

"Oh, God," I cried. "Yes."

"Fuck, Sunshine." Kingston's voice was tinged with sorrow and a mixture of raging lust and pride as he shuddered and jerked in my arms, spilling himself on my belly.

He moved to get off me, but I wrapped my legs around his hips and pulled him closer. I needed this. My wolf wanted more of him. We weren't done.

"What is this feeling?"

"It's your wolf, welcoming her mate home."

"I like it."

"Me too. So fucking much, baby."

He peppered kisses along my neck and throat and then licked up the side, paying extra attention to the spot where he'd marked me. I shuddered, sensation detonating inside me, flooding me with arousal. All I knew in this moment was how great my need for my mate was. I'd denied him for so long. Too long. This was right, how it was supposed to be.

Us.

Together.

Joined.

Even though I was still coming down from my first climax, I was ready for another. From the feel of his erection, so was he.

"Kingston, please."

He rolled his hips, groaning against my throat, teeth nipping the sensitive flesh and nearly making me come apart from that alone. "God, I want you. I've wanted you for so long."

"Yes." My voice was a husky whisper. All I could focus on was Kingston. Nothing else existed.

Not the visions.

Not the choice I was supposed to make.

Only pleasure.

Only instinct.

Only *him*.

My king.

His rock-hard cock nudged between my legs, and he snarled at the barrier of my soaked panties. "These fucking things. A waste of fabric."

He reached down, lightly dragging sharp claws across my skin, making me shiver. Sliding his hand between my legs, he shredded the lace.

I gasped at the feel of those claws so near my sensitive flesh.

"I'm going to make you mine now. Don't stop me. Please." The raw vulnerability in his statement had me arching my back and bringing my pussy up to kiss the tip of him.

"I don't want you to stop." I couldn't tell if it was my wolf answering or me.

"Fuck," he groaned, sliding in a little deeper.

The cool metal of his piercing tickled my slick entrance. With each new inch, a subtle glide of another bar against my internal walls sent tingles arcing across my body. I'd never felt so full, and I said a prayer of thanks to whoever invented the Jacob's ladder. So much pressure in the best possible sense of the word. We'd only just started, and I was teetering on the brink.

"Can you take more?"

Alarm shot through me. "There's more?"

He let out a hoarse laugh which only pushed him in deeper. "Baby, I'm only halfway there." His eyes locked with mine and something passed between us. "Can you take it?"

We were made for him.

My wolf's thoughts merged with mine, and my body responded with a flood of slick, easing his way deeper inside.

"I guess that's a yes."

"I'll tell you if it's too much. Don't stop. I want all of you."

His eyes flared with animalistic hunger. I needed him inside me, all the way to the hilt. It would hurt so good.

"Jesus, God, please," I moaned, digging my nails into the skin of his back.

His laughter washed across my throat. "Just wait. It gets better."

He pulled out of me, leaving me whining for him, desperate to be filled all the way by my mate.

"On your hands and knees for me, Sunshine. I'm going

to fuck you now." He ran his teeth along the length of my neck. "Hard."

I did, instinct causing me to lift my ass in the air and bare my pussy for him. Instead of shoving my dress up my body, he tore the fabric off.

"Normally I'd approve of the lingerie, but not tonight. I'm going to mount you under the moon, and I don't want anything between us."

His claws shredded the bustier, and just like that, I was naked in the forest, about to be fucked hard by an Alpha wolf. My Alpha wolf.

Kingston gripped my hips, but it wasn't his dick at my entrance.

"Just one taste," he whispered.

Then he licked straight up my seam, his tongue piercing adding a delicious friction as he slid all the way across my clit, then back . . . back . . . back . . . oh, God. He went there. I moaned and rocked my hips as the barbell added more than I could handle to this experience.

"Fuck me, Kingston."

He shifted behind me, fisting one hand in my hair and jerking my neck back. "I'm going to fuck you so hard you never forget who you belong to, Sunshine. Or that you're the one who asked for it."

"Well, stop talking about it and do it then."

He slapped my ass so hard, my inner walls fluttered with the barest hint of climax.

"You don't ever have to beg me to fuck you, Sunday. I was born for it."

And then he sank all the way in, in one brutal thrust. I cried out from the pleasure of his cock driving inside me, sliding over all those delicious new nerve endings he helped me discover. But when he pulled back and those perfect fucking piercings dragged along my most sensitive spots, I trembled from the stimulation. He slammed home over and over, hitting me deep and keeping his promise. I would never forget.

His grunts of pleasure joined mine. It was frantic. Desperate. Rough.

Everything I needed.

"I'm not going to last if you keep moving back like that," he bit out. "I'm going to fill you with my cum until it's leaking from you for days."

"Yes."

"I'm going to breed you so hard."

"Yes."

He grabbed me by my hair and pulled me up until my back was resting against his chest. Then he released the tangled strands and slid his palm to my throat, his other hand moving from my hip and down so that his palm pressed against my belly and the tip of his middle finger brushed over my aching clit.

"Come for your Alpha, Sunday. Come all over my cock and scream my name."

The words alone would have been enough, but then he dragged his teeth along my neck and bit down on the tender flesh he'd already marked. Sparks burst through me, a wave of deep pleasure that curled my toes. I screamed his name until my voice went ragged. If he hadn't been holding me up, I would have collapsed in a heap on the forest floor.

He was right there with me, his cries of pleasure harmonizing with mine in the night.

I felt him lengthen, harden even more, as he jerked inside me and filled me just like he promised.

"Take it all, Sunday. It's yours." He kissed the mark on my neck. "I'm yours."

I shivered in his arms, still too undone by the intensity of my orgasm to respond.

"Don't worry," he whispered, running his palm over my breast and tweaking my nipple. "I'll tell Thorne you've come to your senses."

That one statement sent my wolf back into hiding. My head cleared, and everything came into sharp focus. What had I just let him do? I brought my fingertips to the place he'd marked me, the same place Noah had sealed our mate bond.

"Get the fuck off me."

He released me as though I'd slapped him.

"What the hell? Are you actually trying to do a one-eighty on me while my cum is literally dripping down your thigh?"

I was shaking, reeling from the truth of what had just happened. I'd wanted it. Begged for it even. But I hadn't been the one in control. My wolf had been pushing me. It was the first time I'd ever been wholly at the mercy of the animal inside of me.

"You took advantage."

"You begged for it."

"You knew it wasn't me. You knew it was my wolf."

"You. Are. Your. Wolf."

It was a truth I wasn't ready to accept. One I *couldn't* accept.

"No," I said, shaking my head. "No."

"Deny it all you want, sweetheart. You were wet for me. You still are. Your wolf wants this, which means so do you. Stop trying to fight it."

"I'm not fighting anything."

Kingston got right in my face. "Yes, you fucking are. Otherwise you wouldn't be pulling this bullshit right now.

You know what you want. I was inside you. I could feel it. You might be able to lie to yourself, but you will never be able to lie to me. I know the truth now."

Tremors racked my body, my skin itching and burning. Too tight. Too hot. My heart raced so hard it hurt. Hammering filled my head, like horse's hooves pounding hard and fast. Just like when Noah had given me his mating mark and my pulse overwhelmed my senses. I was dying. I was having a heart attack at twenty-three after being mated by two different men in the same night and then fucked to within an inch of my life in the middle of some magical forest.

I gasped, struggling to draw in breath as the tremors turned to what felt an awful lot like a seizure. "Kingston," I whimpered.

"Ride it out. Don't fight it. It always hurts more when you try to resist."

"Resist what?"

But he wasn't a man any longer. A beautiful wolf stared at me, his gaze easing some of the agony as my bones shifted. I realized then what was taking place.

My wolf was coming, and she was ready to play.

It's about fucking time.

"Yes. It fucking is."

And then I was on my hands—paws—on the ground, human no more.

For the first time ever, I was free.

FIVE

W as there a bird in my room? Multiple birds?

"Moira," I groaned, "leave the tweety birds alone."

I squeezed my eyes shut against the sunlight pouring in through my window. I ached. My limbs were heavy and everything felt . . . weird. Not to mention my hips felt like they'd spent the night riding a mechanical bull. Without a break. For hours.

"Did we go to a cowboy bar last night?" I muttered, hoping Moira would get the hint and magic me up some coffee.

"Nope, but you definitely took me for a ride." Kingston's voice brought me out of my sleepy haze. His large, warm palm wrapped around my waist, tucking me into his very naked body.

His very naked *awake* body.

I jerked upright, scooting away from him and that pierced weapon of ass destruction, not paying any attention to the pine needles embedded in my skin.

"Where the fuck are we? Why are you naked?"

Smirking, he cocked a brow. "You're naked too."

Instinctively I covered my bits as well as possible and tried to force my gaze away from . . . what had he named his dick? Jacob?

He groaned, sitting up and putting all those delicious muscles on display as he ran a hand through his tousled hair. "Oh, come on, Sunshine. It's too early for that shit. Don't start playing the amnesia game with me again."

"I'm not playing a game . . ."

"Don't worry. It'll come to you. The first couple of times the wolf takes hold can be rough."

Oh, God. The wolf. I shifted.

Closing my eyes, I let the memories wash over me. It had been so strange to give over control to her, to let her out. My consciousness was still there, but it was like I'd been in the backseat of my own mind, forced to watch as someone else took the wheel. I could hear her thoughts— my thoughts?—merging with my own. They were primal. Raw. Intense. Everything in me driven by instinct and need. There was no logic. No rationalization. Just living completely in the moment.

I blushed.

One long, neverending sexual moment.

How many times had I come last night? How many times had *Kingston* made me come?

He snickered. "There it is."

Turning away, I stalked through the forest, no idea where I was headed but desperate to put some space between the two of us. The fleshy part between my neck and shoulder throbbed.

I lifted my hand, gingerly inspecting the area and

wincing as the soft contact brought a deep ache and then a ripple of unexpected pleasure. I would not groan in front of an aroused werewolf.

"That's my mark, baby. You like it, don't you?"

I glared at him. "You mean Noah's mark."

"Not anymore. I'm your mate. My bite overrides any other. And just to be sure, I put mine right over his. Think of it like a new tattoo covering up the mistake you made."

"Fuck off, Kingston. You didn't get rid of my bond with him."

The air shifted as he approached, one hand sliding around my throat, his jutting cock pressing into the small of my back. His lips brushed the mark, and I had to bite the inside of my cheek to stop my moan.

"I claimed you, and you loved it."

"I wouldn't go that far," I grumbled, shoving out of his arms. "More like a lapse in judgment. A moment of weakness. Something that will never happen again."

"Yes, it fucking will. I could bend you over right now and sink inside your willing pussy. I can smell the slick dripping down your thighs."

My clit throbbed, and my puritanical inner voice couldn't help but berate me. *Whore.*

What he'd said was absolutely true, but it didn't matter what my traitorous body wanted. This could not happen again. Even if my stupid hormones begged for his touch.

Dick drunk. That's what I was. Could you blame me? The things he did with that monster between his legs were legendary.

"Get off me, Kingston."

"Oh, I'll get off. Anytime, anywhere you need me, baby."

I elbowed him in the gut but ended up hurting myself more

than him. He let out a soft grunt of annoyance. That's it? I'd hoped for something more dramatic. My whole lower arm went numb, like I'd cracked my funny bone against a brick wall.

Taking my hair in his fist, he jerked my head back. "Quit sending me mixed signals, Sunshine. If you want to play rough, we can play rough." He nuzzled my neck right over my mark, making my knees buckle as arousal shot straight through me. Then he growled low in my ear. "But I think after last night that pretty pussy of yours might need to take it easy."

I shuddered as pleasure collected in my clit, racing there from that goddamned mark. "I can still feel him, you know."

"My cock? Yeah, Jake has that effect."

The ache deep inside me was testament to that. But I'd never give him the satisfaction of saying so out loud.

"No. I can feel Noah. He's still connected to me, just as strong as ever. You might have put your mark over his, but you didn't do a damn thing to get rid of him."

Kingston pulled me around. His eyes narrowed with suspicion as he glared down at me. "You're fucking with me."

"No, asshole. I'm telling you the truth."

He shook his head. "It's not possible. You can't be mated to different men at the same time. And everyone knows fated mate bonds trump all others. You're mine."

"I don't know what to tell you. But whatever happens next, it's not going to involve you making some primal claim over me. Now tell me how to get back to the university because I stink of dirt and sweat and . . . werewolf jizz."

Emotion flickered in the back of his gaze. Uncertainty, maybe a hint of vulnerability. "If you think you can wash me off you, it's never gonna happen, Sunshine. I'm inside you. Just like my cum. You'll never get me out."

"More like a stain."

He bared his teeth at that but surprised me by not forcing the issue further. "Let's see if you can shift on demand."

"Shift?" I repeated, confused by the change in topic.

"Unless you want to waltz back on campus in your birthday suit?" He raised one perfect brow. "I suppose you could ride on my back. I wouldn't mind your fingers in my fur."

Fuck. What if I couldn't shift? I sure as shit didn't want to walk onto campus naked. I'd done that once before. And I definitely didn't want to ride on the back of Kingston's wolf like we were in some sort of sex parade. That was a line I didn't want to cross.

"How do I—"

Before the question left my lips, my wolf was right there, waiting for me. I could feel her now, sitting beneath the surface. Ready to come to my aid.

"The last time hurt. Will this one?" I hated how timid my voice was, but I wasn't like him. Pain for the sake of pain didn't get me off. Now a good hard spanking delivered by Caleb? That was different.

"The first time always hurts. This will be easier." He stared into my eyes. "I'm your Alpha. Let me help you."

"Wait. I want to try it on my own. You won't always be around. I can't be dependent on you."

"But you can. I'm not going to leave you, Sunday."

"Everyone leaves."

"I'm not your father, your mother, or that fucking vampire. You're the one who walked away from me. I've never chosen anyone but you."

"This isn't about Noah."

It killed me that he was right. All the people that were supposed to be there for me left me without a second thought. But not him. Kingston had always been there. Waiting for me to change my mind. Waiting for me to choose him. Maybe he'd be the one person I really could count on.

I had to shove the thought away, not ready for the tidal wave of emotions that crashed into me right along with it.

"I want to do this on my own. Or at least try. So, what do I need to do?"

He sighed, defeated by my stubbornness. "Close your eyes and ask her to take over."

So I did. I wouldn't admit—even now—that he was helping me. I closed my eyes and she was there, ready for her moment. He was right; the pain wasn't so bad this time. It was more of a hard stretch rather than the cracking of bones.

My senses sharpened as my body rearranged itself. Kingston was everywhere, overwhelming me. The pounding of his pulse as he stared down at me was loud in my ears, thrumming hot and wild. And as I watched, he joined me, seamlessly transitioning from man to beast. It was beautiful and breathtaking.

All the conflicted feelings I had about him fell to the wayside in this form. As a wolf, the only thing I saw when I looked at him was my mate.

Kingston nuzzled me and then gave me a gentle shove with his head, herding me in the direction he wanted me to go.

Play.

Chase.

Run.

I nipped at him. He might think he was the Alpha, but I was the one in control. He could try to lead, but if he wanted me to follow, he'd have to catch me first.

IT'S ALL WELL and good to run through the woods as a wolf. It's another thing entirely to walk into Blackthorne Hall buck naked with blood, cum, and dirt smeared all over you. I was just thankful it was still early morning and most of the students would be sleeping it off after a night of partying.

Kingston strode down the hallway with a proud smile, dick swinging, completely unfazed. Fucking asshole. Not that there was a whole lot to be embarrassed about when your body looked like *that*.

Stop looking. He doesn't need any more of an ego boost.

I tore my focus from the swinging appendage and headed up the stairs, knowing full well my ass was in his face.

He leaned forward, biting one cheek just hard enough to sting but not enough to leave a mark. I hoped. And fuck if it didn't set off more of those little flutters.

I whirled around, digging my finger into his chest. "Behave."

"Make me."

"I hate you."

"No, you don't, Sunshine." He was all wolfish charm and arrogance, which only annoyed me further.

"Go away."

"Never."

Brimming with frustration, I shook my head and continued up the stairs. I reached the landing on the second floor and headed for the final set of steps that would take me home where I belonged. But he gripped my hand and tugged me toward the doorway that would take us out of the stairwell.

"Come on. You're coming with me."

"What? No. Just because my wolf let you fuck me doesn't me I'm suddenly going to live with you in your man cave, Kingston."

"Yeah, you are."

"No. I'm not."

"Fine, I'll arrange for us to move into mated pair housing. It's really not fair to my roommate to subject him to me railing you every night anyway."

My blood simmered, but I'd be lying if I said it was with anger. The fucking fuck.

"Listen to me very closely, Kingston—"

"You called me your king last night," he said in a low, seductive purr. "Do you know how hard that makes me?"

More flutters. I really needed to have a talk with my vagina. This was getting ridiculous. *Focus, Fallon.*

"I live with Moira. That is not going to change. She's my person. She keeps me sane. You should be nicer to her because she keeps me from killing you. In fact, you should *want* me to live with her. But I don't really care what you want, because it's what *I* want. So that's where I'm going."

"I guess I can share space with the witch. We can put a broom out when we're . . . busy."

I rolled my eyes and had to fight a smile at the visual of Moira waiting in the hall while Kingston had his way with me. She'd be more likely to take the broom and shove it up his ass. He'd probably like it.

"I'm going to *my* room. Without you. You are going to

fuck off and leave me alone because if you snarl down my neck for one more minute, I am going to castrate you."

He playfully covered his junk. "Don't listen to the mean wolf, Jake. She's just hungry. She'll feel better after she eats something."

When I reached the third floor, I shoved open the door and spun around as he followed me out into the hallway. I hated how confident he was. How he knew I was fighting with my own instinct and was sure my wolf would win. "Go to your room," I growled.

"Not until I'm sure you get home safely."

"I'm literally five feet from my door."

"Doesn't matter."

I shook my head, not sure what I was feeling anymore other than twisted in knots. Then I scowled. "You just want to watch my ass."

"Guilty as charged. It's a really nice ass. I like how it jiggles. Especially when I—"

The door swung open, interrupting him before he could finish or I could knock. Not like I had anywhere to store my key in everything I wasn't wearing. Moira stared at me, eyes wide, hair inky black and styled in a spiky pixie cut.

"Oh. My. God. What the fuck?" Her gaze traveled past me and landed on Kingston. "Get in here. It looks like we're skipping our morning yoga so you can explain what"—she gestured to my naked body—"this is."

"Don't worry, she's nice and stretched from all our exercise last night."

I glowered at him. "I'm in my room. You can go."

"I'll leave after the door is shut. Gotta get in every second that ass is visible. Maybe next time, I'll come in the back door."

"We don't have a—" Moira started. Then her eyes widened.

Thoroughly mortified, I grabbed the door. "Goodbye, Kingston."

I slammed it in his face with enough force to make the whole thing tremble for several seconds after I released it.

"Girl . . ."

I looked at my roommate and shook my head. "Have I told you lately how much I fucking hate shifters?"

CHAPTER
SIX
SUNDAY

I couldn't look at Moira because I knew I'd have to answer her questions if I gave her my attention. But the witch wasn't giving me an inch. She reached out and plucked a dried leaf off my ass before holding it up and twirling it between her fingers.

"Ignore me all you want, but I'm not the one using werewolf cum for random forest arts and crafts. What is this? A souvenir? Were you trying to make a skirt?"

"Keep it up, Belladonna. You can go on my shit list too."

Moira blew me a kiss. "You love me. Now spill."

Shrugging, I snagged my robe off the back of the door and covered myself. Nudity between wolves wasn't a big deal, but between friends . . .

"What's there to tell? We fucked."

She huffed and rolled her eyes. "Got that. You reek of sex and pheromones. Explain how that happened, please. You left with Thorne and came back with Kingston. How'd you get from point A to point giant D?" She made a face. "Seriously, if it's that big relaxed, does it turn into a damn balloon when it's inflated? It's like a fucking pool noodle.

How did it even fit . . . never mind, we can get to the physics of it all later."

My cheeks burned. "You know what, I need to shower. Then we can talk this over, okay? You said I reek. That means it's time to take care of this situation."

"At least he put it all over you and not inside you. I'm not ready to be a godmother for real. I'm too young."

"Yeah . . ."

"Sunday Fallon, you clearly didn't use protection, but tell me you weren't stupid enough to let him finish inside you? You do know that's how little wolf pups are made, don't you?"

The memory of him bare, filling me like he was meant to, had a shiver rolling down my spine. "It's fine. I'm not . . . fertile right now. Noah said so last night."

Her eyebrows shot up. "He can *tell*? Is that a creepy vamp thing?"

"Maybe? I didn't ask for specifics."

"Wait. You and Noah were together last night, then you let Kingston take you to Poundtown."

I bit my lower lip. "When you say it that way, it sounds bad."

"Dangerous is more the word I'm going for. You've got a cocktail of vampire spunk and werewolf baby batter sloshing around in there, and you needed a vamp to tell you you wouldn't get pregnant. I just think maybe you should be more cautious before riding any more disco sticks."

"You're right." Embarrassment crept through me as her words sank in. "I don't know anything about being a wolf. I just . . . let instinct take over. He marked me and she took hold. There wasn't time for any other considerations."

Moira held up a hand to stop my flow of words. "Hold on. Let me see if I'm understanding this correctly. You didn't just fuck him last night, you mated him? Officially?" She reached over and tugged the neck of my robe to the side. "Is that what this is?"

I wanted to pull away, protect my mark from her gaze, but I resisted the urge. "Yes."

She gently brushed a finger over the space, her eyes narrowing. "Wait. Why are there two sets of bite marks?"

"Um . . . because Noah and I completed our mate bond last night before . . ."

Moira held up her hands, two white flags appearing out of thin air as she started waving them around. "Stop right there. I'm officially calling a flag on the play. Was there something in the air last night, or did you just decide to up and mate every willing Tom, Dick, and Hairy Bastard you found? Kidding, no judgment here. But . . . how is that even possible? Why the fuck would Thorne let you out of his sight long enough for Kingston to do his thing?"

God, this was complicated. "It was only supposed to be Noah. I made my choice and it was him. But something happened after. He left me there—"

"He *left* you? I'm going to murder him." A wooden stake appeared in her hand, replacing one of the flags.

"He locked me in the room because something bad was going down. And now he's gone. I can feel it. He's not anywhere close by. He asked me to wait until the room let me out. He asked me to trust him," I finished lamely.

"Okay, so where did King of the Dick Swingers come into this?"

"When the door opened, he was the one standing there. And well . . . you pretty much know everything that happened after that."

"I can't believe you just rolled over and spread your legs

for him then and there. Something else must have led to that."

I toyed with the sash of my robe, not wanting to meet her eyes. "He saw my mark from Noah and kind of lost it. Then a doorway appeared, and there was a forest, and I ran . . . and eventually my wolf submitted to him."

Moira threw her remaining flag in the air, letting it flutter to the floor, her expression filled with shock. "Your *wolf*. As in, you *shifted*? Way to bury the lead, Fallon."

"It was amazing. Running through the woods, him chasing me, being completely free. As much as I hate him, I also need to be with him. She's a big part of me."

"First of all, you don't hate him. There's hate fucking, and then there's the sex spree the two of you were apparently on all night. Second of all, holy shit, girl, that is amazing! I'm so happy for you. But also . . . your life is a fucking mess. What are you going to do? How will you deal with two mates? If you thought they were possessive assholes before, that's nothing compared to what they're going to be like now."

Unease curled in my chest. "I'm not sure it's going to be a problem. Noah . . . he might not come back."

"He said he would, right?"

"Yes."

"Then he'll come back. He always does."

I hadn't realized how badly I needed someone else to say it. I'd been able to stave off the anxiety gnawing at me because of everything else going on, but the truth was, I was scared. Noah and I had this big, life-changing moment and then bam, he took off again. I rubbed at my chest, still feeling him through our bond, though it was diminished.

"I hope so. And I hope he doesn't hate me for what I did with Kingston."

"He won't. He already accepted that you have a unique relationship with more than one man. Noah Blackthorne loves you, and that means loving all of you."

I sighed and ran a hand through my hair, wincing when my fingers caught on a huge tangle wrapped around a twig. "I really need to shower. Can we pick this up later?"

She nodded and gave me a gentle smile. "I'll get the wine."

"It's not even nine in the morning."

"Whiskey and tea then."

I offered her a grateful smile, my heart brimming with love and affection for her. Without thinking, I reached out, pulling her into a tight hug. "What would I do without you?"

She hugged me back, giving me a couple pats before pulling away. "Probably kick ass and take names, but don't worry. You won't have to test the theory anytime soon. Now scoot. You definitely need that shower." She waved dramatically in front of her nose. "I'm a cat person."

I spent thirty minutes under the spray of hot water, washing out the dirt and dried leaves that had found a home in my hair, then taking extra care to scrub my skin free of Kingston.

Part of me mourned the loss of the wild, free woman I'd been in the forest with him. The evidence of our night together was more than just the side effects of crazy amazing sex. It was proof that for the first time ever, I'd been exactly who I was born to be. How could I go back to just being plain ol' Sunday Fallon? How did I put that newfound part of myself away?

After dressing in a pair of soft yoga pants and a slouchy shirt that wouldn't put pressure on my tender bite mark—

well, marks—I returned to the main room we shared. "There. No more stinky wolf."

Moira crinkled her nose. "Better, but you still smell like him. And a little bit like Thorne too. It's weird."

I frowned, lifting my arm and giving myself a sniff. "I don't smell anything. I mean, besides deodorant and my shampoo."

"Trust me, girl, you stink. But it's okay. I think it's growing on me. You still have that lilac thing, but there's something spicy about it. Like pine and," she tapped her finger to her lips as she searched her mind. Snapping, she added, "Bergamot. That's it."

She handed me a steaming mug of tea liberally dosed with whiskey. "Sit down," she said. "I want to try something."

"Okay." I knew she heard the hesitance in my voice because she gave me a look that said, *you trust Kingston but not me?*

"While you were washing the forest off you, I had an idea. We might be able to find your vampire." Her brows dropped in mock accusation as I perked up. "Oh, so now you're interested."

"How?"

"You're bonded with him. That means we can probably link to him together and do a little . . . astral projection." She rubbed her hands together.

"You can do that?"

She smirked. "Of course I can. I think."

I raised a brow. "You think? Is it safe?"

"Sure . . ."

"Moira . . ."

She gave me an impish grin. "I've never died before, so I say yes. Do you want to find him or not, Fallon?"

That shut me and my protests right up. "Let's do this."

We sat on the floor across from each other, lotus style, knees touching. "Okay, hold up your hands."

I did as she instructed and she mirrored my pose, pressing her palms to mine. "Now what?"

"Close your eyes and focus on him. Bring him to the forefront of your mind."

It wasn't hard. Noah was always there. I smelled him first, that spicy floral scent that was somehow still masculine and dark. My body felt light, loose, untethered, but I could still feel Moira's warm palms anchoring me at the same time.

"Moira?"

"I'm right here," she replied, her voice taking on a dreamy quality. "I can see everything you're seeing."

"That's . . . creepy."

"Hey, it's the only way this works. Now, do you feel your bond?"

"Yes."

"What's it feel like? Explain it to me."

I didn't have the words right away. To me, it just felt like . . . Noah. But as I focused on trying to describe it to her, I realized there was something else. Like a little hook in my chest with an invisible rope attached to it.

"It's a pull. We're . . . tied together."

"Okay, I can work with this. Reach for the rope. Use it as your guide to him."

I glanced down my body and saw it, this translucent line, faintly glowing red and very clearly Noah. Carefully, as though I might break the bond, I wrapped my hand around it, first one, then the other, and pulled myself toward him.

"This is weird."

She laughed, light and melodic. "Yeah, I know. You're

there, but you're also grounded in the real world. Just close your eyes and keep going. It's your spirit moving, not you. It'll take forever if you keep your eyes open. Your brain will insist on being literal as you move, and we don't need to worry about doors and roads. Where we're going, we don't need those things."

Nodding, I shut my eyes and focused on the draw to my mate. Trusting Moira's words, I took a breath and followed the pull until his feelings washed over me. Completing me.

"Sunday?" His voice was broken and rough, filled with despair. "You can't be here. What is this?"

My eyes flew open. There he was, just as devastatingly handsome and perfect as always. Instead of the jail cell I'd been expecting, we were in the middle of a richly furnished bedroom. Confusion ate away at my happiness upon seeing him. "Where are we?"

"Salem."

"Massachusetts?"

He nodded. "My uncle's home, Midnight Rose Manor."

"Wait a second, you said it was about the Council. You walked out on me for an impromptu family reunion? What the hell, Noah?"

He stood from the chair where he'd been brooding and blurred to me, reaching out to cup my face between his palms. I wanted his touch so badly. I leaned forward, ready to close this gap between us, and then nothing. His hands went straight through me.

"What the bloody hell is going on?" His eyes widened. "Sunday, oh, God. Are you . . . did something happen to you? Are you a ghost?"

"Don't be so dramatic, Blackthorne. It's just a little astral projection, not a case of death. Our bodies are perfectly fine back at school. Sunday here wanted to pop in for a visit. She was worried about you." Moira shimmered into existence next to me, casting a disapproving glance around Noah's room. "Not that she should have been, apparently."

"I thought . . . When you left, you made it seem like something terrible was happening, Noah. This looks like the opposite of bad. It's a bed and breakfast."

"You don't understand, love. It's my only choice right now."

"To live in a luxurious mansion with your uncle? Sounds pretty terrible. How noble of you," Moira said, snorting.

"It was that or allow them to get to Sunday. This is the only way to keep her out of the Council's reach."

"Noah, what are you talking about?"

He dragged a hand over his face. "This isn't a holiday. This is a cell. It's a beautiful cell, but it's still a prison. Those windows are barred with silver. The door too. My uncle is keeping me here by my request—"

"Your *request*?"

"Yes, in the room they use to help rehabilitate vampires who go mad after losing their mates. It's the only place I could go that would keep me from you until I figure out how to fix this."

"Fix what?"

"The Council learned of my involvement in Callista's death. Her family wants my head . . . literally. My father and uncle are working hard to smooth matters over, but in the meantime, I'm stuck here. If anyone discovers you, what you are to me, you could be in a world of danger. They will not hesitate to use you to get to me." He took a pained breath, closing his eyes. "Which is why you must leave. You can't be here, Sunday. You can't do this again. It's too much of a risk. The only thing helping me get through this is knowing you are safe."

Guilt hit me hard. Here he was, sacrificing his freedom for our bond, and I'd let Kingston mark me. "Noah, I need to tell you—"

"I can smell him on you." His voice was tight. "Did he mark you?"

Moira's eyes widened, and she backed away even though there was nothing he could do that would hurt her. "I'll just be over here checking out your reading material." The witch moved toward the bookcase in the far corner, pretending she wasn't listening.

I tugged down the neck of my shirt, baring my mark to him. "Yes."

"That bastard," he growled. "He defiled our mark. Remind me to pay him back for that when I return."

"I'm sorry. I didn't stop him. I barely realized he was doing it. He purposely tried to break our bond."

"Don't apologize. And clearly the bond isn't broken. It's not even scratched. But the fact that he wanted to erase me from you . . . I'll just have to marry you when this is over. He won't be able to sully that."

"You keep threatening me with marriage."

"Magic pussy," Moira muttered under her breath.

"I know. I'm trying to wear you down until you're amiable to the suggestion."

"How are we going to fix this?" I hated the wobble in my voice. "We can't get married if everyone wants to kill us."

"Let me worry about the Council." He sighed, balling his hands into fists. "I might hate the bastard, but it's not a terrible thing Kingston completed your bond. There's no one I'd trust more with your life than another of your mates. He'll keep you safe—or die trying."

"You . . . you want me to stay mated to him?"

"I want you alive and well when I come back. That's all that matters to me."

"Noah . . ." I didn't know what else to say.

He stiffened, his focus darting to the door. "You have to go. Right bloody now."

"But—"

"Don't fucking argue, Sunday. Go. Now."

I opened my mouth, wanting to at least tell him I loved him, that I'd be waiting for him. But before I could say anything, Moira grabbed my hands, and we were back in our dorm room.

She stared at me, eyes wide. "Well . . . that was interesting."

CHAPTER
SEVEN

ALEK

I stood in the back of the sanctuary of Father Gallagher's mockery of a classroom. The vampire had taken over for Professor Sanderson after she sustained life-threatening injuries during the attack at the ball. For most, that would mean simply going to her lecture hall and taking her place, but not for the priest. He insisted on this desecrated church as the location for any class he taught. It was bad enough the weather had turned and our daylight hours were waning, but now we had to trudge through rain and wind to get here as well.

I hadn't seen Sunny since Thorne had taken her the other night. I sent a few messages, but other than half-hearted assurances that she was fine, she hadn't really spoken to me. I couldn't quite shake the feeling that something was wrong. Thankfully, she had to attend class which meant she couldn't keep avoiding me.

"Mr. Nordson, I'm not sure how things are done where you come from, but here we *sit* for a lecture."

Father Gallagher glowered from his desk, the rest of the class going silent from the pews where they sat.

"I'm not confident I'll leave these rickety benches intact if I sit here, Father. They weren't built to Novasgardian standards."

There were a few snickers around the church, but annoyance flared in the good priest's eyes. "Sit, Nordson. And if you fall on your arse, we'll see about different accommodations."

My gaze flicked to the doorway in search of Sunday. Why wasn't she here? Thorne wasn't here either. A spark of jealousy ignited in my chest. She must be with him. Lost to the bond no one could deny was building between them.

Kingston sat front and center, one leg kicked out like he was just waiting for Father Gallagher to walk by so he could trip him. I wondered if he was feeling the same sense of loss I was.

"Mr. Nordson, I won't ask you—" he stopped mid-sentence when the tall doors creaked open, and Sunday stumbled through with Moira at her side.

They were both dry, likely thanks to some sort of spell the witch provided, but Sunday was shivering. Her eyes were glassy in her too-pale face. She looked unwell. Not so much so that I feared for her safety, but enough that I wondered why she was out of bed. But also, shifters were usually immune to common human ailments. It wasn't normal for ones such as us to suffer this way.

"Sunny—" I reached for her, but the priest interrupted.

"Thank you for gracing us with your presence, Miss Fallon. You're late. That's just earned you another session."

She sighed, and her shoulders straightened. "With you?"

He narrowed his gaze. "Aye. With me. Would you like to make it two?"

Her eyes narrowed right back. "You know I love it when you make me count for you, Father."

Murmurs filtered through the class, causing Sunny's face to pale even more. Clearly, she realized she'd crossed a line.

"Sit," Father Gallagher said. "All of you."

Sunday glanced around the room, searching for an available seat. When her gaze landed on Kingston, she scowled. He lifted an arm, tossing it across the back of the pew in clear invitation for her to join him. She ignored him, turned, and selected a pew on the opposite side of the room in the back.

Moira and I followed after her, making eye contact and sharing an unspoken seating arrangement. As Sunday settled in the middle of the bench, I took a place on her right side, offering her a smile and a wink as I did. Moira walked around to the other side of the row, ready to take her place on Sunday's left so she'd be flanked by friends. Something wasn't right with her, and neither of us wanted to leave her vulnerable.

Unfortunately, we weren't the only ones with a plan. Kingston rose from his seat at the front of the church and stalked to our pew, not bothering to say anything as he claimed the spot on the other side of Sunday before Moira could.

She huffed at him. "Bad dog."

"If you're quite done," Father Gallagher said, having watched the entire incident play out.

I couldn't help but notice he had been acting oddly ever since Sunday set foot inside the church. He was rubbing at a spot on his chest, his expression troubled. My gaze darted between him and Sunday, wondering why the priest was so interested in her.

In fact, tension filled the church, an edginess that was undeniable. Something strange was in the air, settling in my chest and filling me with restless unease.

I shifted uncomfortably in my seat as Father Gallagher began his lesson. I didn't hear a word he said. With each passing second, unease mounted. It didn't help that Sunday continued to tremble beside me. Her small hands balled into tight fists as she fought against uncontrollable shivers.

"Sunny, what's wrong?" I whispered when I couldn't take her discomfort any longer.

"Nothing. I'm fine." She offered me a tight smile.

"You're not. You have a fever."

She shook her head. "No. Shifters don't get fevers."

"She's fine." Kingston wrapped one large arm around her shoulders, pulling her into his side. "She just needs her mate to warm her."

My brows snapped together. I'd known he was her mate, of course. But last time we'd spoken, she'd rejected the bond they were supposed to share. So what had changed between now and then? She didn't deny his words, nor was she trying to pull away. But she wasn't happy about his possessive claim, either.

"Sunny?"

"It's fine, Alek."

"Balder's foreskin, Sunday. If you tell me it's fine one more time, I'm going to pick you up and carry you out of here. You are clearly not fine. Stop lying to me. I thought . . ." I shook my head, hating that she was pushing me away. Locking me out. I had no claim on her, but we were friends, at the very least. I deserved to be treated as more than an annoying, clingy little boy.

Sunday gaped at me, biting down on her lower lip and shaking her head.

"Yeah, *Alek*. It's fine." Kingston began running his fingers over her collar, leaning closer and inhaling her scent. "Fuck, you smell better today than you did yesterday."

My chest rumbled, darkness clouding my vision. How had he wormed his way into her circle without me noticing? Was this why she'd been avoiding me? And then, the fucker tugged her collar away and exposed the skin at the juncture of her throat and shoulder. A deep purple bruise marred her perfect flesh. He nuzzled her hair as his fingers played across the mark, across the undeniable *bite mark*.

I stood so fast I shoved the pew in front of us forward. The students seated there let out shocked cries and managed to bring their legs up in time to avoid being crushed.

"Nordson!" Father Gallagher shouted. "What the devil is this?"

"Class is over," I growled.

"Not until I dismiss you lot."

I stared him down. "Well?"

"Dismissed."

After casting a few worried glances between a smirking shifter, annoyed priest, and enraged me, the rest of the class scattered.

"What the hell is going on?" Father Gallagher demanded.

I pointed a shaking finger at Kingston, knowing that my control was slipping. I hadn't felt this angry . . . this unhinged . . . ever. If I didn't spill the fucker's blood—soon —I was going to lose it completely.

"He forced his mating mark on her. He fucking raped her."

The wood of the pew Father Gallagher had his hands on groaned under his grip.

"What?" Sunday said, her eyes going wide. "Alek, no—"

"Look at her. She's shaking. He's forcing her to be with him." I reached over and tugged her shirt to the side, exposing the ugly bruise. "Look at what he did to her. Tell me that's what a mating mark is supposed to look like. Because to my eyes, that's not something one gives their lover. That's something a rapist leaves on their victim."

Before I'd finished speaking, Father Gallagher blurred, taking Kingston by the throat and shoving him up against the wall. Stone dust danced through the air from the force of the impact. The priest's voice was ice-cold and filled with menace as he snarled, "If you touched her against her will, there is nothing in heaven or hell that will keep me from exacting a swift and deadly punishment upon you, Kingston Farrell."

"Not if I get to him first," I said, my own voice pulsing with rage.

"Um . . . as much as I'm really enjoying this caveman moment, Kingston didn't force me. My wolf asked for it."

"*You* asked for it," Kingston said. "In fact, I remember the words *please, don't stop,* and *yes* coming from your lips more than once."

Crimson stained Sunday's cheeks as she glared at him from her place beside me. "So what if I did. It was the heat of the moment. I already told you, my wolf took over. I wasn't exactly in control of myself."

Kingston jerked in the priest's hold, trying to shove him off. Sunday's denial, more than any of our threats, had gotten beneath his skin.

"Don't you fucking dare start that shit again, Sunshine.

I was there. I know exactly what happened. Stop denying your part in it."

She stood, swaying on her feet a little before gaining her balance. "I need to go. I don't feel well, and you three are just making it worse."

Moira took her arm, and they exited the pew. Unable to stop myself, I made to follow, but the witch shot me a look. "Leave her alone. She's not feeling good. I'll take care of her. You three figure your shit out, will ya?"

Chastened, I forced myself to let them leave. I needed time with the wolf anyway.

Father Gallagher finally released him once the women were gone. Kingston straightened his shirt, throwing us both a dark look.

"I don't know what crawled up your asses, but you can stop looking at me like that. You heard her. It was consensual."

"Coercion isn't consent."

"She wasn't complaining when I made her come on my cock repeatedly."

The priest glared at him. "Technicalities won't save you in the eyes of the Lord."

"Good thing I don't care about what he thinks."

I stepped forward. "Maybe you'll care about what my fist thinks." I let my fist fly into his face, breaking his nose and sending blood spraying everywhere. "You take advantage of her again, dog, and I will rip your spine free of your body and hang you with it. Do you understand me? Mated or not, you will not abuse her."

Kingston spat blood on the stone floor of the church, his eyes blazing. "I'd never hurt her."

"You call that wound on her neck *not* hurting her?"

"I gave her what she wanted. What she needed. She

finally shifted, for fuck's sake. Her wolf needed me. But I agree, something is off with her. It might have to do with the fact that I put my mark over Thorne's."

"Thorne marked her too?" I asked, but Father Gallagher seemed unfazed, like he somehow knew.

"The fanged fuck should've known better. He could've chosen anywhere else on her body. He had to put it on the spot used by shifters. He was trying to make a point."

"Maybe so, but he didn't try to rip her throat out while doing it. What's your excuse?"

"I didn't. She's fine."

"She is not."

"Enough. You two are worse than a couple of children in a pissing match. I need to do some research on this. You're both going to steer clear of her until we figure out why she's ill." Father Gallagher stared daggers at us as he spoke.

"You can't keep me from her. She's mine. I claimed her." Kingston's words were a low snarl.

"I'll tell you one final time, Farrell. Do not push me. She is sick, and it's your doing. Until I find the cure, you will not touch her. If you'd like to keep your prick where it is, you'll keep it out of her."

Kingston bared his teeth but didn't speak. I could already tell he was planning on going against the priest's edict, which meant the wolf had just earned himself a place at the top of my shit list. If he so much as set foot near Sunday right now, I'd rip his head off and put it on a pike outside my door as a warning to anyone who had a similar plan.

It seemed like the people of Ravenscroft didn't understand who they were dealing with.

But they were about to.

EIGHT

"Hell's bells, Sunday, you need to get in bed. You're sick. You need rest," Moira snapped as she came back into our room, arms filled with supplies for what I was sure would be more tea for me. She'd practically been pouring her witchy brews down my throat, and with every swallow, I grew fuzzy-headed and sleepy, my dreams more disturbing each time I closed my eyes.

"Moira, it's been three days," I whined. "I don't want to sleep anymore. If I don't get some fresh air soon, I'm going to lose my mind."

"You think you're going to lose your mind? Alek has been checking in every few hours. I finally set a spell on him so he'd go away. He's a disaster about you being sick."

"Why haven't you let him in?"

"Because you're giving off some serious fuck me vibes when you're sleeping. The guy can only stay so strong. He might be mad at me when he realizes I wiped his memory of you being sick, but I'll pay the price."

"You can do that?"

She winked. "Try me."

"Then you can magic a way for me to get out of here."

"Sweetie, you can barely sit up without swaying. I'm not letting you leave this room."

"Do you really think you can stop me?"

Moira laughed. "A feather could stop you. Hell, a slight breeze could."

"I'll be fine. I'm just run down. Your sleeping tea makes me have the weirdest dreams. I don't like it. I can't rest when I'm afraid of what I'll do when I close my eyes."

Moira's eyes widened. "Excuse me? Say that again."

"I'm having funky dreams, witch. And it's your fault."

"Sunday, you shouldn't be dreaming at all. These teas are made to induce healing sleep. You should be out cold."

"Well . . . you got the recipe wrong. Turn in your wand and cauldron, your shit's busted."

With a little harrumph, she set her ingredients down on the counter and shook her head. "Nope. You're the one who's busted. What kind of dreams are you having?"

I blushed, a wild and untamed desire unfurling inside my chest. "All kinds. Some good, but some . . . scary."

"Is your mother visiting you again?"

"Again implies she stopped. She still comes to me every night."

"What does she say?"

"Keep going. I'm almost there. They're coming for me. Yadda yadda yadda. Embrace my destiny." I waved my hand. "The usual BS."

She chewed on her thumbnail, a show of anxiety I hadn't seen from her before. "Who are they?"

I threw my hands up in the air, almost unbalancing myself. *Dammit. Moira was right. I was weak as shit.*

"I saw that."

"Hush, witch."

"So, who are they?"

"You think I know? She never tells me anything specific. It's all cryptic nonsense to me."

Moira began to grind various and sundry items with her mortar and pestle as she muttered to herself. "What does she want? Why is she coming to you? How do we make the dreams stop?"

"Are you talking to me, or would you two like to be alone?"

"Since I'm the only one capable of helping you, you might want to reconsider your tone, sweet cheeks. I could easily turn this into a poison."

"You would never."

"You don't know that. I could have an evil plan. *I* could be they," she said in her imitation of a doomsday voice, which for Moira sounded more like a Disney princess.

"What if *they* are the guys?"

She stopped what she was doing, thinking it over and then shaking her head. "No. My visions were definitive. The guys are here to *help* you, not hurt you. Whoever *they* are, they aren't the ones gunning for you. Well, your pussy maybe, but that's about it."

"Stop it." But even those last few words made a wave of unwelcome lust crash over me. Fuck. I was a disaster. I had to get over this bug before I started humping the furniture. "Fine, give me the tea. I need to heal or whatever."

"Praise Jesus, hallelujah."

"You don't believe in Jesus."

"Sure I do. He was a nice boy. Good beard, bad tan lines."

I cocked a brow. "I feel like we're crossing some kind of blasphemy line."

69

"Maybe we should call your priest, and he can swing by and consecrate you." She glanced over her shoulder. "Or exorcise you. You might be possessed, come to think of it."

"You need to work on your material. You already used that joke."

"Have I? Huh. I must be slipping. I'll do better next time."

"Please don't."

Moira wiggled her fingers, and a cup and saucer appeared in her free hand. She dumped the ground herbs into a little silk bag and plopped it into the steaming water. "Give it five minutes, then drink it all down. Try to clear your mind before you go under. Focus on healing. Not anything or *anyone* else."

"You act like I'm doing this on purpose. I don't *want* to think about them. They just take over and do . . . " I couldn't finish my thought. It only added to the ridiculous arousal I shouldn't be feeling.

"Well, don't stop there," Moira said, putting her chin on her fist. "You're just getting to the good part."

"Stuff. They do stuff."

"Sexy stuff? Kinky stuff?" She lowered her voice dramatically and leaned closer. "Butt stuff?"

"All of the above?" I winced, my own voice barely above a whisper as I added, "As a group."

"Oh, my stars and stones. She's out-kinked me. The girl has one night of wild wolf sex, and I've been out-kinked."

I attempted to toss a pillow at her head, but I was so weak it just fell limply to the floor.

Moira eyed it with a pointed smirk.

I huffed. "It's not like the dreams are real."

"It could be. I bet they'd do everything you wanted. All

you have to do is crook your sexy little finger at them, and they'd probably suck each other off while you watched."

Sweat broke out over my entire body at the thought. *Fuck why was that so sexy?* I pictured Noah and Kingston caressing each other while they touched me and wondered what might happen if I asked them to play out the fantasy for me.

"And they'd for sure spit roast you. Or do the Eiffel Tower or whatever it's called." She started listing a myriad of positions on her fingers. "DP. Two-in-one. Hotdogs down a hallway?"

"Moira, do you even know what you're talking about right now? I'm pretty sure that doesn't mean what you think it means."

"Says you." She winked. "From the sound of your dreams, there's some fun stuff to be explored, and a lot of it pushes the boundaries. My sweet baby angel is all grown up and a kink queen."

"We need to change the subject."

But my protest was as weak as my body, my husky voice betraying my interest in the topic. My mind had practically turned into a twenty-four-seven porn site where my four guys and I were the stars.

Oh, the things they'd done to me in those dreams. I shivered. "Is the tea ready?"

She glanced down at the liquid. "Yep. Drink it all. Don't leave a drop. And this time, try to keep the moans down."

I crawled under my blanket. "Oh, God. Tell me you made that up." Pulling the blanket down so only my eyes showed, I gave her my most pleading look.

"You're a talker, honey. What can I say?" She smirked, handing me the teacup. I downed the contents with a grimace. I almost spit it back in her face when she sweetly added, "We're gonna have to chat about Caleb and the pussy slaps once you feel better."

Fuck. How the hell was I going to explain that? But already my eyelids were drooping and my limbs growing heavy. I yawned. "Moira?"

"Yeah, sweets?"

"Turn off the light?"

The room went dark, and only the sound of the wind outside and the rain hitting our window remained. "Moira?" I asked again, groggy and slurring even on the single word.

"Yes, Sunday?"

"He only spanked me once. But I liked it."

"That's my girl."

The dark reminded me of the confessional, which was probably why I continued with my confession. "I'd let him do it again if he wanted to . . . but he doesn't."

"I doubt that. Once you spank a pussy you never go back."

I snorted and wanted to reply, but the darkness pulled me under, a heavy cloak muffling light and sound and the world.

I was aware enough to feel her soft lips brush my forehead and hear her whisper, "Sleep tight, wolfy. If you don't feel better soon, I'll have to bring in reinforcements."

"So fucking wet and tight. I love how your cunt takes my cock, dove." Noah groaned deep in his chest, driving inside me with each bruising thrust of his hips.

"Yes, Noah. God, I need it."

"You know I'll give you anything you need. And right now, that's a good hard fuck. Isn't it, dove?"

He was so beautiful, hovering over me, eyes blazing with amber fire. I moaned and lifted my hips to meet his thrusts. "More. Give me more."

He hitched my legs over his shoulders and slid home so far I screamed. Long, punishing rolls of his hips dragged him out and then pushed forward. "You're mine to claim. Mine to fuck. Mine to ruin."

"Ruin me, Noah." I was so close to orgasm. Right on the edge but never quite reaching the jumping-off point.

Leaning down, changing the angle so that he filled me completely, he layered kisses along my shoulder, and I thanked the gods above I'd been practicing yoga for so many years.

"Gladly. And twice on Sunday."

A breathless giggle escaped my lips. The tiny flutter of my stomach muscles made me grip him even tighter and set off little explosions behind my eyes. "God, Noah. I love the way you fuck me."

"Do you like him deep inside you, *a stor*?" Caleb's voice skated across my skin, pulling my focus from my mate to my confessor.

"Caleb? When did you get here?"

"I've always been here. You know how much I love to watch."

"Just watch?"

"Tell me how to serve you."

I moaned and arched my back as Noah kissed across my mark, his lips sending a tingle straight to my clit. "Touch me."

Holding my gaze, he trailed the tips of his fingers from

my hip up to the side of my breast and then back down. His touch barely more than a ghosting of his skin against mine.

"Like this?"

"Bloody hell, man. Don't you know how to touch a woman?" Noah grunted.

I laughed, that one action sending sparks through me all over again, just like before. I needed to come. I was desperate for it. "Be nice. He's a virgin."

Caleb growled in response, then pinched my nipple—hard. Fuck, I was ready. I wanted this to go on forever even as I begged for release. The harsh breaths coming from Caleb betrayed how on edge he was. He needed relief too.

"Can I touch you?"

"God above, if you touch me I may burst into flames."

"But what a way to go," Noah said.

Caleb steeled himself before giving a short jerk of his head. My gaze zeroed in on the hard bulge at his crotch.

"Show me how much you want me, Father," I whispered.

"Lord forgive me." His words were a muttered plea, but he stood before tearing open his belt, followed by his fly.

His cock was long and thick. Hard and veiny. Mouthwatering. I wanted to taste him. Reaching out, I took him in my hand, slowly gliding over it from tip to root. Caleb groaned, his hips rocking forward, seeking out more of my touch.

"Don't forget me," Noah said, sinking into me and dragging a moan from my throat.

"Never."

"Um, do you two need to be alone?" Moira's voice broke through the lust fog we were trapped inside.

My eyes snapped open, Noah disappearing and my gaze snagging on the sight of my hand moving up a steely thigh encased in dark trousers. My other hand furiously worked my battery-operated boyfriend in and out of my aching pussy. I must have grabbed it from its hiding spot in my bedside table in my sexual haze. I froze, my eyes traveling up until they collided with Caleb's stormy gaze as I slid it out and turned it off.

Not sure what to say, I went on the offensive. "What the fuck, Moira? I thought you were joking about the exorcism."

"I was. I didn't think you'd sexually assault the man. This is getting out of control."

"I-I wasn't. I didn't," I sputtered, sitting up and scrambling back on my bed, shame coiling deep in my belly and sending all lusty thoughts scattering. "Did I?"

Caleb shook his head. "By the sounds you made, only in your mind."

"Oh, thank fuck. I mean . . ."

"What's wrong with her, Daddy G?"

He closed his eyes and let out a long-suffering sigh. "I do not think I'll ever understand your generation's insistence on referring to me as Daddy."

"Trust me, if you watched porn, you'd totally get it."

"I don't watch television. I prefer real life." He stared at me, and my cheeks burned. After our tryst in the study room, I knew exactly what he liked to watch.

Me.

Moira cleared her throat, fanning her face with one hand. "Goddess, I'm starting to get it, Sunday . . . I really am."

I tore my gaze from Caleb to where my roommate still hovered by the door. Our still open door, where we'd been collecting an audience. Three hulking figures stood just outside, their eyes all glowing with feral need, bodies shaking with the effort of controlling themselves. My wolf

75

practically presented herself for them, but she wanted her mate more than anything.

"Kingston," I moaned. "I need Kingston."

Moira's eyes went wide. "Fuck, she really is dying, isn't she, Padre? Sunday never willingly asks for that jackass."

Caleb snapped his focus to the men crowding our door and then to her. "Put up a ward, Miss Belladonna. Right the bloody hell now." Then he turned furious eyes to me. "Why haven't you been taking your suppressants?"

"Suppressants?"

"For your heat," he ground out. "They're a requirement for all female shifters. You know what the heat does to the unmated. You're going to drive them all mad until it's over."

"Um . . . what's a heat?"

"Oh, shiiiiit." Moira shut the door after her ward snapped into place. "That's what this is?"

My thighs were slick with arousal, breasts aching and heavy, womb feeling incredibly empty and desperate to be filled. I reached for Caleb. "Help me with this, please." I didn't know if I was asking him to fuck me or save me. Maybe both.

Caleb jerked out of my reach, his eyes wild. He took a harsh breath, hands clenching and unclenching at his sides. "It's too late now. The heat is already upon her. She's just going to have to ride it out. I'm going to need to take her away from here. The only way to keep everyone safe is to get her out of range. We need to remove her scent—and the temptation—from the main campus grounds, or no one will know any peace, least of all her."

"So this is why they're all acting like such freakshows lately? Even more than usual."

"If by freakshows you mean tense and on edge, yes. I should've seen it for what it was, but then we've never had someone come into their heat before. Female shifters are taught at an early age how to manage such things."

"Shifters with mothers, maybe. I bet no one in her family wanted to have a chat about the wolfy birds and bees with her. Especially since she hadn't managed her first shift yet. Why get into all the uncomfortable details if they didn't have to?"

"Stop talking about me like I'm not here," I bit out before my whole body seized up as a painful wave of need hit me.

"All you're going to add to this conversation is moans soon," Caleb said. "It's going to get worse—much worse—before it gets better. You're too vulnerable here. We need to remove you from this room as soon as possible." He stared at the teacup sitting on my bedside table. "Can you make us a stronger brew of that tea? We can put her under so I can transport her somewhere safe."

"Where are you taking her?"

"It's best you don't know."

Moira scowled at him. "You don't have to protect her from me. I'm hardly the one trying to hump her leg."

"It's not you I'm worried about. Until her scent is cleansed from this room, those men out there are going to be like zombies. They won't stop trying to find her. They may . . . hurt you to get information. And when Kingston finds out . . . "

"He'll do anything to get to her."

He nodded. "Exactly. I'll hold him off as long as I can."

They continued to talk over me. Part of me was annoyed I wasn't included in the conversation, but it was a small part. Smaller by the second, to be honest. My brain was drifting, images from my dreams merging with reality. My body was on fire with the need to be touched. To be filled.

It was unbearable.

I cried out as a twist of desire sent me writhing on the bed. "Why does it hurt so much?"

"Easy now, *a stor*. I'll take care of you."

A cup was brought to my lips, the scent of herbs over-powering and already making my eyes droop. "Drink," Moira whispered. "It'll be okay. I'm sorry I didn't call for help sooner."

"We didn't know."

She brushed my hair off my face. While there was nothing sexual about the action, the soft play of hair over my skin had me trembling.

"It's probably best you don't touch me right now."

Moira jumped back like she'd been scalded. "Shit. Sorry."

"Sleep, Sunday. This will be much more pleasant for you if you can't feel it when I pick you up."

Caleb's voice made me smile, so warm and sensual. That gravel in his words hit me straight in the clit. I wondered if he could make me come just by talking to me. It didn't even have to be dirty. Just a Bible passage or two would probably do it. Maybe a prayer of benediction?

"I can feel you even when you're not around."

Tenderness flashed in his eyes, but his face was still lined with worry. "Sleep."

He started to turn, but my hand snapped out, catching him by the wrist before he could go. "Will you be there when I wake up?"

"I won't be far. But you're already proving to be too much of a temptation for me as it is."

My heavy sigh was laced with disappointment, but deep down, I knew he was right. He wouldn't put himself in a position to take advantage of me when I was like this. But he would care for me.

Exhaustion won out over the lust, and my eyes fluttered closed.

The last thing I heard was Caleb murmuring a quiet prayer in Latin and whispering, " . . . ad perditionem animarum pervagantur in mundo. Amen."

CHAPTER
NINE
KINGSTON

The cool air of the late fall evening did nothing to settle my overheated nerves. I paced back and forth at the lake's shore, working to control the sense of unease that coursed through me, anxious energy prickling at my skin like a swarm of angry wasps. I'd never felt this before.

I hadn't seen Sunday since class a few days ago. I'd been trying to respect her request for space, especially since she clearly hadn't been feeling well, but I was going mad from the separation. When I'd tried to see her, Moira had been worse than a damn prison guard denying me visitation. She sent me packing every single time.

My wolf needed his mate. The longer we went without seeing her, the more unhinged I became. My control over my body was fraying. My wolf was ready to take over and succeed where he thought I was failing. At least, that was what I assumed was happening. I'd never been mated before.

The breeze picked up, sending a faint tease of her scent to me, just enough to make my already aching cock harder

Fuck. I'd always craved her, but now that I'd had a taste of what being with her was like, it was as if I'd lost my fucking mind. She was all I could think about. Was this what it'd be like day after day? Me wanting her, her hiding from me, only for it to end with me losing my shit in a fucking forest at twilight.

Without warning, my wolf let out a howl of denial. The sound ripped from my throat with a savage desperation I didn't understand but could hardly deny.

Why won't she see me?

I had to get to her. For myself and for my wolf. I could taste the pain in her scent. The hunger. The call. My mate needed me. Something was wrong with her. Or maybe something was wrong with me.

I pulled my phone from my pocket with trembling hands. Everything in me was strung tight enough I worried I'd snap. Palms clammy, I struggled not to drop the phone. Shit. Did I have a fever? My head was heavy, my thoughts clouded. Fuck. What if I had whatever Sunday had?

Shifters were supposed to be naturally immune to these kinds of things. But what if this wasn't a normal illness? What if this was something else? Something sinister? We'd just dealt with a hunter attack on the school. Could this be the next way they infiltrated? By poisoning us or dosing us with some new supernatural drug?

Or, fuck . . . what if it was something *I'd* caused by marking her when she'd already been claimed?

There was only one person I trusted enough to ask. He answered on the first ring.

"King, what's up?" Dylan's voice was filled with concern. I never called. Technically, I wasn't allowed to. Dylan had left the pack and become a lone wolf after his mate and firstborn died in childbirth. No one blamed him for needing the space, but rejection was still rejection. And he'd chosen a life that didn't involve us. Which meant we were supposed to do the same.

I'd never been a fan of following the rules. Especially not when it meant I'd have to shun the man who'd always been like an older brother to me.

"I found her. She's here at Ravenscroft."

There was no need to explain who I was referring to.

"Shit, King . . ."

"We're mated."

"What? Are you fucking kidding? She changed her mind? Of course she did. What am I saying? No one can resist the pull."

I ran a hand over the back of my neck, my palm coming away slick with sweat from my burning skin. "I guess."

"When did this happen?"

"A few days ago. She's fucking perfect."

"So why do you sound like you ended up on the wrong end of a jumpy horse?"

I snickered at the expression. "All those years on the ranch are showing, *cowboy*."

"Yeah, you're right. I guess you pick up a thing or two working alongside lifelong ranchers. But this way I can still run, even if it's only on horseback."

"I'm just surprised the horses can stand to be around you. Don't they sense that you're a predator beneath all that sunburned skin?"

"If I started shifting again, sure. But it's been so long, they can't tell me from a human now."

My heart ached for my cousin. I couldn't fucking imagine what it must be like to lose your entire world in one fell swoop—actually, I could, which made it worse.

"But you didn't call to shoot the shit. Something's wrong. What's on your mind?"

"When you . . . mated . . ." I didn't want to continue. I knew it was painful to talk about her.

"Rissa, yeah. It's okay. I can say her name."

"When you and Rissa mated, did you get sick?"

"Sick? What kind of sick?" Concern colored his question.

"Sunday came down with a fever, and she's been out of it for nearly a week. I think it's because I marked her after she bonded with a vampire."

He sucked in a sharp breath. "What the fuck did you just say?"

"It's a long story, but she's mated to a vampire *and* me. Did I . . . hurt her by giving her my mark? I'll never forgive myself if I did."

Dylan blew out a breath, the silence on the other side of the line making my anxiety spike. "Fuck, kid. I don't know. I've never heard of anything like that before. It's possible the two bonds are fighting each other, but as far as I know, fated bonds win out over all others. The only reason I can see as to why yours didn't is that she's destined for you both."

I sat down hard on the ground, exhaustion taking over. "I don't know what to do. I'm edgy as fuck, even more desperate for her than before. How am I gonna live like this? Marking her was supposed to fix things, not make them worse."

"Wait, you asked if *I* got sick. Are you feeling feverish too? Like you want to crawl out of your skin? Maybe like you need to fuck something to get it out of your system?"

Neck heating, I grumbled, "Not that it's your business, but yeah."

Dylan burst into loud guffaws. I pictured the asshole sitting on a hay bale and slapping his leg. I hoped he fell off.

"It's not funny from where I'm sitting."

"Oh, it sure as shit is from my vantage point, boy."

"Why?"

"You're entering the rut. Saddle up. You're in for a wild ride."

Rut? Oh, fuck. As though agreeing, my cock gave a throb. "Why?"

"Sounds like your mark sent Sunday into heat. I'm surprised she wasn't on suppressants, though. Most unmated females are."

Oh. Fuuuck.

"She's in fucking heat," I breathed, the shock of it zinging through me.

"So now you have two options. Hide her somewhere you won't be able to get to her and let her ride it out alone, or serve your mate until it's over. Either way, it's going to be tough."

I jumped up, exhaustion gone, my cousin's words giving my wolf the affirmation he needed. He'd been telling me all along what was supposed to be happening. I'd just been too clueless to understand.

"What would you do?"

Dylan let out a low laugh. "I never left my mate needful. She always got what she wanted, and then some."

I almost hated myself for my next question, but I had to know so I could protect us both. That's what a good mate— a good Alpha—does. "What's it like? Am I going to lose myself? I won't hurt her or anything, right?"

"She's made for this. It's the best sex of your life, times a million. And when you knot . . . well, you'll see. Your wolves

85

will get you through this. They were born for it. Just let instinct guide you and all that."

I took a deep breath and nodded. "Thanks, cowboy. I knew you'd give it to me straight."

"'Course. Now, I'm fixin' to head out and check some fence before breakfast. But I'll leave you with one more nugget of advice."

"Okay, I'm all ears."

"If you really want to drive her wild . . . call her darlin'."

Laughing, I shook my head. "Goodbye, Dylan."

"Have fun, and stay hydrated."

"I intend to."

I hung up and shoved my phone back into my pocket, everything in me humming to find my mate and serve her until I couldn't see straight. Now that I had my answers, all that edginess had turned into anticipation.

Sunday Fallon was going to take my knot, and she'd fucking love it.

"Open this fucking door, Sunday."

Was it the most respectful way to get her attention? No. But I was desperate. She was in pain. She needed me. I hammered on the door hard enough the walls rattled. When I heard a soft moan from inside, I lost it. Shoulder braced, I barreled into the wood, splintering the frame and sending the door crashing inward.

"What the fuck, Kingston?" Moira screeched, her hands flying up to cover her bare tits.

"Put those things away, witch. What the hell do you think you're doing? Sunday is my mate, and no one else should be servicing her. Least of all you."

Her expression shifted from shock to anger to amusement as fast as the accusations flying from my lips.

"First of all, asshole, this is my room. You don't get to enforce a dress code. Second of all, the only person I was servicing was my girlfriend."

"Your *what*?" I snarled.

She rolled her eyes and pointed at the computer screen I

hadn't noticed sitting in front of her on the bed. "Meet Ash. My girlfriend."

The pretty woman on the screen waved at me sheepishly. "Hi."

Realizing my mistake, I wiped a hand down my face. "Fuck. Sorry."

"You should be. We were just getting to the good part." Moira narrowed her eyes and frowned at me. "Now I have to start all over, you clitblocker."

Heat crept up my neck, the embarrassment unfamiliar and unwelcome.

"Call me back later, Mo? I'll be ready when you're done with the dog."

"Sure thing, sweetness. Keep that kitty purring until I can come take care of it."

"Jesus, fuck," I groaned.

Moira snapped the laptop closed and pulled on her silk robe, throwing daggers at me with her eyes. "Nope. You don't get to have an opinion about the things I say to my girlfriend, you fuck. Now why did you go and assault my door? What the hell did it ever do to you?"

"Where is my mate? She needs me."

Her brows lifted, hidden behind a thick fringe of rainbow-colored locks. "She does, does she? Did she tell you that?"

"I can fucking smell it."

Moira bit her lip and hummed. "Well, that sucks. I thought for sure I got the ratio right this time."

"What the hell are you going on about?"

"For the cleansing spell. You shouldn't smell her at all if I did it correctly."

"Wait. Were you trying to hide her from me intentionally?"

"You. The dogs keeping watch in the hallway. Pretty much everybody with a penis, really."

Understanding dawned. It wasn't just me affected by her heat. Every unattached male here must be going crazy. But I doubted they felt the pull like I did. My instinct screamed to rut and claim and fill her. I was at a rolling boil, ready to overflow. They must only be at a simmer, or I'd have noticed. Wouldn't I?

"Tell me where she is, Moira. I need to get to her."

"Sorry, can't," she said, sounding anything but.

I let more than a little of my wolf into the words as I stalked toward her. "You will tell me, or I will make you."

"You all really do lose your fucking minds, don't you?" Moira shook her head and sighed heavily. "I couldn't tell you if I wanted to. I don't know where she is."

"You just let her go without protection? Weren't you the one insisting she be guarded at all times?"

"Callie's dead. What's there to worry about? Also, no one said she was alone."

The mischief dancing in her eyes was enough to have me growling low in my throat. "I'll find her myself."

I strode across the room and grabbed the pillow off Sunday's bed, bringing it to my nose and inhaling deeply. Her scent burst through my body, sending my cock from partially relaxed to rock-hard and throbbing. Whatever *cleansing* Moira had done hadn't been enough.

Feral lust and unchecked desire to serve her hit me all at once. She'd been in this bed, wet and writhing, ready for me to help her through this like a mate should while I'd been off cooling my heels because I thought I was giving her what she wanted. In reality, it had been the exact opposite. That's the last time I let her make the rules. This would never happen again.

Setting down her pillow, I picked up the sheets and rubbed them across my face. She'd touched herself, tried in vain to get off and ease the ache. It wouldn't work. She needed my knot.

But then another scent caught my attention, faint, but there. Incense. Self-loathing. Spice.

"Priest," I growled.

"Kingston . . ."

"No. You will not keep me from her."

"Stop—"

Tossing down the sheet, I shoved past her. "Next time, you should probably get rid of *all* the scents in the room. Now I know exactly how to find her."

"Motherfucker."

"Thanks for the chat, witch. It was very . . . enlightening. Have fun with your girlfriend. Too bad magic can't make your video fuck fest feel like the real thing. I'll have Father Gallagher light a candle for you."

"If you find him."

I cocked a brow. "Oh, I'll find the fucker, and I'll make him talk."

"If you hurt her—"

I paused at the door, snarling over my shoulder, "I would *never* hurt her. That's why I have to find her. I'm the only one who can ease her suffering."

Moira's eyes widened. "You really do love her in your own psycho macho way, don't you?"

"She's my mate. Of course I fucking love her."

Her mouth dropped open as she looked at me, shock visible in her expression. Before she could say another word, I left, door hanging off the hinges, witch staring after me, focused on my one goal.

Sunday.

I TRACKED the priest's scent back to the church on the far end of the campus. Not like it had been hard to find him, I just had to follow the stench of desperation. Not bothering to knock, I threw open the doors and strode inside. The sun had just set, and I knew he'd be here, probably punishing Sunday for her wickedness. Trying to flog the heat out of her.

Rage built in my chest at the thought. He didn't get to share this with her. It was mine to keep. Her heat was my privilege, and I wouldn't be denied.

Father Gallagher glanced up from whatever he was reading, probably the Bible or some shit, as I stormed in. He looked like absolute hell. Dark circles under his eyes, muscles bunched with tension, jaw clenched tight.

Even he, with his celibacy and righteousness, wasn't immune to her pull. Had he touched her? Fucked her? Tried in vain to give her what she could only get from me? I balled my hands into fists as another wave of possessive instinct crashed over me. I'd tear him limb from limb and mount the pieces on the wall if he had.

"Get out of here, Kingston."

"Not gonna happen, Priest. You're hiding my mate from me."

"I'm protecting her."

"Bullshit, you're keeping her for yourself."

His already pale skin leached of color. "What did you just say to me?"

"You heard me. Deny it all you want, but I can smell the truth all over you. You want her. But I'll let you in on a not-so-little secret. Sunday Fallon is *mine*. You will never be able to give her what she needs."

"I may want her, but I have something you don't."

"What's that, blue balls?"

"Control."

I growled, low and deep. "Take me to her, Priest."

"You'll have to go through me if you want to get to her."

Her scent filled the space, and I knew I didn't need this bloodsucking eunuch to help me now. Nothing would keep me from her.

I shrugged. "Not a problem."

I'd pay for this later, but right now I didn't care about things like rules and pecking order. This douche was standing between me and my mate. If I had to kill him to get to her, I'd do it without a second thought.

My wolf rose to the surface, eager to take control now that Sunday was in reach. His strength infused me, fangs filling my mouth and claws breaking through my skin.

The vampire was fast, but in this moment, I was faster. With a strength born of madness, I grasped both sides of his head and twisted, snapping his neck before he could summon another threat.

I let his body drop to the floor with a satisfying thud. "You'll be fine. And trust me, this is the only way to help Sunday now."

Stepping over the priest, I locked onto Sunday's tantalizing aroma, my cock thickening and pushing painfully at my fly. My balls ached. Fuck, everything hurt. I needed her as much as she did me.

"Where are you, baby?" I whispered as I followed her trail through the church, stopping in front of the confessional booth.

I ripped the curtain aside, desperation making me use more force than necessary and accidentally shredding it. It was fucking empty.

No.

I could smell her. She was here.

With that thought in mind, I stalked around the box, her scent growing weaker, then stronger the lower to the floor I was. Bracing my palms on the side of the confessional, I shoved the thing aside. It crashed to the floor and broke into pieces, splintered wood all that remained of the antique. Oh, well. Maybe someone would come along and use a stake to get the priest out of my hair.

As the debris cleared, the secret of the confessional was revealed.

Father Gallagher, you sick fuck.

A staircase twisted down into the bowels of the church, hiding God knew what dark sins and with them, *her.*

She was down there. I knew it without a doubt.

I'm coming for you. And once I find you . . . you'll be coming for me.

I took the stairs two at a time, racing forward in the pitch-black space, not worried about the fact that there was no light to guide me. I didn't need it. I had her. My beacon calling me home.

A soft whimpered moan echoed through the corridor, the whisper of my name reaching me and sending my wolf wild.

I growled, my heart thundering as I prowled down the darkened hall toward the lone door. Without hesitation, I grasped the ancient knob in my hand and tore it straight out. Then I sent the door crashing open and groaned at the sight before me.

Lying on a nest of blankets in front of a fire that was little more than embers was my Sunshine, clad only in a white button-up shirt that definitely did not belong to her.

Her luminous gaze found mine, fevered with lust and pain and need.

"Kingston, please," she moaned.

My cock gave an approving twitch as my hands dropped to unbuckle my belt. A command I'd never uttered sat ready on my lips. I wasn't entirely sure if it was my wolf who was giving the order or me—or if there was a difference at this point. But I couldn't stop myself from saying the word.

"Present."

ELEVEN

S lick arousal dripped down my thighs at the one word that fell from Kingston's mouth.

"Present," he said, voice harder and tinged with impatience that he'd had to repeat himself.

I got on my hands and knees, pushing my hips back and up so my wet folds were on display for him. I needed him now. Everything was swollen and aching, my clit throbbing painfully, my womb cramping. But he could fix it. He could take the pain away.

I whimpered, wondering what he was still doing standing in the doorway. His eyes were locked on my pussy as he undressed at a maddeningly slow pace. Tugging his shirt over his head and baring the carved from stone muscles that made up his chest and abs, then popping the top button of his jeans, he inhaled deep, eyes glowing as my scent washed over him. Instead of shying away from his gaze, I tilted my hips, giving him a better view.

"What are you waiting for?" My breath was thready, desperate. I was burning up, convinced I might actually die if he didn't slide inside me right the fuck now.

I dipped my hand between my legs, reaching for my throbbing clit.

"Stop."

He issued the command like the crack of a whip.

I moaned.

"That's mine. You don't get to rob me of your pleasure, Sunshine."

"But you're not taking me."

"I will. But we're going to have a talk first."

"Now?"

He smirked, but I could see the war behind his eyes. His wolf wanted to rut just like mine wanted to mate. Then with a slight tremble in his hand, he lowered the zipper of his jeans and pulled out that perfect, thick cock of his. The piercings glinted in the light of the dying fire, and I wondered what it would feel like to have that in my mouth.

I licked my lips, as eager to taste him as I was to be filled. I wondered if he'd fuck my mouth with the same driving intensity he'd claimed my cunt.

A bead of clear liquid sat on the tip before rolling down and dropping to the stone floor. I might be dripping for him, but he was doing the same for me.

Reaching between my legs once more, this time on purpose, I stared at him and slid two fingers inside my hole. I moaned low and loud.

"I said stop," he gritted out.

"A true Alpha would already be balls deep inside his mate and easing the pain. I know that much."

His lips twisted in a soft snarl, but his eyes went molten. "You just can't help yourself, can you, Sunshine? You like pushing me to my breaking point, is that it? Do you like it more when I'm angry?"

"I like the way it feels when you fuck me like you hate me."

"Get your fingers away from what's mine, and I'll fuck you like I own you." He ran his hand along the solid length of his cock, pulling out another pearly drop of cum.

My nipples tightened to agonizing points. "Stop talking about it and do it."

"Not yet. Not until you and I come to an understanding."

Shoving his pants down his hips, he continued until he'd removed them altogether, then he stalked toward me and I all but sagged in relief. He was finally going to give me what I needed so badly. What I'd been dreaming about for what felt like for-fucking-ever.

"Kingston . . ."

"I love the way you say my name," he whispered, twisting my hair in his fist and giving it a soft yank.

"I love the way your dick feels when you stretch me out."

"Anything else you love, baby?" He pressed the tip of his cock to my soaked entrance, just that slight bit of contact making me whimper.

"The way it feels when you slide in all the way. It's like I can't breathe, I'm so filled by you."

"Fuuuuuck," he groaned as the tip slid farther in. "Sunday, you're on fire."

"Yes, Kingston. Please. Fuck me. I need you."

He tugged my hair again, making my neck arch. "Not yet. I need you to do something for me first."

"Anything," I moaned, blinded by how good it felt to have him pressing in one fraction of an inch at a time.

Then he pulled out, the length of him nestling against my ass, not going where I needed him so badly.

"What are you doing?" I whined.

"Do you feel that? That aching emptiness?" He leaned forward, his chest flat against my back as his lips brushed the shell of my ear. His voice shook with need and barely restrained desire. He was a man on the edge, his control frayed. "That's what it feels like every time you reject me—reject us. I will take away the pain, give you everything you need, but first I need you to promise that you will never deny me as yours again."

He rocked his hips, giving himself the friction I wanted while denying the thing we both needed all at the same time. The hand that was wrapped in my hair slipped free and clenched my throat as he rutted against me.

"I can make myself come all over you right here and now and then walk away if I need to. I'll ride out my rut alone in my room while you do the same here. Or we can move forward together. It's your choice. And, fuck, Sunday, I need you to make the right one."

His heated words washed over me, simmering in my blood and wrapping themselves around my heart. Yes. *Yes.* He was mine. Ours.

My wolf had absolutely no doubt about her mate. I was the one who kept trying to sit on the fence. But feeling him now, knowing he could take away the pain, that he was the *only* one who could? It made it so much harder to deny the truth. I didn't hate Kingston Farrell. Not even a little.

"Yes," I breathed, pressing back into him. "Yes."

He moved his hand back to my hair and yanked again, a growl in his words. "Yes, what, baby?"

"Yes."

That thick cock pressed against my opening, but he stilled, keeping himself from pushing in. "Say. It."

"Yes, you're mine. You are my king, my mate. I'm yours . . . but I'm his too. I need you to know that."

He ghosted his lips over the mating mark they'd both given me. "I know, Sunshine. But as long as you stop denying that I have as much of a right to you as he does, I. Don't. Fucking. Care."

Relief hit me at the same time unbelievable pleasure did. His teeth sank into my shoulder while his dick slid home, deep and to the hilt. The moan I let out echoed off the walls, and I was thankful we weren't near anyone, or they might've thought something deadly was happening down here.

His ragged, pained grunt joined mine. "Fuck, Sunday. I can't hold off the rut anymore."

"I don't want you to."

"Then grab onto something, sweetheart. This is going to be quick and dirty."

He released his grasp on my hair, sliding his palm down my back until it rested between my shoulder blades, and then he shoved me down. Not enough to hurt, but with enough force, there was no way my body could resist. He was so big, so deep already, but this position sent him all the way to the tender entrance of my womb. It ached in the best way.

He pulled his hips back and then slammed home, making stars explode behind my eyes. The first thrust was a warning because after that, they were relentless, driving into me with the same brutal force but so much faster. In a matter of seconds, we were shaking, on the cusp of a climax that threatened to detonate with the intensity of a fucking bomb.

"I can't stop," he moaned. "I want this to last, but I can't."

"Please don't stop. I need it. I need you to fill me. Please, I'm so empty."

My name left him in a roar as his fingers dug painfully into my hips, holding me in place as he shot jet after jet of his hot cum inside me. I writhed as much as I could, searching for that one final piece that would give me the orgasm I craved.

"Take it all, Sunday. Take my fucking knot."

And there it was. I imploded. His cock swelled at the base, locking us together and sending me into an orgasm that completely obliterated everything else around us. I screamed his name and clenched around him, feeling relief for the first time since this started. Tears streamed down my cheeks. He gave me what I needed, just like he'd promised.

The sound of our panting breaths filled the room. I had no idea how long it was before I came back to myself, only that he was still there, still filling me, and I didn't want it to stop.

"Kingston?"

He leaned down and feathered a kiss at the nape of my neck. "Yes, Sunshine?"

"Can we do that again?"

"Already?"

"Do you need some time?"

He chuckled softly. "You're going to have me again before we leave this room, I promise. But once my knot goes down, we'll need to rest before the next wave."

Alarm shot through me. "The next wave of what?"

"Heat. I'm here to service my mate until her heat ends. That'll be, at minimum, three days. More if we're lucky."

I yawned as soon as I allowed myself to feel anything other than him. I was tired. So tired, everything felt heavy. I hadn't had a peaceful sleep in close to a week, and now it made sense. If I hadn't insisted on shoving him away, on denying what was between us, things might not have gotten this out of control.

"Lie down with me," Kingston said, his voice more gentle and tender than I'd ever heard it.

I nodded and let him take us to the soft blankets together. Then I snuggled against him, my back to his front, as the two of us basked in the afterglow of finally fully coming together with no barriers. I was his and he was mine, and there wasn't anything to keep us apart now.

I DIDN'T KNOW how much time passed as Kingston got me through my heat. All I knew was I woke, I needed him, he served me, over and over. Eventually we moved from the nest of blankets and soft fur rug on the floor to the bed. But I hadn't given a single shit about comfort. The one thing that made me comfortable was him inside me.

The only breaks in that pattern occurred when sharp knocks outside alerted us to the presence of food. Each time Kingston opened the door, Caleb's lingering scent would wash over me, making a different kind of hunger curl in my belly, but we never saw our caretaker. Other than ensuring we were fed, he left us to our own devices.

I should have been worn out, sore, exhausted . . . but I was insatiable. At first, I thought it was just about the sex, but Kingston surprised me. In the quiet moments between our frantic coupling, he'd take care of me. He made sure I was warm even though we both spent all our time naked, covering me in blankets, holding me close, stoking the fire.

I'd never thought of Kingston Farrell as a tender lover, but here he was . . . gentle and sweet.

Warm kisses trailed up my spine, pulling me from my contemplation of how things had changed. "Are you awake, Sunshine? Do you need me again?"

I bit down on my lip, debating my answer. The warm flush of arousal hadn't begun to work its way through my body, but I did find myself wet and willing. The heat had been coming in fast and terrible waves, one right after the other. I expected need to crash through me, the gnawing ache to take over, but it didn't. It was there, but not on the scale it had been before. That alone spoke volumes.

"Soon," I murmured instead. "I think it's slowing down."

"Is it wrong that I almost don't want it to?"

I smirked. "You? Sad about our sex marathon coming to an end? Shocking."

"Sad that I have to give you up when this is over."

My heart lurched. I couldn't come to terms with the differences between the man who had me in his arms and the one who'd made it his mission to destroy me. Staring into the dancing flames as they ate up the logs in the fireplace, I let myself drift and remember who he'd been when we first met and who he'd become.

"What's going on inside your head? You seem lost in thought."

I laughed.

"What's so funny?"

"I never thought you'd give a single fuck about what was in my head."

His fingers curled over my hip, rolling me over so he could peer down at me. "What do you mean? Of course I care what you're thinking. Do you have any idea how many nights I stayed awake trying to figure you out?"

"How are you two different people? I can't keep up."

His devilish smirk had things tightening low in my belly. "I'm the same man I've always been. You just never gave me a chance to show you."

"With the exception of the first time we met, you've been so mean."

Tenderness filled his eyes, followed by apology. "I have. I know. I'd never been hurt the way you hurt me. You broke me. But now, you're helping me put the pieces back together. I don't know if I can really ever go back to the innocent kid I used to be . . . " He laughed, as if the idea of his ever being innocent was hilarious. "But I want to try to at least give you all the same things he wanted to." He tucked some hair behind my ear, his fingers lingering on my jaw, his eyes filled with honest devotion. "You make me want to be him again. For you."

"I'm so sorry." I couldn't look at him as I said the words. My heart ached for all the pain we'd both been through. Pain I'd never meant to cause.

He leaned in and pressed a soft kiss to my forehead. "Me too, Sunshine."

As he pulled me closer to the cradle of his body, I couldn't help but ask, "So is this what I was missing all these years?"

"Maybe. I'm not sure. We never had a chance to be those people, and a lot has changed since then. But this is what we have now. It's not the heat talking. It's you and me."

"Kingston," I whispered, staring into eyes that saw deep into my soul. He saw every part of me. He always had.

I reached up and threaded my fingers through his thick

hair, dragging my nails gently along his scalp and making him shudder as he closed his eyes and soaked up the affection. This man wasn't angry anymore, but he was starved for touch. My touch. Leaning forward, I pressed a kiss to his chest, just over his heart. I could feel it beating, strong and true, for me—his mate.

"Sunday?" he asked, uncertainty in his voice.

"Let me love you."

"That's all I've ever wanted."

I continued discovering him, kissing the hard, inked planes of muscle that made up his chest and shoulders, toying with the piercings in his nipples and loving the soft gasps that drew from him. My fingers played across his tight abs, running down, down, down, until I reached the coarse patch of hair at the base of his heavy length.

He hissed in a breath and rocked his hips. "God, that feels good. I never thought you'd want to touch me like this."

He didn't realize it, but he'd just given me an opening for a confession of my own. "I did," I whispered.

He jerked, lifting his head up to stare at me. "What?"

"I thought about you every day." I continued touching him, not meeting his eyes as I gave him a truth I never thought I'd share. "I never wanted to reject you. When I saw you that first time, God, it felt like my heart was about to explode out of my chest. You were so . . . beautiful. You bared yourself in the moonlight, and I wanted nothing more than to go with you and be yours. But my grandfather . . . I couldn't shame him more than I already had. I couldn't fail to shift in front of the two largest packs in the region." I swallowed through a throat tight with regret. "So I had to give up the only chance I thought I'd ever have to actually be wanted . . . be loved by somebody." I forced myself to look up at him. I didn't want to leave him with any doubt as to my sincerity. "I had to walk away, Kingston, but I never stopped wanting you. Wishing for you and the future we should have had."

He gritted his teeth, eyes shining as he clearly worked to control his emotions. "I would've accepted you. No matter what."

Blinking hard, I let the words land. "Would you?"

He wrapped a big arm around my waist and rolled us together so I was astride him, then he took my face in his hands and pulled me down until our eyes were inches apart. "Yes."

It was my turn to battle against a wave of tears. "Kingston."

"I love you, Sunday. I have since the moment I first saw you, and I've never stopped."

Heart in my throat, I leaned down and pressed my mouth to his, the need to connect with him completely unrelated to my heat or pheromones or lust. This was pure. I wanted him to know exactly how I felt, even if the words couldn't leave my lips yet.

He stiffened under me, his whole body drawn tight as though he wasn't sure what was happening. I opened my eyes while our lips were still locked to find him staring at me, bewildered. Breaking the kiss, I sat up, afraid I'd done something wrong.

"What's the matter?"

"Nothing," he said quickly, blinking a couple of times and giving a quick shake of his head.

Is that a blush?

"I've never . . . I mean . . . Fuck, this is awkward."

"Me kissing you is awkward?" Hurt and confusion laced my voice.

"Fuck, no, that's not what I meant." He groaned, closing his eyes. "I've never kissed a girl—on the mouth, I mean. Sex for me has always been about release, never anything deeper. I'd had my heart broken once. I never wanted to give anyone else a chance, so I didn't . . . I mean, I kept things strictly . . ."

He trailed off, looking supremely embarrassed.

My heart felt like it was about to melt into a puddle at my feet. Here was more proof of the damage I'd done to him, and yet, in a completely unexpected way, it made things so much more meaningful.

He clenched his jaw and opened his eyes, exhaling loudly. "Since we seem to be in a secret sharing mood, you should probably also know that the only way I could get off was if I pretended I was fucking you. I couldn't look them in the face, so I would only fuck them from behind. And if I couldn't look at them, how could I kiss them?" He tangled his fingers in my hair, bringing my face back down to his. "No one gets that part of me but you. It's always been you, baby."

"Oh . . ." I bit my lower lip, thinking back to our first time together in the forest. He'd forced me to get on my hands and knees then too, even though he'd already been halfway inside me when we were face to face. Even now, in the middle of my heat, he'd only taken me on my knees while I'd presented for him. "So . . . you didn't want to look at me either? You still don't?"

His eyes widened. "Fuck, no. That's not . . . I want to look at you all the goddamn time. I've barely let myself close my eyes the last couple of days, worried I'd wake up and find out this was all a dream. I'm afraid it's going to be *you* who doesn't want to see *me*." His voice dropped to a ragged whisper. "What if I give you my broken heart and you realize you don't want it?"

Shaking my head, I leaned close and kissed him softly. "I want it," I whispered against his lips. "I want to unbreak it."

In one move, I reached behind me and positioned his thick cock where it belonged before sinking down on him and taking him all the way inside. His gasp was a thing of beauty. I was so full. So stretched, I could barely move as I adjusted.

His hands went to my hips as vulnerable eyes locked with mine. "Sunday . . ."

"You deserve to be loved like this. To look into the eyes of your mate and know you're safe. That you're wanted. Let me give you this."

He nodded, and the furrow between his brows broke something inside me.

I began a slow dance for him, rolling my hips, dragging my nails across his chest, touching myself as he watched.

"Is this your heat?" he asked, voice hoarse and tight.

"No. This is me. Choosing you."

He shuddered, his eyes closing briefly and then flaring wide as he surged up and grasped my face, sealing his lips over mine. "I love you so fucking much it consumes me," he breathed, before claiming my mouth again.

"I—"

"Don't say it yet. Not until you really mean it."

Instead of responding, I held onto him, baring my mating mark and begging silently for him to remind me where I belonged. He kissed me there, the sensation of his mouth on my tender skin sending an orgasm crashing through me.

"Fuck, Sunday. I'm close."

"Yes."

"Oh, God…please. I can't stop."

"Don't. Don't ever stop."

Fucking me. Loving me. There were lots of ends to that sentence. All I knew was that Kingston belonged to me. He always had. Just like I had always belonged to him.

I wrapped my legs around his waist and rode him as he held me in his arms. His cock jerked inside me, knot swelling at the base, and he let out an agonized groan before calling my name and filling me with his release.

It was more intense than anything we'd done. We'd taken each other so many times at this point, but never like this, never with our hearts involved. Well, never with *my* heart involved.

Collapsing together on the blankets, we held each other, breaths ragged, pulses racing.

He laughed softly before kissing me. "Did that really just happen? I'm not hallucinating because you've drained my balls so many times?"

I smiled, snuggling deeper into his arms. "It really happened." Then my smile faded, and I pressed my hand against his chest over his heart. "I choose you, Kingston. I promise from now on, I will always choose you."

CHAPTER
TWELVE
SUNDAY

"How are you feeling?" Kingston ducked his head and kissed my shoulder as he settled on the bed with a tray of food in his hands.

"Good. Calm. I think it's nearly over." My stomach rumbled, the sound loud in the room, and I laughed. "Also hungry."

He set the tray down beside me with a grin. "Good thing I come bearing snacks then."

My gaze swept the slab of wood the food was laid out upon. A fleeting thought for who had prepared this ran through my mind. Caleb. He knew I was down here, being . . . serviced. The tray was laden with slices of meat, hunks of fresh bread, cheeses, grapes, olives, and even some fresh figs. Where the hell had he gotten those? The scent of the food had my mouth watering.

I reached for a cube of cheese, but Kingston knocked my hand away. "What the hell?"

"It's my job to feed you."

"You brought me the food. That counts."

He picked up the cube I'd reached for and lifted it to my lips. "Not even close, Sunshine."

I accepted the offering with an amused shake of my head, certain this was more weird Alpha posturing. Hard to complain about it when it revolved around pampering me, though.

"Is there anything else to drink besides water?" I glanced at the small table near the door that housed the large pitcher of water we'd been making good use of since this started.

"There's a decanter of wine, but I didn't think you'd want any."

"Why wouldn't I?"

"Your inhibitions are already pretty fucking nonexistent because of the heat." He shrugged and had the grace to look a little abashed. "Wouldn't want you to have any other reason to brush this off as you not being yourself."

A slight frown tugged at my lips. I thought we'd already been over this, but I guess it would take more than my assurances to repair the damage I'd caused. I reached out and cupped his cheek with a tenderness he needed from me. He had to know this was about more than sex. "I'm not brushing anything off. I love you, Kingston."

He jerked back and stared at me, eyes flickering with hope and disbelief. "What?"

"I love you."

His eyes fluttered closed, and a ragged breath escaped him. "I never thought I'd hear you say that."

A painful crack shot through my heart. I hated that I'd caused this. That I'd ever made him doubt he was worthy of being loved. That he'd ever be loved. I vowed then and there to make it up to him. To never give him another reason to feel rejected.

"I'm so glad this happened because if it hadn't, I'd still be wasting time being angry. It all makes sense now."

"Doesn't excuse the fact that I treated you like shit."

"No, it doesn't. But we both made mistakes. All we can do now is make it up to each other."

He held a grape up to me, and as I took it into my mouth, I made a point to overshoot and lightly scrape my teeth over the tip of his finger. The shudder that rippled through him, mixed with his soft moan, had me flushing warm and my nipples pebbling and pulling tight.

Fuck, I thought this was over.

Kingston inhaled sharply, his nostrils flaring and his eyes glowing a brilliant amber. He stood without a word and took the food away, striding confidently toward the table. The door was ajar, but he didn't stop to close it after depositing the tray. Instead he turned toward me, his erect cock jutting forward, glistening at the tip. "Present, Mate."

I did, ass in the air, body burning for his touch. The bed dipped as he joined me, his large palm running up my thigh and over my backside.

He leaned in and pressed a kiss between my shoulder blades. "We have company. If you don't want him to watch, tell him to leave. You have need of me, and no one is going to get in the way of me giving you my knot one more time."

I looked over my shoulder, my eyes finding Caleb standing in the door, staring at me with undeniable hunger. Behind me, Kingston had already lined himself up with my entrance.

"Come in, Caleb."

His whole body shuddered as he fought some kind of internal war. I thought he was going to leave, but then, gaze locked on mine, he stepped inside. Kingston thrust deep, his grunt of pleasure and the force of his entry making me cry out. The flash of arousal on Caleb's face had my walls already fluttering around Kingston's thick cock.

"You like to watch, Priest?" Kingston's voice held a taunting edge. "Have a seat then. I'll show you how it's done."

Caleb sneered, rage twisting his features. "I don't take orders from pups like you."

I reached out and grabbed Kingston's thigh. "I want to turn over. I need to be able to see you—both of you."

A rumble of pleasure vibrated through Kingston. He slapped me once on the ass. Hard. "On your back then."

He flipped me over, making me cry out in surprised laughter. I bounced on the bed but quickly turned serious as the urge to be filled hit me again. I needed him. I needed *them*.

"Please," I moaned.

"You never have to beg me to fuck you, Mate." He slammed inside me before he finished speaking, causing me to arch up with a pleasure-filled gasp.

Breathing hard, I turned my head, my eyes seeking out Caleb's. He stood a few feet from me, his gaze hard and intense, jaw clenched, but under the stoic exterior, I saw the mess of a man who'd been trying and failing to deny himself.

"Touch me, Caleb."

Kingston's long deep thrusts faltered for the barest second, so I rolled my hips to remind him I needed him too. His grip turned bruising around my upper thighs as he renewed the powerful drive of his cock, lighting me up with each slide of those piercings. His way of giving me his own reminder. As if I could forget him.

Caleb stared at the two of us, his focus on me more than Kingston. I wondered if he was putting himself in my mate's place, picturing his cock filling me, him making me moan.

"Please?"

"I can't," he said, his voice low and tight.

"You can."

"*A stor* . . ."

"Please . . . I need you."

His eyes closed and a muscle feathered in his jaw. When they snapped back open, they shone with a determination I'd never seen before.

My breath hitched as he stalked toward the bed. He reached out with trembling fingers, tenderly brushing the backs of them against my cheek.

Kingston huffed out a harsh laugh. "Not like that, Padre. She likes it rough. Give her what she really wants or get the fuck out of here and let me do it."

A ripple of pleasure rolled through me at Kingston's harsh words. He was right. Caleb knew I liked it rough, but Kingston didn't know about what went on in the secret places Father Gallagher took me. My clit pulsed with the need for friction as Kingston's thrusts deepened, and when Caleb gripped my face and slid his thumb between my lips, I nearly came.

"Suck me, little one."

The growled command in his brogue nearly undid me. I'd played out this fantasy so many times without coming close to the nirvana of the real thing. As I did as he asked, I wished it was his cock.

His slight gasp as I sucked hard on the digit had me lifting my hips and picking up the pace Kingston had set. I needed more. My mate was fucking me too slowly, my confessor wasn't letting me have what I really wanted, and frustration crept into my mind. But Kingston could tell. At this point, he knew my body better than anyone. He let out a dark laugh and pressed in to the hilt, stilling his hips and making me suffer.

"Look at that clit, ripe and swollen and begging for attention. I bet it aches, doesn't it, Sunshine?"

I moaned and bit down on Caleb's thumb, making him grunt and step a little closer.

"Do you see what we're doing to her, Priest? She needs us."

Caleb's gaze trailed from my face over my flushed breasts and down to the juncture between my thighs where Kingston had me split open on his dick.

"So pink and pretty," he whispered, his eyes heated with desire. He pulled his thumb free of my lips and let his palm hover over my throat. Then, realizing he'd spoken out loud, he groaned and let out a tortured, "Father, forgive me."

"Your father isn't here right now," Kingston growled. "Make her come on my cock, Gallagher. Make her scream for us."

"Yes," I begged, wanting—needing—exactly that.

I grabbed Caleb's hand and brought it to my breast, moaning as he closed it around the heavy, full globe. My free hand slid between my legs, brushing my clit before my fingers played across the base of Kingston's thick length as he drove in and pulled out. He let out a bark of pleasure that shot straight through me.

"Fuck, if you don't make her come right now I'm going to tear you apart," Kingston said, eyes locked on Caleb's. "This is your one job. Fucking do it."

Caleb's jaw tensed, anger flaring in his irises at Kingston's harsh commands. I could see how much he hated the other man giving him orders, but as I reached out and ran my other palm up his rigid thigh, something else washed over his expression.

His grip tightened around my breast until it was just this side of painful, eliciting a breathy moan from me. Then he released me and trailed his knuckles down over my belly until his fingers rested just above my throbbing, pulsing clit.

Sparks shot through me as he brought those fingers down in a slap, sending the mixture of delicious pain and pleasure radiating from that bundle of nerves. I cried out and bucked, but he responded by rubbing tight circles around the tender flesh.

Kingston groaned. "Fuck, she loves that. Her pussy is clamped around my cock like a fucking vise."

"Yes, please. Again."

Caleb grunted and brought his fingers up before slapping me once more. Fuck, I was going to come. My palm ran along his inner thigh until I brushed over the swell of his rock solid length. He hissed in a sharp breath, the fingers resting on my clit pinching roughly.

Sensation exploded, and I screamed as my climax crashed through me, my hand spasming over Caleb's cock and pulling another tortured moan from him as well. Kingston needed no encouragement, his thrusts punishing as he chased his own orgasm.

"Milk my cock, Sunshine. Take it all. Fuck," he groaned.

Lost to the orgasm, I barely registered the feel of Caleb thrusting into my touch until he took my hand in a fierce grip and shoved it away from him. "I can't. God help me, I want to, but I can't."

Breathing heavily, glistening with sweat, Kingston laughed. "I hate to burst your pious little bubble, but you already did."

"I never claimed I wasn't a sinner."

"No one is asking you to be a saint." I flicked my gaze to Caleb, needing him to know it was okay. That he could come to this in his own time. "I just want you to have everything you need."

His conflicted expression turned tender once more as he lifted the hand still nestled between my thighs and brushed my cheek, filling my nose with the scent of sex and sending a new wave of need careening through me.

"Some of us were born to suffer."

And then he stepped away, that wall he hid behind snapping back up between us.

"Some of us love to play the fucking martyr." Kingston pulled out of me, and I whimpered, already missing him.

Caleb backed away and shook his head. "There are so many things you don't understand, wolf. Maybe one day you will. But true martyrs don't play a role. They do what they must."

My priest left us without a glance back in my direction, his posture tense.

"I've never met a guy who needed to get laid so badly in my entire life."

I huffed out a laugh. "Kingston . . ."

"What? You know I'm right. That guy has the worst case of blue balls I've ever seen." Then Kingston grinned at me, looking mischievous and playful. "Speaking of full balls . . . think we have time for one more round before the heat ends?"

I glanced down at his already hardening dick. "Since you didn't give me your knot, I'd say this round isn't even done."

He growled. "That's only for you. Not when there are other participants."

"I'm surprised you let him join us. With as possessive as you are, I would've thought you'd be all growly and territorial."

"The only thing that matters is giving my mate what she needs. I'm not threatened by a fucking forty-year-old virgin. You told me you loved me and claimed me as yours. I'm not going anywhere."

Happiness settled in my chest. "I'm glad you see that. You are mine. No question."

"Damn right, I am."

CHAPTER

THIRTEEN

KINGSTON

I knew the instant Sunday's heat ended. Her scent had softened. It was no longer settling into my balls and forcing my body to respond to the call to mate. I ran my hand down her spine and pressed a kiss over her mark. She didn't even stir.

My Sunshine was out cold, sleeping so deeply I didn't think a damn earthquake could wake her. Not that I could blame her. After nearly four days of straight fucking, she'd earned a nap.

So had I. Fuck, I was exhausted.

I ached in places I didn't know could hurt. Like my fucking scalp. How could my *hair* hurt? *Oh. Right.* I smirked at the memory of her pulling the strands as I licked her cunt until she couldn't stand it any longer.

"I love you, Sunshine," I whispered against the shell of her ear.

She murmured and burrowed deeper under the blankets. I didn't want to leave, but I'd gone missing for four straight days. I needed to make sure my roommates knew I wasn't dead. The last thing I wanted was a search party finding us like this.

Not wanting to wake her, I carefully got out of bed, picking up my discarded T-shirt and placing the fabric next to her so she wouldn't miss my scent. If I were in the same position, I'd want her to do that for me. I hoped it would also let her know that I wasn't trying to run away. And, bonus, it would give her something to wear since I'd shredded that other asshole's shirt when I ripped it off her in the middle of my rut.

I tugged on my jeans and padded barefoot out into the dark hallway. I couldn't tell if it was day or night in this underground tomb. Priests were a creepy bunch. Who willingly wanted to live in a place like this?

I climbed up the stairs leading back to the main floor, my heart protesting the loss of Sunday with each new step. *Fuck.* I was addicted to her. Would I ever get used to wanting her so fiercely? I hoped to hell not.

"Mr. Farrell. I see you've come out the other side." Father Gallagher's voice was cold and dark.

"You should probably call me Kingston now. Since you've seen my dick and all, *Caleb.*"

A low snarl escaped him, and he blurred from where he'd been hiding in the shadows of the sanctuary. The slight pinch of pain in my neck was my only clue he'd done something to me. Until the numbness spread through my body. I fell to my knees, arms deadened.

"What did you do?" My words lacked the heat of anger, coming out slurred and weak instead.

"Did you really think you could snap my neck and get away unscathed?"

Motherfucker. I hadn't actually, but in the haze of everything else, I had forgotten about that little detail.

"Are you sure it's not because I dominated you while we were downstairs? Whoops," I mocked, unrepentant despite his clear upper hand. "Did I say that out loud?"

"A few days in the well should serve to remind you who is in charge here. I'll give you a hint. It's not you." He leaned close and growled, "And if you ever think to give me orders again, lad, remember this moment. I know exactly where and how to touch her to make her scream. And I don't even have to use my cock or any . . . accessories."

A furious retort was on the tip of my tongue, but whatever fucking drugs he'd injected me with were too strong. A heavy fog settled over my brain, and my eyes rolled back in my head. Leaving me only with the scent of Sunday and Caleb's parting words echoing in my mind.

FOURTEEN

SUNDAY

I stared up at the stone likeness of Persephone Blackthorne, the sadness in her eyes reminding me so much of Noah. The roses twining around her legs, thorns on the stems but never breaking her skin, lent a sinister air to the family's namesake. They resembled shackles more than the delicate flowers they were supposed to be.

Even still, the soft bubbling of water soothed my nerves as I sat with Moira on the edge of the fountain. This was one of my favorite places at Ravenscroft, especially now that Noah and I were separated. But it wasn't until after the ball I realized the necklace Persephone wore was a perfect match to the one Moira magicked for me.

Moira's fingers trailed in my hair as she continued braiding strands of glitter through it. I would end up looking like a faerie if I let her keep going, but if I was honest, it took the edge off.

I hadn't heard from Kingston since I woke up in the bowels of the church alone. Biting my lip, I glanced back down into my lap and the phone that hadn't left my side.

No new messages.

Where is he?

I was now two for two on the missing mate scorecard. I sure knew how to rack 'em up and then make 'em run . . .

"And that's quite enough screen time for you, young lady." Alek's voice slid over me like a warm caress until he plucked my phone from my hands and shoved it in his back pocket.

"Hey! I was using that."

"I know. I've been watching you stare down at it all blasted day. You'd think this damned device held all your darkest secrets."

My neck prickled with the barest hint of embarrassment. It kind of did. My desperate messages to Kingston were on there. Pleas for him to answer me, angry and hurt accusations when he hadn't responded, and then apologies to follow those up.

"Oh no. Not you, too, Týr. She's already got enough stalkers."

Alek laughed. "Nope. Moira, I'm disappointed. I handed it to you already. Are you really that unobservant?"

I glanced between them. "What is he talking about?"

Moira rolled her eyes. "I'm still trying to guess which god he is."

"Is that even a question? He's clearly a Loki. The smirk alone gives him away. I mean, shit, Moira, look at the dimples and those cheekbones."

Her mouth dropped open. "Are you fucking kidding me? He's built like fucking Thor. How can you think he's the other guy?"

I shrugged. "You can't believe everything you see in the movies."

Alek crossed his arms over his chest and laughed, full and loud. "That's my girl. She knows me so well."

"So since I got it right, can I have my phone?"

He shook his head. "I'm sorry, love, it's already gone. Mischief maker and all."

I glared up at him, but there wasn't any heat to it. "I'm going to get you for that."

"I look forward to it."

Why did that sound like sex? Why did everything lately sound like invitations for lots of glorious sweaty sex? My heat was over. Was I just a horndog?

"I need it."

"Not right now, you don't. Whatever you're not seeing on that screen is making you sad. I don't like to see you sad."

Moira stood and stretched like a cat waking from a long nap in the sun. "She's pouting because Kingston boned her into the ground for a week and now he's done a disappearing act."

Emotion flickered across Alek's face. It was too fast for me to get a read on, but I would have sworn I saw jealousy.

"So it's that way between you now?"

I didn't sense any judgment, but I felt the need to explain myself anyway. "Um . . . well, it's sort of hard to explain—"

"No, it's not. The bitch was in heat. See? Done."

"I've heard a heat can be intense, even deadly at times. I'm glad you came through it."

Moira snorted. "Oh, she came, all right."

"Moira," I chastised, but she wasn't wrong.

"And Kingston is missing?" Alek didn't give her any attention, his focus on me. "That seems . . . out of character for a mated wolf."

I bit down on my lip. "I don't have a lot of personal experience, but that's what I've been told too."

"How long has he been gone?"

"About a day."

"And he's not answering his phone . . ." Alek scrubbed a hand down his beard, running his fingers through the golden strands as his eyes narrowed in thought. "Have you tried tracing it?"

Hope lit in my chest. I didn't think that was possible. "No. I can do that?"

Ice-blue smoke swirled around his hand, my sparkly black phone case looking ridiculous in his large palm. He started tapping on the screen without a word.

"Uh, do you need my code?"

He looked up with a smirk. "Now you're just being offensive." His eyes brightened after a few more swipes on the screen. "Ah, there he is. Your wayward wolf is holed up in his room."

"His *room*?" Anger burned in my blood. He'd been in his room. Ignoring my texts. Making me crazy.

I bolted to my feet, snatching the phone from Alek's hand before he could stop me.

"Wait, where are you going?"

"Where do you think?"

He laughed and fell into step beside me.

"What are you doing, Alek?"

"I'm not going to miss this. I needed some entertainment."

"Fine, come on then, but stay out of my way unless you want to get in the line of fire."

He held up both hands in a poor imitation of innocence. "Wouldn't dream of it. I know better after seeing my mother and aunt in action when their mates piss them off. You've got this."

"Your mother argued with a berserker?"

"My mother *is* a berserker."

Holy shit. I couldn't picture the lovely woman with her sweet voice and angelic face from his library mom-date as an enraged she-hulk. *Note to self, do not piss her off.*

I didn't respond; instead I continued across the campus. My goal? Kingston's dorm. The man had some explaining to do.

Alek could have easily beat me up the stairs, but he measured his long strides to match mine. True to his word, he hung back as I pounded on the door.

"Kingston, you coward. Open up. I know you're in there."

The door opened, and Derek stood there, a sly grin on his face. "Well, hello gorgeous." His smile twisted into a frown as he slid his gaze to Alek. "Thor."

Alek crossed his arms over his chest and rolled his eyes. "There's not a stick large enough in this realm for me to be mistaken for my brother."

For a second, I wondered how literal the whole Loki/Thor thing was, but then my brain got caught trying to figure out why Thor would need a stick.

"A stick? You mean like his hammer? Is that a euphemism?"

"He wishes. No, a stick to shove up his arse, Sunny."

"Ohhhh. Gotcha. That makes way more sense." Realizing I'd gotten off topic, I turned back to Derek.

"No cupcakes this time?"

"Nope. I'm not the one that needs to apologize."

Regret flashed in his eyes. "Yeah . . . I guess I do owe you one."

133

"What? You?"

Alek stepped forward, his entire countenance changing as he went from quiet amusement to simmering fury. "Explain yourself."

Derek's eyes widened as they shifted between the Novasgardian and me, his words coming out in a rush. "You know . . . for the whole sniffing around your door trying to mount you and everything."

A low rumble left Alek's chest, causing Derek to speak faster.

"Not that I touched you or anything. But it was super not cool of me. I've just never been exposed to an unmated female in heat. It was . . . wild."

"Honestly, I wasn't even aware of anything that was happening until Kingston got to me. So, apology accepted, I guess?"

"Can you . . . uh . . . call off your Viking?"

"No," Alek answered for me.

I faced him, placing a palm on his chest. "It's fine. He was just acting on instinct. Nothing happened."

"You're damn right. If it had, he'd be dead, or at the very least, dickless."

Derek blanched, looking far less happy to see me than he had when he opened the door. "So, uh, where is Kingston?"

"What do you mean? He's here. Alek tracked his phone."

Shaking his head, Derek left the doorway only to return a moment later with a sleek silver phone. "This fucking thing has been ringing non-stop for the last two days." As he said it, the cell started to go off again, the hauntingly beautiful ringtone catching me by surprise. "See what I mean?"

"Is that classical music?"

"Yeah, that froo-froo piano shit he's always playing. Here, you might as well take it."

I accepted it with a confused frown. "You want me to take his phone?"

"You're his mate. It's basically yours by default, isn't it?"

"I don't think that's how this works . . ."

The phone stopped ringing, the call rolling to voicemail, but a text came through mere seconds later.

D: Kingston, you'd better call me unless you want me to get on the phone with your daddy.

Alek snorted. "Pup got himself in trouble."

Indecision tore at me. I couldn't imagine a scenario that ended well if Kingston's Alpha got involved. *Maybe I should take the phone. To help smooth things over for him, if nothing else.*

I pocketed the device, giving Derek a curt nod. "If you see him, tell him to come find me."

Derek offered a mock salute and winked. "Of course. Bring me some cupcakes next time. Your cherry was delicious."

Alek stiffened beside me. "I beg your pardon?"

"The fuckin' cupcakes, man. Jesus, what the hell is wrong with you people?" he muttered, slamming the door. The audible click of a lock sliding into place punctuated his defensive retreat a second later.

The phone began ringing again, this time vibrating against my ass as the music played. "Should I answer?"

Alek shrugged. "Couldn't hurt."

I pulled the cell from my pocket and slid my finger across the screen to answer, putting the call on speaker so Alek could hear as well.

"Hello?"

A smooth voice with a slight country twang carried over

the line. "Well, hello there, darlin'. You must be the little woman."

Warmth crept into my face at the unexpected endearment. "Uh . . . yeah, I'm Sunday. And you are . . ."

"Dylan Farrell, Kingston's cousin. I take it you two survived then, seein' as you're talking to me. How's he holding up? The first heat can be brutal."

Oh, God. He knew about that? Everyone and their fucking cousin knew about Kingston and me taking an extended trip to Poundtown. I wanted the ground to swallow me whole.

"Actually, I haven't seen him since yesterday. But before that he was in good health."

I cringed, immediately wanting to eat the words. What the hell was I saying? How was I supposed to talk about this with his family member? Did he want a freaking report card? Stamina, A+. Thrusting Power, A++. And a whole lot of extra credit for the real deep dicking.

Fuck my life.

"Settle down. I can hear your nerves jangling over the phone. What do you mean you haven't seen him since yesterday? He should be with you in case there's a new wave."

"New wave?"

"Yeah. Your first time can be unpredictable. Didn't anyone teach you this stuff?"

Motherfucker.

"No. I . . . it's a long story. I went into this whole thing blind."

"Shit. Well, you should make sure he's nearby just on the off chance. Can't you track him?"

"Track?"

"Lord, what are they teaching you at this fancy school?

136

How to stick your thumbs up your asses? Yes, track. You're a wolf. He's a wolf. You're mated. Track him. If he's within a hundred miles, you should be able to find him."

"I . . ." Really should have fucking thought of that sooner. This whole wolf thing was new to me; it wasn't second nature to turn to my beast yet. But it should have been. If someone in my life had prepared me for this, maybe I wouldn't keep ending up in these situations.

"Let me know when you find him."

"Will do."

"And darlin'?"

"Yeah?"

"Take care of him. He's been waitin' on you a long while. There's nothing more life-changing than finding your mate. Except for losing her. He's had to do both."

FIFTEEN

I pushed through the doors of Blackthorne Hall, Alek hot on my heels as I ran down the stairs.

"Sunny, wait up. Where the hell are you going?"

"You heard what Dylan said. I have to track him."

Alek raised a brow. "Is that what you're doing?"

"It's what I'm about to do. You don't have to come with me. I can do this alone."

He clamped a big hand on my shoulder. "You can, but you won't. I'm not leaving you to search for him unguarded."

Rolling my eyes, I sighed and slid my gaze up to his crystal blue irises. "I'm not helpless."

"I didn't say you were. But while you were off . . . doing whatever you were doing"—his cheeks burned pink—"I fought off two demons who attacked a shifter girl outside of *Iniquity*. Sunny, she looked like you. They're coming up from hell faster and more frequently than normal."

That sent a shiver down my spine.

"It could have been a coincidence . . ."

Alek gave me a look. "I don't believe in coincidences. Lilith agrees. She is concerned about the increased level of demonic activity. I may have only been in this realm for a little while, but it's obvious to me you're being targeted. But even if that wasn't the case, even if the woman hadn't looked almost identical to you, I'm not about to let you wander off on your own. Where you go, I go."

His promise wrapped a ribbon of warmth around my heart. "Is that so?"

He nodded. "Deal with it."

"Fine. But you'll have to keep up."

I bolted, running hard away from the main campus and into the wooded area, heading straight for the clearing where Kingston and I trained with Alek. He was right behind me, not even winded as we drew to a stop.

"Why are we stopping?" he asked, glancing around as if searching for a clue he might have missed.

Pulling the phone from my pocket, I tossed it his way before kicking off my shoes and reaching for the hem of my shirt.

Alek caught the phone, but his eyes were locked onto me as I pulled the cotton over my head. "What are you doing?"

"What's it look like I'm doing?" I tossed the fabric on the ground, then shucked my yoga pants before reaching behind me and unhooking my bra.

A wicked smirk twisted his lips as he shrugged and began taking off his own T-shirt. "Ah, a pre-hunt tumble. Excellent plan."

I laughed out loud, but that didn't stop me from raking my gaze over his insane body. Noah and Kingston were built, but Alek was something else entirely. His muscles looked as though they'd been carved from stone, the stacked slabs of his pecs and abs and the deep V cutting down into the waist of his jeans something I'd only ever seen in magazines. No. Not magazines, comic books. The ones that depicted gods and superheroes.

Alek took two steps forward, closing the distance between us as he reached out and ran his thumb slowly along the corner of my mouth. "You've got a little something just there."

Heat raced down my body, making me shiver. Suddenly his plan wasn't sounding quite so silly.

No, Sunday. Focus.

I snapped my gaze up to his twinkling eyes. "Shut up. That's not what this is. I'm shifting."

He pointed between the two of us. "So you don't . . ." He wiggled his eyebrows.

"No. Put your shirt back on."

"There she goes, ruining all my fun."

"You can turn around if it's too . . . hard to see me naked." My focus drifted to the prominent bulge at his fly.

He winked. "Oh, I'm just fine. Besides, I've never witnessed a shifter change."

"Prepare to be underwhelmed. I've only done it twice, once by accident."

"Let me be the judge."

Nervousness flooded my body at the knowledge I was being watched, but I pushed it aside and instead focused on my breaths. I closed my eyes, thinking back to the time in the woods with Kingston.

For a second, I was worried it wasn't going to work without his wolf to summon mine. But there she was. Ready and more than eager to take over.

To find her mate.

To be free.

As my body began to transform, there was still the discomfort of being stretched beyond my capacity, but the shooting pain was gone. It felt more like being shaped and molded into something new and less like I was being remade entirely.

In the span of a heartbeat, I went from standing across from Alek's heated gaze to shaking out my fur. Without Kingston to distract me, I could focus on the world coming to life around me. My hearing was sharper, my vision picked up colors that didn't exist for humans, and my nose . . . God, this was amazing.

I loped over to Alek, burrowing my face against his thigh and drawing in the salty icy tang of the foreign land that was so uniquely him. Now that I had his scent, I knew I'd be able to find him again, no matter where we were. My wolf locked his distinct markers in, and she'd never let us forget them.

Alek dug his thick fingers into my fur, right between my ears. He stroked gently, drawing a happy rumble from me.

"Gods, you're beautiful. I've never seen anything like you, Sunny." He smiled and knelt so he was eye to eye with me. "You're the spitting image of Hati."

I cocked my head and waited for him to explain.

"She's one of the mythical wolves who chases the moon through the sky." His gentle fingers traced a crescent shape between my eyes. "But with Hati comes Ragnarok," he murmured under his breath. If I was in human form, I doubt I would have heard him.

I licked at his hand, making him laugh as I pulled away from the lull of his touch. Nose to the ground, I searched for Kingston's scent. We'd been here often, so I knew I could pick it up. Once I did, I could follow the trail to the place it was the strongest. And then, as I'd hoped, he was there. Strong and musky, the scent of my bonded mate was unmistakable.

I took off, running fast and focused, the sound of my Viking giving chase sending a thrill through me. One day, we'd play like this, but not today. I had to find Kingston.

It was almost easy once I'd isolated the path to him. Confusion fluttered through me as we moved farther and farther from the school and into the thick of the forest.

Why would he be out here?

There were no buildings I could see, at least none nearby.

Is he hurt?

Panic had me moving faster, trees blurring as I tore through the woods in my desperation. The bite of his scent grew sharper, telling me he was close. I pulled to a stop, staring in bewilderment at the surrounding area.

There was nothing—no one—here. Just trees and the heavy cover they provided. Any sunlight from the afternoon was filtered away by the branches overhead, casting this part of the woods completely in shadow.

Hackles raised, I prowled forward, homing in on his scent again. Sitting, I raised my head to the sky and let out a mournful howl.

"Sunshine?" Kingston's voice had my heart racing. He sounded strange, his words echoing and slightly hollow.

Heavy footfalls from behind me told me Alek had caught up, this time his breaths coming in harsh gasps. I'd been too fast even for him.

I shifted back to my human form, calling out, "Kingston, where are you?"

"Down here!"

Where the hell was he? I searched the surroundings and

only saw bushes and trees. But Alek strode straight forward, pulling a shrub clean out of the earth and revealing the stone structure beyond.

The well.

I ran to the side, looking down through the grate, locked with chains and silver. I could just barely make out the top of Kingston's head in the inky depths.

"Who did this to you?"

"That ungrateful bastard, after everything I did for him, letting him join us like that . . ."

At first his mumbled rant didn't make sense . . . until it did.

"Caleb did this to you? I'll have his balls for this."

A soft snicker filtered up from the well. "As much as I love the idea of you riding to my defense, I might have earned it."

"What could you have possibly done to deserve being thrown into the well?"

Kingston let out a harsh laugh. "Broke that fucker's neck."

Alek whistled. "Ballsy."

"Is that you, Viking?"

Alek moved to stand beside me, giving Kingston a little wave.

Shock had my mouth hanging open. It took me a second to process what Kingston had just said. "You broke his neck?"

I could practically feel his shrug. "He was keeping you from me."

I was only just starting to understand a mate's need to be near their fated love. I could only imagine how crazed he'd been. And how desperate. "He should have known better."

"Yeah, well. The good priest is just as territorial over you as the rest of us. He thought he was protecting you. As if you'd ever need protection from me."

"I'll get you out of here. Maybe we can pry the bars off? Break the lock?"

"No. I'll serve my sentence. If you free me, I'll only have to do something else to appease him."

"Did he say how long you'd be down there?"

"One day for each bone I snapped."

"How many did you snap?" I asked, my voice tinged with exasperation and amusement. Why did I get the feeling he was oddly proud of himself?

"Seven. I got every damn one in his neck."

"Am I supposed to get you a cookie?"

"You can let me eat yours when I get out of here."

I blushed, my eyes darting up to Alek's smirking face. He gave me a one-shoulder shrug. "I would have said the same thing. I like cookies."

"Nope. You two don't get to gang up on me. You're not buddies, remember?"

"We've . . . come to understand each other," Kingston said. "Take care of her while I'm down here, Viking. She likes to think she doesn't need us, but she's wrong."

"Already taken care of," he answered, surprisingly serious given his joking manner seconds earlier.

I shook my head. "And I'm what, just supposed to leave you down here to starve? That's ridiculous."

"It's not. The priest is feeding and watering me. I'll be fine."

"You're not a fucking plant, Kingston."

"No. I'm an Alpha. I can survive just fine in the woods. You worry about yourself, baby. I promise you'll be the first person I come see when I get out."

"I never agreed to be a prison wife."

"As much as I like hearing you call yourself my wife, this isn't a prison."

"Feels like it."

"Stop sulking, Sunshine. I'll be okay, I promise."

"Maybe I can talk to Father Gallagher and get your sentence reduced? Time off for good behavior?"

"There's nothing good about my behavior. Trust me." Kingston was such a damn smartass. "I'll see you when I'm out. I promise I'll make it worth the wait."

"We should head back. It's getting dark." As he spoke, Alek's warm palm skated over the small of my back. My *bare* back. God, I'd been standing here naked all this time.

"Fine. I left all my clothes back at the clearing. It'll be night before we get to the campus at this rate. Perfect time for confronting a priest."

Alek held out a familiar bundle of clothes. "I picked these up for you."

"You're just telling me this now?"

He grinned. "I was enjoying the view. But also, you were in the middle of something. It seemed rude to interrupt."

"Uh huh. Likely story, Viking." His smile stretched, forcing me to begrudgingly smile in return. He was too pretty to stay mad at. And he did sort of have a point. Sighing, I said, "Well, you might as well hang onto them. I should probably shift for the run back."

"Or we could take the direct path back to the school."

"The direct . . ." I trailed off, my gaze following in the direction he was pointing. "Sonofabitch."

"In your defense, you had no idea he'd be here. You followed your nose."

I snagged my clothes and dressed quickly. "I can't believe we were so close. What kind of wolf am I? Jesus."

"You're a really pretty one."

"Stop flirting with my mate right in front of me!" Kingston called. "I can hear you."

"She's ours. Get over it." Alek took my hand. "Come on, Sunny. I'll walk you home."

CHAPTER

SIXTEEN

SUNDAY

The rustle of paper was the only sound in my dorm room as Moira and I both lay on our beds, me reading a textbook as I tried frantically to catch up after missing an entire week of classes, her flipping through the pages of a glossy fashion magazine.

"Oh, I love that," she murmured, causing me to glance up from my notes just in time to see her magic herself into a shirt that read 'Peg the Patriarchy.'

"Discreet," I said with a laugh.

"Who's trying to be discreet?"

"You're hilarious."

She lifted her shoulders and offered me an air kiss. "I know. It's one of the reasons you keep me around."

A soft whooshing noise came from the doorway accompanied by a glow that dimmed almost instantly.

"What the fuck was that?" I muttered. I didn't need anything else weird happening. It had been one thing after another these days, and I just wanted a break.

Moira pointed to a pale piece of paper resting at the foot of my bed. "Pixie mail."

149

"Excuse me?"

She shrugged, giving me a look like I was the strange one. "Harry Potter has owls. We have pixies."

"Of course we do."

Moira jumped up, sending her magazine tumbling to the ground. "This is so exciting. I never get any mail." She plucked the letter off my bed and scanned the front, her smile twisting to a frown. "Damn, it's not even for me."

She held it out to me with a noticeable sulk.

"You might as well read it. Not like we have any secrets. I mean, you know all about my crazy sexual habits, so what's a little letter reading between friends?"

She perked back up and blew me a kiss. "That's my best girl."

"I'm going to tell Ash you said that." But her eyes had already dropped to the missive she'd unfolded, reading it with greedy abandon. "Um . . . are you forgetting something?"

"What? Oh!" She laughed. "I guess I should read it out loud, huh?"

I blinked at her. "You think?"

She cleared her throat, deepening it dramatically. "My dearest, darlingest, doviest, most magic vagina-est . . ."

I snatched the letter from her hands with a scowl. "Stop it. He did not write that."

Laughing, she fell back onto her bed. "You never let me have any fun."

"As if I can actually prevent you from doing anything you want, Belladonna."

"True."

Shaking my head, I lifted Noah's letter and started reading.

DOVE,

I KNOW IT'S BEEN A WHILE SINCE WE LAST SPOKE, AND THAT IS MY FAULT. YOU MUST FEEL ABANDONED BY ME YET AGAIN. TRUST ME WHEN I SAY THAT HAS NEVER BEEN MY INTENTION, THOUGH I SEEM TO BE RATHER GOOD AT IT. IF I HAD IT MY WAY, YOU'D BE IN MY ARMS RIGHT NOW, IN MY BED, AND WE'D NEVER BE SEPARATED. BUT SINCE YOUR VISIT TO MY SELF-APPOINTED PRISON, THINGS HAVE SHIFTED AND BECOME MORE TENSE.

I'VE FELT YOUR PAIN AS WELL, EVEN THROUGH THE BLOCK I PUT UP TO PROTECT YOU. ~~ARE YOU WELL?~~ OF COURSE YOU'RE NOT. IF YOU'RE FEELING HALF AS MISERABLE AS I AM, THEN IT MUST BE BLOODY IMPOSSIBLE FOR YOU RIGHT NOW. I CAN ONLY HOPE, AND I CAN'T BELIEVE I'M SAYING THIS, THAT THE OTHERS ARE AT YOUR SIDE, HELPING YOU.

I CAN'T COME BACK TO RAVENSCROFT. AT LEAST NOT YET. POSSIBLY NOT EVER AT THIS POINT. IT KILLS ME TO KNOW YOU'RE THERE AND OUT OF MY REACH. BUT KEEPING YOU SAFE IS THE MOST IMPORTANT THING.

THINK OF ME TONIGHT WHEN YOU SLIP INTO YOUR DREAMS. MAYBE, IF WE'RE LUCKY, WE'LL SEE EACH OTHER THERE.

YOURS,
NOAH

I let the paper fall from my fingers, releasing a heavy sigh. My heart ached. It was almost worse now that I'd heard from him. It brought our separation back into focus, sharpening the edges and cutting me wide open.

"At least he's trying to stay in touch with you," Moira offered softly.

"Yeah, you're right."

"You okay?"

I wiped away a tear with the back of my hand, forcing myself to move past my sadness. "I'll be fine. I just miss him."

"I get it. I really do. I miss Ash like crazy."

"Can she come visit again?"

Moira shook her head. "Not for a while. But we're making it work."

I took a shuddering breath. "What if he doesn't come back?"

"I don't know."

That same whooshing noise filled the room, and another light glowed and faded, this time at the door rather than my bed. Hope lit in my chest. "Another one?"

"Maybe he forgot something?" Moira added, bounding to the door and snatching the piece of paper, but this one was different. It was rolled and wrapped with a deep scarlet ribbon. She opened the scroll, and her eyes widened.

"What is it?"

"You've been summoned to the headmistress's office. Shit, Sunday, what did you do now?"

Unease prickled the back of my neck, settling in an icy patch between my shoulder blades. I only had this feeling when I was in trouble, and here at Ravenscroft, I seemed to be in trouble a lot.

"Maybe it's because I missed so many classes?" I guessed, knowing even as I said it, there was no way it was something that simple. I had a gift for breaking rules I didn't know existed.

"Yeah," Moira agreed, though it lacked conviction. "That must be it."

I kicked my legs over the side of the bed with the same level of enthusiasm one might have when facing a firing squad.

"Do you think I need to dress for a funeral?"

Moira smirked. "Hold that thought." She wiggled her fingers and murmured something under her breath, and before I knew it, I was dressed like a perfectly modest yet absolutely sinful Catholic schoolgirl.

I laughed. "Not quite what I meant, but okay."

Moira winked. "Trust me. That look is going to work wonders for you."

"On the headmistress?"

She shrugged. "In life."

"You're a nut."

"I'm allergic to nuts."

I opened my mouth to protest. After all, I'd just seen her crunching away on a bag of pistachios, but then her joke landed. "Goodbye, Moira."

"I hope you come back alive!" she called after me as I left the room. "Also, bring me some more pistachios from the dining hall if you get a chance."

Shaking my head, I closed the door behind me and headed for the stairs. I caught my reflection in the shiny elevator doors and laughed. Pleated skirt—plaid, of course—white button-up with a Peter Pan collar, even a little tie and headband that matched the skirt. And then there were the stockings. They were navy blue to match my blazer, but instead of coming to my knees, they stopped just above them. The outfit was completed by a pair of heeled Mary Janes—patent leather, shiny, and way too sexy to be acceptable for a uniform.

"Good God, Moira. You need to stop watching Gossip Girl reruns."

I did a little twirl, kind of in love with the overall effect. I'd never pick anything like this out for myself, but I had to admit, the look packed a punch.

I raced down the stairs, all too aware of the air brushing against my thighs under the far-too-short skirt. Especially once I stepped outside and onto a campus buzzing with activity as students milled around between their evening classes.

The sky had darkened to a deep blue velvet as the sun finally sank below the horizon. It seemed obvious to me now that nighttime would be when a lot of students had more energy, even those who could walk in the sunlight. We were creatures granted more power by the moon. All of us. But when I'd first arrived, I'd been operating on an almost human schedule. That's what happens when you live seven years of your life in a fortress cut off from the rest of the supernatural world. You forget what normal is.

I hurried through the quad, smiling as Derek caught my eye where he was playing American football with other members of his pack. Then I spotted a familiar blond head. *Alek.* My smile froze when I saw the sexy valkyrie beside him, and a tendril of jealousy worked its way through me. She was demonstrating something with her wings, posing for my Novasgardian. It wasn't until she ruffled them that she and I both noticed his attention had shifted from her to zero in on me.

His lips curled in a knowing smile, and I realized my jealousy must be evident in my expression.

He tilted his head, gesturing for me to come to him, but I quickly shook mine in response. I couldn't keep Madame le Blanc waiting.

Striding toward the main hall, my skirt swished with each sway of my hips, but I didn't allow myself to look back and see if Alek watched. Even though I wanted to.

I rounded the corner, heels loud on the stone floor. Cool fingers clamped around my wrist, making me cry out in surprise as I was dragged from the hallway and into a small alcove.

"Are ye thinking to tempt me, Miss Fallon? Is that what you're about in this getup?" Caleb's Irish was stronger, nearly breathless as he pressed himself against me and spoke quietly.

My eyebrows flew up. "You think this is for you? Narcissistic much?"

"Isn't it? You fanny about here like you own all our cocks. Funny thing is, I suppose you do. Mine, at least. Even if I try to keep away. There you are, in your short skirt and those damned stockings. You're probably not even wearing knickers."

His impassioned rant sent warning bells off in my mind. *Has he been drinking?*

"Caleb, this isn't like you. What's wrong?" I placed a gentle palm on his jaw, my thumb brushing across his full bottom lip.

He groaned and scrubbed a hand over his face and then nuzzled into me, inhaling deeply.

"I fed from a drunkard."

"On purpose?"

"It was oblivion I was after. To free myself from thoughts of *you*. But I can't escape you, even now . . ." He twirled a strand of my hair around his finger, giving it a sharp tug. "You possess me."

"I'm not . . . it's not on purpose. There's a pull."

"Aye."

"I should go—"

"With me. If it's a man you're looking for, let it be me. I can't take it any longer. The wantin' you." His fingers trailed first over the tops of my stockings and then up until they reached the hem of my skirt. "The needin' you. You unlocked something inside me, and I can't get it back in its prison." His breath was ragged as he dropped his voice even lower. "I don't think I want to."

"Caleb," I whispered. "Stop."

He stiffened for just a moment, then backed away, his touch gone with the flip of a switch. "So that's how it is? You only want me when I'm hurting you?"

"I want you all the time, but not like this. Not when you don't know what you're doing, and I'm late for a meeting with the headmistress." I'd been so distracted by him—like always—that I'd forgotten I had my own bone to pick with him. "And also, I'm pissed with you right now for locking up Kingston."

He snorted, leaning casually against the wall. "The little shite thought he could kill me and get away with it. I won't be accepting of treatment like that from him or anyone. He earned every fecking day in that well. Not a moment less."

"Then maybe I won't let you touch me again until you let him out. That can be *your* punishment."

"I've punished myself enough for the both of us. It's exactly what I need from you, withholding. It's what I deserve. I'm a faithless sinner."

"And I'm a werewolf whore. We make a great team."

He frowned. "You're no whore, Sunday."

"If I'm not a whore, then you're not faithless." I cocked a brow.

My poor priest, I could see the conflict at war in his eyes. He was desperate to believe me, but he thought so little of himself that he couldn't.

"Caleb," I whispered, stepping close. "Loving someone doesn't make you a sinner. It makes you human."

He shuddered, his eyes fluttering closed. "Humans have souls. I'm a monster."

"Then so am I."

"No," he said, shaking his head and opening his eyes. "No, my sweet Sunday." He reached out, cupping my face with both his palms and resting his forehead against mine. "You are a gift. If only God saw fit to give you to me before I made my vows. That's how I know I'm damned. The one thing I want is the only thing I can't have. I'm trapped in a hell on Earth because I can only watch."

"What if I don't want you to only watch?"

He backed away and ran a hand through his dark hair. "I've already crossed too many lines. Don't tempt me."

"Mademoiselle Fallon, are you quite done . . . fraternizing with our priest?" Headmistress le Blanc's voice was a crisp melody on the wind.

I jolted as if I'd been electrocuted, jumping away from Caleb like I could somehow undo the damage of being found with him like this. We hadn't really crossed boundaries—at least not tonight—but if she'd overheard anything we said, we were already screwed.

"It's my fault, Madame. Sunday missed her session with me, and I was scolding her."

There was no mistaking the amusement in the headmistress's voice. "Of course, Father Gallagher. As is your right. I believe Sunday has an appointment with me, but I can send her back your way once we are done?"

"No . . . I'm finished with her." His voice was ice-cold, emotionless, and it hurt.

Words failed me as Madame le Blanc took me by the arm and escorted me away from him. When I looked back over my shoulder, he was still there, standing half shrouded by darkness and his face void of all emotion.

I'd broken him somehow. And it had to have been me. I was the common denominator any time one of my paramours was hurt, and I hated that. Kingston in the well, and my rejection of our mate bond. Noah imprisoned, not to mention his traitor mark. And now Caleb, my professor and a man of God I'd led astray, tempting him to break his vows time and time again.

The only one left for me to hurt was Alek. But it wouldn't happen if I stayed away from him. Maybe I could save him some of the heartache and take it all on myself instead.

"Is something troubling you, Miss Fallon?" Madame le Blanc asked, her voice pulling me from my spiral as we entered her office.

"I'm a little nervous about why you wanted to see me, Madame."

It wasn't exactly a lie.

"Oh? Well, allow me to put your mind at ease. I understand that you went through your first heat. I wanted to check on you and see how you were feeling. If there was anything you needed."

That brought me up short. She hadn't exactly been *nice* to me since I arrived. This woman was distant, cold, but usually fair. Warm and fuzzy wasn't how I would describe her. "I don't understand why you care, Madame. You're not a wolf."

Her face softened, and she took a seat, motioning for me

to do the same. "Perhaps not. But I am a woman, and my knowledge of the world and the creatures in it surpasses most. I know that your mother was not around to discuss these matters with you. It must be confusing trying to figure all this out by yourself. Especially so much later than your peers. Your father did you a disservice by leaving you in the dark."

"It was . . . surprising. But it's over now. Moira ordered me some suppressants to take. It won't happen again."

"Good. That's good. In the meantime, I have something for you as well. It should help . . . regulate things until your suppressants arrive." Without moving, a small bottle appeared on the center of her desk. "You'll need to come see me and drink this once a week until your suppressants have taken effect."

"How long do they take to be effective?"

"At least one full month of pills. Similar to human birth control. We don't want you caught unawares."

"What does that mean?" But my conversation with Dylan sparked to life in my mind, clueing me in to the answer.

"Heats are unpredictable until your body gets used to them at the best of times. Since your wolf was repressed for so many years, you may experience worse irregularity. More frequent and longer periods of need. We can't have that. Our unmated male students won't survive."

"I mated with Kingston." I wasn't sure why I blurted it out except as some kind of explanation that she didn't need to worry about me suffering alone.

"I am aware. He's already put in the paperwork requesting mated pair housing. As has Mr. Blackthorne."

"What?" Noah and I hadn't even sealed our bond until right before he left. How had he found the time?

"Mr. Blackthorne came to me a little over a week ago stating his intentions with you. And your Mr. Farrell applied only a few days after."

Oh, my God. Both of them just anticipated I'd uproot everything and live with them? But if I was being honest, the thought made my heart flutter. Maybe there was a house where all of us could live together.

"Does this stuff prevent . . ."

"Conception? Yes. If taken properly."

"How does someone take it improperly?"

She smiled. "By not coming to see me."

"Understood."

She looked pointedly at the bottle.

"Oh, you want me to take it now."

I pulled the little purple topper off and carefully sniffed the clear liquid.

"I'd be offended by your reticence if you were anyone else. But I must say, Mademoiselle Fallon, I approve of your caution. After the attacks on you, one can never be too careful."

"You know about those? That they were after me?"

"I see all. Remember?"

I held the vial to my lips and looked at her. "I have to drink all of it?"

She nodded. "All. A fresh supply will be waiting for you next week."

I tensed as I tipped the bottle back, bracing myself for it to taste bitter and medicinal. Surprisingly, it didn't taste like anything. Though as soon as the liquid slid down my throat, icy cold moved through my body, making me shiver.

"Very good. You may go now."

I had to force my teeth not to chatter, but I already felt

better. My body warmed itself from the inside out. "Thank you."

The doors opened without me touching them, and I stepped out into the hall, feeling protected, secure, and like I could go back to normal.

That alone should have tipped me off.

When had things ever been normal?

SEVENTEEN

Unease tugged at my senses as I lay on the bed in my gilded cage. In the two weeks since my confinement began, I'd only felt this once before. A restless gnawing in my gut, a desperate hunger I couldn't sate. I craved something but had no idea what that something was. Only that I needed it.

I'd fed, believing that would ease my hunger. It hadn't even scratched the surface. For once, blood was not the answer to this emptiness inside me. I'd been a wild animal, tearing at the walls, frantic as I tried to break out of my cell. Until the sensation vanished like it had never been there in the first place.

But it was building again. Consuming me until I could think of little else. What was wrong with me?

I'd never heard of this happening before. Was it some sort of side effect of being apart from my mate for so long? I knew madness could result from extended separation, but Sunday and I had only just mated. Surely that was too soon for anything, or was it even worse because we were so newly bonded?

Grabbing my phone off the bedside table, I dialed the only person I knew could help me. My father.

He answered before the first ring was half over.

"Noah? What's wrong?"

His voice held the tension of a parent expecting bad news. Cashel Blackthorne always expected bad news from me.

"I feel . . . strange. Off somehow."

"What do you mean? Have you fed? Has Lucas been mistreating you? That cocky bastard probably tossed you an old blood bag and went off to galavant in the woods with his shifter."

"No. Of course not. It's nothing like that. This is . . . different. I don't think it has anything to do with feeding, but something in me is insatiable. A thirst I cannot quench. A pull to get to something."

"I'll be right there. Don't move from where you are."

The concern in his voice had my heart lurching. I couldn't answer him because he'd already hung up.

Two hours passed, and the itch under my skin hadn't eased. I paced the room, anxiety causing me to spiral toward insanity with every second that ticked by. The fucking timepiece on the wall was mocking me. Reminding me of every moment I didn't have my mate. I tore the bloody thing from where it hung and threw it to the floor, denting the glossy hardwood and smashing the intricate clock into pieces.

The crash reverberated off every wall, filling my head with satisfying, discordant notes of chaos. What else could I destroy?

I spied the bookshelf filled with priceless, irreplaceable tomes and stalked over with a dark smile.

Perfect.

Without a second thought, I tore the wood structure free of the wall and flung it across the room, books and artifacts flying everywhere.

And that's how my father found me. Standing amidst utter destruction, pages and random debris raining down around me.

"Bloody hell, Noah. Control your temper. You're as bad as me."

I grinned at him until the panic took hold again. "Something is wrong with me. Isn't it?"

He was a master of self-control, but he couldn't hide the worry that flashed in the eyes that were so like my own.

"Tell me," I gritted out, bracing myself for the worst.

"Do you remember the stories we told you of sun sickness?"

Dread built in my chest. "Yes. It was eradicated. Mother was the cure."

"No. You and your sister are the cure. At least . . . we thought you were."

The way he said it made me shudder. Sun sickness had ravaged the vampire world for centuries, driving the infected mad, causing them to eventually walk into the sun and end their existence in one rash decision.

"Are you saying I have sun sickness?"

My father frowned, looking conflicted. "From what you've described, it certainly sounds like it. As much as it pains me to see you locked up like this, perhaps this is the best place for you until we get to the bottom of it."

"I . . . I'll be fine. I can walk in the daylight. I'm not at risk. What does it matter if I have it?"

"You could infect others. It's a blood-borne virus. Not to mention the madness and uncontrollable strength that comes with it. I watched my mother and brother succumb to this illness, Noah. It isn't pretty. They lost themselves to it."

I sat down hard on the edge of my bed, my breath leaving me in a heavy whoosh. I ran a shaking hand through my hair, not ready to contemplate just what such a diagnosis would mean for me . . . or my mate.

Fuck. Sunday.

"What do we do? How do we confirm this?"

He sighed and dragged his palm over the back of his neck. "Your aunt Callie has a lab back at Blackthorne Manor. We'll take a sample of your blood and test it."

"Aunt Callie is a ghost."

"She's still brilliant, even if she doesn't have a body any longer. It might surprise you to know even I can follow directions."

Something loosened in my chest, a lightness that eased some of the pressure as I thought of my father, the Blackthorne king, taking orders from a ghost. "Take my blood now. I need to know if I put Sunday at risk."

My father nodded and pulled a syringe out of his pocket.

"Carry one of those with you everywhere you go?" I asked, needing to make light of the situation.

"Never know when someone will need a little prick."

A low chuckle rolled through the hall as Lucas approached. "Oh, brother, how right you are. I prefer to bring the big one."

Father's gaze snapped to his younger brother. "Why didn't you tell me he was sick?"

Lucas's brows drew together. "He's not sick."

"Look at him. He's gone feral."

"Wouldn't you if you'd been kept from your mate while she needed you?"

My uncle's words settled in my chest, quieting the maelstrom raging in my mind.

"What are you talking about? I'm mated and can still control myself when Olivia and I have to be apart."

"Cash, you poor pathetic soul. I don't envy that you mated a human. You're really missing out on what it's like to be with your mate when she's in heat."

"In heat?" my father and I repeated at the same time.

Lucas's grin was wicked. "Oh, yes. It's one of the perks of being with a shifter. Briar is wild in the sack normally, but when she's in *need* . . . Let's just say I have to hydrate frequently so she doesn't drain me dry."

Sunday was in *need* of me. She was the one feeling this way, not me. I was tapped into her emotions because of our bond.

"I have to go to her."

My father shook his head. "You can't. Not if you want to protect her from the Council. The Donoghue family is out for blood. If not yours, then hers. You being here is the only thing easing their anger."

I deflated as I let those words sink in. I was here to protect her—and us. If I left, it would only be because she was at risk of death.

"She'll get through it, nephew, I promise. But oh, the fun you'll have next time." Lucas winked. "You could always drop your shields and visit her in her dreams. If she's anything like Briar, those will be just as . . . colorful."

For the first time, I was truly thankful Sunday had Kingston to look out for her. As her wolf's mate, he would know exactly what she needed and see her through it. I, on the other hand, would be left here to suffer alongside her in the meantime.

"Come on, Cash, we should leave him be. I've got a fresh

bottle of grenache blended with the blood of a dastardly politician in the wine cellar. And it looks like our Noah could use a . . . nap."

I watched my father and uncle leave together, relief radiating from both of them. I hadn't seen my father this worked up about something since Mother was in labor with my youngest brother eighteen years ago. The fear that I was infected with sun sickness had been written in every line of his face.

My own relief that these symptoms were related to my mate rather than a deadly illness was equally palpable. Not that I was happy Sunday was suffering so acutely, but at least it was a temporary situation with a specific cure. I only wished I could be the one to provide it.

Settling back onto my bed, I tried to get comfortable among the various books and fragments that had landed there. Perhaps my uncle was onto something. If I couldn't be with her in the flesh, maybe a visit to her dreams would be the next best thing.

CHAPTER
EIGHTEEN
SUNDAY

The library was unusually busy this afternoon as everybody crammed for their mid-semester evaluations. Each student was required to prove what they'd learned so far to their personal advisers, which meant I had to stay focused during a one-on-one session with Caleb if I had any chance of receiving a passing grade. Somehow I didn't think *extra credit* would be on the table. Or under the desk?

The naughty thought made me squirm, catching Kingston's attention. He tugged at a lock of my hair. "Something on your mind, Sunshine?"

"Just thinking about the test."

"Does this test make you wet? I can smell you from here. Do we need to get out of here so I can . . . serve my mate?" His low rumble skated across my skin, but instead of causing the wave of arousal I'd expected, I just felt more on edge.

"No. I need to focus."

"I know a way to clear your mind and help with that."

"Not everything is about sex."

"Sure it is."

"Kingston."

"Okay, okay. Point taken." He sat back, but his gaze never left me.

"What?" I finally snapped, flattening my hands over my book as I looked at him.

"You're . . . not yourself today. Everything all right?"

I didn't know. Everything around me annoyed me. The sounds of people sniffling, the soft clearing of a throat, even Kingston touching me rubbed me the wrong way. I never felt like that about him, even when I'd been pretending to hate him.

If I didn't know better, I'd say I was PMSing. I was uncomfortable in my skin and had that same inexplicable low-boiling rage. I could probably break out into tears as easily as destroy somebody for looking at me sideways. But that made no sense.

And since I couldn't explain it, I was currently smack dab in Denialville.

"I'm fine."

His eyes widened. "Oh, shit. The kiss of death. Second only to 'we need to talk.' You know I have four sisters, right?" He stood. "I'm going to the dining hall to scavenge you some snacks. Maybe steal a heating pad from the clinic too."

He was being so sweet, and it made me feel instantly guilty. He'd done absolutely nothing to deserve my shitty temper, but I just couldn't turn it off.

"I don't need anything. I just need people to leave me alone." I slammed the book in front of me shut so hard a crack splintered through the center of the table. Fuck. Maybe I did need snacks.

Kingston wisely kept his mouth shut. His only reaction

was to brush his palm over the top of my head and press a soft kiss to my forehead. "I'll check in on you later, okay?"

"Fine," I snapped, miserable that I was being such a moody bitch.

I glanced up at him, guilt washing over me at the tenderness in his eyes. When his gaze flicked to the doorway, I followed, catching sight of Alek's hulking form striding in without a care in the world. Must be nice.

Kingston's nostrils flared, and he looked down at me and then back up to Alek with interest. "Oh, I get it."

"Get what?"

"He's the one you need."

"What the fuck are you talking about, Kingston?"

"Your scent changed the second you saw him."

"How many times do I have to tell you to stop sniffing me? It's weird."

"It's a shifter thing. I can't help it." He smirked. "Besides, you're always sniffing me."

"I am not."

"Yeah, babe, that's a lie. You did it just a minute ago even though you seem to want to rip my balls off right now." Reaching down, he toyed with the drawstring dangling from the hood of the sweatshirt I wore. "And you stole my hoodie this morning at breakfast and still haven't given it back."

Embarrassment crept into my cheeks. "If you wanted your stupid jacket back—"

He stopped my hands as I went to pull it off. "Keep it. It looks better on you, and I like knowing you're wrapped up in my scent."

I huffed. He was making it impossible for me to justify my grumpiness with him. Stupid handsome wolf.

"Good. Then I'm keeping it."

One more kiss to my forehead, and he left as Alek walked past. The two men exchanged a look, and I expected my Viking to join me, but he held up his magic mirror and gestured upstairs as he continued on his way. That made me smile. Today must be the day for his weekly chat with his mom. I loved that about him.

After a few minutes of staring at the cover of the closed book without seeing anything, I decided to give up the ghost and follow Alek upstairs. Not to eavesdrop or anything, just to say hi. He was the first person in the last couple of days that didn't seem to set off my 'get away from me' meter.

I leaned against a bookcase, peeking around just to get a look at him as he sat in the oversized chair in his favorite reading nook.

"I see you, Sunny." The amusement in his tone had my body reacting. No trace of irritation. No tension. Just . . . safety and comfort.

"But I was being so stealthy."

He quirked a brow as he looked up, his eyes finding me immediately. "If that's your idea of stealthy, we need to up your training sessions. You're as loud as a wyvern pup learning to fly."

"That's loud?"

"Have you seen a wyvern attempt to fly? They crash into everything."

"Um, I've never seen a wyvern, so . . ."

His lips twisted into a grin. "I'll show you one someday."

The promise of him taking me to his homeland settled something that had become unmoored in me. He made me feel secure—wanted—in a way my own family never had. I inched closer, needing more of his unique brand of Novasgardian medicine.

"I'm not interrupting, am I?"

He shook his head, holding up the compact. "I'm early. I wanted to make sure I could claim my spot. We have time."

One large hand slid around my waist, tugging me close to his body, and everything in me screamed this was what I needed. Until another scream filled the air, this one not from any part of me and decidedly more bloodcurdling.

Alek was on his feet, pushing my body behind his much larger one, immediately on high alert. "Do you smell that?"

"Smell what?"

Even as I asked it, the scent of brimstone and ash filled my nose.

Demon.

I opened my mouth to warn him, but Alek had already put it together.

"Fucking demon," he snarled, his posture changing as his muscles seemed to ripple and swell. I blinked. That couldn't be right . . .

Several more cries rang out from the study section on the ground floor, along with a terrifying, inhuman roar. The shelves and floor shook with what felt like explosions, but they came in such rhythmic waves it didn't take long for me to understand . . . footsteps. The demon was so huge it made the walls tremble and dust fall from the ceiling with every move it made.

Oh, fuck.

"Stay here," Alek ordered, spotting an old suit of armor nearby and relieving the statue of its perfectly preserved broadsword.

My chest hollowed out at the majestic sight of Alek taking a few swipes, testing the blade's balance. He held it like it was an extension of himself, moving it around in some warrior's version of a ballet. Then his eyes flared a blinding icy blue, and he ran his palm down the blade, causing foreign runes to blaze to life along the surface.

"Alek—"

"Sunny, I swear to Odin, if you don't stay put I will tie you to a chair to keep you out of trouble."

"But I can fight. Why do all that training if you're going to bench me when it counts?"

Alek stalked over to me, gripping my chin in his free hand and seizing my lips in a brutal kiss. "Because I couldn't stand to see you get hurt again."

I swayed on my feet from the afterglow of his kiss, then watched as he made his way to the balcony's edge. The way his eyes widened had me on my feet and moving toward him. I couldn't resist. I had to know what we were facing because the expression painted on his features said it wasn't going to be easy.

"Sunday," he growled.

I ignored him, my eyes glued to the monster wreaking havoc below. He was massive. Easily ten-feet tall, his black leathery skin was covered in horrific scars reminiscent of burns. His face was more beast than anything remotely human, a cross between a minotaur and something far more evil. With curling black horns and fiery eyes, he was ripped straight out of my worst nightmares.

"Alek," I whispered.

"Get back." His warning was too late, though, as the beast sniffed once, twice, and then glanced up to us.

"Oh, fuck," I whispered, my voice trembling. It was hard not to want to piss yourself when pinned by the gaze of a creature who looked like he used bones for toothpicks.

The minotaur stared at me, his tail whipping back and

forth, leaving lines of flame on everything it touched. I shuddered at the pure hatred in its eyes.

"Note to self, don't let that tail touch you."

Alek held out an arm, barring me from getting any closer to the railing. "Don't let any part of him touch you. Least of all his tail."

All around him, witches, shifters, and other students worked together to take him down. The witches dealt with the flames, led by the librarian, while the others were busy trying to find his weakness. A fae male I knew named Loren stood on top of the table farthest from the beast, a bow and arrow materializing in his hands. He drew back and released, the arrow headed straight for the demon's heart, but at impact, the deadly bolt simply bounced off the armor-like plates of his chest.

God, we didn't stand a chance.

A few wolves I recognized from Kingston's pack, led by a guy named Chad, shifted and immediately circled him, each one tensing before they strategically attacked one by one. A deep russet wolf leapt forward, teeth bared and ready to strike the tender Achilles tendon just above the cloven hoof, but he didn't see the lash of the demon's tail as it headed straight for his face. I gasped in horror as the whip-like appendage connected, searing through fur and flesh.

The wolf was thrown across the room, yelping in pain before curling up into a ball as the witches extinguished the flames.

Kicking the rest of the wolves out of the way, the minotaur bastard planted his hooves and tensed, knees bent. Then he jumped into the air in one gravity-defying leap, sailing over the balcony and landing directly in front of us, eyes locked on mine.

Shit. The fucker really was after me.

"Sunday, get back!" Alek shouted, already assuming a defensive position with his sword angled in front of him.

The hell I would. I wasn't leaving him to face this monster on his own. Without stopping to think, I called my wolf, knowing she was my best weapon against him.

The shift this time was nearly painless, almost instantaneous. Our minds connected as we focused on one goal, keep Alek safe. I growled deep and low, pulling Alek's gaze from the demon in front of him for a fraction of a second. Then I pounced.

My teeth sank into bitter-tasting flesh at the base of the beast's neck, vile black ichor dripping down my throat and causing tears to prick my eyes as I choked. But I couldn't relent. I'd wounded him. That was more than anyone else had done.

The minotaur wrapped his clawed hand around my much smaller body, flinging me away with an angry roar.

I knew it was bad when the vise-like grip crushing my ribs fell away, leaving me weightless.

Soaring through the air.

Oh.

Shit.

Wolves couldn't fly.

"Sunday!" Alek's panicked cry filled my ears as I began to plummet.

CHAPTER
NINETEEN

ALEK

Sunday went over the edge of the balcony, and the world went red. Primal rage tore through me until all I was left with was the need to destroy.

With a war cry that rivaled the beast's, I shot forward, letting the borrowed sword fall forgotten from my fingertips.

I didn't need it. Not with this unholy fury boiling in my blood.

I took two running steps, jumping up onto an over-turned chair and propelling myself up into the air.

It shouldn't have been possible. Novasgardian or not, there was no explanation for how I managed to land with my thighs straddling the demon's neck.

But I did.

I was running purely on instinct, my hatred for the fiend that dared to harm what was mine fueling me completely.

The demon bucked, but I gritted my teeth and drove my thumbs into the fiery depths of its eyes.

It wailed, shaking its head from side to side as more

thick, oily liquid poured from the pits of what were now only eye sockets.

I bared my teeth, the sound of its pain the sweetest symphony.

It was nowhere near enough. Only its death would satisfy the debt.

I reached up, grasping each of its deadly horns in my hands and pulling downward. My muscles burned, bulging and trembling with the force I exerted, but I clenched my jaw and pulled harder.

The monster began tossing his head in earnest, pitting his strength against my own.

But I would not be deterred.

A roar built up in my chest, tearing through my throat and infusing me with more of that glorious strength.

With a sickening crack, the horns snapped, the creature dropping to its knees as it screamed in pain.

I let the left horn fall. I only needed one to serve my purpose.

With another savage cry, I flipped it in my hand so the pointed edge was aimed straight at the creature's throat, right where Sunday had bitten into him.

"Give Hel my regards," I snarled, stabbing him with his own horn.

He jerked, but I held him by the tuft of fur at the top of his head. He couldn't go just yet. Gripping the base of the blood-soaked horn, I tore through his throat, from one side to the next until I was able to rend his head from his body. I let him fall then, my breaths coming in harsh gasps as I stared at the spoils of my battle.

I wasn't interested in the corpse, only what I could use from it to mark the victory. One of the horns, perhaps?

As I contemplated the option, the body began to smolder and turn to ash.

And then the sweetest voice called out to me.

"Uh, Alek? When you're done bathing in the blood of your enemies or whatever it is you're doing, can I get a little help?"

My heart nearly split in two at the sound of her voice. "Sunday?" I turned, gaze sweeping the area, and found her hanging onto one of the posts that made up the railing on the balcony. From the look of things, the library had been deserted. Its occupants fled, leaving the two of us to deal with the monster on our own.

In two large strides, I was there, reaching for her, hauling her to safety as though she weighed nothing at all.

She was alive.

Safe.

Mine.

"Kærasta," I whispered, sliding one of my hands into her hair and tugging her face down so I could claim her lips with mine.

Her need matched my own. She wrapped her bare legs around my waist, clinging to me as she kissed me with an intensity that brought lust roaring to life inside of me.

I groaned, needing more than her mouth. My palms gripped her arse, holding her completely nude body against my unfortunately clothed one. Walking us toward the closest surface, I pressed her against one of the few bookshelves that remained after the attack and thrust my tongue inside her mouth, desperate to deepen our connection. She sent her hands trailing over my back, then around to the front of my joggers, where she found me straining and hard.

"I want you inside me," she whispered against my lips.

"Fuck, Sunny."

"That's the idea, Viking."

I huffed out a laugh, holding her up with one arm while giving the material at my hips a sharp yank, shoving them down far enough to free my cock so I could take her.

Her damp heat met my battle-fevered skin, and we both moaned. I'd never felt this kind of all-consuming need before. My heart was raging, blood roaring in my ears. If I didn't sink into her right the fuck now, I might die.

"I don't think I can be gentle."

"Who wants gentle?"

"Gods, you're perfect."

She snickered. "You might be the only person on earth who thinks so."

"I doubt that. But right now, you're mine." I took my cock in my fist, notching it at her entrance and pulling back just enough that I could look down into her flushed face. "Look at me, Sunday. I want to watch your eyes as I fill you."

If the groan that tore from my throat when her walls clenched around the crown of me was any indication, I wasn't going to last long once I was sheathed inside her sweet cunt.

I needed to make this count.

I slid in slowly. Agonizingly slow. The glide of her slick walls along my aching shaft, the wetness from her pussy dripping down my balls, was enough to make everything in me tighten in anticipation.

"Fuck, Alek, you're so big," she panted, her nails digging into my back. "I don't think it's going to fit."

"I'll make it fit." My voice was more growl than speech, but I was holding on by a thread. The Viking in me wanted to pillage her body until everything was mine. I wanted her boneless, drenched in my cum, the only word on her lips my name.

"Alek, please."

As if granting my wishes, that breathy moan made me tremble, and I dug my fingers into her tender flesh, tightening my hold but not giving her what she wanted. I was determined to make this last as long as I could.

"Hold onto me, Kærasta."

She wrapped her legs around me tighter and used all her strength to pull me in, sinking my cock to the hilt and making us both cry out.

"That's not exactly what I meant."

"You're taking too long."

"Impatient little thing, aren't you?"

I released her arse so I could get more leverage by gripping the shelves on either side of her head, then I lowered my lips to hers and began moving. The slide of her soft wet flesh over my steel-hard length sent a wash of pleasure through me with each powerful drive of my hips. I was already on the edge of oblivion, ready to fill her with my spend until she dripped with my cream. I wanted her to feel me inside her, remembering this moment and me for days to come.

"God, Alek."

"Yes, that's it. Tell your god who you want."

"You. Fuck, Alek. It's you."

"Damn right it is," I growled in her ear.

"Faster. I know you're holding back. Don't. Take me like you need to."

The bookcase shook, rocking as my thrusts grew wild. She fluttered around me, and I knew she was just as close as I was.

"Touch yourself, Sunny. Rub your clit and make yourself come on my cock."

She snaked her hand between us and began, her walls tightening, even more wetness flooding me in response to her touch. Books fell to the floor with loud thumps, but I didn't stop. I couldn't. My climax was racing up my spine with the force of a freight train, and I wasn't going to be able to do a damn thing until it reached its destination.

Her breath hitched as her inner muscles clamped down hard, milking my cock as she came with a scream. I drove home, my orgasm hitting me and sending my hips pistoning faster and harder. With an ominous creak, the bookshelf began going over, but I didn't give one single fuck. I wrapped my arms around Sunday and rolled so I took the brunt of the fall.

The maneuver had me twisting inside her, sending over another wave of her climax and setting me even deeper as my back hit the fallen shelves.

"Jesus, fuck, Alek."

I grinned up at her, not capable of speech in that moment.

The sound of slow clapping reached our ears, filling me with enough energy to sit up and protectively curl my body around Sunday's.

"Now that's just about the most entertaining thing I've seen in over a century." The ghost floated a few inches off the ground, her spectral form shimmering in the soft light. "Well done, you two. Bravo." Fuck, spirits creeped me out, but I wasn't going to tell Sunny that.

SUNDAY PRESSED her forehead against my shoulder, her back shaking with suppressed laughter.

"Get away, you perverted ghost. You weren't invited to watch."

She shrugged. "If you're going to bump uglies in a library, you're inviting everyone to watch. Let me know next time, and I'll bring some friends."

The spirit vanished, leaving nothing but a chill in the air. I carefully lifted Sunday off me, not wanting to leave her warm body, but also not ready to risk anyone else seeing her like this.

I pulled my bloodied shirt off my back, offering it to her with a chagrined smile. "Uh . . . it's not exactly clean, but it'll keep prying eyes off you."

She laughed. "If I was worried about being clean, I'm pretty sure I wouldn't have just done all that with you."

"Good to know you don't mind getting a little dirty."

As she pulled my shirt on, my cock gave an approving twitch at the sight of her soft curves filling out the too-big cotton. She peeked over at me, pink tingeing her cheeks as she admitted, "I also don't mind an audience. You know, for the record."

I tucked that away, raising a brow. "Do you want me to invite the ghost back?" Gods, I hoped not, but I'd suck it up for her.

She shook her head with a small smile. "No. I prefer my voyeurs to be among the living."

"And do you prefer they only watch . . ."

"They can participate," she whispered. "If it's—"

"One of your men," I supplied.

She bit her bottom lip and nodded. "Is that weird?"

I gestured to my cock, already back at attention. "Does it look like I mind?"

"Vikings," she said, hunger in her gaze. "You're resilient fuckers."

"With massive . . . appetites."

"I'll say." She licked her lips. "Maybe we should go somewhere more . . . comfortable for round two?"

I smirked. "There's going to be a round two?"

"Absolutely, but not until we shower. Then brace yourself, handsome, because I'm planning on going at least seven rounds with you."

A possessive thrill raced through me at her words. I wanted nothing more than to spend the day buried inside her.

I glanced at the library, well, the rubble remaining. Gesturing to the scorch mark on the floor and the pile of ash that used to be a demon, I asked, "Should we talk about . . . this?"

She turned to look behind her, giving a little shrug. "I mean . . . what's there to talk about? We're just students. The people in charge are the ones who have to deal with the aftermath. But if you think we need to, we can do that just as easily in bed."

I wanted to tell her the demon was clearly after her. To remind her the staff had been completely useless. But now wasn't the time. This conversation needed to happen, but I'd require backup. Kingston, Moira, perhaps even the priest. Sunday was in danger, and if keeping her in bed with me meant she'd stay safe . . .

My cock and I would valiantly make that sacrifice.

TWENTY

"Sunny, over here!"

Moira snickered beside me as I glanced over to Alek, who was waving me in like I was a damn airplane he was trying to land.

"I know I'm a cat person, but a golden retriever has never looked more appealing."

I slapped her arm. "Moira, stop. Alek is not a golden retriever."

"True, he's built more like a Tibetan mastiff, but I mean . . . all that good boy, puppy energy. He's just so damn eager to please." She snickered. "I've heard of being dick drunk, but girl, you have that guy so pussy possessed . . ."

My cheeks burned as I thought back to the marathon after-battle sex we'd had, both in the library, then back in his room. It ended up being ten rounds, not seven.

"Have I mentioned how athletic he is in bed? The things he did to me . . . I'm glad I do yoga."

"Tossed you around, huh?" She grinned. "Good to know those muscles are for more than show. Oh, speaking of, you should have him show you some of his moves in the gym. Defies gravity, I swear."

That had my eyebrows rising. "It must be something special if you took note of it."

"Trust me, girl," she said as we slid into the row with Alek and Kingston. "You want in on that magic. Thank me later."

Kingston's gaze locked with mine from where he sat, with one seat between him and Alek. The cocky wolf looked like I was a foregone conclusion, and he was right. One arm was thrown across the back of the empty chair, his knees spread, a smirk on that handsome, rakish face.

"Miss me?" he asked.

Alek let out a soft chuckle. "I don't know if you were on her mind at all recently."

Kingston cocked a brow. "I'm always on her mind. Just like she is for me. It's a *mate* thing."

There was no outward reaction from Alek to the reminder that while Kingston and I were mates, Alek and I weren't. But I could feel the angry tension coiling in him. His building rage was icy, and it made me want to thaw him back out.

I slid my hand over his balled-up fist, weaving my fingers through his. "He's just trying to make you jealous."

Alek smiled. "I woke up to my dick inside you. I have no reason to be jealous."

"Sleeping through it, huh? Wow, you must be a boring as fuck lay, Viking."

"Not the word I'd use to describe it," I said, giving Kingston an annoyed glare. "Stop trying to be the bully. You took that mask off when you agreed to work together to stalk me."

"Not stalk," Moira tossed in from the other side of Alek. "Protect. There's a difference."

I rolled my eyes. "Maybe to you."

Kingston leaned in and ran his nose across my mark. "I've missed having you close."

A shiver ran up my spine at the contact and the sweet words. "Me too."

He inhaled deeply, a low growl rumbling in his chest, almost a kind of purring noise. "You . . . are you in heat?"

I stiffened. "What? Why would you ask me that?"

He took another long sniff, running his nose from my mark up to the spot just behind my ear. "Because one whiff of you has me rock-hard and ready to mount you. Which, to be fair, is pretty standard, but this feels different."

"Are you trying to tell me your hard-on is special?"

His grin had me squirming. "Isn't it, though?"

I pushed him away, too concerned about why he thought I might be in heat. Maybe it was because Alek had just spent the last twenty-four hours vigorously fucking me until I was boneless in his arms. I'd showered. I gave a cursory sniff.

"I'm not in heat. I was just . . . worked up after fighting that demon with him."

Alek leaned in and winked. "My people call it the blood-lust. When it takes hold . . . well, if we're not fighting, we're fucking."

That sounded about right to me. My blush deepened. I wasn't sure why I was feeling so exposed all of a sudden, casually talking about having sex with both of them out in the open like this. It felt too . . . normal. I didn't trust it.

"Maybe that's what it was for you, Nordson. But not for her. Sunday is a wolf, not a Novasgardian."

"She's still a warrior. You should have seen her yesterday," he said, his eyes raking over me and burning with pride, "she was utterly fearless."

"I wish I'd been there. She wouldn't have had to fight at all. I could've defended her like a mate should."

I knew the blow landed because Alek flinched.

"Alek killed that thing with his bare hands, Kingston. Trust me, he did just fine protecting me all on his own."

Kingston wrapped his large palm around my shoulder and tugged me closer. "I can't believe I wasn't there for you. It . . . I shouldn't have left."

That softened me. He might've been taunting Alek, but it was only because he'd been scared for me and beating himself up about not being there.

"Stop," I said softly, cupping one of his cheeks with my free hand. "I'm right here. I'm safe. You don't need to get twisted up about this."

"Isn't that one of the perks of this poly thing you guys have going on?" Moira asked, drawing our attention back to her. She resumed braiding the butt-length oil-slick colored hair she'd chosen that morning, speaking as if it should be obvious. "I mean . . . one of you can always be there for her. Picking up the slack, or whatever. We all know a guy on his own is pretty much doomed to fail. It's inevitable. But four guys"—she pursed her lips—"seems like that could be the recipe for perfection."

Kingston snarled at the implication that he was said slack, but Alek seemed to think she made an excellent point. Except there weren't four of them right now. One was decidedly absent. And the other . . .

Caleb sat beside the headmistress, his broody gaze trained right on me. As soon as our eyes collided, he looked away. I sucked in a sharp breath at the zing of attraction that one simple action sent through me. He didn't want me to know he'd been staring, and with his vampire hearing, he probably heard every word we'd just said. Which meant he had to know about Alek . . . and he didn't look happy about it.

An eerie silence fell throughout the audience as a spell cloaked every one of us. I knew without trying that I wouldn't be able to speak and be heard.

Madame le Blanc stood, her crimson velvet gown seeming a little extra if I was being honest. Especially with the matching feathered fascinator she had pinned into her hair. God, she looked like a character straight out of a Gothic horror film. I half expected a British aristocrat to ask for my hand in marriage just so he could lock me up in his creepy old mansion.

A small smirk lifted my lips. Technically, Noah fit that bill.

"Bonsoir, students. I apologize for interrupting your schedules, but as you have probably heard, Ravenscroft has come under attack." Her intense stare raked across the crowd, and I didn't think it was my imagination that it lingered a little longer than necessary on me. "Yesterday, a demon was summoned right here in our library, where he then went on to kill two of your peers and maim one other. I take this assault as a personal affront. It is my sacred duty to keep you all safe while you matriculate. To that end, we will be conducting an investigation on campus. Magic abilities will be held under strict lockdown until we find the culprit. That includes in your rooms as well as common spaces."

Moira shot me a stricken glance over Alek's bulk. Her eyes were wide with panic as she stroked her long braid. "My hair," she mouthed.

Leave it to Moira to miss the point entirely.

"As some of you witnessed, two of our students heroically took down the demon, vanquishing him from the library and saving countless lives."

I squirmed. We'd done that and fucked like wild animals right after.

"Sunday Fallon and Alek Nordson, we are in your debt. I have little doubt many more would have fallen without your bravery. There is no way to repay such actions, so I humbly offer you my vow. If you ever find yourself in need, call on me, and if it is within my power to help, I shall without question."

I could feel the eyes of every single person in that room fall on us. I slouched low in my chair, hating the attention.

"The wards will be strengthened, and we've already begun the task of tracking the trail of the summoner," Caleb said, standing with hands crossed in front of him. The picture of piety. "Until they are found and punished, a strict curfew will also be enforced."

I could feel the collective but silent groan from my classmates.

"That includes leaving school grounds. Everyone must be in their rooms by ten p.m. No exceptions."

Madame le Blanc chimed in. "Any classes held after curfew will be rescheduled or suspended for the time being. That goes for extracurricular activities as well. Please check your personal emails for further details."

She stared down at me, and the weight of her gaze had my heart racing. I wondered if extracurricular meant sex, because we didn't have any sports teams or school clubs. "You are all dismissed. Please return to your dorms to begin our first night of curfew." The spell lifted, and hushed voices returned to the air around us at once. "Mademoiselle Fallon, a word."

Fuck.

Kingston rose right along with me, his arm around my shoulders, holding me close.

"Not you, Mr. Farrell. I assure you, your mate will be fine."

He reluctantly released me, but by the set of his jaw, he wasn't leaving me alone with her. He'd wait.

The headmistress beckoned me with a crook of her finger. With a heavy sigh, I gave him a quick kiss on the cheek. "I'll be fine."

"But of course you will. How silly to think otherwise," she said as I left a glowering shifter, curious witch, and intense demigod behind.

Their gazes weighed on my back as I approached Madame le Blanc. My neck prickled, and I glanced to the left where I spotted Caleb lingering in the shadows, his gaze locked onto me as well. It looked like our conversation was going to have quite the audience.

"Do we have to do this here?"

She waved a hand, and my ears popped as the air pressure changed. "There. No one can hear us. Have you forgotten something?"

My eyes widened as I thought over the events of the last week. "No?"

She crossed her arms, looking supremely disappointed in me. "Have you really forgotten so soon? Did I not convey how gravely important it was for you to take your weekly tonic?"

"Oh! *That*. Well, the demon—"

She waved a hand, cutting off my excuse for the missed appointment. "And after the demon?"

Why did it look like she was trying not to laugh? No

way in hell was I telling her I'd been participating in an epic fuck fest.

"I got distracted."

A delicate snort left her. "Distracted. Well, you are lucky the dose I gave you was strong enough to remain effective for several weeks. I was under the assumption you might be as irresponsible as most young women your age. And look, I was correct."

My eyes narrowed at the burn. Even though she was right, the need to defend myself came roaring to life. "Well, it doesn't matter because the suppressants arrived."

Thank you, Moira, for leaving those on my bed. They're really coming in handy, helping me save face right now.

"Is that so?"

I nodded.

"Well, why didn't you say that from the start? If you've begun taking them, then you have no need of the additional elixirs. The strength of the first dosage is enough to protect you until the suppressants take full effect."

I squirmed, thinking of what Kingston said about my scent. "And what if . . . it comes back?"

Her brows rose. "I'm assuming you're referring to your heat?"

"Yes. I . . . well, sometimes I think I feel it." It was a truth I hadn't wanted to admit to Kingston earlier, but what Alek called bloodlust seemed a lot like a weaker version of heat now that I thought back on it.

"It is said that shifters often have . . . relapses the first time."

Dylan had warned me of the same thing. I guess minor flare-ups were normal. My cheeks burned.

Thank God I had so many men willing to service me.

"Things will level out soon. And with the precautions in

place, you won't have to deal with males acting like feral idiots around you. I could always put you in the well if they do."

I balked at the thought. "It seems a little harsh to confine me over something I can't control."

"The safety of the school is always more important than the comfort of a single student. I will not allow you or anyone else to jeopardize that."

I balled my hands into fists, trying to contain the frustration building in my chest. I wouldn't be put in a hole in the ground. "Are we done here? I'll do my best to keep my legs closed. No promises."

Amusement flared in her dark gaze, but she simply nodded. The air shimmered as she released the spell she'd placed around us. "Perhaps an extra session or two with Father Gallagher will help you center yourself and regain some composure."

I flicked a glance over my shoulder where Caleb stood, his focus burning into me. My thighs clenched on instinct. I didn't think he'd be helpful at all.

Before I could reply, Madame le Blanc vanished in a cloud of smoke.

"What the fuck was that about, Sunshine?" Kingston stalked over to me, Alek and Moira right behind him.

"She likes to check in on my progress to report back to my grandfather," I lied, not ready to admit I had conversations with the head of our school about my reproductive issues. "Though, half the time I can't tell if that woman wants to help me succeed or see me fail."

"Madame Moody has that effect on people," Moira said with a sympathetic smile.

"Come on, you're hungry. I can tell." Kingston threw an arm around me.

"How do you know?"

"You're my mate. I can sense these things. You need me to feed you, then fuck you, and we can go from there."

His possessive words sent heat flooding my core. I couldn't help my smirk as I asked, "How do you know it's you I need?"

Alek laughed, wrapping an arm around my waist and pulling me against him. "I guess one taste has her addicted. Sorry, wolf."

Moira rolled her eyes. "At this rate, you just need to all get a room and have an orgy. Then maybe you'll stop feeling the need for these public pissing contests."

Alek's smile didn't dim. "It's all in good fun. And I'm up for anything Sunday wants. How about you, Kingston?"

Kingston's hand slid across my hips. "If my mate wants two of us to satisfy her, I'll gladly give her what she asks for. As long as she cries my name, I don't care who else is making her moan."

Alek's eyes glittered. "Shall we make a bet of it? See which one of us she cries out for?"

Moira gagged. "And with that display of disgusting testosterone, I'm out. Good luck being the only hotdog bun at the sausage fest. I'll light a candle for your vagina."

A low dark chuckle floated on the wind from behind us. Caleb stood in the shadows, arms crossed over his chest, a smirk on his devastating face. Maybe he'd like to watch?

I didn't think the guys were serious about running off and actually having a threesome. But now that Moira had planted the idea in my mind, I couldn't stop thinking about it. Or how much I wanted all four of my men at the same time. How would that even work? Hands? Mouth? Hands and mouth? Hands, mouth, and . . . other places?

I shook my head as arousal punched me straight in the

clit. "Okay, no one needs to light a candle for my vagina. She's just fine. Kingston's right. I'm so hungry I could eat a horse."

"Or a Viking," Moira called as she walked away from us. "Weren't you just telling me how much you loved his Norwegian foot-long?"

"Not helpful!"

She cackled all the way down the moonlit path. Alek took my hand and lifted it to his lips. "I'll give you my foot-long whenever you want it."

Rolling my eyes, I forced myself not to laugh. "How generous."

"What can I say? I live to serve."

"Don't we fucking all?" Kingston asked, startling the laugh right out of me. "Come on, asshole. Let's get our girl something to eat."

CHAPTER
TWENTY-ONE
SUNDAY

I threw myself on my bed and groaned dramatically as the headache I couldn't escape continued its dull assault.

"Alek really rode you hard, huh?" Moira asked from the small desk at the end of her bed.

I turned my head and opened one eye in question.

"In training. God, get your mind out of the gutter," she said.

"He did, but that's nothing new. I never leave one of his sessions without ending up sore and sweaty."

Moira snickered.

"Now whose mind is in the gutter?" I snapped.

"Gee, you're testy today. For someone getting laid regularly, you sure are tense."

"I'm sorry. I'm tired, okay? Can you magic me up some ice cream? I need something sweet."

Moira's expression soured. "You know I can't. Magic embargo, remember?"

I winced. The magic ban was really getting to my little

203

witch. She'd been forced to have the same hairstyle for a week now, and she was not handling it well. "Sorry."

"Don't apologize. I'm sorry I can't help you with your cravings. Are you PMSing or something?" Her eyes brightened. "Oh! We're syncing up! You're basically my sister witch now. All our cycles happen at the same time."

Dread snaked through me as I did some scary mental math.

When I didn't immediately answer, Moira's eyes widened dramatically. "Sunday Fallon. When was your last period?"

"Uh . . . six weeks ago? But that's normal for me. I've never been regular. The pack doctor said it was because of my wolf." I said this all in a rush, not sure if I was trying to reassure my roommate or myself.

"Oh shit," she whispered. "Oh shit. Oh shit. Oh shit."

"Stop freaking out. I'm not pregnant."

"How do you know? You went into heat, and Kingston shot how many loads of shifter spunk in you?"

I shook my head. "I can't be. No way. Noah said I wasn't fertile, and that was the night Kingston called out my wolf."

"Right. And then you went into heat," she emphasized, throwing a pillow at my head. "The only reason for a heat is to breed, you dummy."

I swallowed, feeling incredibly nauseated. "Why wouldn't Kingston have mentioned it?"

"He probably didn't think about anything other than getting his dick wet."

"Oh, God. I might puke."

Moira jumped up and raced over, wrapping me in a surprisingly strong hug. "Don't freak out. We don't know anything for sure. I'm going to sneak out and get you a test. Okay?"

I nodded. "Get two. Or five. Just so we can be sure."

"You know . . . if I had my fucking magic, we could take care of this right now," she grumbled, muttering under her breath as she grabbed her shoes and a jacket. She tore open the door and practically growled at whoever was on the other side. "I'm leaving, and don't you dare try to stop me. You men are good for nothing but anxiety, I swear to the goddess."

My belly clenched. If it was Kingston, I didn't know what I was going to say to him. Hell, he'd probably pound his chest and howl at the moon with wolfish pride if he'd knocked me up on the first try.

Fucking Alpha asshole.

Caleb's low voice washed over me, interrupting my mental rant. "Is that so, Ms. Belladonna?"

I craned my neck toward the door in time to see my pixie of a roommate poke him in the chest. "Don't think your God will save you from my wrath, priest-man."

"What did I do?" he asked, truly baffled.

She huffed. "You have a dick. Right now, that's enough. Be back in a flash, babycakes." Then she winced. "Sorry. Poor word choice."

The door closed behind her, leaving Caleb and me alone together. I stared at the handsome, brooding vampire with my heart in my throat. I would not cry. I wouldn't. But I did.

Before I could stop them, tears trailed down my cheeks.

"What's wrong, *a stor*?" he asked, at my side in a blur of motion. Tenderness he hadn't shown me since I'd been injured at *Iniquity* radiated from him.

I didn't know how to answer. I couldn't say the words out loud. All I could do was shake my head as more tears fell free.

His arms were around me, pressing my head against his

chest where I could feel the strong thump of his heart. He'd never held me before. Not like this. I clung to him, seeking more of his strength.

"Tell me what's happened. I'll do what I can to fix it for you."

I shook my head, his shirt wet from my tears. "I don't think it can be fixed. I was stupid. Kingston and I were reckless."

He stiffened, stepping back slightly. "Sunday . . ."

"Please don't scold me. Not right now."

"But you're not—"

I jerked back, heart galloping. "Not what?"

He looked confused, like he didn't understand why I was upset and was weighing if his words would be welcome or not. "If you're thinking you're pregnant, that's not the case."

I laughed. "Oh, are you an OB-GYN now too?"

"I've helped birth a babe or two in my time."

"So you can just, what . . . smell it on me?"

"I'd hear the heartbeat."

Vampire. Right.

"Not if it was too soon for that to be detectable."

"And . . . yes, I'd smell it on you. You're not pregnant, Sunday. I'd know."

I wanted to believe. God, did I want to. But until I saw the proof with my own eyes, I knew I wouldn't stop worrying.

"She went to get me a test. Just to confirm." I stared up into his eyes and waited for some kind of argument.

"I'll stay with you until she returns."

Confusion swirled within me. "Why are you being nice to me?"

"What?"

"You're broody, stern, angry. Never nice."

"That's not true."

"It isn't? Do you even have friends besides me and God?"

His lips quirked. "Is that what we are? Friends?"

"I don't know. It's not like I can just call you my spanking buddy. And you don't like it when I call you my daddy."

He glared at me, his eyes darkening with hunger. "It's not that I *don't* like it."

I swallowed.

Oh.

"I call you my confessor, in my head."

"I suppose that's accurate." He ran a hand through his hair. "I call you my temptress."

"Look at us. Revealing all our secrets."

"Hardly. My sins are for God's ears."

"I tell you all mine."

His fingers twitched, and he clenched that beard-shadowed jaw. As he stepped toward me, the door burst open, and a bedraggled Moira rushed inside the room.

"Okay, I got five tests and some ice cream, either for celebrating or wallowing. God, I hate human stores."

Caleb stepped back, and I knew whatever he'd been about to say or do was gone. The moment was lost. "I'll leave you two."

"You're not staying for the results?"

"I already know the answer," he said. "Enjoy your ice cream."

He left without another word, and Moira simply shrugged and shoved the bag of tests into my hands. "Go. Pee. I'll wait."

Three minutes later, I stared down at the two tests I'd

taken. My eyes filled with tears and my hands shook as I opened the bathroom door.

"Well? Am I a godmother for real?" Moira called.

"Negative."

Moira whooped and then laughed. "Since the danger has passed, I feel like I can admit this now. I was kind of excited about it. How weird is that?"

I could hear her moving around, dishing out ice cream as I stared at the tests in my hands.

It wasn't weird. As relieved as I was, I couldn't deny the little disappointed twist in my chest.

In the whirlwind between finding out being pregnant was a possibility and then learning it wasn't, I'd run the gamut of emotions.

I was supposed to be happy about this . . . right?

My body wanted one thing, my mind another. Stupid biology. Stupid heat. Stupid ovaries.

With a deep breath, I tossed the tests into the trash and washed my hands before joining Moira. As I walked back into our bedroom, I burst into laughter.

"Moira, what the hell is this?"

She gave the ground filled with inflated condoms a proud look. "What? I got you some balloons."

"Gee, thanks."

"Well, someone has to use them. You're clearly not."

"I guess I could start."

"You could." Then she cocked her head. "But your suppressants will prevent pregnancy better than anything. And even if these guys are your mates, you don't know where they've stuck their wieners. They probably need to wrap it up in general."

"Supernatural STIs don't exist. It's one of the few things I was taught about sex."

Moira snorted. "Of course it was. That's some patriarchy bullshit right there. They only care about it if it'll make their dick fall off."

We sat together, each of us digging into our ice cream in silence before Moira looked at me pointedly.

"So tell me about the piercings."

TWENTY-TWO

The hum of voices in Sanderson's classroom filled my ears, people buzzing with nervous energy. We'd become used to weapons & defense being held in the church since Caleb took over, but an hour ago, an alert went out to every student scheduled to attend this class that we were to report here instead.

"Something is up. I can fucking smell it," Kingston said, his voice a low, uneasy growl.

"What else is new?" I muttered.

Alek laughed beside me. "You're starting to sound like a Viking."

"Why's that?"

"Nothing fazes you anymore."

"In my defense, over the last couple of months, I've been stabbed, attacked, turned into a wolf, and mated to two men. I think I'm pretty desensitized at this point."

"You're sensitive where it counts." Kingston nuzzled my neck, right over my mark, and I couldn't stop the shiver of need that ran through me at the contact.

Alek grunted his agreement. "That she is."

I squirmed out of the sexy man sandwich. Class was so not the place to get turned on. Not when half the room would be able to smell it on me. Especially when one of them was my teacher.

Speak of the devil . . .

Caleb strode into the room, gorgeous in head-to-toe black. All he was missing was his collar, and I hated myself a little for wanting to see him wearing that tiny bit of white just so I could take it off him.

As if he could read the naughty thought, his stormy gaze found mine. I hadn't seen him since he popped in during my spiral the other night. Without stopping to think, I lifted both my hands, giving him two thumbs up and a grin. His lips twitched, and he shook his head but continued walking to the front of the room.

"What's that all about?" Kingston asked.

"Nothing."

"Bullshit."

I saw no reason to let these two in on my pregnancy scare. Knowing Kingston, he'd probably just try to trigger my heat again so he could put his spawn in my belly. Farrell was his last name for a reason. And, my traitorous body reacted to the thought of him breeding me again. Because as scary as that future was, my instinct wanted it.

Craved it, even.

Kingston stiffened beside me, his hand sliding across my lower back to grip me hard as he inhaled deeply. Fuck. He could smell me. I knew it. Damn hormones. Maybe we could sneak away and take care of this problem before we were noticed?

Before my thoughts could travel too far down that rabbit hole, Caleb addressed the class.

"Demons are among us."

His words rang out in the space, a booming echo that made me think of his time spent with a congregation at his mercy. Everyone went silent, our attention on him. It made me glad we weren't in the church today. The sinister topic, combined with the religious sanctuary, would have been overkill on the scary factor. Likely making us fear for our immortal souls instead of just our lives.

"They claw their way out of the depths of hell, and until now, it was a rare piece of filth that escaped. Unless, of course, a weak soul summoned one of them. Ravenscroft is under siege. *You* are in danger."

Caleb stared straight at me, as if his words were for me alone. I reached out for Alek, seeking his strength. He took my hand in his, giving it a comforting squeeze. So far, the demon attack had been easy to dismiss, but hearing Caleb speak on it now had a new kind of anxiety settling in my bones.

All around us, people shifted in their seats, the mood in the classroom dipping dramatically. No one here had ever had to worry about being prey before. These were the monsters, at least the ones humans feared. We were supposed to be the ones invoking fear. Not the ones who were afraid.

"Until now, they haven't been able to breach our walls. Break our lines of defense. But as we saw in the library, that is no longer the case. We cannot allow them to gain a foothold here. A girl was attacked outside our borders, another two killed on this very campus, and the scent of brimstone is strong in the air. The fissure in our protection is widening, and that means more demons are on the horizon. We must be ready to fight them."

A petite shifter girl named Hope raised a hand. Caleb turned his intense stare to her.

"Yes?"

"Why now?"

"The battle between heaven and hell is eternal, like a game of chess where each strategic move can have catastrophic consequences. Their fight for souls acts like a pendulum constantly swinging back and forth. The balance between them is always shifting, and recently it tipped again. Things are changing. It's going to get worse before it gets better."

"But . . . which side are we on? We're not exactly heaven's favorites."

Caleb let out a dark chuckle. "If you don't know what side you're on, you shouldn't be here."

She practically melted into her chair at the tone of his voice. I felt a little sorry for her, but her question had merit.

"What are we supposed to do then? Kill them?" I called out, not bothering to raise my hand. "Douse them with holy water?"

"Miss Fallon, you'll hold your tongue unless I give you permission to speak."

His chastisement was harsh and cut across me like a whip's lash. I'd missed him.

"Excuse me, Father, but it's a little naive of you to assume we will just know how to fight them. If you're going to scare the shit out of us, I think the least you can do is give us a few pointers."

"That's exactly what I'll be doing, Miss Fallon. Patience is a virtue. Has no one ever told you that?"

I should have been embarrassed. A few months ago, I wouldn't have baited him. But that was before I knew how much my disobedience turned both of us on. And doing it here, surrounded by people when he couldn't punish me for it . . . well, it was a bit like throwing gasoline on a fire.

"Oh, I've heard it. But I prefer instant gratification. It's so much more satisfying, and life is too short to spend it hanging on the edge."

"That's quite enough from you. I'll see you for your session this evening, and if you keep mouthing off, it'll be every night this week."

Excitement built in my belly. I could keep this going and get all the time with him I wanted. But Alek leaned in and whispered in my ear, "You're poking the bear in front of everyone. Wait until you have him to yourself so they don't catch on, Sunny."

Spoilsport. Didn't he realize the potential for getting caught was half the fun? But he was right. I didn't mind getting myself into trouble, but Caleb was another matter.

With a huff, I settled back into my seat. "Sorry, sir," I grumbled.

The flare of hunger in Caleb's eyes at the honorific had me filing it away for later use.

"Now, as I was saying, and as Miss Fallon so helpfully brought to the class, you'll need to be prepared to fight. These hellspawn are vicious—some beasts, others tricksters, and many as beautiful as angels. They were born to manipulate you, to feed on your sins and use them against you. Magic is of no use against them, except for temporary containment. The only way to send them back to hell is to kill them."

"But won't they just come back?" I called out, still not raising my hand and earning a sharp look from him once more.

"Aye, they will. Evil always does. But our goal isn't to end them for eternity. It is to stop them from overrunning the mortal plane. Keep them at bay. Stay alive."

I swallowed. This sounded like we were playing a losing game.

"So if hell's demons are on the loose, where is heaven's army? Why is this even our problem?"

That came from Kingston, and I was surprised he'd piped up. He'd perfected the 'everything is beneath me, and this is a massive waste of my time' expression long ago. I don't think I'd ever seen him willingly participate in class unless it was a physical assignment.

"People are dying all around you, Mr. Farrell. What part of that sounds like it isn't your problem when next time it could very easily be you?"

He shrugged. "People die every day."

"And so you continue to prove exactly how self-absorbed you are. For a future Alpha, I'd expect your concern for others to be greater, Mr. Farrell. How disappointing for your pack and your mate to have a leader who cares so little."

Shots fired. I was used to being on the receiving end of Caleb's tongue lashings, but this was the first time I'd seen him eviscerate someone else. I winced in sympathy.

Kingston growled low in his throat. "I'd die to protect them. And her."

"Care to prove that point?"

"Name the time."

What the fuck? This wasn't a duel to the death, but it sure sounded like the two of them were meeting at sunrise. I was half-expecting Caleb to demand Kingston choose a second. And with the way Alek was bristling beside me, I was pretty sure I knew who'd volunteer.

I needed to take the focus off the rapidly boiling antagonistic energy between these two. "Okay, so what are we supposed to do? What have you dragged us all here for? Just to yell at us about hellfire and brimstone?"

His eyes narrowed at me once again butting in. I was in for it that evening, but I'd much rather his temper focus on me than anyone else.

And no, that wasn't because I was selfishly looking forward to his special brand of punishment and missing his attention.

At least, not entirely.

"Today, we will practice. You are all going into the city, armed with nothing but your wits. You'll encounter foes and innocents and will be forced to make a choice. If you fail, and an innocent dies, you return to face me."

"Can we use our magic?" a warlock called.

"Did I not just say you will be armed with nothing but your wits? Clearly those have escaped you. In the real world, should you come in contact with a demon, your powers will largely be useless. As those of you who were present for the attack in the library have already learned. Brute strength and deadly force prevailed there."

"What about weapons?" Chad asked.

Kingston's gaze snapped to his packmate, and he shook his head. "Fucking idiot."

Caleb pinched the bridge of his nose, muttering an exasperated, "Jesus on the cross, what did I do to deserve this?"

"What? It's a good question," Chad continued.

"Do you regularly walk around the city armed to the teeth?"

"Well, no . . ."

"Then there's your answer."

"Who needs to bring weapons? Anything can be deadly in the right hands," Alek added with a smug smirk.

"That is only true if you can manage to keep your *wits* about you, which with this lot is proving less and less likely," Caleb said with an annoyed shake of his head. "Now, if there are no more unnecessarily stupid questions..."

"I thought there was no such thing as a stupid question," I said, just because I couldn't help myself.

"Keep talking, Miss Fallon. We'll make it two weeks, shall we?"

I clenched my thighs together in response to the promise in his words.

Caleb paced the floor and pulled out a small bottle filled with deep purple liquid. He opened a door on the other side to reveal a supply closet and tossed the vial inside, the crack of breaking glass hitting my ears before a cloud of violet smoke filled the space. Then the sounds of a city filtered in through the opening.

"Remember, if an innocent dies due to your negligence, you return...to me."

He stood by the door, waiting as the class filed through one by one. I found my way to the back of the line, hoping for a moment alone with my confessor.

When we were the last two in the room, disappointment sat heavy in my chest. He wasn't even looking at me as I approached the threshold between our classroom and the city beyond.

Then he grabbed my wrist, tugging me back and shoving me against the wall, his other hand coming up to roughly grasp my chin.

"God save me from you and your smart mouth, Sunday Fallon." His voice was tight as he leaned close and stared down at my lips.

My tongue darted out, wetting them as arousal pooled low in my belly.

"What am I going to do with you?" he whispered.

"Excuse me from this assignment, and I can spend some time under your desk showing you."

His eyes flashed and he grinned, fangs glinting in the light. He looked a hair's breadth away from losing control. "That would be one way to shut you up."

I smirked. "Oh, there's all sorts of fun sounds I can make with your dick in my mouth, Father."

A low groan was his only response.

I tilted my chin up and locked eyes with him in challenge. "Go on, you know you want to let me stay back and play."

"What I want is irrelevant. This is important. You need to know how to fight these creatures."

"I already fought one."

"And by the way I hear it, you would've died if Alek hadn't been there to send the beast back to hell."

I huffed in annoyance. "I was the first one to draw blood. Alek wouldn't have even known where to hurt him if it wasn't for me."

Probably.

Tenderness flickered in his gaze. "My fierce little hunter. You have no idea what you are, do you?"

"I guess not. Tell me, Caleb. What am I?"

"Everything," he whispered so softly I wasn't sure he meant for me to hear it. Then he leaned down and closed the distance between our mouths. The kiss was intense, searing, and over far too soon. Lips still on mine, he breathed one word that sent chills down my spine. "Mine."

He shoved himself off the wall, pushing away from me. "Now go," he ordered. "We can continue this conversation during your session."

I lifted my hand to my lips, which still tingled from his

kiss. I slowly started moving, my gaze trained on him as I did.

His palm cracked down on my ass. "Now, *a stor*."

"Yes, sir," I said with a saucy wink.

Then, with a final glance over my shoulder, I strode through the doorway and found myself in the middle of a city I recognized.

"Of course we'd be in LA. What could be more appropriate for a priest to choose than the City of Angels?"

TWENTY-THREE

Sunday stepped around the corner, her hair mussed, cheeks flushed, and eyes dark with arousal. My wolf snarled deep in my chest, annoyed that our mate looked that way because of another man.

"Kingston," she said, not a flicker of guilt in her eyes at getting caught by me. "What are you doing?"

"What the hell do you think I'm doing? I'm waiting for you." I knew she could tell by the bite to my voice that I'd been waiting a while. And that I knew the reason for her delay.

She came close, standing up on tiptoe to press a kiss to my cheek. "You didn't have to wait."

"Why wouldn't I? No way I'm going to let you roam around by yourself when you're the personification of demon bait."

One brow cocked, she stared at me. "Demon bait? Really?"

"Yeah. Look at you. If I were a demon, I'd be all over you by now."

"Not to mention you were singled out in the library attack," Alek drawled, stepping out of a nearby alley.

"What is this? An intervention?" Sunday grumbled.

"We're here for you. It's my job to keep you safe."

Alek cut me a glare. "*Our* job. I might not be able to mark her, but she's mine. I feel it . . . here." He placed a hand over his heart. "We're linked."

Sunday's eyes went soft at his words, but her voice was still tinged with exasperation. "I don't remember hiring any bodyguards."

"You didn't. It's the perk of being one of your lovers."

I rolled my eyes. "Enough. You can write her a fucking poem later. Let's go."

As if we'd done it a hundred times before, we moved into position. Sunday at my side, Alek guarding our flank. I'd never admit it out loud, but having the Viking at my back made me feel more relaxed.

The stench of *city* filled my nose, my sense of smell heightened even through the barrier keeping me from shifting. My wolf was part of me, even if he couldn't get out. The sickly sweet scent of rotting garbage overpowered everything, and when I glanced into the alley, I found overflowing dumpsters and a bedraggled transient man picking through the trash. It was night here, just as it had been back at campus, which told me this was a simulation and not the real deal. But fuck if it didn't smell like it.

A low rumble hit my ears as a car approached. Even from a distance, I could hear the heavy bass from the subwoofer. It drew closer, and I grabbed Sunday by the hand, pulling her off the road and onto the sidewalk. Then I positioned myself on her left, keeping her away from traffic. The car rolled past, windows rattling from the volume of the music.

"What are you doing?" Sunday asked when I wouldn't let her switch sides with me.

"Keeping you safe."

"By doing what exactly? Shoving me into buildings?"

"Standing between you and the cars. Never know when one might go rogue and come up onto the sidewalk. This way, it will crash into me before touching you."

She blinked at me, clearly not expecting the answer. "That's . . . sweet."

Alek snickered. "Now who's the one writing poetry?"

I glared at him. "It's not poetry. It's chivalry, you asshole."

Sunday linked our fingers, the connection at once soothing me. I hadn't realized how much I liked holding her hand until this moment. The casual intimacy was a rush more potent than sex. I was starting to crave the moments with her when she'd brush her lips against my cheek or wrap her arms around my waist so she could rest her head on my shoulder. If someone had told me even a year ago I'd live for those moments, I would have laughed in their face right before punching it, but now . . . fuck.

Alek put a hand on my shoulder, stopping us. "Wait. Do you smell that?"

I frowned, confused, senses on alert. "What?"

"Brimstone," Sunday whispered.

Closing my eyes, I let the scent wash over me, faint but there. I also heard a low growl, deep and barely audible.

I spun around, eyes scanning the horizon for the source of the animalistic sound. "Where are you, you piece of shit?"

I shoved Sunday behind me into Alek, only a little surprised when he repeated the move and bodily pushed her behind him.

Sunday grumbled, and I knew she'd probably try to chew us out later, but for the moment, she was staying quiet. I only hoped she'd let us do our jobs as her protectors.

"Do you see anything?" I asked.

"No," Alek grunted, sounding as frustrated and on edge as I felt.

"Blood," Sunday whispered. "Can't you smell the blood? Copper and salt."

I couldn't. "Fuck, Sunshine, did Thorne partially turn you or something?"

"No?"

The hesitation in her answer, as if she wasn't quite sure, sent unease stabbing straight through me.

"Stay with her," Alek ordered, stalking ahead.

For just a second, I could easily imagine him with a battle-ax wearing leather armor and furs while releasing a savage war cry. He moved a little ways down the block, and it was all I could do to keep Sunday from following.

She ducked under my arm, intent on going after him. I snagged a finger through one of her belt loops, tugging her back with no little force, but she refused to stay where I wanted her. Shielded. Safe. Protected.

"Not so fast, Sunshine. You heard the Viking. You're with me."

"But he might need help."

"He single-handedly killed a demon not even a week ago. He'll be fine."

"It wasn't single-handed," she muttered.

Alek stopped near a pile of black garbage bags, his brows pulling together as he stared down at something. Then his face paled, expression stricken as he looked back at us. On instinct, I stepped in front of Sunday.

The odor of blood and brimstone filled the atmosphere, coating my tongue as though I'd tasted it.

"Sunday!" Alek shouted, rushing toward us, fear and rage warring for control of his face.

She cried out, and I wasn't fast enough to do anything as the transient from earlier grabbed Sunday by the hair and pulled her down. He stared straight at me as he did it, his eyes glowing a pale red as the pupils narrowed and stretched into goat-like slits. His smile spread far wider than anything remotely human as it revealed row after row of yellow fangs.

"Sonofabitch," I swore, furious at myself for not realizing it had been a demon in disguise. Everything in me screamed to rush forward and rip her from his grasp, but I already knew even the hint of such a move from me, and he'd tear her throat out before I got to him.

He dropped his glamour entirely then. His human facade shimmered into something skeletal and black. He was neither beast nor man, but something uniquely in between, with long fur-tipped ears and deadly sharp claws.

"Get off me, you asshole." Sunday kicked and squirmed, but the demon had a tight fist in her hair, limiting her mobility. "God, you stink. Ever heard of a breath mint?"

"You smell like sweet cream and sex. Maybe I'll keep you instead of delivering you to my master." The demon leaned in and licked a trail up Sunday's throat with a slimy forked tongue.

"I doubt you could even get it up."

His clawed hand ran over her lower belly, then up until he cupped one of her breasts. Rage exploded through me, and I searched the surroundings for something I could use as a weapon. But Sunday was faster. She drew her elbow back, aiming it straight for his demon dick.

Apparently one truth was universal—if it had balls, it hurt like a motherfucker when they were struck. The demon let out an unearthly wail as he released his hold on her, curling in on himself.

Sunday spun, grasping the demon by both ears and tugging his head farther down as she brought her knee up, slamming it into his pig-like nose. The crunch was satisfying even from my vantage point. Black blood poured from the bastard's face, and he howled, lashing out with razor-sharp claws.

Sunday screamed as three deep wounds opened on her left forearm, blood welling instantly.

She shouldn't be bleeding. This was a simulation. But as the blood dripped down her arm, there was no denying the truth.

"Fuck."

This was real. He was real. *Motherfucker.*

Together, Alek and I rushed him even as he clamped a hand around her throat and lifted her into the air.

"You're going to die for that. I don't care what my master does to me for killing you."

She reached for his head, thumbs pressing against those goat-like eyes. Alek grunted in approval.

Before either of us could react, a shadow blurred out of the alley, slamming into the demon and sending him flying. He lost his hold on Sunday, but instead of hitting the ground, she was cradled in the arms of a familiar dark-haired priest.

"Caleb?" she whispered, blinking rapidly.

"Aye, *a stor.*" He turned to us, his expression livid. "Take her while I deal with the creature."

Alek moved faster than I did, gathering Sunday in his arms and tucking her into his body.

I didn't watch the priest as he took his revenge on the demon. The squelching and tearing sounds coming from behind us said it all. Caleb was playing the role of avenging angel, destroying him for touching our Sunday.

"Sunshine," I whispered as I brushed her hair away from a face streaked with grime and sweat. "Fuck, are you okay?"

Instead of answering, she asked a question of her own. "How are we supposed to fight those things when we walked right by him without even realizing what he was?"

"Don't worry about that right now," I murmured.

"She has a point," Alek said, his voice tight. "Without our powers, we're little more than humans."

Caleb returned as Alek finished speaking. The shock of seeing him covered head to toe in demon blood, eyes wild with hunger and chest rising and falling as he fought to catch his breath was enough to make even me take a step back. The priest was fucking terrifying. Who knew he had it in him?

"Put me down," Sunday said, squirming in Alek's hold. The Novasgardian tightened his arms, but he relented when Sunday growled at him. Without a second's hesitation, she went to Caleb, flinging her arms around his shoulders and hugging him. "Thank you."

He pushed her away with a hand on her hip. "We need to be going." Caleb's voice was calm and controlled, even if he appeared crazed. "This exercise is over."

"There's a dead girl in the alley." Alek's words stopped us all. "She looks like Sunday."

Sunday shook her head. "That's not real. None of this is."

"The demon was fucking real. Look at your arm," I snarled.

229

She held out her arm, still bleeding freely, and Caleb sucked in a sharp breath in response. "Won't it stop when the illusion is broken?"

Caleb pulled out another vial like the one from earlier and threw it into the street. Purple smoke filled the air before everything around us disappeared, leaving a blank room, students in mid-fight, and a dismembered demon who was rapidly crumbling to ash.

The four of us turned to the place where Alek had stood by the garbage bags. Even as I prayed for there to be nothing remaining, I wasn't surprised by the mangled corpse. Her dark hair was strewn about her, her body the same size and shape as my mate's.

"Get her out of here," Caleb said, his voice a low, scary rumble. He locked eyes with me. "You know where."

Sunday was working up to a protest, I could feel it in her, but Caleb roared, "Now!"

The rage coming from him was enough to stun Sunday to silence and make Alek and I kick into gear.

"Where are we going?" Sunday asked as I caught her hand in mine and took off in a flat-out run.

"Somewhere we can keep you safe."

TWENTY-FOUR

T error and dread jolted me from my uneasy sleep, leaving me shaking with adrenaline, a sick feeling twisting my gut.

"Sunday." The room echoed with the sound of her name falling from my lips. Something was deadly wrong.

Phantom pain tore through me, but instead of fading away, the sensation intensified. It was like acid burning a path in my veins. I had to get out of here. To help her. I dropped my shield and linked with her mind, knowing the risk I was taking but unable to stop myself.

All I saw was blood and fire and death in her mind. It was reminiscent of the night she shared her dream with me, but worse. Far worse. Pounding hoofbeats filled my ears, so loud I feared my eardrums would burst. And on their heels, the wail of three furious battle cries.

I didn't know what it meant, only that I was terrified for my mate. She was being hunted. Little did the predators know, I was the only one who could hunt her. But I didn't mean to kill her. I meant to love her. Sunday was mine.

"Lucas!" I called, my voice booming. He'd hear me. He

could hear everything I said and did in this house. I stalked to the silver-lined door and pounded my fists into it until they burned. "I know you can hear me, you bastard. Let me out of here."

The small window in the center opened, revealing my uncle, clad in a disheveled tuxedo with lipstick on his collar and a bite mark on his neck. "You'd better have a bloody good reason for this. You startled Briar mid-feed, and now my shirt is ruined."

"My mate is in pain. Something happened. I need to go to her."

Conflict warred in his eyes. "Noah . . ."

"Please, Lucas. You know I would only ask if it was a matter of life and death."

He hissed in a breath.

"You know what you would do if our situations were reversed. What you already *have* done for Briar. Please. Do not deny me."

He sighed and crossed his arms over his chest as he leaned against the wall across from the door. "You're putting me in a very difficult position, you little wankstain."

"Call me what you like; just let me out of here. She is my everything, and she's . . . I think she's dying. Please, Uncle?"

Briar appeared next to him, her long blonde locks falling over one shoulder. A bite mark on her neck betrayed exactly what they'd been up to when I interrupted.

"Who is dying?"

Lucas shrugged. "His wolfy mate."

"What happened?"

I gritted my teeth. "I don't know. But I feel it. Let me free."

Briar placed a palm on Lucas's forearm. "If you don't let him out and she dies, he'll never forgive you."

"I've been hated before."

"I'll never forgive you," she said, her tone serious. "Remember when I died? Remember how it shattered you? You changed completely. Don't make him go through that."

Lucas rolled his eyes. "Fine. Call Silas and Natalie. We'll need a witch if we're going to get him to his mate before it's too late."

Relief made me sag against the door, alleviating some of the pressure in my chest, but not much. Until Sunday was in my arms, I didn't think I'd breathe easy again.

"Thank you, Briar."

She pressed her palm over the window. "No one should ever come between mates. Save her, Noah. And then bring her to meet your family once it's safe."

A swell of affection for her hit me in the chest. My uncle was an asshole on most days, but she made him better.

AN HOUR LATER, I stood outside Ravenscroft's church. It was bloody useful having one of Salem's most powerful witches on speed dial. Thanks to Natalie's portal creation skills, I'd made the trip across the pond in under five minutes. I just had to find Sunday.

At first, I tried to follow our bond, but Sunday was still lost to her nightmares. Instead, I had to rely on my other senses. Her scent was oddly absent, but I knew if she'd been hurt there was no way that fucking wolf wouldn't be by her side. Thankfully, his scent was strong here, and it was no trouble following his trail into the church and then lower, deep into the forgotten depths. Prior to my grandfather taking control, monks had resided here. I imagined them using the small rooms as dormitories or for storage. Either way, they were well hidden. Finding Kingston, and thereby Sunday, was simply a matter of locating the correct door.

Light at the end of the long dark hallway had hope humming through my veins, and Sunday's scent finally filtered to me. It was changed, weaker somehow, tinged with the bitterness of brimstone. Oh, bloody hell, she'd been attacked by a demon. I was all too familiar with that stench.

I picked up my pace, running full tilt toward her. Murmured voices from the room told me both Alek and Kingston were there, and then the Irish lilt of Father Gallagher joined in. All of them? It must've been dire if they'd all banded together.

Heart in my throat, I pressed my palm against the cracked door, pushing it slowly open.

Three snarling alpha males stared back at me, but I only had eyes for the woman on the bed. Why hadn't they helped her yet? She was clearly suffering. I could feel the pain rolling from her.

"Move aside. If you're not going to fucking heal her, get out of my way." My voice was dark and brimming with violence as I stalked toward the priest who hadn't done the only thing necessary to fix this mess.

The three of them parted, opening my path to her. My stomach churned at the sight of her wound, my own forearm giving a sympathetic throb as the memory of her pain raced through me. Swollen, jagged gashes went black around the edges as death crept from the inside out. These would be fatal to any creature. The flesh surrounding the wound was red, hot enough I could feel the warmth radiating off her without touching her skin. I reached for

Sunday, but the priest grabbed my arm before I could make contact.

"Her blood is tainted, Thorne. Don't touch the wound," Father Gallagher warned. "It was a pestilence demon. I can't heal her."

That sent ice down my back. A pestilence demon? A tendril of forgiveness for the priest's inaction unfurled in my gut. His blood would do little to help her. But mine? As a born vampire, mine was stronger than that of a human who'd been turned.

"She needs me."

He nodded, but before he fully moved away I was shoving him back, kneeling at her side and tearing at my wrist with my fangs.

"I'm here, dove. You'll be good as new as soon as you drink from me." I pressed my bleeding wrist to her lips, cradling the back of her head with my other hand and supporting her.

Sunday whimpered, but when the first drop of my blood fell past her lips, she moaned and latched on.

"That's it, my love. Good girl." My words were nonsensical, falling out without conscious thought. The smell of wet dog hit my nose, making my lip curl. "Not the time, pup."

"Trust me, we're going to have words about where the fuck you've been once she's in the clear. For now, just know that if you turn her, I will end you."

"I'm not going to turn her. And I've been away to keep her and everyone else safe. Believe me, it's a choice I wish I hadn't had to make."

"You seem to do that a lot. Abandon her." The censure in Alek's voice cut through me.

My free hand balled into a tight fist. "I didn't abandon

her. She knows exactly where I was and why I left. I had the strength to leave her because I love her. Unlike others in this room . . ." I shot a glare at the priest who couldn't seem to stay away from her.

He met my angry stare without flinching. "Not all of us have the luxury of that choice."

"Stop fighting. It's going to give you wrinkles." Sunday's voice pulled us away from our argument. I hadn't even noticed she'd released my wrist from her hold.

"Are you all right?" I let my gaze trail over her arm where the festering wound had been. All that remained were faint pink lines, no trace of the poisoned gashes.

The tip of her tongue darted out, licking off the smears of blood dotting her lips. "Perfect, now that you're here."

Her voice was breathy and just this side of . . . was that arousal?

She sat up and reached for me, pulling me down on top of her with surprising strength, but all thought vanished from my head as her lips found mine. I hadn't kissed her in far too long. Fucking hell, I'd missed her.

"I love you," I murmured against her mouth. "I'm sorry."

"Don't." She arched into me, clearly not caring that anyone else was around. "I need you. I need you so badly it hurts, Noah."

"Fuck," Kingston said, the sound of a belt being unfastened ringing out in the small room. "Looks like we're in for a wild night, boys."

I tore my mouth from hers even though it pained me to do it. Sunday let out a wanton moan, trying to pull my face back to hers.

She was in need of me. My mate ached for me. I could smell it.

"What are you on about?"

"Heat." Alek's eyes were locked on Sunday, hunger blazing in them.

Kingston pulled his shirt over his head and tossed the fabric onto the floor. "Saddle up, bloodsucker. Our mate needs us to serve her."

"All of us?" I asked, shock rippling through me.

What the hell had I missed since I'd been away?

Apparently, your mate needs a hell of a lot more than she let on. Serve her and show her how much you love her. Enough to share her with as many men as she needs.

"Yes," Sunday breathed. "Don't leave me. I need all of you."

Her eyes were locked onto Caleb, who'd been trying to escape the room unnoticed.

"*A stor*, you know I can't."

"Then watch, Priest, since you love it so much. But our woman asked you to stay, and so you will."

As I spoke, Alek moved to stand in front of the door, blocking Caleb's escape. It was an empty gesture. We all knew the priest could leave if he wanted. My bet was he'd stay.

Caleb swallowed but took his hand off the doorknob, then with a sharp nod, he pulled the hard chair from the corner and sat, eyes locked on Sunday.

"Breed me, Noah," she whispered, and that one soft request sent me from hard to throbbing.

"As you fucking wish."

CHAPTER
TWENTY-FIVE
SUNDAY

I moaned and rubbed my thighs together as I watched Noah rub one hand over his still fully clothed cock. That wasn't what I needed. I needed his thick length deep inside me. I needed his hands on me.

"Fuck me, Sunday." Noah licked his lips and spared a glance at Kingston. "You've ridden this out with her before? Was she this needy?"

"It was worse the first time." Kingston reached out and cupped my breast, rolling my taut nipple between his fingers. "She was insatiable."

Alek brushed my hair off my face. "That last is true for the second time as well, isn't it, Sunny?"

"Fuck," Noah said again, though this time it sounded reverent.

Every single place they touched me burned with hunger. I had to have more. "Please don't make me wait."

"Seeing as how I missed the first two occasions, I think I will. I think I'll draw this out until you're writhing beneath us, begging us to let you come. How does that sound?"

"Terrible."

"I wasn't asking you, dove."

"Fuck that, you're not going to make her suffer," Kingston growled. "If you won't man up and fuck her like she needs, get out of the way."

"No," I protested. "I need Noah. It has to be Noah."

"My pleasure, but I'll be doing this the way I want. And it's been too long since I've been inside you. For my own sake, I have to take this slow, or it'll be over before I can serve you the way you need."

Kingston snorted. "So you're saying you're a two-pump chump. I thought that might be the case."

"Fuck you, wolf. Fast doesn't mean better. Haven't you ever heard of delayed gratification? There's a lot to be said for edging. The antici . . ." Noah ran his hands up my thighs, touching me everywhere but the place I desired, " . . . pation can be the most exquisite form of torture."

He hooked his fingers in the waistband of my jeans and tugged, sharp and quick, filling the room with the sound of tearing denim. The cool air hit my bare flesh, sending my heart racing as sensation overwhelmed me. Already? How was I going to survive him?

"Look at how turned on she is," Alek said in his low grumble.

"Her knickers are so wet I can see her pussy through them. Can you see, Priest? Do you want a closer look?" Noah stared down at me like I was his treasure. I was going to combust. He'd kill me just by looking at me.

"I can see just fine right here." Caleb's voice was distant, but thick with desire. I couldn't see his face over Alek's massive frame, but there was no missing the way his hands grasped the arms of the chair like he was at the edge of his rope.

I could picture those strong forearms of his, corded with

veins and muscle, tense and flexed as he tried to control himself.

Alek's fingers gripped my chin and tugged my face toward him, forcing me to look into his ice-blue stare. "Watch me while he eats your pussy. I want to see the light catch fire in your eyes."

A flood of liquid heat rolled through me at the words, and I was a slave to his command. He slid his hand down so that it cupped both my throat and my jaw as he rubbed his thumb along my pulse point.

"Make her writhe, Thorne. I'll hold her steady."

Noah's soft grunt of agreement hit my ears the second his lips met my inner thigh, and it was all I could do not to tear my gaze away from Alek's stare to watch what my vampire prince was doing to me. My God, these men. When Noah sliced through my panties with his teeth, I jerked, but Kingston's hands settled on my hips, stilling me, anchoring me.

"Hold her, gentlemen. I'm starved."

I moaned, feeling a surge of slick heat rushing out at his words. I was powerless against my need for him—for all of them. A slave to my body and my desire. The heat brought everything to the surface. I may be helpless in the face of its pull, but these thoughts, these wanton urges were all me.

"Noah, please."

He hummed and slid his nose across my clit, making me scream in frustration. "I could die happily surrounded by your fucking scent."

"I'm going to *actually* die if you don't fuck me with some part of you right now."

His fangs scraped either side of my clit as he started to move back down to my throbbing core. "Gladly."

The tip of his tongue traced my center.

"More," I begged.

"You'll take what he gives you." Alek's deep voice was so filled with desire I barely recognized it.

I begged him with my eyes, but he wasn't relenting.

Beside me, Kingston unzipped his pants, his voice gravelly and his words harsh. "If any of you don't want to see me jerking off and covering our girl in my cum, you better walk the fuck away right now. I won't stop once I start."

My nipples tightened so fast I cried out. And when Kingston's hand left his thick cock and came to the collar of my T-shirt, I arched into him.

"Ah, ah, ah, little wolf. You'll move when we want you to move. Now hold still, or I'll make one of them keep you down." Noah's warm breath brushed across my over-heated and sensitive flesh, amping up my need even more.

I took a moment to collect myself and locked gazes with Kingston as he tore my shirt straight down the middle. I would need a whole new wardrobe if things kept going like this. Alek curled one of his thick fingers around the center of my bra and tugged, the burn of lace sharp and hot as it tore in two.

"That was expensive," I panted.

Alek's grin stretched. "Put it on my tab."

I was going to retort, but a talented tongue connected with my clit and sent all my focus straight there. I cried out, Alek still holding my face in his hand, Kingston running his palm over my belly, between my breasts, and back. And then there was Caleb, I couldn't see him, but I knew he hadn't left. I could feel him. Sense him. Fuck, I could smell him.

Just when I thought I couldn't take another assault on my senses, Noah slid two fingers inside me, curling them as though beckoning me as his tongue played with the swollen bundle of nerves at the apex of my thighs.

I cried out, feeling like a creature born only of need.

Noah worked me faster, bringing me right to the brink before pulling away.

"No," I moaned, trying to jerk my head toward him, but Alek held me hostage. "You bastard," I whined.

"You'll love me again in a minute." Noah's tender promise made me wish my hands weren't currently being restrained by a naked werewolf.

"We'll see about that," I protested.

But he was right, because the instant Noah slid deep inside me, I loved him. I shuddered and came as soon as the tip of his cock kissed my womb.

At the feel of his torturously slow thrusts, I blindly reached out, running one hand up Kingston's thigh and the other curling around Alek's waist before sliding down and grasping his firm ass.

Alek sucked in a sharp breath and kicked his hips forward just enough that his swollen cock nudged my cheek from where the monster was restrained behind his fly. Magic brushed over my skin as he removed his clothes.

He widened his stance, allowing my hand to traverse between those two sculpted globes to reach between his legs, and he moaned as my fingers brushed his heavy balls.

"You fucker, you could have done that to my bra."

"It's not nearly as satisfying."

I glared at him, but he ran the tip of his length over my lips, leaving a bead of sticky precum behind. I licked it off and moaned at the burst of flavor.

"How do you taste so good?"

He smirked down at me. "I'm a god, remember? Ambrosia has to come from somewhere."

245

I was pretty sure he was lying, but also, who the fuck cared?

Noah continued his slow, toe-curling thrusts while Kingston grabbed my hand and pressed my palm to his hard dick. The deep rumbled groan he let out sent a wash of pride through me. It was difficult to keep track of every sensation these men evoked, especially once my orgasm started to build.

They might be working together to make me come undone, but I was doing the same for them. I could hear it in the hitch of Caleb's breath and feel it in the increasingly wild pump of Noah's hips. The agonized groan from Alek as he slid the tip of his massive cock past my lips tapped into something primal inside me. But it was with the feral grunt from Kingston as each barbell piercing his shaft ran across my palm that I truly lost myself.

With my mouth full of Novasgardian dick, I couldn't tell them what I needed, but they didn't require instructions. They moved as a unit. Alek took his hand from my throat and moved it back behind my head, where he gripped my hair and shifted me into a position that worked better for us both. He knew I couldn't focus enough to do this right, not with Noah deep inside me.

"Let me take the lead, Sunny. Fuck, your mouth feels so good."

He slowly thrust, not deep enough for me to gag, but enough that I had to force myself not to think too hard about it.

Kingston's large palm gripped my thigh and spread me wider, allowing Noah deeper access, even though my vampire prince was already bottoming out inside me with every roll of his hips. Or so I thought. That one adjustment had me seeing stars as Noah pounded into me, his groan ricocheting off the walls.

"Keep your hand right there, Sunshine. Let me do the work for us both." Kingston pumped his hips and ran his erection across my hand. Then he wrapped his free hand around himself, helping me jerk him off.

"I'm on the edge, dove. I can't hold back much longer, but I want your walls fluttering around me when I fill you with my spend. God, I want to see it leaking out of you."

Alek groaned deep in his throat, his hips working harder as he chased his own climax. "Come for us, Kærasta. Let us have your pleasure."

I wanted to. God, I was trembling with need. But something held me back. My focus slid to the man sitting in the corner, watching me with a gaze that burned as hot as the fires of hell.

He reached for his cock, palming it through his trousers and breathing heavily. But when he commanded, "Make her come," in that dominant way he had, I tumbled off the cliff.

I came with a strangled moan, and Caleb's eyes widened with panicked pleasure as I did. His hand rested between his thighs. Thighs that tensed and released as he fought the need to come.

My orgasm triggered the others'. Alek spurted down my throat as my hand worked along the crack of his ass. Kingston spilled all over my chest and belly, his hot cum dripping everywhere. As for Noah, the second I detonated around him, he came with a feral cry that rivaled Kingston, his release filling me so full I knew I'd be leaking with it just as he'd wished.

As hot and fast as it had been, there was a certain magic to it. All of us had finished within seconds of each other, my pleasure the gatekeeper of their own. If I'd ever had any doubt this was right, that they were mine, it was gone in that second. Erased by the perfection of having all of them at the same time.

The wave of my heat that had taken over receded as we all came down from our combined pleasure. Who knew how long it would be before it began to rise again, but for the moment, it was perfect. We were perfect.

Noah pulled out of me, making me whimper at the loss of him.

He smiled lazily. "Don't worry, my darling, I won't be gone long. I belong right here with you."

Alek was the next to leave me. He pulled back, grunting as he left my mouth. "Fuck, Sunny. I can't wait to do that again." Then he leaned down, claiming my mouth with his own. He hummed in appreciation as he backed away. "I can taste my cum on your lips. That's fucking hot."

Kingston left without a word, and for a moment, I worried he was pissed about something. Before my anxiety could really start to spiral, he was back, a towel in his hand. He ran the warm damp cloth down my belly and between my legs, cleaning up the evidence of our fuck fest.

Then he leaned down and feathered a kiss over my lips, surprising me. "I fucking love you, Sunday Fallon."

"I love you, too."

His eyes shone with pride as he kissed me again, this time leaving no doubt that he was staking claim. He might be willing to share me, but there was no denying he owned a part of my soul.

When he backed away, I frowned up at him. "Why does it feel like that was a goodbye kiss?"

He grinned. "Because it was. Thorne will see you through the rest of this heat. Alek and I need to go make sure the grounds are safe for you. We can't risk letting demons find you, not when they're clearly out to kill pretty brunettes."

I bit down on my lip, not wanting them to leave but understanding why they had to go. Plus, this way I would have some time alone with Noah. My gaze sought out my confessor, but he was already gone. Disappointment left a bitter taste in my mouth, but I wasn't surprised he'd left. Caleb was a watcher. Maybe one day he would join in, though I wouldn't hold my breath.

If this was all I could have of him, I told myself it was enough. Even though I knew it was a lie.

I wouldn't force this choice on him. He needed to come to it on his own. Just like the rest of my mates had.

And while he couldn't mark me in the same way, there was no doubt Alek was my mate. I felt it in the electric buzz in my veins whenever he was near.

As the two of them left the room, closing the door behind them, Noah strode to the fireplace where the once blazing flames were now nothing but dying embers. He tossed more logs into the hearth and brought it back to life, the glow of the blaze as it licked the wood casting him in a beautiful symphony of shadow and light. He was stunning as he walked naked toward me.

"Are you tired, dove?"

I scooted over and let him join me in the bed, fighting my yawn. "No."

His low laugh warmed something inside me. "Sleep. I'm not going anywhere."

"You've said that before, then the Council took you away from me."

He pressed a kiss to my temple. "Never again. They'll have to drag me from you."

"And what if they do?"

"I'll rip their fucking heads off."

"How are you here now? Is it over? Did you figure out how to get them off your back?"

He shook his head. "Now is not the time. We'll talk about it after your heat has passed."

"Promise you'll tell me?"

"I promise. Now sleep, little wolf. I'll watch over you."

I tried to fight it. I'd missed this—him—so much. But just like it had been with the others, the side effect of my heat left me exhausted, and soon my lids were fluttering closed without my permission. Leaving me to fall asleep in the arms of my vampire, his tight hold and the steady thump of his heart the only things I was aware of as I faded away.

CHAPTER

TWENTY-SIX

CALEB

I hadn't even touched her, but the scent of Sunday's arousal continued to torment me. Even now, hours later, my dick was still hard, still aching for relief. The fecking sounds she made as they'd had her right in front of me echoed in my mind. I'd pulled sounds like that from deep inside her, I wanted to then as well, but I hung onto my resolve by the thinnest thread I had remaining.

The way she'd looked at me, begging me with her eyes to touch her. To taste her. God above, it was nearly my undoing. Did she have any idea what she did to me? How little control I had when it came to her? How every time I touched her I swore it would be the last, even when I knew she'd make a sinner of me the next time we crossed paths.

"Is something burning?" The words intruded on my thoughts, the angel Gabriel's voice holding annoyance as he looked at me. "Caleb, your hand."

I blinked, my thoughts of Sunday dissolving as reality came crashing back down. I glanced at my hand where I was clutching a rosary, the silver cross embedded into my palm. Thin curls of smoke rose from where the metal

continued to burn my skin. I removed my personal imple-
ment of punishment and tucked it away into my pocket, the
shame of my failure to control my lust hitting me hard as
God's own messenger stared me down.

Beside me, Lilith smirked, her eyes glowing as she fed
on the lust I'd tried and failed to push aside.

"You," I growled.

She blinked, feigning innocence. "What? You know I'm
not one to turn down a free buffet, sugar." Then she licked
her lips, letting out a lusty sigh. "Delicious, by the way.
Forbidden fruit always is."

Gabriel's lips twitched from where he stood in the
center of our gathering. "If you're quite done with . . . whatever that was, we have business to which we must attend.
Business that is taking me away from other matters I'd
much rather be focused on."

"Like that book in your pocket?" Lilith asked with a
sultry curl of her lips. "I do love a good smutfest."

"I've said it before—"

"It's not smut if they're in love. Yes, I remember." Lilith
was a ballsy one; I'd give her that.

For a demon and angel, two celestial beings that played
on opposite sides, they certainly had an interesting friendship. The same could be said for most of the people in this
room.

"I'm with the angel. I have the safety of my pack to
concern myself with. We were fine until you brought the
half-breed here, Fallon." Ronin Farrell's booming voice
filled the space from where he was seated.

The circle of society members seemed so out of place
in the basement of *Iniquity*. The room was nothing but a
box with peeling wallpaper and empty shelves as decor, a
single pendant light hanging from the center of the

ceiling and illuminating all of us in sickly light. Well, almost all of us. The Seer remained cloaked in shadow, her hood low on her face as she stood just outside of the group.

"She was brought here to keep this from happening. Instead it's gotten worse. Blackthorne's son can't keep his dick away from her." The growled words from Niall Fallon vibrated through me.

"You will refrain from speaking of my son that way," Cashel Blackthrone snapped, his fangs on full display. "We did what we could to keep them apart. I know from experience, a mated pair like them will not be stopped."

"My, if I knew there'd be a dick measuring contest, I would have brought my popcorn." Quinn Satori was an enigma, the Novasgardian ambassador new to our secret group. She smirked, looking every bit as devious as the demon sitting next to me. "Nord never mentioned how much fun these little meetings were."

"What do you have to say for yourself, Priest? You were charged with keeping Sunday safe. You failed. The seals are opening." Cashel's eyes burned molten amber, so like his son's.

"I cannot be with her twenty-four hours out of the fucking day. Even if I could, she's a grown woman. I do my best, but she makes her own choices. As you bloody well know."

"But you want to be," Lilith muttered under her breath. I was going to hang her up by her toes if she didn't stop taunting me.

"We really have taken every precaution. No one anticipated demons would return to the surface. Or that they would single her out so quickly." Antoinette le Blanc's words almost sounded like a defense. One I hadn't expected. The headmistress and I rarely saw eye to eye on anything.

"This isn't about the fucking demons. It's about the seals. My granddaughter is going to end the world, and since no one would let me kill her when she was born, there's nothing we can do to stop it."

Rage boiled in my blood. If anyone harmed a single hair on her head, I'd tear their heart from their chest and feast on it while they watched.

"Careful, Priest. Your feelings are showing." Lilith looked pointedly at my hands, knuckles white as my fingers dug into my knees.

"The girl is an innocent. She doesn't deserve death. She requires saving." Gabriel glanced around the room, his eyes singling me out. "She needs a guardian who can keep his personal emotions in check."

Especially if he wants to redeem his soul.

He didn't say the words out loud, but I felt them in every cell of my body. It's why I was here, after all, part of this motley crew. I was not one of the members, but a servant to their cause. If I succeeded, my reward would be my soul. Gabriel himself had promised to go into purgatory and bring it back to me.

And yet, I continued to fail at every turn. I couldn't keep my fecking hands to myself.

"She will open another seal before long. The beast will be freed, and she will die."

The Seer's voice was soft and eerie. She only spoke when having a vision. She was the reason we were all here. She'd come to us individually and told us we'd been called upon by fate. Lucky us.

"She will die?" Fin, one of the fae princes of the Shadow Court frowned as he repeated the most important part of her statement. "Doesn't that negate the issue then?"

"I say kill her now and get it over with. Rather solves the issue of the seals, doesn't it?"

I glared at Blaire Belladonna. The old woman might be the head of the most powerful coven of witches since Salem, but I would slit her throat where she sat if she thought to act on her impulsive words.

"If she dies this will all be for naught. She has to stay alive, or the seals will all open at once." Antoinette's voice was clear and strong. "My research has confirmed this to be true."

"What we need to do is ensure the seals remain closed." Ronin spoke with the authority of an Alpha, sitting back in his chair with the same cocky assurance as his son.

"That's a lot easier said than done when we don't know what the fucking seals are." The fae's frustration matched my own. It was the same issue I'd been running into.

"Isolate her. Put her in the well until we figure this out," Blaire offered.

"That won't work. Noah will free her the moment he realizes what's been done to her. They're bonded mates." Cashel ran a hand through his hair and sighed.

Knowing I would likely be right there beside the Blackthorne heir, I couldn't resist adding, "Besides, Niall already tried that, and look where we are now. You can't just lock her up and throw away the key. We can't just sit around with our heads buried in the sand and pretend this isn't happening."

"Oh, I don't know, I kept her locked up for the better part of twenty-three years and managed to keep any seals from opening aside from the first one when she was born. Now that she's under your care, we have three of seven open. Two in a matter of months." Niall stared daggers at me, his disdain dripping from each word.

"I still can't believe you tried to mate her with Kingston knowing she was the Harbinger of the Apocalypse," Ronin spat.

"I thought we could stop it if she found her wolf. Why the hell do you think I've been trying so damn hard? Why do you think I finally gave in and sent her here?"

"Fate always finds a way. Such is the way of destiny."

The Seer's words had a shiver of premonition racing down my spine.

"Excuse me," Quinn said, raising her hand as if she was a student in one of my classes. "I know I'm new here, but what's the point of doing anything if this is already fated? You just said it yourself—fate always finds a way. So what can any of us do to stop the inevitable? We could just tell the poor girl what's happening. Maybe that will help?"

"We can't tell her. If she knows, she'll go mad trying to stop herself from making a misstep." I hated the idea of Sunday suffering with the guilt of who—and what—she was.

"What gives us the right to make that decision for her? She might surprise you. It's amazing what a woman can do when her back is up against the wall and the fate of the world rests in her hands. Trust me, I know a couple who came back swinging."

"This is different, Satori. She's a bomb with an unpredictable fuse," Ronin said. "I can't believe my son is tied up in this."

"They'll take her on the path to her destiny. There's no way to stop it. The world will end in fire and flames, with screams and blood and pain." The Seer's interjection silenced everyone, and we all turned our attention to her hooded form.

"Well," Gabriel said, clapping his hands together. "Lovely. This is where free will gets us. I'll never understand why you Earth dwellers are His favorites."

"I do." Lilith's voice was tinged with amusement. "Mortals burn so brightly because their lives are finite. They feel everything so deeply. It's irresistible. We are burdened with eternity. It's rare any of us feel anything. There's such beauty in mortality. Don't you agree?"

"Why are you looking at me?" I snapped.

"You were once a human man, with human . . . needs. Surely you can appreciate how fleeting life is."

"But what is the fecking point of all this then?" I turned my attention away from the succubus and back to the soothsayer in our midst. "Why are we here, Seer? Give us something useful for once."

The room was suspended in silence. All of us waited for her answer.

"One of her mates must die so the world as we know it survives."

Blaire laughed, wicked and cruel. "So choose one and kill him. Boys, you can draw straws to determine which of your sons will be sacrificed for the cause."

Cashel and Ronin both got to their feet, rage etched in each of their faces. "You will not touch my son," Cashel snarled. "I'll burn the world down myself if anything happens to him."

"The same goes for me," Ronin added.

Quinn stood, surprising me with the furious cast of her expression. I didn't understand why she was here until that moment. She practically vibrated with the depth of her anger. "If you try to murder my godson for your silly games, you will call down the wrath of the Old Gods. Trust me when I say this, you will stop your apocalypse only to find yourselves on the brink of a war you will never win. And you should pray for that option, because otherwise you'll be answering to *me*."

"One of them will die," Gabriel said, resignation in his voice. "It won't be at our hands. I can promise you that much." He glanced from Quinn to Cashel, then to Ronin, before his gaze landed on me. "I am so sorry."

The air in the room shifted, and my ears popped as the angel vanished. The sensation was unsettling for all of us if the way the rest of the group tensed was any indication. With a soft rustle of fabric, the Seer walked away from us, not headed for the stairs but straight into the wall, where a portal opened for her alone. She was gone in an instant, and I finally relaxed my shoulders a fraction.

The fae prince leveled his gaze on me. Eyes that should be kind were now hard and calculating. "As the only person remaining without a vested interest in this girl or her mates, what do you plan to do? My children's lives hang in the balance, and I will not take risks with them."

"Whatever I have to."

"This is nice," I said as I leaned against Noah's chest from where we sat on a blanket by the lake. "It's . . . normal. That's weird."

His laughter rumbled from deep within him and made me sigh happily. "Normal is what we make it."

I twisted in his arms. "I didn't mean a picnic by the lake was weird. Just the not being hunted by demons and almost killed part. It's sort of become the status quo."

He kissed the tip of my nose. "I knew what you meant, but thank you for clarifying. I figured we both could use a little R and R after the . . . excitement of the last few days."

Plucking a grape from a nearby plate, he popped it into my mouth. I crunched down on the fruit, biting through the skin to release the burst of flavor. Everything tasted and smelled better lately. I wondered if it was because he was here and all my men were finally with me.

"Well, isn't this a pretty picture?" Kingston's rich timbre washed over me, and I stiffened.

We hadn't seen each other since all of us had done . . . things. So many delicious things. I was worried about how everyone would react to each other now that the heat had passed.

"A picnic? Nice. I'm fucking starving," he said, not waiting for an invitation before plopping down and stealing a piece of meat off the plate.

Noah sighed, rolling his eyes and shifting to pull the little cooler he'd brought closer. He nudged it toward Kingston. "I had a feeling you might stop by."

"Where she goes, I go. Even if I don't realize it's happening until I find her." He shrugged. "It's a mate thing."

"I'm well aware," Noah drawled. "Seeing as how I'm her mate."

I cleared my throat, preparing to intervene. But Kingston surprised me.

"So you can sympathize. We're pussy whipped."

"Moira says you're pussy possessed."

They both laughed, the sound like music to my ears. "Possessed, obsessed, take your pick. As long as it's never rejected again."

I reached over, taking Kingston's hand and squeezing. "Never. I promise."

He grinned, scooting closer so he could press a kiss to my lips. It started sweet but quickly turned heated.

Noah coughed. "Unless you want an audience, you might want to tone it down. A crowd is starting to gather."

Kingston grumbled but didn't stop kissing me. Instead he murmured against my lips, "Let 'em watch."

"What's this, a picnic?" Alek's voice broke through the silence, and I pulled away from Kingston with a laugh.

The Novasgardian had already claimed a spot on the blanket, his shirtless body misted with sweat and his hair pulled back in a topknot. He must have been out for a run.

His finger trailed over my bare foot as he inspected the offering of food.

"Not a feast, but it'll do." He snagged a fig and took a bite.

Noah released a heavy sigh. "I must have left my mead in my other jacket. You'll have to slum it with the rest of us, I'm afraid."

"Did you pack any communion wafers in case the priest shows up?" Kingston asked.

"I think we're safe since the sun will be up for a few more hours."

Disappointment gnawed at me. This would have been a truly perfect moment if Caleb had been here with us.

Then Noah made me laugh by pulling a baguette out from behind his back. "I did bring some bread, though. Just in case."

"Wait, so you have emergency bread but not wine? What kind of picnic is this?" I asked with mock indignation.

"I never leave home without my emergency loaf," Noah quipped.

Alek reached into the pocket of his joggers and pulled out a flask. "I am also prepared with my emergency mead."

"What about you, boy scout? What mystery supplies did you bring?" I asked Kingston.

He pulled a condom out of his back pocket. "The usual. Much more useful than bread."

Noah's expression went deadpan. "I was kidding."

I smirked. "Kingston, I didn't think you even knew what a condom looked like."

"I've watched porn. Besides, you never know when you might need one."

Alek let out a low laugh. "Planning on fucking a human? They're the only ones who need protection from you."

The idea of him with anyone else made my gut churn, but Kingston's reaction immediately soothed my ruffled fur. He took the condom and tore it open before flinging it at Alek's face.

"Good point. Here, you take it."

We all erupted into peals of laughter as the latex landed across the bridge of Alek's nose. The Viking used his magic to turn the condom into a flopping fish before throwing it into the lake.

Eventually we eased into a happy silence as we continued our picnic. The chill of fall had me shivering as the minutes passed into hours and the sky darkened. What had once been a landscape of oranges and reds as the leaves dropped from the trees lost its color to the dimming light. Kingston wrapped me in his arms, warming me instantly, as Noah took my hand and Alek rested his palm on my knee.

"This was nearly perfect," I said on a happy sigh.

"Nearly?" Noah asked. "What could've made this better?"

I felt guilty as Caleb's name sat on the tip of my tongue. I didn't want them to feel like they weren't enough for me.

"Her priest, of course," Alek murmured, saving me from the confession.

"Ah yes. We'll have to make our next family gathering a moonlit one then, so he can take part."

The easy acceptance brought tears to my eyes. I'd been so worried about what the dynamic between us would be like now, but it had been for nothing. It was just like all of them had promised me. The only thing they seemed to care about was my happiness, so long as they were part of it.

"You know, next Thursday is Thanksgiving." I sat up a

little taller, feeling silly even mentioning the holiday when we were in the midst of demons taking shots at me.

"We don't celebrate Thanksgiving here," Noah said.

"But you live in America."

"Sure, but vampires rarely do holidays, you know."

"That's just stupid," Kingston offered. "Any excuse to eat, count me in."

"Me too." Alek stood and stretched, putting all those muscles on gorgeous display.

Excitement flooded me. "Do you all want to join me and Moira for our little friendsgiving?"

"I was hoping you'd ask," Kingston said, kissing me. "I want you for dessert."

"I'd like an appetizer." Noah nibbled my neck and sent shivers down my spine.

"And you, Viking? What would you like?"

Alek grinned down at me, stopping my heart with one word.

"You. Just you, Sunny."

～

"Next time I get the bright idea to grow my hair out, I need you to remind me of this moment."

I glance at Moira, trying hard not to laugh. "Hate to break it to you, Belladonna, but you didn't grow it out."

"Right, but if I'd known I was going to be stuck with ten pounds of sweaty blanket on the back of my neck, I wouldn't have bothered," she grumbled.

I wandered across the school's massive kitchen to the professional-grade range where Moira stood. She wore a pink apron tied around her waist and huffed her annoyance at the turkey she was basting. "It helps if you pull it up, you know. As a long hair owner, I've perfected the art."

Her hair stuck to her face from the heat of the oven. "Then help me! It's your harem coming to eat all this food. I've never cooked this much in my life."

"I can get the scissors and give you an edgy bob if you want."

She glanced back at me over her shoulder, looking horrified at the thought. "No offense, sweets, but I don't trust my hair to just anybody. The thought of you wielding shears gives me the heebies. I'll suffer."

My laughter filled the kitchen as I collected the heavy locks and began braiding the strands down her back. When I was done, I stared at the oil-slick colored braid that hung to the base of her spine. "God, that's a lot of hair."

"Never again."

"No one anticipated a magic ban."

"True, but I'm not going to let myself be unprepared. Apocalypse ready at all times from here on out."

I snickered, watching with no little awe as my pixie of a roommate hefted heavy pots of potatoes as if they weighed nothing at all. She may be used to doing mundane tasks with magic, but she certainly knew her way around a kitchen.

"How can I help?" I snagged the other apron Moira had not so subtly set out on the counter, this one pale blue with lace trimming the edge.

"Pie or sweet potatoes?"

"I'm better with baking. Less chance for error with exact measurements."

Moira cackled. "You only say that because you've never seen my aunts in a kitchen. Those bitches can ruin anything."

"I might be those bitches."

"No way, your cupcakes came out great."

"Because you were there over my shoulder the entire time."

"Well . . . don't fuck it up, I guess, and we'll be just fine."

"Good pep talk."

"What do you want from me? I'm kinda in the middle of fisting a turkey."

I stared at the half-roasted bird. "I think you're past the fisting stage. Unless you want second-degree burns."

Moira grumbled under her breath. "Goddamned demons fucking everything up."

"It smells fucking amazing in here, Sunshine," Kingston called as he strode in like he owned the place.

"Oh look, the King of the Assholes has arrived."

I locked eyes with him and was surprised to see a little flash of hurt at Moira's barb. "You know, he's not that bad."

"Sorry. Old habits die hard and all that." Moira blew him a kiss, which he sneered at. "Watch it. I'll take my apology back."

He continued to glare at her and then surprised us both by blowing her a kiss. "Fine."

I was still gawking at him when he came around the stainless steel island to where I had been flipping through a cookbook in search of a recipe. He wrapped his arms around my hips and pulled me back into the cradle of his body, brushing a kiss over my mark.

"What are we cookin', baby?"

"I've been assigned pie duty."

"Mmm, your pie is delicious. I have firsthand knowledge."

The way his hum of approval vibrated against my skin made me shiver.

"Nope, veto. I'm not slaving away over here listening to sexual innuendos all day. Keep it in your pants, Kingston. The only sausage we're having in this kitchen is the one I'm putting in the dressing." Moira's words were playful, but she meant business.

His lips twitched. "No promises, but I'll try to stay on my best behavior."

"What are you doing here? I thought you had plans to run with the pack?" I asked, skimming over the pie crust instructions before grabbing what I'd need.

He shrugged, taking the ingredients out of my arms and carrying them over to my workstation. "I wanted to help you."

My heart tumbled. "Really? I thought guys usually played football and avoided coming inside until it was time to eat?"

"I'm used to spending Thanksgiving in the kitchen with my mom and sisters." Color tinged his cheeks, and he ducked his head as he deftly began following the recipe, proving just how much experience he had. "I like cooking."

My chest squeezed. "Oh, my God, that is so cute."

He growled and slapped my ass. "I'll show you cute. Now stop teasing me before I break my agreement with Moira."

"We wouldn't want to do that," I whispered, heat pooling in my belly.

His smile turned wicked. "Definitely not."

"*Definitely not!*" Moira called from the sink, where she was busy washing yams.

I stared at all the dry ingredients he'd mixed in a big bowl, and anxiety raced through my veins. "It says to cut in the butter. What is that supposed to mean?"

The low laugh that escaped him didn't embarrass me; it

endeared him to me even more. He pulled the cold butter toward him and began cutting small pieces of the creamy goodness into the flour mixture.

"Use your hands and combine it. You want to get the butter mixed in until it looks like peas."

I loved this side of him. It was thrilling to know that while he could be this gentle giant, he could also rail me so hard I couldn't walk straight the next day. I hoped I'd see that side of him later.

We continued to work together, Kingston doing most of the job, until the pie dough was chilling in the fridge.

"Now what?" he asked, looking at me expectantly.

I glanced at the bushel of apples Alek had oh-so-help-fully picked from Ravenscroft's magical ever-producing orchard the day before. "I think we need to get to work on those. I have a feeling our Viking was making a not very subtle request."

"Apple is easy. Wash, peel, slice, and cook."

"The last time I dealt with more than one apple, I almost cut my finger off," I admitted. "The knife got all slippery."

"Don't worry. I've got this. You wash. I'll handle the sharp stuff."

I was no Cinderella, and he was hardly Prince Charming, but damn if that didn't make me swoon.

"Why are you looking at me like that?"

"I just never expected you'd . . . I don't know, be so domestic."

"What can I say? You tamed me." He smirked. "Sun-shine, this is what life between us is supposed to be like. I'm your mate and your Alpha. I'll always take care of you. I was *born* to take care of you. I'll slay your monsters and your apples too."

"I'm going to vomit," Moira announced, arms crossed over her chest as she smiled over at us.

"Do it somewhere else. I'm baking," Kingston said, never taking his eyes off me.

Kingston stayed and helped us finish cooking the entire meal, serving as official turkey lifter, assistance which Moira appreciated but only grudgingly accepted. And before long, the table was filled with beautiful food and people I loved. I might not have told them all, but I did love them.

Seeing Alek, Noah, and Kingston talking and laughing as they passed food around filled me with joy. It made me so happy to see them working together, acting like friends, not just allies. Family.

My family.

The first one that ever truly accepted me exactly as I was.

My eyes pricked with tears.

"Stop it, you're going to ruin my casserole," Moira whispered, giving me a squeeze.

"Shut up, Belladonna. I'm having a moment."

Moira gave me a kiss on the cheek. "Love you too, babycakes."

"Stop, or you're really going to make me cry. And then Ash will be mad at you."

"Not to mention the rest of us," Noah added, proving once again just how attuned to me and my emotions he was. I'd thought he'd been deep in conversation with the others, but he'd been completely aware of me too. "None of us like to see tears in your eyes."

He reached over and squeezed my hand while Moira beamed at her girlfriend, who'd surprised her by showing up for the weekend. I was still patting myself on the back for helping arrange that.

The only person who was missing was my priest. He'd been distant even during our sessions, keeping me out of arm's reach, barely making eye contact. It stung. I'd dropped off a handwritten invitation a few nights ago, hoping he'd bite, but he clearly wasn't interested. Maybe that night we'd all been together had been too much for him. Had I pushed him too far?

Before I could fall completely down the anxiety spiral, the sound of footsteps at the door had all of us shifting in our seats.

My breath caught. Caleb stood in the doorway, his hair still wet from the shower, dressed formally in a dark suit with a bottle of wine in his hand. "Sorry I'm late. I wasn't sure what to bring. This is my first Thanksgiving. I didn't know the protocol."

"Oh good, the priest is here. We can get the blessing out of the way and start eating," Kingston said, his eyes twinkling with mischief.

Caleb handed me the wine and leaned in, pressing the barest kiss to my cheek.

"I thought you weren't coming," I whispered, overcome by emotion.

"I almost didn't, but then I thought of how sad that might make you. Especially after your sweet letter asking me to join you. I might be a grumpy arse, but I'm not that bad."

"Here, take my seat," Moira said, standing and moving around to the end of the long table where the turkey proudly rested.

Just as she sliced down the breast, Alek jerked in his

chair, pulling a familiar compact out of his pocket. "Shit, sorry. I need to take this."

The worry in his eyes robbed us of our lighthearted banter.

"Has anyone else noticed he can still access his magic while the rest of us can't?" Kingston asked in a low voice.

"His god-power must be stronger than the wards," Noah said.

Caleb looked concerned by the prospect.

As for me, I was too worried about Alek to care either way. He'd moved away from us, but we had no trouble hearing both sides of the conversation.

"Aunt Quinn? Is everything okay?"

"Alek, listen to me. You need to get as far away from that girl as possible. You need to come home. Right now."

His gaze shot to me and my gut clenched, appetite gone, heart turned cold.

Fuck.

Just like that, the happy bubble I'd been drifting in popped.

I knew it had been too good to last.

CHAPTER
TWENTY-EIGHT

ALEK

Sweat dripped down my face and spine as I pushed my body to its breaking point. I slammed a massive log onto the chopping block before bringing my ax down and splitting the piece with such force each half was launched across the small clearing I'd made my own. I'd been at it for hours, giving up on the gym after I broke three of the machines. They didn't provide enough of a challenge, and the forest was better suited to me anyway.

The music I'd selected matched my mood. Frustrated. Tense. Driving me on and fueling my workout until I was a man possessed. The speaker blared, volume as high as it would go without rendering the device useless. I wanted nothing more than to take my mind off everything going wrong in my world.

Usually, an hour or two of pushing my body this hard would clear my mind. Help me find my balance, but today nothing was working, and I was running out of wood to split.

'You need to get as far away from that girl as possible. You need to come home. Right now.'

My aunt's words ran through my mind on an endless loop. Not what I wanted to think about, but still, they persisted almost a full day later. Leave Sunday? Abandon her? I couldn't. I was hers in more ways than one. Her protector, her guardian, her lover . . . her mate. But was I?

I gritted my teeth as more sweat trailed down my face. That was the crux of the matter, wasn't it? Sunday already had two mates, both with tangible proof of their claim. I wasn't sure why that fact bothered me so much. Okay, that was a lie. I knew exactly why. I felt every bit as connected to her as they did, but I didn't get the benefit of a physical mark. I wanted my mark on her. I wanted everyone to know she belonged to me every bit as much as I belonged to her.

Possessive? Fuck yes. I didn't care.

Thoughts of my conversation with Aunt Quinn intruded on my wallow, setting my nerves on edge. I'd left the table, given myself privacy because of the look in Sunny's eyes when she overheard Quinn's order for me to return to Novasgard. Hurt. Fear. Sadness. I never wanted to be the cause of those emotions in her.

'She is going to bring your death if you stay,' Quinn had said.

Whether that was true or not, only the gods could say. As for my thoughts on the matter? So what if she did. Because the thought of returning to a realm without her felt like its own kind of death sentence. Valhalla was waiting for me, no matter what. I'd rather go because I lived out my days with Sunday than after a life spent hiding behind Novasgard's walls.

I flung my ax away, needing to change to something more . . . physical. But the gods' cursed blade connected with my speaker, pulverizing the thing in one blow.

"Odin's sweaty sack," I yelled as I picked up the last log

I had and ripped it in two with my hands, letting out a growl of savage frustration as I did.

"Oh." The little whispered word stopped me in my tracks, sending a thrill through me.

I spun around, spotting Sunday at the edge of the clearing, her eyes wide and her lips parted in awe.

"Did I just witness a Viking temper tantrum?" she teased, though the playful words were belied by the flare of hunger in her gaze as it traveled down my body.

Using my forearm, I wiped the sweat from my brow. "Vikings don't have temper tantrums. We have manly rages."

"Uh huh. And what else do they do during these *manly rages* besides making firewood with their bare hands?"

I glanced down at my already large pile of logs. It would see a family through the entire winter. Feeling embarrassed and not knowing what to say, I shrugged, tugging my hair down from the knot I'd twisted it up into. The golden strands fell down past my shoulders, obscuring my face.

Sunday sucked in a breath. "You really do look like a god with all that hair and those glistening muscles."

I peeked up at her, giving her a wicked grin. "A god of what?"

"Sex."

"Oh, really?"

She slid her fingers over my arm, then up until she trailed her fingertips along my neck. "Really. I wonder what it would look like, having you over me with your hair hanging down, brushing my body."

"Why wonder? Let's find out right now."

Her pupils flared, but she pressed a palm to my chest. "Actually, before we distract ourselves with mind-blowing sex—"

"That's my favorite tactic."

She rolled her eyes. "Why am I not surprised?"

"It's very effective."

"It is. But I wanted to talk to you."

"What if I don't feel like talking?" I asked, taking a step closer to her and crowding her with my body.

She had to tip her head back to hold my gaze. I knew she wanted me; she was practically vibrating with it. But she was also determined not to give in. Her eyes searched mine, a small furrow appearing between her brows.

"Why are you avoiding me?"

"I'm not avoiding you." *Liar, liar.*

"So it's normal for you to dine and dash then? You couldn't get out of dinner fast enough last night. You didn't even eat or say goodbye. You just answered your special magic phone and bolted. I texted you on your not magic phone, but you didn't answer. I'm worried."

Guilt ate at me, bringing everything bubbling back up to the surface. "I know, I'm sorry. I just had a lot to think through."

"About going home?"

Her voice was so hesitant, her body held so carefully, as if she was bracing herself for terrible news. It physically hurt me to see her like this. The need to reassure her filled me, even as my own insecurities buzzed in my head like a swarm of angry bees.

I rested my palm against her cheek, weaving the tips of my fingers through her hair. "Yes."

Her eyes shuttered. "Oh."

I swept my thumb over her lips. "I was trying to figure out a way to explain to my family why I'm not going back."

Hope turned her eyes a brilliant cerulean. Gods, she was so fucking beautiful it made my heart ache.

"You're not? But that woman said—"

"I know. I'm not afraid of what she said. I'm afraid of losing you."

"You're not going to lose me."

The promise was everything I wanted to hear but not enough to assuage my own doubt.

"Are you sure you want this? I can't make you choose me over your family. I know how much they mean to you. I don't want to damage your relationship with them."

"You *are* my family. And if they love me like I know they do, they'll understand. They'll accept my decision. Even if I'm not as connected to you as I want to be."

"Alek?" she asked, seeing straight through me.

I stepped back. "It's nothing."

"No, it's not. What is that look in your eyes? Why do you look like you're pulling back even though you just told me you're staying?"

Because I am, dammit.

This kind of insecurity was new to me. It had me doubting my place, questioning my worth. I was born a damn prince of my people, for Odin's sake. I've never doubted my value in my entire life. And yet here I was, desperate to carve out a space for myself in her heart. Worried I didn't matter enough to belong there.

My focus landed on the mark on her neck, fully healed but still present, now two raised sets of bite marks.

Her brows dropped low, and she nervously fingered the proof of her double bond. "Do these bother you?"

"Bother me? No. And yes." I sighed, shoving my hands through my hair.

"Why?"

"Because it's the one thing I can't give you!" The words exploded out of me. I tore my gaze from her, ashamed that I

281

couldn't control my emotions. "I can fight for you, fucking die for you, but I can't bond with you like they did."

"Alek..."

I squeezed my eyes shut, not wanting to see pity in hers. But my Sunny wouldn't let me. She grasped my chin and forced me to look down at her. To anyone who might've seen us, we must've made a strange picture. My hulking form controlled by her smaller one. A beauty taming a beast.

"A mark won't change how I feel about you. But if it's something you need to feel secure so you know you're just as important to me as they are, then let's do it. You don't have to bite me. Let's make our own marks. Something that holds special meaning for the two of us. Whatever you want. We'll do it together." A sheepish expression flitted across her face.

"What?"

"As long as you don't want to pierce me."

That made a wave of amusement rise in me. "I only want to pierce you with one thing."

She rolled her eyes, but a blush crept into her cheeks. "You don't pierce me with your dick. You split me in two."

"Damn right."

But the mention of piercings led me to something I should've thought of before. Something permanent, meaningful, powerful.

"A tattoo," I murmured, my focus landing on her arm.

Her eyes brightened with interest. "I've always wanted a tattoo."

"It will be a first for both of us."

"Oh, goodie. We'll lose our virginity together. Do I get to pick the spot?" she asked.

"No," I told her, my voice firm. Lifting her arm, I gently traced the place I knew I wanted to mark her.

"Not even for yours? I mean it is mine to give."

"You're right. You should choose where you want to stake your claim on me."

She crossed her arms over her chest and tapped one finger on her chin. "Hmm . . . I think I need to thoroughly inspect my canvas before I choose."

I chuckled as she walked in a slow circle around me, trailing her fingers over my body, making me lift and lower my arms. At one point, she even dipped her fingers into my pants as if she was going to remove them. Once she stood in front of me again, I asked, "Well? What have you decided?"

"Here," she murmured, running the tips of her fingers down my ribcage. The touch was gentle as she trailed the line of my torso until she reached the waistband of my joggers. "Yep. Right here. I want you to shiver just like that every time you think of me and remember where my claim is."

"When can we do it?"

She bit down on her lower lip as she considered. "How about right now?"

"Gods, I was hoping you'd say that. I don't want to wait another second." I lifted her up, making her squeal with laughter as I tossed her over my shoulder.

"Where are we going?"

"I'm sneaking you out of here where my magic is stronger. I can do a lot of things even with the wards in place, but this requires more control and focus." I stopped, shifting my hold on her to bring her face back down to mine. "Unless you don't think it's safe to leave the campus right now."

Sunday feathered her lips over mine. "I'm not sure any place is safer than with you."

My heart swelled, brimming with pride that she trusted me so much. I claimed her mouth with an intensity that robbed us both of breath.

If I had any doubt about staying here with her, it was gone now. Sunday and I were fated, just like my parents had been, and there was nothing in this universe that could part us now.

TWENTY-NINE

"I'm surprised it doesn't hurt," I murmured, staring down at the runes marking the inside of my bicep.

"It's magic. That's kind of the benefit," Alek teased, lifting my arm and pressing a kiss over one of the sigils, which sent electric tingles racing across my body. "I love seeing my name etched into your skin, and knowing it didn't bring you pain only makes it better."

I tugged up his shirt, trailing my fingers down the side of his ribcage where he'd marked himself with my name. "Me too."

"It's a shame I have to wear a shirt and cover it up."

"I always think it's a shame you don't walk around naked. Then again, it's probably safer for the female population that you keep all that Grade A Novasgardian beef under wraps."

Alek laughed, his eyes sparkling with delighted mischief. "I'll endeavor to be naked around you more often since you find it so … appealing."

"Only me. I can't guarantee the safety of anyone else I

catch ogling you. I'm a wolf now, remember? We're possessive."

Alek grasped me by the waist and lifted me up so we were nose to nose. "That makes two of us, Sunny. I may not be a wolf, but I am a beast in my own way."

His lips brushed mine in a gentle kiss, but I threaded my fingers around the back of his neck and deepened the contact. I wanted to make sure he knew, tattoos or not, that he was mine. When I'd sought him out that afternoon, I hadn't known what to expect, but there was no denying the sense of rightness that had settled in my bones when we'd solidified our claim on each other.

Even now, almost an hour later, I felt invigorated. Filled with a strength and boundless energy that had me ready to scale trees and jump over buildings. Something similar happened every time the connection between me and one of my mates was accepted.

Noah was my peace. Kingston was my home. Alek was my superpower. And Caleb . . . well, I guess we'd find out if the infuriating priest ever decided to take that step.

Alek set me back on my feet, and we approached the stretch of stone wall that lined the edge of Ravenscroft's campus, the wrought iron spikes at the top looking far more ominous on the way back than they had when we left.

"You ever notice this place looks like something straight out of a horror movie?"

Alek laughed. "We don't have a lot of those back home. But don't worry, I'll protect you from the big bad monsters."

"Uh, Alek . . . we *are* the big bad monsters."

"True. But some things are worse than others. Like fucking demons."

He held his palm up to the stone, closing his eyes as he focused, a furrow between his brows.

"What is it?"

"Wards on this side. Don't worry, it'll just tickle. They're not trying to keep us out, just the demon filth."

"What does it do to them if they try?"

"I'd assume it hurts like hell."

"But does hell hurt them? I mean, it's their native realm, so how bad can that really be?"

Amusement twinkled in his icy blue irises. "So maybe it hurts like heaven?"

I bit the inside of my cheek, loving that he was being playful with me. "That sounds more appropriate."

Threading his fingers together, he crouched by the base of the wall and held out the step he'd created with his hands. "Ready?"

"I always wanted to try this," I admitted.

"Sneak back into school?"

"Well, sneak out and back successfully. It's a lot easier with a partner in crime."

"I'm your partner in all things."

We shared a brief kiss that warmed me from the inside out. "Heaven yeah, you are."

"Valhalla," he corrected with a wink.

"Sure. That one." I steadied myself with one palm braced on his big shoulder while I stepped up onto his hands.

I expected him to lift me up, just give me a boost. Instead, the Viking launched me into the evening sky. On instinct, I tucked into a ball as I flipped through the air, landing on two feet but stumbling as searing pain ripped through my gut. I was pretty proud of my landing, considering I hadn't been prepared to bust out my inner gymnast, but I'd be willing to bet the Russian judge was less of a fan of my dismount. Also, how the hell had I done that without breaking a bone?

A heavy thud from right next to me pulled my attention to Alek, who'd landed on his feet as though he'd simply hopped off a counter.

"Showoff."

"It takes practice."

"You really are a troublemaker, aren't you?"

He winked, then linked our fingers. "And you love it, Kærasta."

Heat bloomed inside me, as it always did when he used the unfamiliar endearment. "What does that mean? You call me that sometimes but I don't understand."

Alek looked adorably shy. "It's what my father calls my mother, and his father before him. The meaning has changed over time, but for us, it's the equivalent of beloved, or sweetheart." He reached out and tucked a piece of hair that had escaped from my bun back behind my ear. "We only ever use it when we find our fated mate."

My heart swelled, pushing away the lingering pain in my belly from crossing the wards. "You've been calling me that for a while."

His smile was slow but blinding. "The first time I said it, the word came out without permission. It took my head a while to recognize what my heart knew from the start. I should have realized it straight away. I never would have been able to heal you after that fight otherwise."

"So what do I call you? Is there some special nickname I should have for my Novasgardian mate?"

"You could say 'elskan mín'."

"And what does that mean?"

"My love."

I couldn't stop the rapid fluttering in my ribcage at the tenderness in his voice. "Elskan mín."

The pride shining in his eyes had me lifting up onto my toes and kissing him hard, my fingers working their way under his shirt so I could trace the raised edges of the runes running down his side.

"I really like the sound of that," he murmured against my lips, his voice rough with desire before claiming my mouth again.

"What in God's name do the two of you think you're doing out here?"

Caleb's angry Irish lilt hit me like the lash of a whip. Alek broke our kiss, putting a protective arm across my chest as we turned to face my confessor's wrath.

"You. Mischief maker. What part of the fact that we've warded the surroundings did you not recollect?"

"I needed to access my magic," Alek answered, as if it was the most justifiable reason there could be. Which I suppose for him, it was.

"And so you play fast and loose with the life of the woman you've sworn to protect? I expect these shenanigans from her and the others, but I thought you were smarter than that."

"Hey," I protested, but Caleb shut me up with an angry glare.

"Apparently not." Alek crossed his arms, staring Caleb down. "But I assure you, she's fine."

Caleb's gaze burned hot as he zeroed in on the tattoo peeking out from under my sleeve. It was cold outside, but being with Alek kept me warm enough my jacket was wrapped around my waist. Now I shivered, but was it because of the weather or because of Caleb?

Caleb's hand shot out, and he grabbed me by the wrist,

his favorite way to get my attention, it seemed. "My office. Now. You and I have something to settle."

I clenched my thighs together at the pulse of arousal those words sent shooting straight to my clit.

Alek began to follow as Caleb pulled me along with him, my protective shadow looming nearby. But Caleb turned on him.

"Not you, Mr. Nordson. Back to bed with you. I'll see to our naughty Miss Fallon."

Alek's eyes were stormy, and I could tell he wanted to come to my defense, but I reached out, grasping his fingers. "It's all right. I'm used to his snarly ways. He's all bark, trust me. I'll be fine."

"He has fangs. Don't let the collar fool you."

"That collar doesn't fool anyone but him."

Caleb's eyes flared at that, but he didn't respond as we continued to walk. Alek pulled gently on my hand, bringing us to a stop, because for all his grouchy demeanor, Caleb wasn't going to hurt me. Not unless I asked him to.

"Let me know when you're safely returned to your room, Kærasta."

I went up on my tiptoes to kiss him. "I will, elskan mín."

A long-suffering sigh left the vampire next to me, and I felt Alek's lips quirk into a smile beneath mine.

"You might be in a position of power over me on these grounds, Priest. But don't forget who I am. If you mistreat her, you will answer to me."

Caleb glared at Alek as he turned and strode toward Blackthorne Hall, but I could have sworn I saw a flicker of respect in his dark gaze. His fingers tightened on my wrist as he snapped his focus to me, his eyes locking on mine.

"Shall we, then?"

"What, like this is a date? Your courtship skills need work, Father."

"It's been a long time since I've courted a lass. And believe me, if I'd been courting you, we'd already be wed, and you'd not be leaving our bed for another."

My heart did backflips at the thought. "You sure seem to think highly of yourself for a virgin who's been celibate for the last eighteen hundred years."

He smirked and leaned in. "I'm not that old. And you don't seem to have any complaints about my virginity if your moans are anything to go by."

The way his lips brushed the shell of my ear as he whispered made things tighten in my belly.

"I'd never have given my vows to God if he'd have let me find you back then, *a stor*. I'd have married you and made you mine, filled you with my children, made a life with you. But that's not where we are now, is it? So this is the life I'll lead. One full of want and guilt and sin."

My heart was beating erratically. *This is it. This is your moment.*

"Caleb, it doesn't *have* to be that way. You could give in. There's no shame in what you feel for me. You don't have to deny yourself what you want. What we both want."

He glanced around the open space as we reached the door of his office. Then, tearing it open, he shoved me inside and closed the heavy wood quickly. "You don't know what I want, Sunday."

Be bold, Fallon.

I stepped up to him until the tips of my breasts brushed against the solid wall of his chest. "Yes, I do. It's the same thing I want."

He gripped my chin and forced me to stare into his eyes.

The hunger I saw there made me squirm in anticipation of what came next.

He was the last piece of the puzzle. I needed him to see it as clearly as I did. I couldn't back down.

"And what do you want, Miss Fallon?"

"You. Inside me. Where you belong. Don't you know that you're mine?"

A flash of panic raced through me because I'd finally said it. There was no going back now.

"I can't be yours."

"You already are, Caleb. You're denying fate. That never ends well."

He growled, a low, tortured sound deep in his throat. "Sunday. You're a bad girl, aren't you?"

I pressed my palms to his chest and sighed. "Yes, Daddy. It's the only way to get your attention."

His eyes fluttered closed, and with a groan that was surely defeat but sounded only like surrender, his lips claimed mine.

The kiss burned through us. Finally, his walls were down, and he was letting himself have what he needed.

Our tongues tangled together as he held me in that bruising grip, dominating my mouth and exerting his control in that long-suffering way of his. His thumb pressed hard against my tattoo, the touch not hurting, but sending a tingle through me and making me gasp.

He broke the kiss, pressing his forehead to mine and breathing heavily. "I fucking hate that he's given you his mark, that *they've* all done it. But most of all, that I bloody well can't."

"Yes, you can," I said, tilting my head. I presented him with the smooth, untouched skin on the other side of my neck. A temptation. A gift. An offering.

He shuddered against me and leaned down, pressing his lips to the pulse point I'd just presented to him. "God in Heaven, I want to taste you again. I've had dreams about this. About taking your blood and fucking your cunt just like *he* did."

"How do you know about that?" My clit throbbed at the statement even as I asked the question. It was my fantasy. He was my shadow man. But had it been real all this time?

Dark sapphire eyes found mine. "Because I was there. I've always been there. But you already know that, don't you, *a stor*?"

"I'd hoped, but I wasn't sure if it was really you. I wanted it to be." I trailed my fingers down his front, feeling the rippling muscle underneath his shirt, wondering what he'd look like without the fabric covering him. "You don't have to hide and watch anymore. It can be you and me, right here, right now."

His breath was ragged as it left him in a rush. He was close, so close to giving us both what we desperately craved.

A knock at the door sent my hope scattering. Caleb jerked against me, his eyes wild with panic.

"Underneath the desk," he hissed, shoving me none too gently in that direction.

"Father Gallagher? Are you in there? I need to speak with you." I recognized Professor Moriarty's voice instantly. He was hard to mistake for anyone else.

Caleb shot me a fierce look that sent me diving under the oversized desk before he sat down, his knees inches from my face. I thought sitting was an interesting choice until I spotted the unmistakable bulge between his legs.

My, my, Father Gallagher, what a big stick you have.

I nearly giggled out loud when I responded for him in my head, *the better to fuck you with.*

"Come in," Caleb called. Despite the welcoming nature of the words, his tone was anything but. It soured further when the door opened, revealing the source of our interruption. "Eugene, I told you to stop bothering me after hours."

"I know, but it's important."

"What do you want?" The tension in Caleb's voice was undeniable.

"Something set off the wards. You were on duty tonight. Why didn't you alert us?"

"I checked. It was nothing more than a few students fooling around near the wall. Stupid children making stupid decisions."

Stupid, huh? If he thought shoving me under the desk while he was hard as a rock and tenting his trousers was smart, I'd show him. I ran my fingers across his ankle, grinning when he jerked at my touch.

"We have to do something about them," Moriarty said, followed by the distinct sound of a cork being pulled and liquid splashing.

Oh, joy, the man was making himself a drink. Maybe I could get Caleb to kick him out before he got too comfortable.

"We are doing all we can. The wards keep the demons out, but the students aren't prisoners. As foolish as they behave, they are adults. We cannot keep them here against their will."

As he carried on his conversation, I ran my palms up higher, laughing to myself when Caleb's hand snaked down and gripped my wrist like a vise.

"Here. It's rude to make your guest drink alone," Moriarty said.

Caleb's tense thigh had me licking my lips. This was fun. Maybe Moriarty should stay.

"I'm ready to send them all home for their own good. Some of them don't know how to take care of themselves."

I rolled my eyes at Moriarty's blatant dig. *Maybe it's because we're too busy taking care of each other.*

I thought he was done, but he continued. "And then there's that Fallon girl, strutting around with every man who'll pay her any attention. Did you know she wasn't on suppressants? She had half the male population here panting after her. Something needs to be done."

Dick. Heat flooded my cheeks. It wasn't like I was asking for it to happen. And while it was true I'd been sleeping with more than one man, outside of my mates, there wasn't anyone else I would even consider being intimate with.

And then Caleb came to my defense and snuffed out any shame Moriarty's words brought to life.

"It's not like she did it on purpose, Eugene. No one ever told the girl what would happen. She can hardly be blamed for biology running its course."

Professor Moriarty tutted, and I actually feared for the man's safety. How did he miss the undercurrent of violence running through Caleb's voice? It sounded like he was seconds away from ripping the toady man's head off.

"If you ask me, she's trouble. Someone should send her home."

"She deserves her spot here just as much as anyone else."

That had me smiling. Caleb's fingers loosened on my wrist, and I fought a gasp as the pad of his thumb rubbed gently against my skin.

"You have to admit, she's a danger to us. We don't know what she is."

"She's a wolf."

"Half of her is. But what about her mother? For all we know, she's a succubus who hasn't come into her power."

I stilled, wondering if he could be right. I never even considered the possibility that my mother wasn't a shifter. I'd always just assumed.

Caleb chuckled. "She is quite . . . seductive."

Oh, I'd show him seductive. I slid my free palm up his thigh until I made contact with the swollen length of him. The way his hips twitched and he sucked in a sharp breath sent pride through me.

"Everything all right?" Moriarty asked.

"Yes. That is just an intriguing thought. A succubus on campus would be something."

"Could explain the wards going off. A half-demon wouldn't be bound by them in the same way. This really deserves proper looking into. We should run tests."

I slowly tugged Caleb's zipper down and reached inside. *Oh, Father Gallagher . . . no undies? How naughty.*

He grunted. "We're not going to start treating the girl like a bloody science experiment. Besides, no one said it was her messing around."

"You're going to tell me it wasn't her? She defies the rules at every turn. Spoiled, pampered princess. Just like the rest of them."

I stroked Caleb's cock, rolling my palm over the crown. The slight moan he let out had me wet and aching.

"I think you're putting too much stock in this." His voice was tight, and when I licked the head of his cock he kicked his hips forward involuntarily. The hand holding my wrist prisoner let go, and he threaded his fingers through my hair, trying to keep me still.

"Doesn't matter. The possibility alone should be investigated. And if it wasn't her, there's still the chance some other hellspawn half-breed is to blame."

I took him fully into my mouth, loving the feel of the velvet soft skin surrounding the steel-hard shaft of his erection. He couldn't hide his gasp this time. His hand tightened in my hair, and he thrust up, sending himself deeper.

"What? What is it?"

Caleb started coughing, like he was clearing his throat. "Nothing, just swallowed funny."

I snickered to myself. *Smooth move, Priest.* From the feel of things down here, it wouldn't be long before I was the one doing the swallowing.

"Here. Drink some of this. It will sort you right out."

"I don't have time for this, Eugene. I need to get back to work."

"But I just poured myself a new glass . . ."

I sucked harder, swirling my tongue around him as I worked over his length, my hand cupping his balls and making him clamp down on my hair harder.

"Jesus and all the saints," he muttered.

"Fine. I'll leave, but I'm taking your chianti with me. Ignore this if you want, but it isn't going to go away. Sunday Fallon is a problem we need to sort out."

"I'll sort her. Now get out."

I worked Caleb harder as Professor Moriarty's footsteps moved away, wanting to see if I could make him come before the door shut. His cock throbbed in my mouth, breaths coming in sharp pants with every passing moment.

"Oh, by the way, Caleb," Moriarty started.

"Fecking hell, Eugene. Leave me be."

He was swelling in my mouth, thighs trembling, and I knew he was about to blow. Maybe I could send him over the edge and win this little game of mine. I let go of his balls and moved my hand farther back, sliding across his taint and exerting pressure as I did.

"If you don't take care of her, I will. You should know that." Moriarty's words were cold, but I wasn't focused on the implication in them. I had a priest to defile.

"I said I'd handle it, you great bloody wanker. Now fuck . . . off!" Caleb roared. The sound of shattering glass alerted me to the fact he'd just thrown his drink at the other man. I wonder if he'd been aiming for the wall or if he was distracted.

The door creaked open as Moriarty huffed. "You really are an arsehole."

Caleb's balls tightened up as my finger probed the tight ring of muscle at his ass.

The door slammed shut, the wood protesting the force of it.

And then his entire body tensed, a tortured moan leaving him as he swelled further in my mouth and spilled jet after jet of his cum down my throat.

His taut muscles went lax with his release. He was still breathing heavily when he pushed his chair back to look down at me. I couldn't stop my smirk, and when I reached up and ran my thumb over the corner of my mouth where some of his spend had escaped, he whispered, "Christ almighty, Sunday."

"Forgive me, Father, for I have sinned."

"Yes, you have. Repeatedly. Now get out of my office before I do something I'll regret."

Prior to tonight, I might have been stung by his dismissal. But still alight with the glow of my victory, I ignored the brusque words and focused only on the affection in his gaze. He could send me away as many times as he wanted. I would just keep coming back.

He couldn't resist me forever. Especially when I knew he didn't want to.

"Miss Fallon."

"Oh? Already calling me back? I thought you were kicking me out."

"There's the small matter of your punishment we have to see to before you leave."

"Will it require me to get back on my knees?"

His eyes flashed. "No, actually. It will require you to keep your hands to yourself."

My eyebrows shot up. "What?"

"I can smell your wet cunt from here. But the only one who gets your orgasm is me. I figure it's only fair since you just stole mine without permission."

"You didn't tell me no. And your fingers in my hair held my head in place as you fucked my mouth. Don't tell me I stole anything."

Sharp eyes locked on mine, fire flickering in them as he continued like I hadn't just schooled him. "So go home. Get in your bed. And think on your sins. And if you make yourself come before I tell you to, I'll know, and you'll be in even more trouble. Trust me. You don't want to find out what happens if you break my rules."

Yes, I do. I really, really do.

Instead of protesting, I smirked, my voice coy and teasing as I started back for the door. "Goodnight, Daddy."

His growl made me grin.

Caleb could deny it all he wanted. He was mine.

And I would have him.

CHAPTER
THIRTY
SUNDAY

I was dreaming again. Fuck.

It started the same as they always did, nothingness interrupted by the thundering sound of hoofbeats. I braced myself for the oncoming terror, for flames and death and the nightmarish landscape I'd become accustomed to. Instead, the world around me was lush and green, a peaceful creek cutting a path in front of me. The sun was high in the sky while birds sang from the trees.

"What the hell?"

"Eden, actually," my mother's voice corrected.

I spun around to find her wading through the water, an apple in her outstretched palm.

"I think I've heard this story. The person with the apple isn't to be trusted."

"It's good for you. An apple a day. Isn't that the saying?"

"Why are we here? What's going on?"

My mother's serene expression twisted, and a bolt of fear shot through my heart. Then I blinked, and she was smiling once more. "I've been trying to tell you, to show you the truth, but we're running out of time. You need to feed, daughter."

"I don't like apples unless they're in a pie. I'll pass."

The apple vanished. "Do you always take things so literally?"

It was the first time she expressed genuine frustration with me. "Oh, excuse me for not speaking in metaphors. I like it best when I can understand what the fuck people are saying to me."

"You want me to speak plainly? Fine. Let us out. Stop fucking around and do what you were born to do. You *need* to feed."

"I'm. Not. Hungry." I stepped into the creek, the water so cold a chill ran up my spine.

"You are. Your wolf side might be sated by that pup you're mated to, but the part of you that is born from chaos, from me . . . *she* is insatiable. She'll die without the sustenance she needs. You've felt it. You've given her a taste. She needs more. Needs to be strong. It will only get worse if you deny her."

I threw my hands in the air, sending droplets of water flying in every direction. "I'm not denying myself anything."

"Yes. You. Are. You act like a human, wavering between what is acceptable and right. You are so much more than those mewling worms. You were born to rule. A god does not ask for permission. A goddess takes what she wants. When she wants. Stop worrying about insignificant matters. Claim what is yours."

"And what happens when I do?"

"You can be reunited with your true family. With us."

Confusion and longing flickered in my chest. I'd always wanted to belong to a family.

"What are we?"

My mother smiled. "I was not born, but created. The beginning and the end. Infinite. I hold chaos in my palm and wield it as my sword. I am the one powerful men bow down and submit to. The one who hears their prayers. The queen can move in all directions once freed from the interference of the pawns."

"Great. More metaphors."

"You asked me a question. I gave you the truth. It's not my fault you're too stupid to understand it. But you will. Do as I say, and all will be revealed. The game will be won."

"So I'm one of the pawns?"

She laughed. "No, darling. You are the chess master."

Unease coiled in my stomach. My mother had always intimidated me, but now I was genuinely afraid of what she might be.

She moved closer, cupping my cheek in her palm. "Darling daughter, you have nothing to fear from me. All I want is to walk at your side as you rule your kingdom. Do as I say. Take your knights. Feed your demon."

She kissed my forehead, sending lightning zinging through my veins.

I gasped at the blinding pain racing through me and sat up in my bed, the garden around me gone, the birds no longer singing. Gulping in air, I worked to push aside the tingling burn in my limbs, kicking free of blankets that tangled around my legs like shackles.

Moira sat up, lifting her eye mask and sending its obnoxious fake lashes fluttering as she blinked sleepily at me. "Sunday? What's wrong?" Then her eyes widened as she really saw me, and she swung her legs off the bed and rushed to my side.

I hated the tremors rocketing through me, making my

teeth chatter as the dream faded from my memory. All I remembered was one statement, loud and clear in my brain. "Moira, I think I'm a demon."

She paled, but God bless her, she didn't back away and run screaming from the room. "Why do you think that?"

"My dream . . . oh, God, and Moriarty. It makes sense."

"Glad it does to you, but I'm still in the fucking dark, babycakes."

I gulped, my mouth tasting like ash. "The heat. It's like a hunger with no end. And Moriarty said he thought I was a succubus the way I was luring all these men against their will. Then in my dream, she said . . . she told me to feed my demon."

"Who said? Your mom?"

I nodded, feeling like the world was crashing down around me. "Do you think it's true? Do you think I've been f-feeding on Noah and Kingston and oh, God, and Alek?"

She bit her lower lip and turned on the lamp at her bedside. "I really don't know. Do you feel stronger after you're with them?"

My stomach clenched. "Y-yes."

Every time I was with one of them, it was like a surge of adrenaline straight through me. Afterward, I was stronger. Faster. More powerful in every discernible way. Each of them gave me something different, as if they were the keys that helped me unlock my true power.

"Shit. Maybe."

"Am I the one summoning the demons? Oh, my God. Am I the reason those people died?"

Moira grasped my hand, squeezing it tight. "I don't know, but there's someone who will."

"Lilith," I breathed, a little frustrated with myself that I hadn't thought of going to her sooner. Of course she would know if I was her kind. "But the portal is locked. The wards . . ." The wards. They'd hurt me when I crossed them. My heart sank. *Shit.* I was a demon. Lilith was going to confirm it. Then where did I go from here?

My roommate smirked. "I was saving these for a special occasion. Don't tell anyone where you got it."

She handed me a ball roughly the size of a bath bomb, but something told me it wasn't going to fizz and bubble if I dropped it in a tub of water. "Moira, won't they be able to track it? You'll get in trouble."

She rolled her eyes at me. "So what else is new? Some things are more important than rules. I think my bestie finding out she's a secret sex demon qualifies. Now put on something less . . . sweaty, and go get your answers."

After cleaning myself up, I dressed in a pair of tight jeans and a long-sleeved sweater with a low neckline. I wanted to be comfortable but still fit in at a place like *Iniquity*. Moira gave me her seal of approval then said, "Just toss it on the floor and think of where you need to be."

I did as she told me, a swirling green portal opening in front of me. "Okay, here goes nothing." Before I stepped inside, I pulled Moira into a hug. "Thank you. I don't know what I'd do without you."

"You'd be a mess. Well . . . a bigger mess."

Rolling my eyes, I released her and took a deep breath. Then I stepped into the portal in search of answers.

~

"What the bloody hell good is a security team if random bitches in heat can just pop into my office unannounced?" Lilith's sultry British voice was laced with annoyance as her head snapped up and she found me standing awkwardly in the corner of the room. She blinked, her expression morphing into surprise. "Oh, Sunday, it's you."

I was too busy staring at her desk to do more than lift my hand in some semblance of a wave. Well, the man acting as her desk. He was almost completely naked and painfully erect. He had a ball-gag in his mouth, and a horse's tail hung between the taut globes of his ass. An ass that was bright red and marked with welts. He was big, heavily muscled, with a light dusting of hair over his legs and chest. Lilith sat behind him on what appeared to be a small throne, which made sense since *Iniquity* was basically her Queendom. A black book was open across his back, her riding crop held in one hand and a red-feathered quill in the other.

"I . . ." I had no idea what to say.

The man's gaze flicked to me, then back to where he'd been focused. But Lilith didn't miss a beat. She trained her attention on me and said, "I'm in the middle of a scene. If you don't want to witness me punishing him for looking at you, you should leave now."

I turned on my heels and walked out the door, just as the sound of the riding crop connecting with his ass and his sharp grunt of pleasure filled the room.

My heart was racing, and no longer from my nightmare. *Jesus.* I wasn't sure what I expected just waltzing into a succubus's office, but I feel like I should have been prepared. I hadn't been. Not even a little.

At least I was feeling more than anxiety-induced fear when she stepped out and joined me in the hallway a minute later.

"Now, dear one, tell me what has you popping in unannounced? You look flushed." She trailed her fingers across my cheek and offered me a sweet smile.

A shudder of arousal raced down my spine. I'd forgotten how potent she could be. "I needed your advice, or I guess your opinion really. I think I might be, that is, I had a dream and . . ." My words were jumbled, the result of my fuzzy brain and nerves.

She made a shushing noise in her throat and moved to stand behind me, massaging the corded muscles in my neck and shoulders. "It's all right, dear. Just relax. I don't ever want you to fear me. There's no need. I never intend to scare you, only arouse you." Her seductive laugh bounced off the walls as her fingers worked their magic.

"Am I a succubus?" I blurted, trying to push through the haze of attraction she always coated me in.

"What?" Her hands left my skin, and she came back around to face me.

"You heard me. Am I . . . like you?"

She leaned in and took a long breath, inhaling my scent deep into her lungs. Her eyelids fluttered closed as she stepped back. "Has anyone ever told you how delicious you are?" She hummed softly, a noise of pure pleasure. "Honey. Lilacs. Ice and the ocean." She ran her nose up my throat. "Moss and cedar as well. And some delicious citrus with roses. Oh, it's delectably convoluted. It shouldn't be so appealing." One more sniff had her shuddering. "Blood and brimstone."

"Brim-brimstone?"

"Just a hint of it. I know you came searching for answers, love, but I don't have the ones you seek. You're not a succubus, but there's definitely something dark in you."

"What is it?"

She fingered a lock of my hair and inspected the strands. "I don't know. But it's dark and it's hungry."

My gut clenched at the same time as a wave of heat

washed over me. Her nostrils flared as she picked up on the abrupt shift of emotions.

"Here, let me see if I can help. Hunger is one of my specialties, after all. She laced her fingers around the back of my neck, her blue eyes turning into a swirling endless black as she peered into mine. My heart stuttered, and I forgot how to breathe as she unleashed her power on me.

"Show me what you desire, Sunday. What is it you crave above all else?"

I didn't say a word, but her gaze sharpened, then her brows lifted. "Ah, there it is. I know what you need, darling. Go on to your room. You'll feel much better after you do."

I opened my mouth, but she stopped me with a black-tipped finger on my lips.

"Let Lilith take care of you. It's why you came, isn't it?"

"Okay," I agreed, feeling the same lightheaded euphoria that usually accompanied a good buzz. Man, if Lilith could bottle and sell whatever she was exuding, she'd make a killing.

In a daze, I made my way down the stairs, not even seeing the other patrons who must've been at the club. My heart was pounding, head spinning as need careened through me, just like it had with Kingston. Intense and nearly taking me to my knees. Why was this happening again? If I wasn't a succubus, why couldn't I be sated?

As always, when I reached the room, the door swung inward. My breath caught at the sight before me, the room looking like nothing I'd expected and everything I secretly desired.

CHAPTER
THIRTY-ONE
CALEB

My fecking phone buzzed in my pocket, an intrusive annoyance I should've removed before I knelt in my chamber of atonement. The skin of my back still smarted from the last of the lashes I inflicted after once again giving myself over to the remembrance of Sunday's perfect mouth around my cock. I groaned.

"What?" I growled as I answered the call.

"Oh, he's grouchy. I like it when you're mean." Lilith's voice washed over me, sending dread and excitement through me at the same time. My traitor of a dick twitched in anticipation. She only contacted me for one reason.

"Where is she?"

"Waiting. In the room. In need."

"Where's Blackthorne?"

"He's not the one she needs right now, Priest."

If I wasn't already hard, I would be. "It can't be me."

"But it is."

I closed my eyes as longing nearly as painful as the wounds on my back swept through me.

"It's what her heat requires. No one else will do. If you deny her, you will leave her in pain. It may even kill her. Need this intense is . . . dangerous."

Gritting my teeth against the overwhelming urge to fix Sunday, to heal her and serve her, I stood and strode up the stairs. "Fecking hell, I'm on my way."

I tossed my phone on the desk, the very desk Sunday had swallowed my cum underneath, and sat on the edge, my entire body trembling. Reaching up, I pressed my palm over the marks on my chest, three now. Was I about to be the reason for the fourth?

I should let her be, let this run its course and see what fate had in store for her. If I didn't help her, see her through this, would she die? Would that stop this?

The instant the thought appeared in my mind, pain sliced my heart. If I was a stronger man—a better one—I would have put the needs of many before hers. But I had never been a very good man. Or a good priest, for that matter. I was a sinner through and through. Locked in a cycle of eternal atonement destined to fail.

"Forgive me," I whispered as I stared at the crucifix hanging on my wall. "I know exactly what I'm about to do, and I can't stop myself."

I closed my eyes, wishing God's voice would come to me, that I would feel His presence and unconditional love answering my prayers. Reassuring me that I had not strayed so far from the path of righteousness as to be denied that mercy.

Instead, it was a woman who answered. *Help her, Caleb. She is yours.*

Was it an angel or a devil whispering in my head?

I snagged my shirt off the back of the chair where I'd left it and slid the fabric on. Then, with shaking hands, I buttoned it as I steeled myself for the war I knew I was destined to lose.

The night blurred around me as I raced across the campus grounds to the secret tunnel that was my personal access point to Lilith's lair in the city. Once I was outside the door that separated me from her club, I pressed my hand against the aged wood and closed my eyes, gathering my strength once more.

This time I didn't know if I was hoping to resist or praying that I wouldn't.

Either way, I was determined to see this through. She needed me, not them. And tonight, she was mine alone.

Temptation, thy name is Sunday Fallon. And like a siren who lures her prey to their deaths, I am helpless to resist your call.

Lilith didn't greet me as she usually did. In fact, no one spoke a word to the depraved priest skulking in the hallway. They left me to my destruction, and I was thankful. My heart hammered in my . . . wait.

My heart.

It wasn't Sunday's pulse in my head; it was mine. The small miracle held me captive. I hadn't felt my heartbeat since the night I lost my soul. Was it possible it had been my heart all this time? Was this the sign I'd been searching for?

Lifting my face to the heavens, I closed my eyes and whispered, "Is this you? Are you showing me where I'm supposed to be?"

I stood outside the door to my room, my place where I watched her live out her desires with Noah Blackthorne. But nothing happened. The door didn't open for me.

"What?" I shoved at the heavy steel, but it wouldn't budge.

Confused, I wandered a bit farther down the hall, intent on finding the succubus and demanding she stop playing her games. Before I took more than a few steps, a door swung inward, and Sunday's scent overwhelmed me, beckoning me inside.

She faced me, eyes wide, cheeks flushed, lips begging to be kissed.

"Caleb." She whispered my name like a prayer, and it sent righteous hunger through me.

I swallowed as I crossed the threshold, unable to speak as I took in her surroundings. I knew this place. My gaze traveled the space, stone walls I'd laid one by one, painstakingly, with reverence. The rocking chair my mother used to sing me to sleep in, given to me in hopes my wife would do the same with our children, Mam's old patchwork quilt resting on the back. And beside it, the table and chairs my father had carved by hand as a wedding present for his bride.

I had built this home from the ground up with my bare hands and filled it with my most cherished belongings when I believed the path before me included a wife and children. Before God had shown me another way. It was simple, modest, and had been mine.

Sunday stood in the center of the room, fulfilling every bit of my fantasy future. It was painful and beautiful all at once. A gift I never thought I'd receive.

A fire already danced in the hearth. Sunlight spilled through the wide windows, gauzy curtains fluttering as the scent of my homeland drifted in on the ocean's breeze.

"*Éire*," I murmured in awe. I was home.

Sunday whimpered, the sound of her pain triggering my instinctive need to protect. I shot forward, catching her as her knees buckled.

She stared up at me from the cradle of my arms, pain in her eyes, but something else there that I dared not name. "Your eyes look different in the daylight," she said, wonder in her voice.

I jerked, my gaze shifted to the window and the beam of light shining down upon us like a holy spotlight.

This is how you die. With everything you've ever wanted within reach and the woman you love in your arms, only for them both to be ripped away. A taste of heaven before the reality of hell. What a fitting end for a habitual sinner.

I braced for the pain I knew would come . . . but it didn't. Instead of fire's angry burn, I felt only a long-forgotten warmth.

Laughter bubbled in my chest. I steadied Sunday on her feet and then grasped her head, cradling it between my hands as though she were a cherished gift. Then I kissed her, pouring every ounce of my joy into the moment.

If I could stay here forever, I would. I'd live out the rest of my days as a human man, with Sunday at my side, in a cottage by the sea.

"Caleb, please," Sunday said, her voice a raw whisper.

I bent down, scooping her up like she was my bride as I carried her into the adjoining room I'd built to contain my marriage bed. The room was as I'd last seen it, a four-poster bed covered in a plain white coverlet the star of the space, then a desk in the corner with a hard wooden chair. Simple pleasures all waiting for the love of a good woman to make this house a home.

I knew Sunday was that woman. The one I'd always hoped for.

I couldn't love her.

But I did.

"Lie back, *a stor*. I'll care for you."

317

I set her down gently, feeling only a moment's nerves as I stared down at her. In this moment, she was my wife, given to me by God Himself. We were coming together the way we were meant to. This was how my life should've been.

I slowly stripped her clothes off, baring her to me, every lush curve ready to be savored by my mouth and hands. She was mine.

The way she writhed for me, her legs sliding together, the slick arousal glistening on her inner thighs, had me throbbing in my pants. I needed her just as much as she did me.

"Please, God."

That one word stopped me, bringing my vows crashing back to the forefront of my mind. I'd given God my solemn word. Promised that I would remain celibate for all my days so I could serve Him. I'd come this far and nearly crossed the line so many times, but I'd never broken my vow. Up until now, I'd remained chaste.

But I hadn't. Not really. I'd been lying to myself and allowing the falsehoods to dictate how far I'd step with Sunday. I'd found release time and time again with her name on my lips, her lips on my cock, her scent my only saving grace. Somewhere along the way, Sunday Fallon had become my religion. The only one I'd sworn my eternal devotion to.

All that remained was my virginity. I was teetering on the edge, but I would not cross it. I'd already lost so much, I couldn't lose that final part of myself. It was all I had left that was pure. I needed it to believe I was still worthy of redemption.

"Caleb, I need you. Please help me. I hurt."

The knowledge she was in pain, pain without the added

benefit of pleasure, sliced me to my core. I was here for a reason—she was in need of relief. I couldn't serve her in the same way her other mates had—even though I fiercely wanted to—but I could help. I could take away some of the need.

"Spread your thighs, Sunday. I'll take away the ache."

She was quick to do so, her body visibly reacting to my gaze. Slick arousal slid down her plump lower lips and sent my cock weeping with need. She reached for me, her hand palming my length and squeezing.

"Feck, you're a bad girl. No touching."

I would never last if she touched me. I cast my gaze around, searching for something to bind her with when it was clear she was beyond obeying the simple request.

A golden stole rested on the back of a chair in the corner of the room. She moaned as I stepped away to grab it, though hunger flared in the depths of her eyes as I grasped her wrists and tugged them above her head.

I secured her to the headboard and couldn't fight the smirk that twisted my lips. "That should keep you from wandering. My good little lamb. Let me guide you safely through this."

She writhed, testing the hold and begging me with her eyes to touch her. She was incapable of more than wanton moans when I leaned down, my hands on either side of her as I suckled the rosy bud of her tight nipple. Sunday Fallon, naked and restrained in my bed, was too much to bear without touching the full curves of her perfect breasts.

"I can smell your wet cunt from here," I murmured. "Were you a good girl? Did you do as you were instructed? Did you save your climax for me?"

"Yes, Daddy. I did as you commanded. Please let me come."

"That's my good girl. You are so needy. It drives me wild."

"Not wild enough," she complained. "Fuck me, Caleb."

"No, my gorgeous girl. I won't. But I promise I will make you feel so good you won't miss my cock."

She shook her head. "Not true. I need it. You don't understand what this is like."

I trailed my fingers down her belly, slipping through her slick folds. "You think I don't know the taste of hunger? The burn of need? I've been mad with it for longer than you've been alive. Have resisted the call. Until you."

As I said the words, I filled her with my fingers, making her back arch as she cried out.

"There it is. The sound I dream of. Give me more, Sunday. Let me hear you."

"Oh, God, more. Please."

I continued to circle her clit with my thumb and pump two fingers inside her, curling them up and knowing I hit the right spot when an answering flood of wetness coated my fingers.

"More." Her voice was a breathy plea, a woman on the edge who needed someone to push her to fly.

I spread her legs wide, using more force than necessary as I dove between her thighs and feasted like a starving man. I wasn't sure which one of us groaned louder. Sunday at the feel of my tongue lapping at her, or me at the taste of her.

My beauty was rolling her hips in search of the *more* she kept asking for. I needed her to come more than I needed blood to survive, but she couldn't get there. My thumb toyed with the tight ring of her arse, pushing against the muscle just as she'd taunted me under my desk. As I sucked her clit between my lips, she sobbed my name, but still, those walls didn't flutter with pulses of pleasure.

She was so wet, her arousal dripping down between her cheeks, so there was little resistance as I slid my thumb in deeper, past the tight pucker.

She screamed my name, hips bucking as she rode my tongue and finally found her release.

I ached to be inside her. My cock leaked, leaving a wet spot on my trousers. This was nothing short of torture. How fitting. It was far more painful than any session I'd ever had with my flogger.

"Caleb, I need you. I need more of you. All of you."

I'd seen her in heat before. I knew it would hold her in its clutches until she got what it demanded of her, but I wasn't sure how much longer I could deny myself.

"Just a little. Just your skin on mine," she pleaded. "I need to feel you."

She looked like the most beautiful angel, spread before me on the bed, cheeks flushed, hands bound, lovely pink pussy bared.

"Fuck," I groaned, reaching for my fly.

The light in her eyes as she watched me pull out my cock had me swelling even more. She was hungry for me. Only me.

"Inside. Please, inside."

I shook my head. "No, *a stor.*"

She whimpered, biting down hard on her lip but nodding to show me she understood. It was her heat that made her beg, but my Sunday wouldn't push me farther than I was willing to go. If she only knew how badly I wanted to give her everything she asked for.

I stroked my length from root to tip, arms shaking as I did. With my free hand, I grabbed a pillow, and she lifted her hips on instinct, knowing exactly what I was after. I tucked the pillow under her arse, then positioned myself closer to a woman's cunt than my cock had ever been.

"I need your cum."

"Fecking Christ on the cross."

I didn't know how I was going to get through this. Heat was driven by the body's biological imperative to breed. And there was only one way for that to happen. Sunday needed my cum inside her sweet cunt. Just like she was begging me for.

I could do that without penetrating her. I would come all over those glistening lips, and then I'd just slip some of my seed into her tight channel to satisfy her need. It would be enough.

It had to be.

Her name was ripped from my throat as I slid between those slick folds, coating the crown of my shaft in her hot cum. "Jesus wept," I whispered as I braced myself over her, rolling my hips slowly and desperately working to keep my dick out of her.

"C-Caleb," she stuttered, her head thrashing on the pillow.

I slid back and forth, the temptation to sink inside nearly more than I could bear. Every pass over her opening was an exercise in control. It would be so easy to push in, to give her exactly what she wanted.

My thrusts grew wilder as she matched my speed, my balls tightening with my own impending orgasm.

"Come for me," I ordered, needing it to happen so I didn't give in to my desire to feel her clench around my length. If I had to listen to those wild moans of hers, watch her tits bounce as she arched her back in search of me, I'd lose hold of myself and break my vow.

"Come with me," she begged. "I need to feel it."

"Fuck."

I wish I had been strong enough to ensure her climax before mine took over, but that desperate command was as irresistible as the woman who gave it. I was spilling myself all over her belly and pussy, rope after rope of cum shooting out as she joined me. Pleasure chased away all my guilt and made my eyes roll back in my head as I continued to slide through her folds, mixing my spend with her slick. My oversensitive cock gave a jerk at the heat of her, and I knew this was far from over.

I wasn't sure when she'd gotten free, all my attention had been zeroed in on the place where our bodies touched. The hand no longer bound to the headboard reached down between her legs, traveling through our combined releases and ghosting over my still hard cock. I sucked in a breath as I watched our cum slip inside her, chased by her fingers.

She arched her back. "I'm sorry, Caleb. It wasn't enough. I can feel it building again. I need you inside me. It's the only way to end this."

God, why are you testing me? I am going to fail.

"I can't. Not all the way."

"The tip then. I just need to feel you. Please."

I closed my eyes and forced myself not to look at her cunt, to keep Caleb, the human man with human needs, out of this. I'd been a vampire a long time; I should have had the control to stop this. But my heart beat hard, just like it had when I was human. It begged for us to connect. I needed her just as much as she did me.

Lining the head of my cock up with her entrance, I shuddered at the warm, wet, perfect feel of her. The muscles inside of her pulsed with need, as if they were trying to draw me in.

Christ, I am the biggest fool.

Swallowing and filling my mind with every prayer I'd ever been taught, I let myself sink in only the barest inch.

It wasn't enough. Fuck, it was nowhere near enough. But it had to be. Any deeper and I would fuck her with the kind of abandon I'd always dreamed about. This wasn't about me or my needs, though, only about seeing her through her heat.

This had to be enough. It was all I could give.

I grasped her hips, pressing them down into the pillow so that she couldn't take over and pull me in deeper.

"Touch yourself," I gritted out. "Make yourself come around me. I can't move, not if I don't want to fill you until you see stars."

"I want to see stars."

I growled, giving the slightest roll of my hips, then pulling myself from the welcoming heat of her. She moaned, and her brow furrowed. "Do as I say." I slapped her pretty pussy with my dick, right on her clit, and she cried out but brought her fingers down her body.

Then I slid inside again, stopping before I breached her fully. It was beautiful torture. She fluttered around me, her inner muscles tensing as she worked herself toward another climax.

I wanted to know what it would feel like to have all of her clutching all of me, milking me. I shivered with the need to drive forward and fill her full of my cum. I'd known hunger, but never like this.

"Kiss me, and I'll come for you."

I was helpless to resist. I leaned down, claiming her mouth with mine and groaning as the change in position shifted our angle, sliding me in just a fraction more.

"You temptress," I breathed, realizing she'd asked for

that exact reason. "Stop trying to control this. You're not the one in charge."

"Aren't I? Untie me, Caleb. Let me show you how good it is. Please, Daddy?"

Fuck. I untied her in one quick jerk of the fabric, and one hand went around my back, thighs wrapping tight around my waist. She didn't move her hips, seeming to honor my request—at least for now.

Freedom for her hand meant she was able to bring those sweet lips of hers up to my ear, where she whispered, "You're so big. I can't imagine what it would feel like to have you in my ass instead of your thumb."

I groaned because I'd thought about that very thing more than once. "Come, little one. You promised."

She nibbled my earlobe, and my arms trembled as I held myself up to keep from thrusting home. Sunday chuckled, trailing her kisses down the side of my neck. I could feel her hand still working at her clit. She circled faster as she ran her teeth over the muscle joining my neck and shoulder.

"I'm close, Father Gallagher. Pray for me."

I would've laughed, but she moaned and her orgasm took over. Her walls clenched around me, milking the head of my dick for something I couldn't give her. I had to pull out, to leave my release painted on her skin.

But then she bit me, marking me, and my whole body tingled as a climax raced through me.

I grunted, moving my hips back, desperate for the euphoria and afraid of it at the same time. I came, rolling waves of pure pleasure sending my vision white, my fangs extending, my cock deeper into her rather than away. It was the most incredible orgasm of my existence and the weakest moment I'd ever had as I filled her with my spend.

Sunday released me, running her tongue over the bite she'd given me with a happy murmur.

"Now you're mine."

Her whisper was sleepy, her body shutting down after the intensity of her heat.

I leaned back, my heart a mangled mess inside me as I watched her battle to stay awake.

"I love you," she whispered as she lost the fight.

I squeezed my eyes closed, still inside her as her words crashed into me.

Oh, God, what have I done?

THIRTY-TWO

SUNDAY

"Mmm, Caleb," I murmured into my pillow, rolling over and reaching for the man I'd finally claimed as mine. It was the last piece clicking into place.

My body ached with delicious tingles. Not from being railed into next week by my hot as fuck priest, sadly, but from the intensity of the three back-to-back orgasms he'd given me. As I stretched and rolled over, I did a quick mental inventory.

The heat was gone, completely. Like a switch had been flipped and I was my normal self again. I knew, with a bit of sadness, that it wouldn't return for a long time. But that didn't mean I couldn't coax another orgasm out of Caleb before we rejoined the real world.

I cracked one eye open, turning my head on the pillow to look at him.

He wasn't there.

Sitting up, I glanced around, but the lovely cottage-style room was gone, replaced with something utilitarian and not remotely familiar. The only thing besides the bed and me in the simple space was a single piece of paper.

That motherfucker.

He did not just Dear John me.

My hands shook as I reached for his note. Maybe he went to get breakfast? An egg McMuffin for me and a bag of blood for him?

But as soon as I saw the scrawl of his handwriting across the page, I knew. He'd left me.

THIS CAN NEVER HAPPEN AGAIN.
WHAT WE DID DOESN'T LEAVE THIS ROOM.

He didn't even sign it.

My lip quivered and tears pricked my eyes, but I refused to cry. Even though my heart felt like it was breaking. I crumpled his bullshit letter in my fist and chucked it across the room with an angry scream. It bounced harmlessly off the wall, rolling into the corner as a single tear escaped down my cheek.

The door opened then, revealing Noah, heartstopping, strong, and wonderful Noah.

"What's all this?" he asked, his voice tender but cautious. "I got a message that you needed me, not that you were upset."

I shook my head, too frustrated and sad to speak and not wanting to admit to my mate that I'd just had an unintentional one-night stand with Caleb.

He spotted the note and crouched down to pick it up. "Do you mind?"

I shrugged, and he took that as permission to read it. Honestly, it wasn't like he couldn't smell Caleb all over me. He had to know what had happened.

As he scanned the two lines of text, his face darkened like a storm cloud. Jaw clenched, he shook his head. "The absolute git. He thinks he can come in here and shag you all night, then leave like nothing happened? He's wrong."

"It's complicated, Noah."

His eyes flashed with possessive anger. "Fuck that. Don't make excuses for him. It's complicated to love a woman who loves three other men too, but I do it. It's bloody complicated to abandon my family because I know I can't be without you and stay sane." He slid his shirt sleeve up, exposing the traitor mark he bore for me. "I welcome the complications because the reward is worth everything. You are worth everything. Don't let this coward make you believe you deserve this."

He pulled me into his arms, and the tears I'd been fighting broke free. I just wasn't sure if I was crying over losing Caleb before I ever really had him or because of Noah's heartfelt declaration. I guess it didn't really matter.

By the time my tears had dried up, I was sure I looked as shitty as I felt, but you wouldn't know it the way Noah gazed at me. He kissed each of my cheeks, cupping my face in his warm palms and then pressing his lips over my eyelids.

"I wish I were enough for you." He whispered the words so softly I almost missed them.

My heart clenched. I hated that I was hurting him. "I'm sorry."

"Don't be. I know you need more than me. I understand this isn't a choice. You are fated to be bonded with all of us. I can't change it. I just wish . . . well, if I were enough, you'd already be happy."

"Noah, you *are* enough. I couldn't love you any more

than I already do. I don't ever want you to feel like my loving them means that you're lacking something. Because you're not. You're as much a part of me as the blood running through my veins. Now that I know what it's like to be loved by you, I can't live without it."

"I promise you'll never have to." He kissed me, soft and tender, not demanding anything more than I was willing to give. "I love you. As you are. Simply. Completely. Without limitation."

Pressing my palm over his chest, I let his heartbeat soothe me just like his words did. "Can we get out of here? I'm ready to be somewhere . . . else."

"Of course. Let's get you home."

"To yours. I don't want to be alone."

A smile spread across his face, pride in his eyes. "Whatever you want, dove. I'm at your mercy."

AFTER A SHOWER and Noah's surprise of Eggs Benedict with asparagus, I felt marginally better. Less like I'd just been sucker-punched by one of the men who was supposed to love me, and more like I'd just gone a few rounds with Alek in training. Still sore. Still shaky. But recovering quickly.

"What would you like to do today? I'm at your disposal." Noah lifted a coffee mug to his lips and watched me carefully.

"Sleep for five years. Can you make that happen?"

Concern drew his brows together. "Are you feeling ill?"

"Just really tired. I think it's a side effect of the heat ending. For good this time, I hope."

"Did you call for him? When you went to *Iniquity*?"

I shook my head. "I went to see Lilith. To ask her a question about what I am."

He raised a brow at that. "What you are?"

"I think . . . thought, I was part succubus. So I went to the only one I know. She couldn't give me any answers, but she told me she knew what I needed. A few minutes later, Caleb showed up."

"Why would you think you were a succubus?"

"These crazy heats, plus the things my mom said in my last dream. It all came to a head after the dream."

"Show me."

"I don't remember much, just a few of the things she said."

"Show me," he insisted.

I didn't actively keep any mental barriers between us anymore, so it was as simple as recalling the parts I did remember while he focused on my mind.

He sucked in a harsh breath and backed away. "Bloody hell, Sunday."

"What?" Dread slinked down my spine, a cold wash of fear and apprehension.

"I think your mum is Lucifer."

I laughed out loud. "What? No, she isn't. That's ridiculous."

"The apple, Eden. The things she said."

"What?" I could feel the color draining from my face. I'd thought he'd been making a joke to make me feel better, but his expression was deadly serious. "I don't remember any of that."

"I saw it all. Right there in your mind. I don't think she can be trusted, Sunday. If she is Luci, she's the master of all manipulators. You need to try to stop letting her into your mind."

Nausea clutched at my belly. "I don't know how to stop her. I'm not exactly in control of my dreams."

"The witch will know what to do. You need to ask her for help. Anything is better than nothing until we get to the bottom of this."

"Moira won't be able to stop this. The last time she tried to help she was pulled into a vision she barely escaped. Plus, her magic is bound the same as the rest of us because of these stupid wards."

With a sharp nod, he stood and began pacing, reminding me of a caged lion. "I'll call my cousin Silas, see if his wife Natalie can help. Perhaps she can put us in contact with the Siren Coven. They stopped Lucifer once before. They might be able to do something."

Everything was making a horrible, grim sort of sense. The demons coming after me. The wards reacting to me and not Alek. Why I'd never met my mother. Why she was asking me to free her.

Crap. I was the literal spawn of Satan.

"I . . . oh, God, Noah. I can't be here. I can't . . ." My breaths came in harsh gasps as panic clawed at my throat, my blood humming with anxiety.

Noah pulled me into his arms, pressing his lips to my forehead as he murmured reassurances against my skin. "It's going to be all right, dove. I don't bloody well care who your parents are. You're mine, and I won't give you up. Not even for the ruler of the underworld herself. We will figure this out. We will keep you safe."

It was hard to miss the plural there, and his intentional usage of it warmed me. I wasn't alone. I may not have Caleb, but I still had three other mates willing to stand at my side and protect me.

"I think I'm calling the demons to me. It's not safe for

you to be near me. None of you. You should lock me away in the well until we know how to stop this. I'm a risk to be around."

"No, Sunday. Absolutely not. You are not a threat to anyone. You've done nothing wrong."

"But—"

"No. If anything, you are a victim. Locking you away and leaving you unprotected is the worst thing we could do. I won't hear of it."

"Noah, if I'm the literal Antichrist, I think I should be treated like a dangerous ticking time bomb, not a victim. Handle with care, but also wear a bomb-resistant vest."

He laughed. "Sweetheart, I'm pretty much bomb-proof. I think I'll take my chances."

A frantic giggle escaped me. "God, we're like the beginning of a bad joke. The Antichrist, a vampire, and a priest walk into a bar . . ."

"We're the beginning of a beautiful forever, dove. There's nothing bad about what we have."

"How can you say that when—"

He shut me up with a kiss, proving with his body what I wouldn't hear with his words.

He loved me. He believed in me—in us. He wouldn't listen to anything else.

I melted against him, some of the fear ebbing in the wake of his unshakable faith. "Okay. I'll trust you for now, but at the first sign of this going tits up, I want you to lock me away. I don't want to hurt anyone or be the reason they get hurt."

"Sunday—"

"Promise me, Noah. Promise you'll do it."

He sighed, looking like he would rather do anything than agree. But eventually he did. "Fine."

His arms tightened around me, lips ghosting over the crown of my head as he held me close. Then he stiffened, his head turning, focus on the bank of windows to his left.

"Something's going on outside," he murmured. "Stay here."

"Yeah, okay," I said, rolling my eyes and following him.

When did that ever work? Was there any situation in any reality when someone didn't go see what was causing the ruckus?

The instant I glanced out the window, I wished I wouldn't have. Derek and Chad, wolves I knew ran with Kingston often, were carrying something across the grounds. They were both stained and battered, covered in blood and dirt.

"Oh, my God, Noah. What happened to them?"

"Demons," he answered grimly. "Two of them this time."

I didn't question how he knew. His hearing was far superior to mine, and with all the conversations happening down below, there was little doubt he'd overheard them. A sickening twist in my belly had me fighting the bitter taste of bile in my throat.

"But how?"

He shook his head, his expression tight when he looked back at me. "That's not the worst part. Sunday . . . it's Kingston."

"What? No, it's not. He's fine. I'd know if . . ." But even as I stared down at the bundle they carried, wrapped in bloodied cloth, I knew the truth. The blanket covering him fell away just enough a part of his tattooed chest came into view, a ragged slice cutting through skin, exposing bone. "No."

"Go. He'll need his mate. Go to him now, dove."

He didn't need to tell me twice. I was already running for the door. My heart felt like it had just been ripped from my chest for the second time that day.

Don't be dead. Please don't be dead.

I can't lose you too.

THIRTY-THREE

KINGSTON

Motherfucker, what the hell happened to me?

My chest was on fire, my head throbbed like I'd repeatedly smacked it into a cement wall, and my mouth was drier than the fucking desert.

If I just went ten rounds with a grizzly, why didn't I remember?

I tried to take a deep breath, to clear my mind, but that hurt like a sonofabitch too. I shifted, trying to alleviate some of the ache, but even that was too much for me. Instead, I let out a groan that was far too weak to have come from me.

A small weight at my side disappeared, and I mourned the loss instantly.

"Kingston? Kingston, are you awake?"

Her voice was frantic. Exhausted. Tinged with desperation.

"Sunshine? What are you doing in my bed? Did you miss me?" Was I drunk? I sounded drunk.

She made a sound halfway between a hiccup and a sob.

"No. You almost died, you asshole. You've been unconscious for three fucking days."

"So you missed me."

"I thought I was going to lose you."

I let out a happy sigh. "She missed me."

Fuck, I was definitely on something. I hadn't felt this zen since that one time Jennifer Tate slipped some molly in my drink at a new moon party.

"How are you feeling?" Sunday asked, her voice finally prompting me to open my eyes.

"Terrible. Where'd the bear come from?"

"Huh?" she asked, her face adorably scrunched. "What bear?"

"The one I was wrestling."

"You didn't wrestle a bear." She glanced behind her. "Did he?"

"It kinda looked like a bear, but bigger and meaner." Why was Chad in my bed too? I didn't want Chad in my bed. Only my Sunshine.

Blinking a few times, I saw him standing in the corner, arms crossed over his chest.

"It was a bear." I made a face and tried to mime claws. "Grrr."

My Sunshine stared at me in shock and then giggled. "How much of that stuff did you give him?" she asked Chad.

"Enough that he shouldn't feel any pain for a while."

"Not enough. So much pain."

"Can you give him any more?" Sunday's sweet fingers ran through my hair, easing some of the throbbing in my head.

"Not if you want him to keep breathing."

"I like breathing. It smells like you, Sunshine. It makes me hard."

"Uh, I think I've got it from here," she said, flicking her gaze to Chad.

"I'm on watch."

"Do it from outside," I demanded. "Sunday might wanna open the present I have for her underneath my sheets." Did I just say that out loud? From the look on her face, yeah, I sure as shit did.

"Fine. Call if you need me."

"We won't. If the bed's a' rockin' . . . " I couldn't figure out how to finish that sentence. My brain was too fuzzy.

"Christ," Chad muttered, but he left.

"There will be no rocking, Kingston. You're hurt."

"Swaying then. I'll lie back, and you just ride me like your prized stallion."

"Your chest was nearly split open. How are you horny right now?"

I waggled my eyebrows. "God-given talent. I'll be good. Won't move at all. You do all the work. Don't I deserve it after almost dying?"

"You must be feeling better if you're going for coercion now."

"It's because you smell so fucking good."

She leaned down, and I thought she was going to kiss me, so I closed my eyes. But her lips missed and landed on my cheek.

"You missed," I grumbled.

"I didn't."

I lifted my hand and pointed to my lips. It took a couple tries before I found them. "My kisser is right here."

Leaning forward, she brushed her lips on mine. Not enough. Not even close.

341

"I'm so glad you aren't dead. I was so scared, Kingston."

Her voice was soft and small. It made my heart twist in my chest. I didn't like the sound of her fear.

"I'd never leave you. Not even to die."

"You can't control that."

"Yes, I can. I'll come back as a ghost and fuck you with my big fat ghost dick."

"Just what I want. Ghost jizz. Sounds fun." The sarcasm in her voice made me laugh, which hurt like hell.

"It's less sticky. Just tickles a bit."

"And you know this how?"

I shrugged. "Everyone knows it."

"You're high."

"So what?" Then another thought occurred to me. "How's my scar gonna look? Badass?" I tried to glance down my body, but that did not feel good at all. The world dipped like I was on a boat, making my stomach roll.

"Oh, yeah. You're a real He-Man."

"I thought you liked scars. Every girl likes scars."

"I like you whole and healed."

"Han Solo had a scar. I bet you like him."

She rolled her eyes. "I like you better. And yeah, I'm sure your scar will be badass and sexy, okay?"

I chuckled. "Fuck you, Han. My girl likes me better."

She kept playing with my hair, which did absolutely nothing to calm my dick down, but I didn't want her to stop. I needed her touching me.

"Tell me what happened." Her tone was filled with a plea for honesty.

My gaze locked on hers, the pain in those beautiful irises breaking my heart a little. "Honestly, it's a blur. We were running, trying to work off some tension."

"We?"

"Me, Chad, Derek. They're going to be my betas. When I take over."

"And?"

"We can't shift, but we still need to run. So we hit the woods. I should've smelled the brimstone, but I didn't. Fuckers came out of nowhere."

"Fuckers? There were more than one of them?"

"Two . . . I think." I lifted a hand to my head with a groan. "That's really all I remember. My brain feels like scrambled eggs. Mmm . . . eggs."

"I can see about getting you something to eat," she offered.

"No. I don't want you to go anywhere."

"I'll come right back."

"What if I fall asleep? I want you to be the last thing I see before I close my eyes. The first thing when I wake up. Always."

Her smile was so beautiful it lit up the whole room. "Then rest. I'll stay here and keep watch."

She was running her fingers through my hair again, making it impossible for me to keep my eyes open. "I don't want to sleep. I want you."

"You need to rest."

"Need to come."

"Later. If you're good."

"Party pooper."

"That's me. No fun Sunday."

"Oh, you're my favorite day of the week. That's why we say twice on Sunday. Cause we like you."

She let out a soft laugh. "You're not even making sense now. Go to sleep."

"Will you be here? Will you stay?"

"I promise."

343

"Sunshine." I couldn't remember what I wanted to tell her. "Now I know what that song means."

"Which song?"

"That happy one. My Sunshine."

The title was wrong, but my head didn't want to work. She knew what I meant. She had to. But just in case, I started humming the melody, off-key and lazy. I'd always look to her when the sky turned gray. Always.

"And you call yourself a singer," she teased, but tears were rolling down her cheeks.

"I'll sing for you. Wrote you a song." I tried to say more, but I wasn't entirely sure I'd even said that much because I finally lost the battle to keep my eyes open.

I drifted to sleep with her touch on my skin and her scent wrapping me like a blanket. It was the only thing I wanted. Thank God I had my Sunshine to keep me warm.

My blood hummed with unease as I abandoned the book I'd been reading for the third time in as many minutes. I was anxious, restless, my thoughts racing. I hadn't seen Sunday, nor had I heard from her since she left to be with Kingston days ago. I could've gone to check in, but Alphas were notoriously edgy when they were vulnerable, and Sunday didn't need the added stress of dancing around our egos while worrying about her mate. And if I set aside my own desires enough to be objective, the two of them needed space alone to deal with what happened.

I let out a heavy breath, raking my hand through my hair and working to calm my pounding heart. Closing my eyes, I reached out to my mate with my mind, needing some kind of connection to her, if only for a moment. We'd already been parted for far too long once before, and I wasn't strong enough to go through that willingly again.

Even knowing the cost of my selfishness.

My sister Roslyn had chosen to give up her freedom in place of my own. The Donoghues had insisted on a Blackthorne alliance or my death, and they'd gotten what my family thought the lesser of two evils. But instead of me marrying Callista—I refused to let my aunt Callie's name be attached to that creature—I'd killed her, and now it was Rosie shackled to their oldest son Gavin. The sweet lamb didn't stand a chance in that den of vipers. She was too pure for their darkness. More human than the rest of us, never changed, never fed. And because of my love for Sunday, she'd be their prey.

I'd made my decision, and there was no going back.

My soul craved hers. Nearly as much as my body.

Sunday's awareness brushed against mine, bringing with it the scent of pine and cool night air. She was outside. Alone. At risk.

Straightening, I dropped my book on the sofa and got to my feet before I began pacing.

Should I go to her? Would she welcome me?

Annoyed with myself, I scowled. When the hell had I ever cared about such things? I'd accompanied her on moonlit strolls more than once without her knowledge. First because I was curious, then because I was hunting her. Now? Because I bloody loved her.

Snagging my heavy black peacoat, I shrugged it on. Not that I was cold, but if I knew Sunday, she'd escaped outside on instinct without a care for the unusually cold December weather.

Now that I had a plan of action, my unease settled. It was as if the promise of seeing her again was all I needed to feel whole. Or at least as close to whole as I could be without her in my arms.

I barely registered my own movements as I blurred to the stairs, forgoing the elevator in favor of speed. In mere moments I'd reached her proximity, keeping myself out of her line of sight until I was sure she wanted me.

She stood as she often did at the side of the lake, her face tipped up to the night sky, eyes closed as a light dusting of snow drifted over her cheeks. It was an enchanting sight. Something an artist would choose to immortalize with their paints. Innocence and sensuality. The untamed wild. Beauty in its purest, rawest form.

I almost didn't take that step forward into the moon-light simply because I didn't want to disturb such a peaceful moment, but then she shuddered and her breath hitched.

She was crying.

My feet moved of their own accord, drawing me closer. I couldn't stand by and watch her suffer. Not when I was there and could offer her comfort.

She flinched at the feel of my hands on her shoulders, then instantly relaxed. "Noah."

Taking off my coat, I wrapped it around her, cocooning her in its warmth and my scent. Staking my claim even as I cared for her. That might make me a bit of a selfish bastard, but then I never pretended to be otherwise.

"What are you doing out here all alone? There are demons afoot, you know."

She let out a light laugh, but there wasn't any real amuse-ment in her tone. "Afoot? Is this a Victorian romance now? Or are you playing at being my very own Sherlock Holmes?"

"We do have a mystery to solve together. Although I don't imagine those stories were intended to have such intimate moments as the ones you and I share."

She leaned back into me, resting her head on my chest and taking a long shuddering breath.

"How is Kingston? Is it bad?" I asked, wrapping her in my arms.

"It was touch and go there for a while, but he finally woke up today. I . . . I think he's going to make it."

Her uncertainty gave me pause. "Is he not healing?"

"He can't shift, and the demon's claws contained some kind of poison. It's been slow going, even with his supernatural blood. It'll be weeks, maybe longer, before he's back to normal."

"Have you gone to the headmistress with this? If word gets out to the Families, they'll rake her over the coals. She should lift the ban if only so he can heal."

She shook her head. "Not yet. I just left his room. That should probably be my next stop, though."

"Perhaps after you shower. You smell like . . ."

Her shoulders stiffened, and she turned in my arms. "Go on. What do I smell like, Noah?"

"A very earthy version of yourself."

The slight twitch of her lips and the laughter in her eyes eased something in me. "Well played."

"I do try. Come on, I'll walk you back to your room. Or . . . if you'd rather, you could come to mine?"

She looked torn. "I should probably go back to mine. Moira's likely worried sick. Not to mention Alek. I don't even know where my phone is. I need to check in with the troops."

"You know, this is a problem we can easily solve. If we all lived together, everyone would remain in the loop."

Her brow furrowed. "All of us?"

I shrugged as though it was the most natural thing in the world. "Yes. Your very own pack of misfits. Family is what you make it, dove. You've created yours, now you have to tie it all together."

She snorted. "Can you picture Alek and Kingston sitting around a breakfast table? Sharing small talk over a cup of coffee? I can't."

"They've shared a meal before, at your dinner. What's so hard to believe about it? They love you, Sunday. We all do. We just want what's best for you. I'm certain I'm not alone when I say it would make me feel better to know where you were each night."

"Would you just . . . draw straws to see who slept in my bed?"

Smirking, I winked. "Or we get a bed large enough we never have to choose."

Her eyes heated, and I had no trouble seeing just how much the idea appealed to her. Flashes of her desires filled my mind. All of us together, touching her, kissing every inch of her body, filling her at the same time.

"What if I wanted alone time?" she asked. "Or to be with only one of you?"

"Then each of us maintains his own room for such an occasion. It's not rocket science. No need to overcomplicate it."

"And you'd really be fine with that? Having to listen while I was with one of the others? Without you?"

"Your moans of pleasure are never a bad thing. Maybe I'll take up voyeurism as well. It has its appeal."

The mere suggestion of Caleb cooled her desire. The light in her eyes faded, as did her smile. I mentally punched myself in the face.

Good one, Blackthorne.

I couldn't believe I was about to defend the arse, but here we were. With a sigh, I hugged her tight, resting my chin on her head. "He'll come around, dove. It can't be easy for a man to let go of vows he's clung to so fiercely. His entire world is shifting. That takes time to wrap your head around."

"I know. It just . . . hurts. The rejection."

Wherever he was hiding, I hoped the priest was in misery for hurting her. "Do you want me to track him down and show him the error of his ways? I'll be happy to teach him a lesson."

She smiled at the thought. "Best not. We don't need anyone else sent to the well for breaking his neck."

"Anyone *else*?"

"When my heat first started, Kingston snapped his neck to get to me. Caleb sent him to the well in retaliation. It was a whole thing."

"Seems like I missed some things when I was away."

Her cheeks flushed as she stared at me. "You missed too much. Don't go away again."

That made my chest flutter like I was a fucking teenager. "I won't. I swear it."

"Even if you think it's the right thing to do?"

"I will burn the world to ashes if I'm faced with the choice between you and it. You are the only right thing in my life. The Council has tried and failed to stop me from being yours. I've made up my mind. My choice will always be you."

She kissed me, her lips tasting of salt and snow. "I choose you, too."

"Well, I bloody well hope so. It's too late to change your mind now."

She laughed, cuddling into me. "So you're saying you're stuck with me?"

"No, love. I'm saying you're stuck with *me*. So if I need to start shopping for a five-person bed, just say the word."

"But what about Moira? I can't just abandon her."

"I doubt she'll have any interest in the bed, but we can always make sure she has a room of her own if she wants to stay over."

A happy little noise escaped her. "Thank you. I love you."

"And I you. Now, let's get you cleaned up and ready to face off with Madame . . . what was it you called her?"

"Madame Moody."

"Yes, that's the one. If anyone can persuade her, it'll be you."

We walked back to Blackthorne Hall hand in hand, and for the first time in three days, the part of me that had been restless was finally calm. Things were far from settled, the world was practically going to shit all around us, but for now, at least, I was at peace.

Because of her.

As long as she was safe, nothing else mattered.

I idly wondered when Sunday Fallon became the center of my entire universe. And just as the thought occurred, I realized it didn't matter when. Only that it was true.

THIRTY-FIVE
SUNDAY

"Sunday Amadeus Fallon. You are in BIG trouble."

I froze in the doorway of the bathroom, the knob still clutched in my hand, wet hair in a towel. I wasn't sure amusement was appropriate with the way Moira was glaring at me, but I couldn't help the little shakes of laughter working their way through me. "Amadeus?"

"Well, I don't know your middle name, but this kind of trouble requires a full name's worth of chastisement."

"Rose."

She rolled her eyes. "Basic and boring. I'm changing it."

"To *Amadeus*?"

"It was good enough for Wolfy. It should be good enough for you."

"I'm not following."

"Mozart."

"I didn't realize you were on a nickname basis with dead composers."

She raised a sculpted brow. "Who says he's dead, smartypants?"

"Uh, history?"

"Wrong. The greatest composers and artists of our time faked their deaths when they were turned."

Turned. Vampires. Well, shit.

"What about Elvis?"

Moira mimed locking her lips and throwing away the key.

I shook my head, giving in to my laughter. "Moira, you are a nut. Now get over here and give me a hug. I've missed you."

"I've missed you too, you bitch."

We moved toward each other, embracing tightly, neither of us wanting to let go.

"I heard about Kingston," she murmured.

"It was awful."

"How are *you* doing? What'd Lilith say?"

Shit. A heavy weight settled back on my shoulders. Talking about Lilith meant talking about Caleb. I wasn't ready to get into that again.

"Not a succubus."

"Huh. I thought for sure we were onto something."

Now didn't seem like a great time to mention I might also be the devil's daughter. *God, when did things get so complicated?*

I never thought in a million years I'd ever think this, but I was really starting to miss my days in the tower. At least things were simpler then.

"You're keeping something from me," Moira said, narrowing her eyes.

"Kind of. Until I have more information."

"I don't approve."

"I know. But this is a tell-as-few-people-as-necessary kind of thing."

"How dare you!" she screeched, pulling back to stare at me. "I'm not people, you hooker."

"Hooker? Wow. I see. Encourage me to build a harem, then slut shame me the minute you don't get all the info."

She scowled at me and waved her hand in the air. "That's not what I meant, and you know it. Fuck whoever you want. I don't care. It was the nicest thing I could say to you without actually causing harm, unlike what *you* said. That really hurt. I'm not *people*. Random bitches are people. I'm your fucking person."

Guilt hit me hard, taking me down at the knees. I sat on my bed, tension settling in my chest as I looked into her eyes. "Okay, I'll tell you, but you're going to need to sit down."

Over the next hour, I filled her in on everything that had happened since I'd gone to *Iniquity*. Lilith's desk. Caleb. Kingston. Noah's revelation about my mother. All the dirty, ugly details.

It was a testament to our friendship that she was still sitting beside me, holding my hand by the time I finished.

"Okay, so you weren't kidding. You've been a busy girl. I'm not even sure where to start with . . . all that."

"You see why I was trying to spare you?"

"But on a scale from one to wrecked, how good was Daddy Caleb? Before he was an absolute asshole, I mean."

"God, it was so fucking intense. We quite literally played 'Just the Tip,' and it was the sexiest fucking moment of my entire life."

Her brows lifted. "That's saying something considering your other sexcapades."

"I know. It was just so . . . perfect. And then he took it all back. Like it was nothing. Like *I* was nothing."

And that's what hurt the most because that moment

with him had been *everything*. The culmination of what I'd been searching for my whole life. The last puzzle piece finally sliding into place.

And then he ripped it away.

"Ugh, you two are the most forbidden pair *ever*."

"Are we, though? He's not really a priest anymore. I mean, he's my professor, I guess."

"He will always be a priest, even if he and God are going through a rough patch. But I was talking about the fact that you're the daughter of his sworn enemy. How's that for some conflict? Shakespeare, who?"

I blew out a heavy breath. "Crap, I didn't even think of that. Man, he's really going to lose his shit when he finds out. If he hates me now, he'll despise me after that."

"What if he knows? Oh, shit. What if that's why he left? He figured it out. Or did he know all this time?" Her eyes sparkled with the possibilities.

"If he knew and didn't say anything . . ." I'd . . . I had no idea what I'd do. Murder him in his sleep? Nail him to a cross? Fury built in my chest as the prospect of him betraying me so completely sank in.

The last time I'd felt this bloodthirsty, I'd tried to single-handedly take down a demon in a library. Caleb was lucky he'd tucked tail and run, because if he came anywhere near me right now, he might not be shown as much mercy as the demon had been. Alek ended that beast quickly. I would have made him suffer.

"Um, Sunday . . . are you okay?" Moira's voice shook as she asked the question.

"Yes. Just working through some rage."

"Your eyes . . ."

"What about them?"

"They're pitch-black. Everywhere."

Dread curled in my gut. That's how the demon's eyes looked when we'd fought it. Dead, soulless, black holes of nothing.

Panic hit me like a bucket of ice. I blinked, jumping up and running over to the full-length mirror Moira had placed against the wall. I'd expected a monster to be staring back at me, but it was just me . . . just Sunday.

And wasn't that the scariest fucking thing of all? A monster hidden behind a human facade.

"What is wrong with me?" I asked, my voice barely above a whisper.

Moira came up behind me, pressing her small palm on my shoulder. "Nothing. You're still you. Just a little, um, scarier."

As we stood there, the black faded from my eyes. "Moira, I'm scared."

"I know, sweetie. We'll figure it out."

"I don't want to hurt anyone. I mean . . . not innocent people. Just the bad guys."

"You won't. I swear. I think you might just be coming into your power, you know? Everything hit at once. Your wolf, your mom, the visions. It's a lot. And bear in mind, you haven't hurt anyone who didn't have it coming."

I thought back to Callie, who had actively been trying to kill me, to the hunter who kidnapped us I'd left eviscerated on the dirty warehouse floor. They'd been trying to hurt me and the people I loved.

"I need to turn myself in to the headmistress."

"What? Why?" She didn't even try to hide her shock.

"Because I'm pretty sure I've been inadvertently summoning these demons. If she has me under lock and key, she can give everyone back their magic. Kingston can shift and heal. I'll be safe from myself. You can change your hair."

I reached out and twirled a long lock in my fingers.

"It's not you. I'd know."

"How?"

She shrugged, looking so tiny and so fierce. "I just would. Dark magic has an oily aura it leaves behind. I'd feel it on you when I touched you. Right now, I feel lots of conflicting energy, but not darkness."

Her calm assurance brought tears to my eyes. I rarely cried, but I seemed to be a human sprinkler today. Moira was right, though. The last few days had been a lot. I don't think I'd really had a chance to process any of it. I was a damn mess.

"See. This is why you can't leave me for a bunch of men. Who will talk you off the ledge when things get crazy?" Moira's gentle gaze told me she was only teasing.

"I told you we already decided you'd have your own room."

She wrinkled her nose. "On the other end of the house, right? I don't want an accidental strip show. I've already seen Kingston's elephant trunk waving in the breeze."

Just because joking with her like this made me feel normal, I couldn't resist tormenting her a little more. "Wait until you see Alek's God Rod."

Moira gagged. She actually gagged, which in turn made my stomach roll as nausea hit me hard and fast.

"Oh, don't do that, please."

"What? Vomit?"

In the mirror, I caught sight of my complexion, pale and tinged a little green. "Yeah. You'll make me puke."

"Aw, I didn't know you were a sympathetic puker."

"Me either," I said, clutching my stomach.

"Sorry. I'll stop."

I closed my eyes and took a few deep breaths until my belly stopped trying to revolt. "I need to go talk to the head-mistress."

"Not yet. Don't throw yourself on the fire until we know what's really going on. I have an idea."

I cocked a brow. "I'm listening."

"Alek mentioned you talked with Kingston's cousin."

"Dylan, yes."

"Call him. Tell him what's happened. Or better yet, call Kingston's father. The minute Ronin Farrell hears his son is being forced to suffer, he'll insist she drop the wards."

"You beautiful genius."

She beamed. "Thank you. I accept." Snagging my phone off the charger, she handed it to me. "Go on. I'll wait."

I didn't have Kingston's father's number, but I pulled up my newly added contact for Dylan and called him, nerves jangling in every cell.

He answered after three rings, just when I was about to give up. "Hey there, darlin'. To what do I owe this pleasure?"

His warm voice made me smile, setting me at ease, just like it had the last time we spoke. "Bad news. Kingston's hurt, and he can't shift and heal himself."

"Fuck. Are you serious? Why can't he shift?"

"There have been demon attacks. The headmistress has locked down all magic. None of us can shift."

"What do you want me to do?" The resolve in his tone comforted me instantly.

"I know you don't exactly talk to your uncle, but—"

"Consider it done. Your headmistress is in for a rude awakening."

Relief made me lightheaded, and I sat down with a

breathless laugh. "Thank you, Dylan. I know we haven't met—"

"You're family. That's all that matters. Now I best go make that call. I'll let you know once it's done."

He hung up without waiting for me to say goodbye, and I simply sat, staring at the phone, praying he was successful. Kingston was a sitting duck right now, and none of us knew when the next attack was going to happen.

"Darlin'?"

I shrugged. "He's a cowboy."

"Just how big is this harem of yours going to get?"

Laughing, I shook my head. "I can't handle any more than what I have."

"Uh huh. That's what you say now, but what happens when the next sexy beast comes into town?"

"Trust me. Four dicks is enough."

She wrinkled her nose, making me laugh. "Why don't you get some rest? You look like you're dead on your feet. I'll wake you up if anyone calls."

I laid down on top of my blankets, exhaustion settling over me the moment my head hit the pillow. Before long, the tendrils of sleep wove their way into my mind, taking me under into another kind of torment.

My dreams.

THIRTY-SIX

SUNDAY

I hated my fucking dreams. Even now, in the middle of one, I knew it wasn't going to be good. I balanced on the edge of knowing this wasn't real and falling into the abyss.

I didn't recognize this place. The white and black marble floors echoed with the sound of my footsteps as I walked down a seemingly endless hallway. Gossamer curtains fluttered in an invisible wind, the scenery outside the same rolling green hills and craggy cliffs that greeted me the night Caleb broke my heart.

Before the pain of his absence could grip me fully, the thin wails of a baby crying sent my pulse racing.

"Hello?" I glanced around, searching for any other sign of life and coming up short.

Why was there a baby here?

What little furniture there was stood covered in white sheets, like ghosts wandering the space, searching for home. Cobwebs covered every free corner, ancient and collecting dust. This was no place for a child.

The cries pierced the air once more, insistent and needy.

I moved faster, desperate to find the poor thing. Where was its mother? Who would abandon their child in a place like this? My breaths came in harsh panicked rasps as I ran toward the sound, the pull between me and the infant strong. What if something was wrong? What if I was too late?

I finally reached the end of the hallway, spilling out into a room that hadn't been there the second before my foot hit the pristine carpet. Everything in here was white. The walls, the floor, the crib. Everything except the woman in the center of the space with her back toward me. She was shrouded in blood red, a dramatic statement, appropriate for her.

"Mother?"

She turned in slow motion, the red gown cutting into the white room as though she'd been sliced into it with a knife, beautiful and bloody.

A gasp was torn from my throat. Not because of her presence here. She was a foregone conclusion in my dreams these days. But because of the baby cooing in her arms.

"What are you doing to her?"

My mother stared down at the child, expression softer than I'd ever seen. "She was all alone. She needed me." She stroked one finger over the chubby little cheek before booping the baby's nose.

This was wrong. This was all wrong.

My mother, my very *not* maternal mother, should not be anywhere near an innocent child.

But I couldn't remember why. My thoughts were cloudy in this dream world. I knew that my mother made me uneasy, but not the reason for the sheer panic spiraling through me.

"What is this place?"

"Why, it's your home, of course."

I shook my head. "No. I've never been here before. I don't know what you're talking about."

"You will."

The infant gurgled, and my eyes dropped back down to her bundled form. Then she began to cry, her high-pitched thready sobs stabbing me in the chest. My breasts ached, suddenly heavy, nipples tingling in response to the cries of hunger. Then and there, I knew the truth but couldn't admit it.

"Who is she?"

My mother was slow to look up, mischief dancing in her eyes. "Darling Sunday, don't you recognize your own daughter?" She tsked. "What kind of mother are you? Leaving her unattended for just anyone to happen upon."

Palm sliding over my belly, I sucked in a sharp breath. "Give her to me."

A wicked smirk twisted my mother's lips. "No. I don't think you're ready quite yet."

My panic only grew at her refusal. "I said give her to me. Now."

My mother's face hardened into a horrific visage I hadn't seen before. The promise of carnage and brutal violence shone in her eyes. "A gift such as this must arrive at the requisite time. Patience is a virtue, after all. Just ask your priest."

"Give me my fucking daughter."

A cackle came from her throat, villainous and terrible. "If you want her, you'll have to get to her first."

I lunged for my baby, desperate to touch her, to make sure she was all right. I needed to see her, to look into her eyes. Each step that should have brought me nearer at a rapid speed seemed to cause the distance to grow instead of lessening. Inch by inch, I drew closer, and the blanket began to fall away from where it had obscured her face. I was almost there. I reached out, ready to take her.

Before my hand brushed against the soft cotton, the image of my mother vanished, only to be replaced by my night-darkened bedroom. I was awake and alone, breathing hard, tears dripping down my cheeks.

"Moira?" I called, my voice cracking in a mix of fear and distress as I turned on my bedside lamp.

What I saw couldn't possibly be real. I couldn't be . . . I wasn't . . . there was no way.

Wild sex aside, I'd been taking my suppressants religiously. They were supposed to prevent this from happening.

So I couldn't be pregnant.

I couldn't.

I reached up and cupped my breasts, the memory of needing to feed my child still burning in my mind. But nothing was out of the ordinary.

"Why are you cupping your tits?" Moira asked as she came back into the room through the bathroom door.

I shook violently. "Nightmare."

"Was someone after your boobs?"

"Kind of?"

She shrugged. "Sounds like a typical day at the office." Padding to the kitchenette, she began filling the kettle.

"What are you doing?"

"Tea. I can't sleep, so I'm making tea. Want some?"

I nodded and swung my legs to the side of the bed before standing. God, I was fucking woozy. My stomach churned, my head throbbed.

"You don't look so hot."

Sucking in a huge breath, I gave her the truth. We'd

weathered this particular storm together before. No point hiding it now. "I think I need to take a test."

Her face scrunched for one second. "A test? Are you still sleeping?" But then she blinked, her face draining of color. "Shit, Sunday, I thought we talked about this."

She grabbed me by the elbow and ushered me into the bathroom. Despite her words, her touch was gentle. She was in full caregiver mode. She pulled one of the spare pregnancy tests from the cabinet and handed the box to me.

"Aren't you taking your pills?"

"Yes. It was just . . . this dream felt so real."

Her eyes widened. "You dreamed you were pregnant?"

"I saw the baby. I felt it."

I took the test out of the box and had to fight the wave of anxiety crashing through me before I could tear open the package.

"I'll just be in the kitchen." Moira crept out of the bathroom carefully, as though any sudden movements might break me.

Pulling my pajama shorts down, I did my business and set about waiting. My palms were sweaty, my stomach a roiling ball of nerves. In short, I was freaking the fuck out. I did my best to block my emotions from Noah because the last thing I needed was a panicked vampire at my side right now.

My feet bounced, tapping out a soft beat on the tiled floor as I waited. My brain was surprisingly empty. I wasn't able to think about anything other than what the results of the test would be.

Not how I'd feel about it. Not how my mates would feel about it. And definitely not why I was dreaming about babies in the first place.

369

A soft knock on the door had me glancing up as Moira peeked in with a mug of tea in her hands. She offered it with a gentle smile.

"Anything?"

I winced. "I haven't looked."

"Want me to?"

Nodding, I brought the cup to my lips and inhaled the soothing chamomile scent.

Moira carefully picked up the test, holding it between her fingers. I stared at her face, trying to read the answer through her expression alone. After a second, she set the test back down.

"Well?"

She beamed at me. "Not pregnant."

Tears streamed down my cheeks without my permission. I couldn't tell if I was relieved or sad. A torrent of emotions hit me all at once. "It was so real. She was real."

"Hold up. Do you *want* to be pregnant?"

"No. Not yet. It's not the right time. But eventually, yes."

"Then why are you so upset? This is good news."

"I know. It's just . . . I saw my daughter, Moira. She was right there and she was crying for me, and there was nothing I could do to save her. My mother had her, was keeping her from me—" The words came faster and faster until I was hyperventilating and she took the mug from me.

"Sit down. Slow your breathing. You're going to pass out."

I did, working to calm myself as she rubbed my temples. A loud banging on the front door had us both jerking our attention out into the hall.

"Who the fuck is that?" Moira grumbled.

I knew. It was one of them. Maybe all of them. I'd lost control of myself and was sure I'd dropped my walls.

"Let me in, Sunday. I'll stand here all night if I have to," Alek's voice boomed.

Moira glanced at me. "I'll send him away."

"No, don't. It's okay." The thought of his strong arms around me sounded pretty perfect right about now. I always felt safe with Alek around.

She eyed the test she'd set back on the counter. "You going to mention that?"

"No."

She picked it up and tossed it into the trash, then unrolled some toilet paper, crumpled it, and added that to the top. "There. No one will know."

I stood on shaky legs and walked to the front door.

"Sunny, please," Alek said, his voice softer this time.

Opening the door, my gaze found his piercing blues, and the relief that filled his face made my heart lighter. He didn't give me an inch. He simply strode inside, wrapped me in his embrace, and held me close.

"I felt your fear," he mumbled, his cheek pressed against the top of my head. "I had to see for myself that you were okay. What happened?"

"Nightmare."

I couldn't trust myself to say more than that. Thankfully, Alek didn't seem to require further explanation. With a slight nod to Moira, he hefted me up in his arms and carried me back to my bed, laying me down with a reverence that made my belly flip.

"Then I'll lay here and watch over you until the sun rises. Monsters won't dare to disturb you while I'm here."

And fuck if I didn't believe him.

CHAPTER
THIRTY-SEVEN
SUNDAY

"I hate you," I said through my heaving breaths as I worked to keep up with the Norse god running in front of me.

Alek stopped, a boyish grin on his handsome face. "That's not hate you're feeling, Sunny."

Since he stopped I didn't feel bad about bending over at the waist, glaring at him with my hands on the tops of my thighs as I tried to catch my breath. "Don't be so sure about that, Loki. You fuck like a champion, but I'm ready to push you off a cliff right about now."

"Oh, she's talking dirty. Bringing out my government name."

I laughed, then coughed because my lungs weren't ready for any more exertion. "Government?"

"You know, official. Like on those birth certificates of yours. Ridiculous practice. Writing it down on a piece of paper doesn't make it real. The fucking baby does. I don't have a birth certificate, but I'm here. I exist."

I shook my head. "You're ridiculous."

"And you have spaghetti arms."

"Rude. No need to get personal."

"I thought we were simply stating the obvious."

"I do not have spaghetti arms."

He sauntered over, lifting my arm from the wrist and immediately letting go. Laughing when it fell limply to my side.

"Well, you have . . . um . . . great big tree trunk arms."

Alek flexed. "I really do."

"Humble."

"You're the one who brought it up. I'm simply agreeing with you."

"Is everyone in your family this . . . honest?"

"Everyone but my brother Tor. I sometimes wonder if Odin bestowed our gifts incorrectly."

I cocked a brow. "So he's the mischief maker?"

"The liar." He wrapped his arm around my shoulders and tugged me close. "I'll never lie to you, Kærasta."

I gave him a sweaty one-armed hug. Hardly sexy, but no less grateful. "I appreciate that about you. Any more tidbits I should know about the other Nordsons?"

"My father is basically a king, even though he originally turned down the title. That makes me a prince." He waggled his eyebrows.

"Great, just what I need. Two princes."

Alek waved a hand. "Blackthorne isn't a real prince."

"Apparently neither are you, and you're still trying to claim the title."

He released me before his palm connected with my ass, making a little squeak of protest fall from my lips. "Run home, Sunny. Before I catch you and put that pretty mouth of yours to use elsewhere."

Flutters shot through my belly. "Don't threaten me with a good time."

He growled, a perfect imitation of Kingston's Alpha growl, and it had my wolf perk up and take notice. She may not be able to come out and play, but she was intrigued by the blond Norseman who sounded so much like her mate.

Thinking of Kingston, my playful smile slipped. "Actually, I should probably head over and see how King is doing."

"Oh, so he gets to be a king, but I can't be a prince?"

"I didn't say you couldn't." Leaning close, he ducked his head and claimed my lips in a sweet kiss. "I enjoyed waking with you in my arms this morning. We should do that more often."

"Blackthorne mentioned looking into a place for all of us. It could be a daily thing soon enough."

A twist of excited energy unfurled in my belly. "You'd want that?"

"Any excuse to see you naked is high on my list of things to do."

I rolled my eyes. "Men are all the same. Show them a pair of tits, and they're happy."

I attempted to turn on my heel and flounce away, but Alek caught my wrist and spun me around. He was pressed right against me, forcing me to tip my head back to meet his gaze. His eyes devoured me as he grasped my chin with his thumb and forefinger.

"I intend to spend the rest of my life with you, Kærasta. I don't care who else shares our walls. I intend to share your bed. And your days. And your nights. You are mine. Where you go, I follow."

"Just like that?" I asked a bit breathlessly.

"Just like that."

I couldn't hide my grin. "Okay, someone put his swoony pants on this morning."

He kissed the top of my head and patted my ass gently this time. "Go check on the wolf. I'll find you later."

I still had butterflies the size of hamburgers flapping around in my stomach, so I knew my smile was a little dazed. As I nodded my agreement, he walked away in the direction of his favorite training spot.

My Viking was a swoony motherfucker. Who'd have guessed?

I'd have put my money on Noah being the one who busted out roses and poetry, but all my men seemed to have inherited the gene.

Well, except for the priest. But we weren't thinking about him right now. He was dead to me. Sort of. My heart hadn't exactly gotten the memo yet, but we were working on it.

With my chin held high and my ponytail swinging, I strode confidently in the direction of Blackthorne Hall.

I cut through a courtyard, walking around the fountain and giving Persephone a little wave as I did. When I reached the shaded walkway that would lead me to the hall, a hand reached out and pulled me deeper into the shadows.

"What the fuck, Caleb?" I exploded. "You can't just keep doing that. It's rude. And creepy."

"You've never complained before. You must not remember just how much you enjoy it when I steal you away to dark corners."

"Maybe before you did your ghost impression. I'm less of a fan of all things *you* these days." I crossed my arms over my chest, trying to put more space between us because damn him, he was right.

"I'm doing the right thing. Trust me. This is what needs to happen."

"Screw you and your self-righteous sermon. You don't get to decide that for me. You don't get to put your dick—"

His hand shot out, wrapping over my mouth, but I was pissed, so I licked him until he let me go with an annoyed grunt.

"I gave you what you needed. Served you when nothing else would help. I never promised you anything more than that. It can't happen again. It won't."

"Yeah, I read your note. I got the message."

He dragged his fingers through the wavy mess of dark hair I loved so much. Then he sighed. "It was a coward's way out, I know."

"You think? And here I thought you were the grown-up."

His eyes hardened. "I'll not be lectured by you, Miss Fallon. I'm here to check and make sure you're well and to deliver a message."

"You sure you don't want to leave it on the edge of my bed? Or better yet, slide it under my door so there's no chance of running into me at all. You don't want to risk me accidentally falling on your dick. Tell me, Caleb, why go face to face when you're such a master of the written word?"

His jaw ticked as he clenched against whatever retort was on his lips. Then he looked away from me, his whole body tight. "Tonight at moonrise, the headmistress will be lifting the magic ban on Kingston. So he can shift and heal."

My heart leapt. "She is? That's fantastic."

"Don't get excited. It's going straight back on him as soon as he's done."

"Maybe she shouldn't be so hasty. Clearly this plan of hers isn't working as well as she'd hoped."

"That's not for us to decide."

I wiggled my way past him and tried to get free, into the beam of morning sunlight where he couldn't continue to break my heart with his proximity. Part of me wanted to confide in him about my dreams, about the fears I had of my origins, who I might be. What I might be doing. Instead, I shut down and closed off that part of myself he'd once held in the palm of his hand. I trusted him to keep my heart safe once, and he'd thrown it right back in my face. I wouldn't give him the chance to do it again.

Before he could say anything else, I gave him a sarcastic little salute. "Thanks for the news, Father. Next time, send me a text. Or better yet, anyone else."

I'd only just fought my tears back by the time I reached Kingston's door. Letting myself in, I spied Chad sitting on the couch in the living room, his phone in his beefy hand, a scowl on his face.

I simply headed for the door to Kingston's room, needing to get inside and see my mate, but the guard I'd assumed wasn't paying attention stopped me.

"You can't go in there."

I scowled. "What? I'm his mate. Of course I can."

"No. I'm his guard, and I say you can't."

"Listen, Chad. You can try to stop me, but Kingston will be very unhappy with you if you do."

"Doubt that. He's the one who said no visitors."

"He didn't mean me."

"I wouldn't be so sure. He doesn't sleep when you're around. He's too busy trying to impress you by playing the Alpha, but he can't heal without his wolf, and he's in pain when he's not asleep. Some mate you are, making him suffer like that."

"What?" I couldn't believe what I was hearing. Kingston hadn't said a word.

"The doctor has been in three times trying to do something about the infection. If he doesn't heal soon, he might make a turn for the worse. So, little wolf girl, let. Him. Sleep."

"Can you at least tell him I stopped by?"

Chad smirked. "Sure will. Now get out of here before he wakes up and smells you. You reek of pheromones and . . . Viking."

I blinked at the beta. It was about the only thing he could have said to me that would have made me walk away without seeing Kingston. But thanks to my run-in with the Mr. Darcy of priests, I knew Kingston would be able to shift tonight. I could wait. I'd see him later. He'd get better, and we'd put all of this behind us.

I made my way to my floor, laughing a little as I wondered if Noah might pop out of the elevator and make my mate run in a full sweep. But he didn't.

Probably for the best, I was still sweaty from my run with Alek. I opened the door to find Moira still in bed. She lifted her eye mask with one hand as she groaned and flailed dramatically.

"Wake up, sleepyhead, the sun is shining and the birdies are singing."

"Oh, look, another lovely morning. It makes me sick."

THIRTY-EIGHT

KINGSTON

My chest felt like it had been carved like a fucking pumpkin. A deep ache blended with the burning pull of tight, slowly healing skin. My meds must have worn off. Fuck. I'd never been hurt like this. Not for this long without being able to shift and heal.

On shaky legs, I shuffled out of my bedroom and into the living space. I'd never been as thankful to have gotten one of the apartment-style dorms as I was now. My pack members shouldn't have to see me like this unless I wanted them to. I thought about Sunday's room, small and shared with the witch, and shook my head. No. That would never work in my situation.

Chad looked up as I came into the room. "You shouldn't be up."

"I can't be in that bed."

"Dude, you look like you're about to keel over." He jumped up and made like he was going to grab me, but I glared at him, stopping him in his tracks.

"You touch me, and I'll knee you in the balls."

The dickhead had the audacity to smirk. "You really think you have the strength or balance for that?"

"Enough for that."

He barked out a laugh. "Please be my guest. You're as weak as a damn pup. I'd love to watch you fall on your ass."

Fucker might have a point, but I still managed a growl anyway. Sweat dotted my brow, and my knees were starting to wobble. I dared him to say anything as I leaned my back against the wall to help support my weight.

"You need some more meds?"

I shook my head, even though fuck, yes, I did. "It makes my head foggy as shit. My senses are fucked."

"How?"

"Well, like right now I smell Sunday, but she hasn't been here in what, a couple of days?" I looked to Chad for confirmation. It was hard to keep track of time when I kept going in and out of consciousness.

"Yeah, something like that."

"I should call her. Something might be wrong." I glanced around the space, searching for my phone. "Where the fuck is my phone?"

"It was smashed in the fight. Fucking obliterated."

Crap.

"Besides, she's fine. She's been all over Blackthorne. They're moving in together."

Wait. What?

"When did that happen?" Jealousy hit me like a lash from a whip.

Chad lifted one shoulder in a shrug. "How the fuck should I know? I've been here with you."

"Then how do you know they're moving in?"

"I overheard him ask her on my way to the gym when Derek took over for me. She seemed really happy about it. I don't know why living with a leech would make her happy, but I don't understand her at all anyway."

A part of me seethed at the shitty way he was talking about my mate. The other part was too busy being ripped to shreds by irrational jealousy. She was mine every bit as much as his. He shouldn't have more access to her than I did.

"She's mine," I growled without thinking.

"Doesn't look like it."

"She wears my mark."

"And a vamp's."

I snarled at him. He was just stating the facts, but I didn't appreciate his honesty right now.

"And I'm pretty sure she and that Viking got matching tattoos. I saw him at the gym with fresh ink down his side. Looks a lot like the tat on her arm."

My stomach clenched. "What tat? Sunday doesn't have any ink."

His brow lifted. "Yeah, dude, she sure fuckin' does." He trailed one finger along the inside of his bicep. "Runes or some shit. They look like smaller versions of his."

What the fuck? No wonder she hasn't stopped by; she's been too busy running around with everyone else. Probably hadn't thought of me once.

Had I lost her already?

"She marked him?" I said, more to myself than to Chad.

"Looks like it. Fuck, dude. I'd be pissed if my mate gave some other jerkoff her mark before she returned mine."

I flinched. I hadn't told anybody about that, not that it was easy to miss the lack of bite on my neck. "We've got time. I didn't want to rush her."

"Seven fucking years isn't rushing."

"Well, it's not like Sunday really marked Nordson. It's just a tat. It doesn't mean anything."

"Yeah, okay, buddy. Keep telling yourself that while she makes a fool of you."

I gritted my teeth against the urge to take a swing at him, but he wasn't wrong. Also, I didn't have the strength to hurt him.

"Look, you're gonna be better soon. One night under the moon in your wolf form, and you'll be good as new. Then maybe she'll come around. She clearly forgot the whole for better or for worse part of being a mate."

"It's not like we made vows to each other."

"Doesn't matter. She's your mate. She should know better. Or at least fucking act like you matter. I don't know how you stand it, dude. Your girl, rubbing all up on these other guys. Putting out for them. Seems like some bullshit to me."

I grabbed him by the collar of his stupid yellow polo shirt and pulled him in, fury winning out over my self-control. "Don't. Talk. About. Her. Not ever again."

Chad took me by the wrist and removed my grip easily, but he backed down all the same. "Sorry, man. Just telling you what other people are saying. Didn't mean to strike a nerve."

"Yes, you did, you prick."

"Truth hurts. Speaking of truth, you're fucking ripe, dude. Think you can manage alone in the shower?"

"Why? You offering to wash my balls, bro?"

He shrugged. "I've done worse."

I grabbed a pillow off the couch and smacked him in the head with it. "Fuck off. I can wash my own balls."

"Glad to hear it. Just don't jack off in there. You might pass out, and I draw the line at touching your jizz."

I couldn't respond because if I did, he'd hear how much pain I was in after hitting him with the pillow. Moonrise couldn't come soon enough.

Carefully, I made my way to the bathroom, thankful for the fact that we didn't have a tub, just a shower. I wasn't sure if I'd be able to step over anything higher than this.

I turned on the water and cranked up the heat until steam filled the room. The spray was hot enough to scald, but I didn't turn it down. I needed the sting of pain if only to offset how fucking torn up my insides were. And I wasn't talking about the cut over my chest. Hearing everything Chad had to say about Sunday had me reeling.

Despite all the assurances she made to me, she still hadn't done the one thing a mate should do for her other half. I expected she'd come to it on her own; instinct should drive her to want to mark me as hers.

I hadn't thought about it too much, just being with her felt fucking amazing after the way things had been just a few months ago. But hearing about her and Thorne and her marking herself with something distinctly Alek's had all the old insecurities rearing their heads. Why them and not me?

Didn't she want me? Or was she still fighting against her wolf?

I shook my head, trying to clear the intrusive thoughts. Standing under the water, I let the heat wash over my body, hissing with every rivulet that ran over the raw healing wound. Even still, the memory of being with Sunday had my cock jerking. I'd been tortured by fever dreams of her, waking up hard, wishing she'd do something to ease the ache, but knowing beyond all doubt that wouldn't happen. I couldn't. Not until I was healed. Maybe that was part of this. I knew I couldn't serve her as her mate should.

I was weak. Less than. Not deserving of her. Especially

since Blackthorne could give her what she needed. So could Alek. Fuck, even the damned priest could give her more than I was able to right now. No wonder she'd abandoned me.

Resting my fists against the wall, I hung my head, the water running down my face. Embarrassment and shame swirled inside me as tears pricked my eyes. At least no one was here to witness me falling the fuck apart. All this time I'd never shed a single fucking tear over her.

But this . . . her choosing them over me? It was the thing that was going to destroy me. And there was nothing I could fucking do about it.

A swirl of blood ran to the drain, mixing with the water, and I cursed under my breath. I'd probably torn my stitches. I hated this. Hated being broken. Being less than what she needed. Knowing she was happy with them while I was here alone. Hurting. Wanting only her.

But it wouldn't be long before I was back to my true self. I'd be healed and whole, and then I'd tell her she had to make a choice. Because I couldn't go on like this. The laughing stock of my pack. She was my mate.

Mine.

And I wouldn't give her up without a fight.

THIRTY-NINE

I stared down at my phone, pacing back and forth across my room, frustration mounting with every passing moment. He hadn't answered any of my messages. Was Kingston still sleeping? He shouldn't be sleeping this much, should he?

Me: How are you feeling?

Me: Are you awake?

Me: I need to see you. Please let me know when you feel up to a visit.

Me: Kingston.

Nothing except that little notification under my messages that said, *read.*

Me: If you're going to leave me on read, you should just turn off your fucking phone.

Three little dots appeared, dancing on my screen and telling me he was typing. And my stupid heart did a somersault. Well, at least that one seemed to have gotten his attention.

Good. I wasn't going to sit around playing these games with a grown-ass man. One fragile male ego was more than I could handle in a day, and after Caleb's nonsense, the last thing I needed was Kingston backsliding into old patterns.

Especially when I hadn't done anything to deserve it.

King: I don't know what to say to you.

Me: What the hell is that supposed to mean?

King: I just don't want to see you right now.

Me: What? WHY?

King: Because this whole thing is your fault, and the longer I sit here stuck in this fucking bed, the more pissed I am about it.

Me: I don't understand.

King: You're a liability, Sunshine. I don't think right when you're in my head, taking up space. It damn near got me killed.

A knife to the chest would've been less painful. He couldn't have known it, but he'd just thrown my grandfather's words back at me. He'd softened the blow some, but not by much. And it fucking *hurt* coming from him.

Me: I'm sorry. I've been trying to give you alone time so you can rest and heal. I'm just worried about you. I needed to know you were okay.

King: Panic texting me four times in a row sure looks like it. It's fucking desperate. You aren't getting enough attention from your other fuckboys?

Me: EXCUSE ME.

King: You read that right.

Me: What the fuck is wrong with you? Did you fall down and hit your head or something? What's this bullshit really about, Kingston?

King: I'm done. I never wanted to share you in the first place. Do me a favor, stop hanging around outside my door like a bitch in heat. We already handled that. I don't want to see you anymore. You have plenty of other willing dicks you can use.

My heart cracked open. First Caleb, now Kingston. My throat tightened, angry tears clawing their way up, trying to break free.

This was such bullshit.

Me: Stop it. You don't mean that.

King: I think I know what I feel better than you.

Me: You told me you loved me.

King: I lied. I just wanted to fuck you and leave you. Just like you left me. How's it feel now that the shoe's on the other foot?

Me: Fuck you, Kingston.

King: No thanks. Already been there. Didn't enjoy it the first time.

Hot tears blurred my vision. I screamed in rage as I hurled my phone against the wall, my wolf just as angry, desperate to get out and run. Why was this happening? I'd finally brought them together, started to feel whole.

My front door burst open, a hulking Viking and angry vampire prince standing there, gazes trained on me with laser focus.

They spoke at the same time.

"What's the matter?"

"Who hurt you?"

The two of them were at my side in the blink of an eye, each with a tender hand touching me.

My voice wavered. "I think Kingston just broke things off. With a fucking text message."

Noah's brows pulled together. "He can't have done. That doesn't seem like him."

I let out a bitter laugh. "Really? It seemed just like him to me. The old him anyway. Angry at the world. Hateful."

Alek trailed the pad of his thumb over my cheek to wipe away a tear. "We'll get to the bottom of this. If he thinks he can break your heart and get away with it, he clearly hasn't been paying attention."

Noah reached for me, pulling me toward him so he could tuck me against his chest. "If he wants to end things, he owes you the courtesy of having that conversation with you in person."

"I don't want to look at him right now."

"You don't have to," Alek said soothingly.

"It might be better if you do. It would make you feel better to clear matters up. Or, if he really does want out, then he can fuck off. Alek and I will take care of you."

The thought of seeing Kingston right now tore me in two directions. On one hand, I wanted to give him a piece of my mind, show him what he was throwing away. On the other, I might not be able to see him without breaking down. For all his jealousy, he still owned so much of me. How could he not understand that? What had changed between me leaving his bed and now?

I wiped away the tears still trailing down my cheeks. "You're right. I need to hear him say it. Otherwise a part of me will always feel like maybe there was something else I could have done. And when you love somebody, you fight for them, right? Even when they act like total assholes."

Alek cupped my cheek and leaned close, kissing my temple. "That's right. We fight."

"Come on, we'll go with you."

"That way we can punch him in the throat if he gets out of line," Alek said with a grin just a little too bloodthirsty for his words to be a joke.

"He's not in his room. Moonrise was five minutes ago. The headmistress lifted the ban for him so he could shift and heal." I glanced at the window where, even covered by clouds, the moon made the sky glow.

"Lead the way then, dove."

The three of us walked hand in hand down to the clearing. We arrived just in time to see figures standing in shadow, my gaze immediately locking on Kingston as he pulled a pair of sweats up over his hips.

As hurt as I was, I couldn't deny the flutter of arousal the sight of his mostly naked body triggered. His gorgeous chest was on full display, healed and perfect, and the sight brought no small amount of relief to me. The light of the moon as it peeked out of the clouds caught on the nipple piercings I loved to swirl my tongue around and tug on with my teeth.

Taking a deep breath, I willed myself to focus and stop thinking with my vagina.

"Wow. Way to show up for your mate," Derek said, standing off to the side and looking at me with far more ice than I'd ever seen in his expression. He tossed Kingston a shirt, but my surly wolf didn't bother covering himself.

"I figured you'd skip it tonight, Sunshine. I'm surprised to see you here." Kingston's voice was cold and detached, a note of hurt hiding in the depths.

"After the shit you said to me in your texts, it can't come as that much of a surprise."

His brows snapped together. "What texts?"

"Cute, Kingston. Playing dumb in front of your friend. Nice, real mature."

Derek stiffened, his eyes flitting from me to his Alpha. "Do you two need some privacy? I'm picking up some serious tension."

"We're not going anywhere," Alek said, arms crossed over his chest.

"You can go. They're no danger." Kingston draped the shirt across his shoulders like it was a towel, somehow looking even hotter than before.

With one hesitant look back, Derek left, the silence between the four of us deafening.

"What were you saying about text messages?"

"Come on, Kingston. Grow up."

His eyes narrowed, temper leaking into the hazel depths. "You're the one playing fucking games. My phone was destroyed in the fight. I don't know what fucking messages you're talking about because I didn't send them."

The ache in my heart intensified, but not because I was sad. I was so flooded with relief my knees buckled, and Alek put an arm around me to keep me steady. He always seemed to sense my emotions before I could process them.

Kingston's gaze tracked our movements, jealousy turning his irises so dark they were nearly black.

"King, please stop this. I don't know why you've started acting like this again. We had it all figured out. Things were good. Amazing. What happened?"

"I'm not doing anything, Sunshine. I've been in bed for days."

"I know that, asshole. I was there with you for most of them."

"Most," he agreed, the word oddly weighted. As if it was significant somehow.

"Yeah, most."

"If our roles were reversed, I never would've left you." His eyes blazed with accusation, and Noah slipped his palm across my shoulder, fingers trailing over the mark before he gently massaged the nape of my neck.

"She was a wreck when she left you. I found her walking alone, beside herself. It was all I could do just to get her to go to her room and shower."

Kingston's focus landed on Noah's hand around the back of my neck. "But she had enough energy to go brand herself with a tattoo? Don't lie for her."

"What? That happened before you got hurt. The only

reason I didn't come back is when I tried to visit you Chad sent me away saying that's what you wanted. Even then, I tried again, but he sent me away *every* time I came to see you."

His gaze narrowed as those words landed. I could tell he was warring with himself as my statement brought to light something he never considered. That one of his pack mates might not want me around. He gritted his teeth and growled, eyes glowing amber.

"Fucking Chad. I'll deal with him later." He looked into my eyes, hurt still swimming in the depths. "But why do you think he'd keep you away?"

"He's an asshole? Most Chads are."

"Or maybe he's protecting his Alpha from a mate who doesn't seem to understand devotion."

"What are you really angry about, Kingston? You've never doubted Sunday like this before." Alek's voice cut through the pettiness of our argument, and I was thankful for it because the fact that Kingston came to Chad's defense hurt.

Kingston started to pace, raking his hands through the thick locks of his golden hair and tugging hard. I could tell he was losing control, fighting against his wolf and trying to stop it from taking over. There was only one explanation for such a battle between beast and man. Emotional turmoil. And I was the cause . . . Again.

Please don't run. I willed the thought to take shape and find him. If he ran, I'd lose him. My wolf let out a mournful howl inside my consciousness, and as though he heard it, he snapped his attention to me.

It didn't look like he was going to answer, his eyes hard and the lines of his face drawn with tension. And then it all crumbled, anger shattered by his pain, his shoulders slumping, hands balling into fists at his sides.

"She claimed you both."

All the air left my lungs at the broken, hollow sound in his voice.

"She claimed you as well," Noah said.

"No. It's different for shifters. It's not as simple as a tattoo or a little blood. She let me mark her, but . . ."

Realization had me pulling out of the arms of the two men at my side and going to my beautiful, tortured mate. "I never marked you."

He flinched as I reached for him. "Just tell me why."

"I didn't know. I wasn't taught . . ."

"You mean to tell me your father, your *grandfather* never explained how it worked? I find that hard to believe. They had us paired up from the time we were kids."

"Do you remember how I found out about my heat? My grandfather only spent time with me when it couldn't be avoided. Family heart to hearts weren't a thing for us. If he wasn't belittling me or shaming me, he was ignoring me entirely. And my father was drunk off his ass ninety percent of the time. I had no one, Kingston. No one to talk me through all the things I needed to know about being a wolf, because they didn't think it was worth it." I shoved him, not enough that he moved, but enough to make a point. "Why didn't *you* tell me?"

Guilt swam in his eyes. "I couldn't bring myself to beg you to want me again."

I cupped his cheek. "Kingston. You can't be afraid to tell me what you need. My shifter education is clearly lacking, so you're going to have to help me fill in the blanks. I need all of you to help me. I can't do any of this alone. We're supposed to be a team, but I can't be the partner you deserve if you don't help me out."

"I'm sorry," he whispered. "You deserve so much better than me."

Stepping closer, I wrapped my arms around his waist and pulled him against my body, instantly feeling more at ease because I could hear his heart beating, steady and strong, beneath my ear.

"No. That couldn't be farther from the truth. Now how do I mark you? I'll do it right here."

A deep rumble came from Kingston, the vibration rolling right through me. "It's not exactly something we should do in public. And you need to be able to shift, at least partially, to do it."

Noah stepped forward. "I might know a way around that if you're interested?"

Kingston gave him a wary nod, as if being vulnerable in front of my other two mates physically pained him.

"Go to *Iniquity*. It will provide you with privacy and a safe space. Sunday can access her magic there. It will ensure you both have everything you need and make the moment truly memorable. Like it was for us."

"Noah, that's a wonderful idea." Looking up at Kingston, I asked, "Will that work?" I hated not knowing if there was some special ceremony or circumstance that would be required. But I had to rely on my mate to teach me.

"Only if we can go right the hell now. I need this. I'm on edge and hungry for my mate."

"You're always hungry," I teased.

"It's worse now that my wolf was freed after not shifting for so long."

I smirked and rose up on my tiptoes to kiss him. "Then sneak me out of here so we can make sure you are sated."

"I'll give Lilith a call, let her know you're coming."

"Not yet, but we will be," Kingston growled in my ear. "I fucking love you, Sunshine. I'm sorry I doubted you."

"Me too. Those messages really got to me. I shouldn't have believed they were you."

"What did they say? Can I see them?"

I pulled out my phone and handed it to him. Expressions rapidly flitted across his face as he scrolled through the wall of text. Horror. Disgust. Fury. One right after the other.

"Sunshine . . ."

"It doesn't matter. I love you. And after this, I hope we never have a reason to doubt each other ever again."

CHAPTER
FORTY
KINGSTON

C had and I were going to have a little chat the next time I saw him. Punctuated by my fist in his stupid fucking face. That asshole. What the hell did he think he was doing coming between his future Alpha and his mate? He'd be lucky if he could walk by the time I was done with him.

But for now, my thoughts were on Sunday and what we were about to do. The step we were about to take.

I hadn't been to *Iniquity* since I claimed Sunday as mine in a fit of unbridled need and magic. But the room, Sunday's room, was the only place I wanted to be at the moment. The thought of her claiming me, giving me her mark where everyone could see, sent a thrill through me. I'd proudly wear her brand. Show it to anyone who asked. Take her home to my pack and prove to them I was always worthy of her love.

Sunday squeezed my hand as if she could feel the anticipation buzzing through my veins. As if she was feeling the same.

"I wonder what will be waiting for us in the room," she murmured.

"What do you mean?"

"Haven't you noticed? It's always different depending on the needs and desires of the occupants."

I hadn't, but only because until I set foot in Sunday's room, I hadn't even ventured down this hallway. I'd never been interested in intimate, private moments with the women I'd hired as poor replacements for my mate, so I'd always stayed in the public area.

She ran her thumb gently along the underside of my wrist as we walked down the long hallway of doors, and that small touch, the gesture of affection, filled me with longing. How could something as insignificant as the stroke of her thumb on my skin affect me like this?

Because you've craved it for as long as you can remember, dumbass.

The sarcastic cut of my own inner voice made my lips curl up in amusement. I was an asshole even to myself. But the truth was, Sunday owned every part of me. She could bring me to my knees if she wanted. All she had to do was ask.

I should have been scared by the thought of my submission. I'd been raised to believe that Alphas didn't bend to anyone. But I would—I have—for her.

Maybe that was the way of true mates. Hadn't my father done the same for my mother? He worshiped her. Gave in to every whim unless it was going to risk her life. They fought often, butted heads, but in a way only those closest to them would see.

To everyone else, she was a perfectly submissive Omega. Nurturing. Dutiful. Obedient. Behind closed doors, she tried and tested him. Knowing which way to turn his head if she needed to. That was how my youngest sister was born. She'd wanted another baby, but he'd said no after he'd nearly lost her in childbirth the time before. They went away for a weekend, and nine months later, Tessa—Trouble, as I called her—was born.

I wondered if it would be the same for Sunday and me. If the power dynamic between us would be in constant flux, each of us bending to the will of the other. I fucking hoped so. I'd dominate the fuck out of her, then show her my throat and let her take the reins right after. Jesus, I was rock-hard and ready just like that.

"Did you . . . not want to go inside?" Sunday asked, her voice breaking through my fantasy.

I had to clear my throat before I could answer. "Just picturing all the ways I was going to take you."

Her cheeks flushed, and her eyes darkened with desire. "Then what are you waiting for?"

Scooping her into the cradle of my arms, I carried her over the threshold and into the room I didn't plan on leaving for the next twenty-four hours. The instant we set foot inside, the space changed from four bare walls to a night garden filled with fragrant blooms, all bathed in the pale glow of the moon.

"It's so beautiful." Her voice was soft and reverent. "Perfect for this."

I wanted to tell her that she was perfect, but my throat was too tight with everything I was feeling. I could already picture her, bathed only in shadow and moonlight, filled with me, writhing in pleasure and crying out my name.

"So how do we do this?"

I smirked. "Well, we usually start by taking off our clothes. Then you lie back and—"

"And think of the queen?"

"Fuck no, Sunshine. When my dick's inside you, the only one you're allowed to think about is me. And when I make you come, it better be my name on your lips."

Her eyes sparked with lust. "Sign me up for orgasms. I want you so much, Kingston. I've been dying for you."

"I could be inside you every fucking day and still not have enough of you. It's not just my wolf who wants you. The man in me aches for you."

She reached out and trailed her fingertips over my chest, stopping just above my piercing. "Do I have to be a wolf to claim you? You weren't."

"I wasn't a man either. It was more like something in between."

"I don't know if I can partially shift—at least not on purpose. I'm sort of an all-or-nothing girl."

. "You can. Trust me. When the time is right, your wolf will take over. She'll claim what she wants."

Sunday's eyes flared with hunger as she nodded. "Then what are we waiting for?"

I couldn't ignore the throbbing of my thick cock in my pants anymore. I hadn't been inside her in too long, hadn't felt the heat of her squeezing me, milking me for all I was worth. That was over now. This time was ours, and when she marked me, any doubt of our bond would be gone.

"I can't be gentle with you," she said, her voice a throaty rasp.

"Fuck, who asked you to be, baby?"

We lunged at each other, crashing together in a tangle of limbs, mouths devouring each other.

It felt like coming home.

In mere seconds our clothes were a pile of fabric on the soft grassy ground, and I had her in my arms, her legs wrapped around my waist as I positioned myself at her welcoming entrance.

"Hold on tight," I murmured, a little breathless.

She threaded her fingers in my hair and pulled, the pain making me thrust upward as I sheathed myself inside her all the way to the hilt. Then I walked forward until her back was pressed against a thick tree trunk so I could drive deep and fill her so full she'd miss me when this was all over.

She moaned, arching her spine and pressing her tits into my chest as she raked her nails down my back. "Fuck I've missed you, Kingston. The way you fill me up. It's perfect."

"Is my mate already going to come?"

"Yes. Keep going."

I braced my palms on the tree, claws already coming out and embedding into the bark. Her legs around my waist and the drive of my hips were the only things holding her up. Her walls clenched, nipples tight points against my skin. I needed her pleasure like I needed my next breath. I wanted to smell her sex and desire, taste it in the air, worship her like the fucking goddess she was out here under the moon.

"Shift, baby. Just enough so you can bite me. I'm already so goddamned close to coming."

Her eyes were wild, her beast shining through as it took hold of her. It was fucking beautiful. She was moonlight and nature. Wild and free.

Mine.

And then she made me hers.

Sunday brought her lips down, feathering them lightly over the pulse thrashing in my throat, and then she pressed the sharp points of her fangs against my skin. Licking me once, playfully, before sinking in and marking me.

I came instantly, the pleasure erupting through me so fierce I thought I was going to break the tree in two with the force of my frantic thrusts. I needed to be deeper. All the way inside. Leaving a piece of me behind. And when she cried out and fluttered around me, that familiar pulse of her orgasm drew out every last drop I had.

"Fuck," I groaned as the release continued to roll through me. I could die like this and never even realize it.

Sunday lapped up a small trickle of blood that must have dripped from the bite. I could already feel the wound start to heal when she pressed a gentle kiss on top of it. She pulled back, cupping my face in her hands and staring deep into my eyes.

"I love you, Kingston. Always."

"I love you too, Sunshine. So fucking much."

My cock gave a happy twitch, and she moaned. "You're mine now."

"Yes. Forever."

She sighed and let her head fall back to rest on the tree, then a laugh rolled through her, and I followed her gaze.

"What?"

"There's a bed."

I chuckled, hands cupping her ass, dick still half hard and inside her. "Round two?"

She grinned. "This time I want to be on top."

I went from half hard to fucking stone at the thought. "Yes, ma'am."

I woke with Sunday in my arms, contentment unlike anything I'd ever felt filling me. At first I didn't know what woke me, but as I laid there with her sleeping peacefully beside me, I felt an inexplicable need to explore.

I trailed my fingertips across her cheek, tracing her perfect lips before murmuring, "I love you. I didn't think I could love anyone until you made me yours." I slid out of the bed, whispering, "I'll be back, beautiful."

If I'd stopped to think about why I felt the need to explore a magical room on the bottom floor of a sex club, I might have been a little more hesitant, but I couldn't explain why I felt such an intense pull. Only that I knew something was waiting for me. And this place was a sanctuary to all who came in search of their deepest desires. Nothing could happen to us here. The only real danger was losing yourself to the pleasure until you starved.

It wasn't long before I came across a gazebo. Roses and ivy crept up the wooden beams, grown so thick it appeared to be constructed out of nature itself.

This is what I was supposed to find.

I walked up the shallow staircase, discovering a glossy black grand piano in the center of the structure. It stood out in the middle of this earthen garden. Pristine and unmarked by age or abuse. The shafts of moonlight that filtered in through the open sides of the gazebo bounced off the lacquered finish on the perfect instrument. I itched to touch the heavy ivory keys, to run my fingers over their familiar texture.

Music had been my escape for as long as I can remember. A safe place to express the emotions threatening to destroy me. There was only so much I could purge from my system in my wolf form. Even after running myself near to the ground, the anger and pain lingered. Which is where music came in.

For the first time, I didn't need to purge anything. I wanted to revel in it. I couldn't help but wonder if it would feel different. Playing when I was happy and to express joy rather than to give a voice to the raw burn of my heartache.

I sat on the bench, my heart pounding with excited anticipation as I closed my eyes and slid my fingers over the keys. Then the music simply began to pour from me, the notes filling the air and floating away on the light breeze running through the garden.

The song was a familiar one, but it felt different now. It sounded . . . hopeful. No longer dark and ominous, the soundtrack to my broken dreams and shattered heart. My song had been reborn, forged not in heartbreak but in love. It was the one I'd written for Sunday. One I thought she'd never hear.

I sensed her the instant she stepped behind me, her warmth radiating straight to my soul. But when she ran her palms over my shoulders and down my chest, I damn near cried with relief at her touch.

"You don't have to try to seduce me anymore, King. I'm yours."

A laugh rumbled through me. "You think this is seduction?"

"You sitting nude at a piano, looking all broody and dark. Yeah. Seduction 101."

"I was restless. Something called me here."

"That's funny. I woke up and you were gone. I followed the music like aural breadcrumbs. Somehow I knew they'd lead me back to you."

She leaned forward, her hair tickling me as she kissed her mark. A shiver of longing ran through me, causing my cock to jerk and desire to rush to the forefront again.

"Something on your mind?" The teasing note in her voice only added to my rising hunger for her.

"There is now," I growled, twisting and grasping her hips in my hands before plopping her down on top of the piano. Her heels crashed against the keys sending a flurry of discordant notes ringing out in the night.

"Aw, but the music stopped."

"We'll make our own. The way you call out my name is my favorite song."

I skimmed my palms down her legs, my stomach clenching with anticipation at the sight of her arousal, glossy and beckoning me. My mouth fucking watered at the scent of her. Heady, more wild than usual.

"I thought about you like this a lot. Legs spread for me while I played for you."

"Oh yeah? What else happened during these fantasies of yours?"

"Usually I was punishing you," I admitted, still running my hands up and down, fingers drawing closer to her dripping center with each glide but never quite touching.

"Punishing me?"

"For not loving me. I would play for you, make you ache for me, and then not let you come."

"Ass."

I gave her a wicked grin. "I did say it was a punishment."

"Did you get to come?"

"Every fucking time. Usually all over this perfect pink cunt of yours."

She gave a little whimper as my fingers brushed the lips of her pussy. "Kingston," she whined.

"Tell me what you want." I leaned in and kissed the inside of her knee. "Tell me what to do to you."

"God," she moaned.

"I don't think He's here right now. It's just you and me."

Her eyes flicked to the side as if she was looking for something, but then I drew my fingers down her center, skimming her entrance, and her attention returned to me.

"I want your tongue. That piercing. I want you to suck on my clit until I come on your face."

A low growl rumbled from deep in my chest. "Mmmm. Then that's exactly what you'll get."

I dipped my finger inside her, making her squirm. Then I pulled it free and sucked her slick arousal from the digit, savoring the flavor of her. I didn't know if it was the completed bond or not, but she tasted incredible. Richer somehow. Like now that we were connected in the most intimate way possible, there were so many more flavors I could taste.

"Fuck," she moaned. "More."

I dove in, unable to stop myself and drag it out. My fingers slipped inside her, curling just the way she liked, hitting that special spot that made her go boneless. As my mouth latched onto her swollen clit, I had to fight a grin before I began humming my song for her. I knew exactly what I was doing. I could play her body better than any instrument.

She came hard, her orgasm flooding my fingers. As her walls fluttered and her toes curled, I released her clit and slid out of her, enjoying every bit of the slick she gave me.

What I'd only just started to tap into with that first taste of her came roaring into focus. Monumental. Life-changing. Our future.

"Sunday," I whispered, absolute reverence in my voice.

She panted as she looked down her body at me. "What is it?"

How could I tell her? Did she already know?

So many questions and emotions collided within me. The only thing I knew for certain?

Nothing would ever be the same.

"Tell me what you want." Kingston's words hit my ears as I entered my private den at *Iniquity*. I'd tried desperately to avoid coming here after the last time. My weakest moment and my most revisited memory. She was the sin I couldn't give up.

He had her spread out on a piano, legs splayed wide, body on full display. Her slick pink cunt dripping for him. "Tell me what to do to you."

"God," she moaned.

The sound of her breathy plea had me rock-hard and aching, the memory of the last time I'd heard her say the same sending a bolt of lust so potently spiraling through me I almost dropped to my knees in benediction. My cock jerked, balls tightening and throbbing.

"I don't think He's here right now. It's just you and me."

But that's not the truth, now is it?

Sunday glanced to her left, and I knew her thoughts mirrored my own. My favorite sin was searching for her confessor. Knowing she wanted me, perhaps even hoped I was here, despite the angry words she hurled my way earlier, had my cock weeping.

My palm slid down my chest, but I stopped myself just shy of my belt buckle. I would not give in. Not after I'd already broken my vow and forsaken my God for her. I was never going to free my soul from purgatory at this rate . . . but maybe having her instead was worth it.

"I want your tongue. That piercing. I want you to suck on my clit until I come on your face."

Jesus wept. How do such filthy words come out of a mouth so sweet?

A low growl rumbled from Kingston, an unwelcome reminder he was there. "Then that's exactly what you'll get."

I watched, muscles tensed in an effort to stay under control, as he dipped his finger inside her. Oh, the wolf didn't know how fecking lucky he was. Memories of her flavor burst across my tongue, almost as if I'd been the one to touch her, to taste that perfect pussy.

"Fuck," Sunday moaned. "More."

"Yes. More." My words were tight as I shook with the need to palm my cock.

Envy curled in my chest as Kingston feasted on her. The look of pure hunger flitting across her face only added to my desire. She was an angel playing the part of a damned woman, and as she reached her pinnacle, her fingers delving into his hair and pushing him closer, deeper, I couldn't keep my breaths even.

Her eyes flicked up from the man servicing her to meet mine. I knew she couldn't see me, but the almost panicked look of pleasure and the ragged moan she let out sent an unexpected and uncontrollable orgasm racing up my body.

I came in my pants like a bloody teenager, and I couldn't stop it.

As the edges of release faded, my breaths calming while I watched her, Kingston's posture tensed.

"Sunday," he whispered, shock and awe lending his voice a breathless quality.

She panted as she tore her gaze away from mine and back down to him. "What is it?"

"You . . ." He backed away and ran a hand through his hair.

"Kingston, you're freaking me out."

"How long have you known?"

No. No. No. This could not be happening. I knew with a clarity that sharpened every passing second what he was going to say, and it was the most dangerous thing he could utter.

"Known what?" Her brows knitted together in confusion too genuine to be feigned.

"You're pregnant."

A roar was ripped from my throat as I picked up the chair beside me and hurled it into the thick glass. The window shattered, shards raining down as the world as I knew it imploded.

She could not be carrying a child. The consequences were far too dire.

Fear skittered up my spine because as much as I wanted to deny it, I knew it was entirely plausible.

Worse still, there was every chance I could be the father which would place the blame for this travesty squarely on my shoulders.

My torment knew no end.

I'd failed.

My God.

My mission.

Her.

I wasn't worthy of redemption, and this proved it beyond all doubt.

With a howl of despair, I tore out of the room and knew there was nowhere on this earth far enough away to protect me from the hell that was about to be unleashed. The Society couldn't know. Not until I'd explored all options. If they found out, they'd come for her, and it wouldn't be isolation in the well. It would be death.

I'd failed her completely, but I wouldn't be the means of her destruction. Not if I could avoid it.

I couldn't stop the Seer's blood-soaked visions from coming to pass.

But fuck if I wasn't going to try.

CHAPTER

FORTY-TWO

SUNDAY

"You're pregnant."

My world stopped. I stared at Kingston, heart in my throat as an earth-shaking clap of thunder filled the air. Fat drops of rain fell from the sky, now pitch-black with clouds.

"No, I'm not. I took a test. *Two* tests."

"You suspected, and you didn't tell me?"

Crap. I bit down on my lip. "Um . . . yes? But they came back negative, so there really wasn't any point."

"What the fuck, Sunday?"

"Well, I didn't want to freak anyone out until I knew for sure. And it was only because I was having these mood swings and hadn't got my period and you know the creepy dreams."

"What dreams?" he growled.

Shit, this was really turning against me.

"Sunday. What. Fucking. Dreams?"

"I can't talk about them right now. I promise I'll tell you, but . . . not right now." Tears swam in my eyes. I wasn't really a crier . . . until recently. It all made sense now. I'd been hormonal. Kingston had filled me with his wolfy spawn. My belly lurched. Or Noah. Or Alek.

Then nausea took hold, stronger than it had over the last few weeks. I ran for the bushes, rain soaking my skin as I fell to my knees and waited to empty the contents of my stomach.

Caleb.

It could be Caleb's, and I couldn't say a damn thing.

Kingston ran his warm palm down my spine, soothing me as shudders racked my body.

"Shit. Sorry, Sunshine. I didn't mean to upset you. I don't, fuck, I don't know what to do."

"I don't know either. I did everything I was supposed to do. I took the suppressants. She said they would also act as birth control."

"They're supposed to," he confirmed. "You know I'll take care of you, right? Both of you. No kid on this fucking earth will be more loved than our baby."

I brushed back my hair and looked up at him, hating that I had to give voice to the question but needing his answer.

"What if it's not yours?"

"No matter what, if it's part of you, it's mine."

Tears clogged my throat. "Kingston."

"When did you start the suppressants?"

I got to my feet, letting him help me as the two of us walked back to the gazebo. "After the first heat."

His lips twisted into a smirk. "Well, mystery solved then." He placed his large warm palm over my lower belly. "Mine. You weren't on anything when I knotted you."

Even brimming with tension from his revelation about my pregnancy, I still got turned on instantly when he mentioned that first time I'd ridden his knot.

"But I took a test after that. And another one not long ago. They were both negative."

"Did you take a human test?"

"Yeah, is there any other kind?"

He sighed, as if this should be obvious. "Sunday . . . human tests don't work on shifters."

"But Moira—"

"Is a witch, not a shifter. She's human, with a little added flair. She wouldn't know better. This is why you should have come to me."

"Don't let her hear you call her magic a little flair. She'll castrate you."

One of his hands protectively curled around his junk. "The fuck she will. I have more babies to put inside you."

"Kingston."

"What? I'm excited, okay? I've always wanted a big family. A whole pack of our own."

My chest squeezed. "Really?"

"Yeah, of course. You carrying my pups is the hottest fucking thing I can imagine. Your body is going to be even more breathtaking because I'll know you're taking care of our baby."

"How many pups are we talking about here?"

He wrapped his arms around me and pulled me close. "At least four. Mmmm, maybe I put more than one in you this time." His cock swelled, pressing against me. "God, your tits are going to get huge."

There it was. This was Kingston talking; even his sweetness came with an edge. But I loved it. Hearing how excited he was, how badly he wanted this, took my fear away on a cloud of possibility.

Instead of worrying about who the father was or how the hell I was supposed to juggle everything, I was starting to picture a little boy with eyes the color of a summer forest. Or perhaps a sweet dimpled little girl with eyes of amber or glacial blue.

While unexpected, life-changing, and way earlier than I'd ever planned, this didn't have to be a bad or scary thing. It could be amazing.

It could be perfect.

We stood there together, me in his arms, now facing away as the two of us watched the torrential rainfall and the lighting arc through the clouds. It had been a wild raging storm when it had first begun, but now, as though linked to my own thoughts, the thunder rolled farther in the distance, the lightning strikes were less often, and the rain softened. Calming as I did.

"I don't want anyone else to know yet, Kingston. I need to figure some things out first."

He tensed behind me. "Like what?"

"What I'm going to do. How this is going to work. Take your pick."

His hand shifted back to my belly, cupping it as if he could protect the tiny bundle of cells within from whatever I was about to say. "Do about what?"

"Babies take money and time. I can only go to Ravenscroft for so long until everyone sees I got knocked up. Not to mention the logistics. How am I going to manage classes with an infant in tow? And I'll need to find a job. I don't want to go back home and rely on my family. God, can you imagine what my grandfather will say?"

Kingston relaxed at my words. "You're not in this alone, Sunshine. I already told you, I'll take care of you. How about you come home with me for the holidays and we'll figure it out there? Together."

"You want to take me home to your parents?"

He grinned. I could feel it against my mark as he nuzzled me. "Of course I do. You're my baby mama."

I groaned, but secretly loved the possessive quality of his voice. "Secret baby mama."

Those lips trailed over my mark, making me shiver. "It won't be secret for long. You'll start showing, then everyone will know what I did to you."

Heat bloomed across my skin. They would. I had to admit, that wasn't a bad thing.

"You don't want to tell Noah and Alek?"

I shook my head, knowing I wouldn't have long. Noah would be able to hear the heartbeat with his stupid vampire ears. But I wanted to hold onto this for a few days. "Not yet."

"They're not going to like that."

Shrugging, I leaned back into him. "They'll have to deal with it. I'm not going to keep it a secret for long. I just . . . I need time to let it sink in. If you hadn't been the one to sniff it out, I wouldn't tell you yet either. A woman needs time to wrap her head around something this big before other people get all up in her business about it."

A low growl of disapproval rumbled from his chest, vibrating into my back. "Sunday, you and I don't have secrets."

"Oh, stop with the Alpha bullshit. There's a tiny wolf-vampire-god growing inside me. I'm just asking for a few days. You know this isn't something I'd hide from any of you. I just don't want to"—I bit my lip—"jinx it."

"It's a wolf," he growled sulkily. "But fine, I get it. This is our secret. For now."

"You just want to tell everyone you knocked me up, don't you? Strut around campus with your big virile dick swinging?"

"Technically, it's my big virile balls."

"Gross."

"You love my balls."

"Shut up."

"You love me."

"Dammit, I really do."

He wrapped my hair around his fist and tugged until my face was tilted up toward him. Then, just like he'd claimed my body time and time again, Kingston Farrell laid claim to my lips like a fated mate should.

FORTY-THREE

I snickered as Sunday tugged on the neckline of the leather corset she was wearing as we approached Blackthorne Hall. We'd hopped the fence and no one seemed the wiser, but I couldn't ignore the flash of discomfort that had washed over Sunday's face as we breached the wards.

"You okay?"

"Leave it to Lilith to dress me up like a dominatrix," she huffed.

"She didn't have to provide us with any clothes. Then we'd be arriving back here like Adam and Eve leaving the Garden of Eden."

"You wouldn't be so cavalier about it if she handed you a pair of assless chaps or something." A smile twitched across her lips, there and then gone.

"Wouldn't I? Saddle up, darlin'."

She laughed then, warm and open and exactly what I needed to hear. "You have to stop shredding my clothes."

"Nope. Never gonna happen."

"Then you better be prepared to start replacing them, mate."

"A sexual incidental fund? I like the sound of that."

"Emergency sex fund. We'll make sure to label the account so we know exactly what it's for."

I wrapped my arm around her, tugging her into my side, inhaling her scent. How had I not noticed the difference in her before? The richness of the honey over the lilacs. The heady aroma making the changes in her body known.

"I love building a life with you. Including the mundane shit like special accounts to replace clothes and baking pies together."

"Pretty soon it'll include changing dirty diapers and sleepless nights."

That made my chest go tight and heavy all at the same time. "I can't fucking wait."

She shook her head, her nose adorably scrunched as she studied me.

"What?"

"I just can't believe how easily you slid right into the daddy role. It's kinda hot."

I waggled my eyebrows. "Oh? You got a daddy kink, Sunshine?"

Her cheeks went crimson. "No . . ."

I snaked my arm around her waist and nipped at her neck. "Liar."

Before I could do more than tease her, a scream tore through the night air.

"What the fuck was that?" I tensed, head snapping toward the sound.

"Someone messing around?"

"With all the attacks around here lately? Not fucking likely. Come on, let's get you inside."

But then chaos erupted all around us. Creatures shuffled out from the shadows like a small swarm of demonic insects, except infinitely larger and more terrifying.

My heart stopped. There was no way I could protect her on my own. Not in this form.

"Motherfucker," I whispered. "Get behind me."

Every instinct I had alerted. I needed to guard my mate, my child. If anything happened to them, I'd burn it all down until hell itself was nothing but cold ashes. My wolf fought to free himself from the constraints of the magic blocking my shift.

The courtyard directly in front of Blackthorne Hall had once been a peaceful place where we'd gather. Not now. Students flooded the grass, makeshift weapons at the ready to defend their territory from the filth attacking us. But without our magic, we were no match for the hellspawn.

Cries rang out, and brave supernaturals lost the battle against the demons. Blood spread across the grass, turning the dark green blades black in the night as my classmates fell.

The swarm surged forward, focused on me and my mate. They were coming for her. But they'd have to go through me first.

"Stop them! They're going to kill the Alpha to get to her." That screamed order from Derek had me shoring up my energy, prepping myself for hand-to-hand combat with something I could never beat.

Glass shattered somewhere above us, and I looked up in time to see a figure hurtling down from the sky.

Sunday's hands tensed on my waist where she held onto me. "Noah!"

Thorne landed in a crouch, his vampiric agility more than a match for something as basic as gravity.

"What the hell kind of superhero shit was that, Noah Blackthorne?" Sunday screeched, smacking his arm with the flat of her hand.

"I felt your fear. I could hardly leave you to fend for yourselves, could I?" He smirked. "Besides, this is what being mated to a vampire can do for you."

I wasn't mated to the bastard, but I was glad for his sudden appearance. I could use the help protecting our girl. Now, where the fuck were the Viking and that priest?

A flash of red from above caught my eye, tearing my attention upward to the woman standing on the balcony of the headmistress' tower. Madame le Blanc was fucking terrifying as she stared down at the carnage. Her hair was a vibrant, flame red rather than the black it used to be. Even in the moonlight, I could see the color as the long locks blew in the wind. But it was her eyes, glowing with fire in the irises, that had my gut curling with dread.

Holy shit . . . is she controlling these monsters?

I didn't want to believe it, but there was something about her, waving her hands through the air like a conductor guiding an orchestra that had the hair lifting at the back of my neck. Her lips moved, but I couldn't make out the words.

The clock at the top of the tower struck midnight, its bells ominous as they rang out over us. And with it, a shockwave on the twelfth strike.

I could actually *see* the air coalesce and expand, moving with enough force to knock students and demons alike flat on their backs. Instinctively, I curled my body around Sunday's, Thorne doing the same. As the air washed over us, I felt the change. Magic surged through my veins, and it felt as though I could finally draw in a full breath after surviving off small pants.

My wolf was free.

She'd lifted the magic ban so we could fight. So we had a chance.

"Stay with Thorne. You won't be able to shift fully." I murmured the words into Sunday's ear, desperate for her to understand the seriousness of her situation. With her pregnancy, she'd be unable to do more than partially change until the baby was born. She was a sitting duck.

"I love you."

Then I released her, my back burning as a demon lashed across the skin with sharp claws. I turned on the creature, a feral growl ripping from my throat just before I shifted into my wolf and lunged.

FORTY-FOUR

SUNDAY

War wasn't pretty as a rule, but something about this scene called to me, holding me hostage while it forced me to watch with a grim sort of fascination. The epitome of not being able to look away from a train wreck. Except the train was my friends, and there was nothing I could do to stop it from happening.

I hated standing on the sidelines, forced to watch them fight for their lives. I itched to join them, but without my wolf I would only be in the way. So I stayed back, an unwilling sentinel to the chaos.

Something no one ever tells you is that battle has a scent—but not one anyone would ever want to wear. It's ugly and powerful, darkness blended with the righteous will to survive. The air around me, heavy with magic and rage, held the sharp bite of ozone, tinged with the coppery taste of blood. All mixed with the rancid stench of sulfur. What could have been mistaken for nature's blend of brutality was corrupted by the unmistakable taint of demonic energy. It covered everything in an oily sheen of evil thick enough I felt it crawling up my throat.

What had started out as a surprise attack quickly turned into an all-out battle. Everywhere I looked, I saw someone I recognized engaged with one of the foul creatures.

My pulse raced, an electric current of anxiety in my veins at the sight of Moira as she hurled a ball of blue flame straight into the chest of an advancing demon. The creature faltered, then exploded into nothing more than ashes. Moira caught my eye and smirked as she mimed dusting off her hands but quickly armed herself once more as another came at her.

"No, dove, you can't go to her. Don't even think about it," Noah warned, his large frame blocking my path.

"I can't just stand here and do nothing."

Kingston, still in his wolf form, pounced on a demon who had just torn the arm off one of our classmates. His jaw locked on the beast's throat, and he tore the flesh with vicious shakes of his head until the demon went limp. My mate was brutal, fierce, and beautifully terrifying. I ached to join him.

"Why did Kingston say you can't shift?" Noah turned to face me and stared into my eyes.

"I . . ." But before I could answer him, pain sliced his features, a soft grunt leaving him. "Noah?"

He staggered forward, pushing me into the unfamiliar arms of somebody behind me.

"Take her. Guard her with your life," Noah ordered, his face twisting into a mask of rage as his fangs snapped down.

"No! Noah—"

"Stop fighting and come with me if you want to live."

I ceased my squirming, tilting my head back to look up into Chad's face. Of all the people for Noah to hand me off to, he had to pick the Lord of the Douches? But there wasn't time for a lengthy debate, and despite my personal dislike of the guy, he was Kingston's second-in-command.

"Fine."

Chad grasped my elbow and wrenched me hard until I followed without protest. While we seemed to have a focused path, he wasn't rushing. Why weren't we running from the scary demons?

"Where are you taking me?"

"Shut up. Do you want them to follow us?" His voice held a note of pure annoyance, the twang of his southern accent coming through. Louisiana maybe? Who cared? The guy was a dick. I really hoped Kingston demoted him. Derek would have been my choice for next in line.

"No." I shrank into myself at his harsh chastisement. My emotions were still all over the place after the day's revelations, and I didn't have it in me to snap back with my usual biting retort.

"Good girl. I didn't want to have to punish you before we got to the good part." A chill ran down my spine. "Although from what I've heard, you like that."

I tried to yank my arm out of his hold, not wanting to be with this asshole any longer. "Not with you."

"Oh, come on, Sunday. I just saved you from a horde of demons. The least you can do is show a little gratitude. We'll find a nice quiet spot while the fight winds down and you can . . . show me what your mouth feels like."

I finally seemed to have found my inner badass because this time, the words came easy. "The only way you'll get my mouth on you is if I'm biting out your throat, jackass."

"Oh, she's feisty. I like it." He jerked me down a darkened path into the woods. "Keep walking, or I'll have to carry you. I don't want anyone to see us until I get what I deserve."

"Come a little closer, Chad, baby. I'll give you exactly what you deserve." My words were all growl, filled with the beast whose form was denied to me because of the child growing in my womb. Somehow, I didn't think that was going to be a problem. I wanted to tear this guy apart with my bare hands. He was giving me a serious case of the creeps.

We reached a small clearing, and my gut churned as the circle burned into the earth came into focus. In the center, an altar with an athame rested across the stone.

"Chad? What is this?" I hated the wobble in my voice.

He shoved me into the circle with a dark chuckle.

I fell down hard, not prepared for the attack. If Alek could see me right now, he'd be so fucking disappointed. I pushed myself up, but Chad was right there, picking up my wrist with one hand and grasping the sacrificial dagger in the other. He cut a burning path through the fleshy part of my palm, spilling blood everywhere.

"Hmm, not enough," he muttered before wrenching my arm out to the side and sinking the blade into the tender skin of my bicep, tearing through muscle and destroying the inked runes marking me as Alek's.

Then he flung my hand down as I cried out in pain, tipped the dagger so it pointed down as a stream of ruby drops splashed onto the outer rim of his circle. The walls went up instantly. I could see them, just a thin faint sheen of red preventing me from leaving.

"What are you doing?" I screamed.

"Come on, Sunday. I thought you were smarter than that. Don't go and play stupid on me now. I don't have time to explain. My demons are on their way with your mate."

"Your demons? You're the one behind this? But how could you summon them while there was the magic ban?"

"Why do you think we're all the way out here? It took me a while to find a weakness in the wards, but it was there. And I was . . . motivated."

"Why? It doesn't make sense. Do you really hate me that much?"

He snorted. "Of course you'd assume this is about you."

"It's not much of an assumption when women who looked like me kept showing up dead, and the demons always seemed to target me."

"Not you. Kingston. That fucking sorry ass excuse for an Alpha. The most powerful pack in America is going to be led by a goddamned cuckold? I don't think so."

And then it clicked. He was trying to take out his competition. He wanted to take Kingston's spot.

"You ungrateful piece of shit," I growled.

"Yeah, well, you're a stupid bitch. Like I give a fuck what you think. I can't wait for the big finale. I'm going to make him watch as I kill you. Oh, but maybe I'll fuck you first and then slit that pretty throat of yours while I fill you with my seed. It probably won't bother him. He's used to sloppy seconds."

I gagged at the thought of him anywhere near me. But he continued, and the words he uttered sent lightning surging through my veins, filling me with an unholy fury. I'd never felt a soul-deep need to kill before, but the thought of Chad harming a single hair on Kingston's head had me ready to tear him apart limb from limb.

"Then I'm going to tear out his heart and eat it before claiming my rightful place as Alpha."

"Tor is concerned about you." My mother's voice was calm and measured, but I knew her. She wasn't happy.

"Tor believes it's his gods-given right to worry."

Usually my dry insults made her laugh. Not today. "Quinn's report has everyone worried, including me."

I stared at her in the mirror, catching glimpses of Aunt Quinn as she paced in the background, the familiar walls of our family home making me long for the quiet peace of Novasgard.

"We've been over this. I'm not leaving her. Where would you be if Father took off at the first hint of danger? We don't leave when things get rocky. We protect. It's in our blood, Móðir."

"It's *my* job to protect *you*."

"I don't require protecting."

"You might be six-plus feet of Novasgardian ego, but you're still my baby. I will always protect you. I may be retired, but I can still kill a man with my bare hands."

"And I can kill *every* man using only my words. Don't forget who raised you, Tiny."

I flinched at Aunt Quinn's use of my nickname. The woman had called me that from the day I was born, simply because I'd been a few ounces lighter than my brother. She never let me forget it.

"Maybe it's time you trust in the man you helped raise and stop doubting my ability—"

I cut myself off as the scent of rotten eggs cut through the clean pine smell of the forest.

"Aleksandr."

Something was amiss. The air felt . . . wrong. I closed my eyes and searched for Sunday's presence. It was a sensation I felt constantly, just a little tickle in my heart where she'd stolen a piece without even knowing.

Instead of the soothing warmth I associated with my Sunny, there was a frantic tingling like the anxious buzz of bees or the angry hiss of a serpent.

"I have to go."

My mother's face went pale at whatever she saw in my eyes, but I snapped the mirror closed and was running before she could give voice to any more protests. Sunday needed me. I would not fail her.

I ran through the brush without care for whether there was a path or not. The quickest way to get from point a to point b was a straight fucking line. I moved so fast I was barely aware of the forest around me. A massive tree loomed straight in my path, but with my current speed, there wasn't a chance to dodge it, so I simply shoved it down, felling the ancient pine with what seemed like barely any effort at all.

Every cell in my body felt charged. Adrenaline coiled in my gut, swelling with each step that brought me closer to my mate. My skin was too tight, stretching taut over muscles that trembled with unreleased energy.

"What are you doing?" Sunday's voice hit me in the chest, her scream ratcheting up my fury.

"Come on, Sunday. I thought you were smarter than that. Don't go and play stupid on me now. I don't have time to explain."

Who the hell was this sonofabitch, and what was he doing to my mate? As the bastard continued with his speech, I placed the voice, and my understanding of the world around me fractured. All I knew as the filth before me came into view threatening to rape my woman was white-hot, blinding rage.

As he continued to spew his foul words, I rushed forward, my body acting before my mind could register what it intended to do. I stepped around him, grabbing him by the throat and lifting him until his beady eyes were level with my own.

"You. Hurt. Her," I growled, not recognizing the voice that escaped my throat.

"Alek!" Sunday's panic-laced voice cut through the night, but I couldn't look at her. The glimpse of her splayed on the ground, blood pouring from a wound bearing my name, was already more than I could comprehend.

Chad drew his nails down my hand, but the scratches only fueled my need for vengeance. His skin turned a mottled purple as he gasped and gurgled in my hold, but it wasn't enough. I needed to inflict greater pain. I needed to make it hurt.

With a roar that continued to vibrate in my chest long after the sound shot through the night, I swung his bulk down toward the ground, smiling in primal satisfaction at the crack of bones breaking.

Chad screamed, his twisted body still twitching as he called on his gift to try and heal himself. I crouched down, putting my lips beside his ear. "It's too bad I can only do this once."

The musky scent of urine perfumed the air, making me laugh with unnatural glee.

"No. Please."

The sound of his begging only made me more eager for the kill. I needed it. My veins were screaming for it.

Staring him straight in the eye, I lifted my foot and brought it straight down on his face. Again. And again. And again.

Until Chad was nothing more than a smear on the forest floor. An offering for the woodland creatures he'd preyed on in his other form.

My chest rose and fell in an attempt to draw air into my lungs. A small whimper from my left had me spinning back toward Sunday. The barrier around her had collapsed, but she was still bleeding heavily.

The sight of her blood sent something primal screaming through me. A beast rattling the cage of my bones and begging to be unleashed.

"Alek, you . . . your eyes." She looked at me with a mixture of fear and intrigue as she stood.

Footsteps crashed through the trail behind me, the sound harsh in ears far more sensitive than they should be.

A feral growl filled the air, but from the labored breathing accompanying it, I knew something wasn't right. I shoved her behind me, protecting her with my body.

Five demons broke through the trees, black blood streaking their skin, the one in the back dragging a bound wolf behind him.

"No!" Sunday cried out, and her distress only added to the rage pumping through my veins.

Destroy.

Once again, my body acted purely on instinct. I grasped the arm of the closest demon, and when the burn of its tainted blood met my skin, I knew nothing but violence. It was my birthright. My destiny. My reason for being.

Sunday's scream echoed in my ears, calling me back from the bloodlust that had taken over. I held a man by the throat, just as I had done with the other shifter who'd tried to hurt her. Around us lay dismembered demon parts, crushed and torn, unrecognizable. The man in my grip gasped for air, kicking at me all while Sunday begged me to release him.

"Please, Alek. Let him go. Kingston won't hurt me. I'm safe now."

I blinked, a shudder racing down my spine as some semblance of rationality came crashing back.

I dropped Kingston, staggering away from him.

What had I done?

Sunday came to my side, her small palm resting on my shoulder, but I flinched away, unsure if I'd lose control again. "Take her," I growled at Kingston. "She's not safe. There could be more of them."

As Kingston wrapped an arm around Sunday's waist and pulled her trembling body against his, the air beside me began to shimmer and shift. I recognized the effect instantly. They were coming for me.

Before my mind could give name to the magic, a portal stretched open. Two familiar faces peered out at me. One apologetic. One brutally determined.

My uncle . . . and my father.

The Warrior of Odin was here for his mischievous son.

Fuck.

CHAPTER
FORTY-SIX

CALEB

The uneven stone floor cut into the bare skin of my knees as I knelt in front of the cross in my purification room. I hadn't even started, and already my weakness was getting the better of me.

Usually the ritual of entering this chamber was enough to quiet my mind so I could focus on my punishment, but not tonight. Tonight my thoughts raced with Sunday. Whether that was because I'd been negligent in my absolution or because of what I'd just learned, I wasn't sure. Only that it was true. This time, punishment wasn't a choice. It was a requirement. I *needed* to purge the sin from my veins.

"Pregnant," I whispered. "You fool of a sinner. How could you do this to her?"

As a man, I knew better than to be so stupid. I was supposed to take measures to ensure my woman was cared for. Protected in all things. Yet when it mattered most, I'd managed to forget the most basic way of doing it . . .

But she wasn't my woman. She couldn't be. Somehow, my heart and mind were at odds. I'd succumbed to the moment and lost myself. Lost hold of the convictions and vows that made me who I was—who I thought I was destined to be.

A small voice in the back of my mind offered up a tiny piece of hope. *What if your destiny is not what you thought? What if she is your destiny?*

I snuffed it out before it could catch fire within me. I couldn't afford to entertain the idea even for a second. I'd seen countless priests fall in love, leave the priesthood, marry and go on to live their days out with the woman they found. But I wasn't a priest any longer. I hadn't been for decades. The simple truth was, I wasn't even a man. I was a monster. One of the damned. I didn't deserve her. But even still, I'd managed to taint her with my seed. Leave my abomination growing inside her.

Even now, just the memory of her heat around the crown of my cock, milking me, begging me to sink deeper, had that familiar ache building between my legs.

"No," I snarled, flicking my hand and sending the weighted ends—silver-tipped this time—of the flogger flying into my back. I hissed in pain, the burn offering no edge of pleasure.

Over and over, I rained lashes across my skin until blood ran between the grooves of the stones in the floor and the only scent in the room was my shame.

I was ruthless, striking not only my back and shoulders but my thighs and calves as well, going far longer than usual until I couldn't maintain my grip on the blood-slick leather handle. It fell to the ground as I drew in ragged breath after ragged breath. Unfortunately, my mind was nowhere near closer to calm or repentant. Her lips, plump and parted, flashed across my vision every time I closed my eyes. The wanton sound of her voice calling out my name rang out in my ears, the melody of a favorite song. Lilacs, freshly picked and dipped in rich honey, filled my nose, overtaking the tang of my own blood.

I was consumed by her, the method of my destruction, the beautiful instrument of damnation, the sin I couldn't help but commit.

And now . . . the mother of my unborn child.

I pushed myself to my feet, leaving my flogger forgotten in the rapidly cooling pool of my blood. I stumbled over to the stool by the base of the stairs, moaning as I slid my trousers over my ravaged skin.

I should leave Ravenscroft. For my own sanity. For her safety. For my soul. But now, there was more at stake. They couldn't find out about the babe. Not until I knew more. I needed to talk to the Seer, find out if she had any information about what this meant for the prophecy.

As soon as the intention crystallized, a now all-too-familiar burn seared into my chest, ringing out a cry from my lips as I fell to my knees on the staircase I'd been limping up.

No.

No. No. No. No. No.

Four. Four fecking seals were open while I'd done nothing to stop them. That was more than half, and they were breaking faster with each one.

A scream of pure rage tore from my throat as I got to my feet and headed for the cool night outside in search of the only person who could've opened another seal.

Ignoring the pain surging through my body and the agony tearing through me with each step, I raced off into the night. It was as if my heart knew exactly where to find her because I ran without thought, not slowing or stopping my steps until I approached the clearing. The heart hammering in my chest was an unsettling sensation, but the feel of it grew stronger the closer I drew to her.

"Alek!" Her cry of the Viking's name had me moving faster, breaking through the treeline and stepping into utter carnage.

It only took a quick scan to put together what was happening. Alek's eyes were bottomless pits of black, his already massive form rippling with the infused strength of his heritage. But even if I hadn't recognized it, the pile of desecrated bodies scattered at his feet was testament to the truth.

Berserker.

It should have been an impossibility. The legendary warriors had died out. His existence could only mean one thing.

He was the fourth seal.

A blond man who matched Alek in stature stepped out of a portal, the same flickers of lightning flashing in his own inky gaze.

"Aleksandr." His rich, accented voice held pure authority and heartache as he uttered the name.

"Faðir? I don't know what's happening to me."

Quiet fury rolled off the man I'd only heard about in rumor. Nord. The last of the original berserkers. Odin's chosen warrior. Alek's father.

Despite the pulse of his anger, his voice was a controlled storm as he answered, "I never wanted this burden for you."

"Who are you?" Sunday asked, her words thin and shaky.

Nord's gaze slid to her, his expression a careful mask of control. The instant his focus landed on Sunday, Alek began to shake, his body seeming to swell and ripple as a deep snarl of warning left his lips and eyes that had started to fade from black bled dark once more.

"No." Nord uttered the one word with such command the world around us fell silent.

He stared at his son, his gaze narrowing just slightly as thick chains wound around his wrists like coils of a snake before solidifying into two heavy shackles. But still he struggled against the hold on him, as though his monster couldn't relinquish control.

"You would hobble your own son?" Alek's rasp was filled with venom.

"There's nothing I wouldn't do to save you."

That one statement took all the fight out of Alek. He dropped to his knees, his head bowed in what appeared to be shame.

"What are you doing to him?" Sunday screamed, attempting to run to Alek, but held in place by a bloodied and bruised Kingston.

"What I must."

"It's okay, Sunny."

"No, he's hurting you." Tears shone in Sunday's eyes.

"He's protecting you because I cannot."

"But you can. You just did. I just watched you destroy five fucking demons in less than two minutes."

"Sunny . . . the berserker can't be trusted. I looked at Kingston and saw only a monster. In that moment, he was nothing more than a rival, a threat. What if it had been you? What if I hadn't stopped?"

"No, you were just trying to protect me."

"And I'd do it all over again. But if you knew the stories I'd been told. The people caught in the crossfire of an untrained berserker . . ." His voice broke, and he flicked his gaze to his father.

Nord strode forward, the rings on each of his fingers catching the light as he placed his hand on top of his son's head. "So you understand what needs to happen? *Why* it needs to happen?"

"Yes, Faðir."

"Then stand and come with me. It is not safe for you here now."

"What? No. NO! Alek!"

Sunday thrashed in Kingston's hold, narrowly breaking free, but not in time to stop what was happening. I caught her in my arms, keeping her from doing something she couldn't take back. She'd be killed on sight if she went through that portal uninvited.

"You can't, Sunday. I'll not allow it."

"I hate you," she spat at me, her words harsh but deserved.

I clenched my jaw and tightened the hold I had on her, not letting her see how deeply those three words cut me.

As he got to his feet, Alek turned his head and leveled Sunday with a tortured glance. "I love you, Sunny." His eyes locked on mine. "Take care of her."

And then he was gone. Vanished through a portal as if he'd never been there at all.

Sunday became a wild thing in my arms. A tempest bound in flesh.

"*A stor*, you need to calm down."

"No, you just let them take him."

She twisted, slapping me as she broke my hold with a strength she shouldn't possess. When she stepped back, chest heaving and hands balled into fists, I caught the bottomless black of her gaze and the warning flicker of lightning.

My stomach bottomed out at what it meant.

She was changed. No longer a shifter without her wolf, but something more. Something *other*. It was clear in that moment. This was the danger the Seer had warned us of. Sunday was so much more than my temptation.

She was the woman whose destiny was tied to my eternal soul's freedom.

The woman I was sworn to sacrifice if all the seals were opened.

The woman I could never let go.

Sunday Fallon.

Harbinger of the Apocalypse.

~

To be continued in Possession . . .
keep on reading for a sneak peek!

SNEAK PEEK

POSSESSION: CHAPTER 1
ALEK

Two months ago

K *ærasta.*

I still couldn't believe that word left my lips. Sunday wasn't my mate. I didn't have one. Fated mates were rare and precious. The fact that my parents found each other was the stuff of fairy tales. The odds of lightning striking twice for my family were less than zero. But here I was, uttering an endearment I'd never been called to speak before.

At least she had no idea what it meant.

The fuck of it all was I wasn't even supposed to be here. Tor had been slated for the mission. As the twin with a perpetual hard-on for following the rules and proving himself, he'd been the clear choice for this military assignment. Which made it even more surprising when Cora, the Satori matriarch blessed with glimpses of the future, told me I needed to be the one to go.

We'd learned early on never to question one of her *feelings*. So there'd never been any doubt I'd take her advice. Even though I didn't have any interest in this kind of responsibility.

Every few months, a Novasgardian would be sent to Earth for a full trip around the sun to learn and report back on any magical or technical advancements. We never wanted to be caught unawares when it came to growing powers in the supernatural world. Not after the casualties Novasgard sustained in the battle against a foe who'd been left to his own devices for far too long. These last twenty-five years we've been much more involved, increasing our visits to Earth, refusing to ever let another enemy rise to such heights.

I only had to make this work for one year. Gathering intel on the future leaders of the supernatural Families at Ravenscroft shouldn't have been hard. They were ripe for the picking, all full of misplaced pride and puffed up like peacocks showing off for their future mates. Easily distracted, ready to boast about their power. I'd have them filling my book with intel before my time here was half over.

But then *she* happened and everything stopped.

Gods, if she was my mate, how the hell was I supposed to leave her?

My limbs vibrated with an unfamiliar sensation. Was this . . . panic? My breaths were strident and labored, as though I'd gone twelve rounds with a wyvern and it was winning.

Kærasta.

The word echoed in my mind again. *Mate. Beloved. Destined.*

Fuck.

Hands shaking, I pulled the spelled mirror out of my pocket and ran the tip of my finger over the runes etched into its frame. They lit up as my skin passed over them, the magic sparking to life once all ten of them were activated.

My mother's concerned face appeared within seconds. "Alek? I didn't expect to talk to you today. What's wrong?"

"How did you and father know you were mates?"

She blinked. "*That's* why you called?" Relieved laughter escaped her, and she ran a hand through her hair. The slight quiver of her fingers betrayed her own nerves. I'd worried her by calling out of the blue.

"I'm sorry, Móðir. I . . . I didn't know what else to do."

Her frown returned and she peered out at me, eyes searching. "You never need to apologize for calling me. What's got you worried about mates?" Then her eyes lit up, excited by the possibility. "Have you met someone?"

Swallowing through a throat tight with nerves, I tried to put my thoughts together into some form of coherence. But I also didn't want to give her false hope that I'd bring home a daughter-in-law either.

"I'm just curious . . ."

She raised a brow, not buying my bullshit anymore now than she had when I'd been little. "Curious. About how to know when someone is your mate. Well, for your father and I, we knew immediately. Not that it was easy. Recognizing you've found your mate is only the first step. Earning your place beside them is something else entirely."

"So there was no doubt?"

"No. Our eyes met, and something in our souls shouted 'mine.' But it took us a while to get from there to where we are now. For Odin's sake, he wouldn't even be tempted when I walked out in only a—"

I held up a hand. "Okay, that's enough detail. I don't need to know more about . . . that."

"The point is, once we found each other, even before we came together, we couldn't be parted."

"What would have happened if you were?"

She laughed, long and loud, wiping a tear from her eye when she finally caught her breath. "That's funny. You've seen your father in the midst of one of his rages. Do you think he would have allowed that to happen? I mean, not even death kept us apart." Her eyes got dreamy and she bit her lip. "One could argue death is what brought us together. How else do you explain a ghost being brought back to life after decades only to find their soulmate?"

"Sounds like destiny."

"Exactly. And I learned to never fuck with fate. Trust me. Besides, if you found your mate, why would you *want* to be parted? True mates are a rare and wonderful gift."

Knowing I was getting dangerously close to spilling a secret I wasn't ready to share, I asked, "What if fate deigns to give someone more than one mate?"

She was quiet for a second, and my heart beat frantically as I waited—with no little dread—for her answer. "I've never seen it, but your father once explained to me his ancestors' belief about the soul. How it can split into many parts only to come back later. Perhaps twin flames are not the only kind. Fire spreads and burns. Why couldn't a soul have more than one mate?"

Is that what I am? A missing part of her soul? Are all of us? What are the odds Sunday would find her mates at the same time in the same place? What does fate have in store for her that requires more than one?

"Alek? You've gone quiet, minn son."

I shook my head to clear the troubled musings. This

was more than I bargained for. "It's a path I hadn't considered."

"We are rarely prepared when fate comes calling. All we can do is adapt. Just look at your father. He threw every plan he had aside the second his soul recognized mine. And when our bond was threatened, he fought a seemingly unwinnable battle to save it. One does not walk away from the promise of true love, Alek. Rather, we do anything in our power to keep it. Remember that, perhaps it will lighten those heavy thoughts of yours."

I didn't know how to respond. Instead of telling me I was making a mistake, she'd only reaffirmed my instinct. Sunday was my mate. She was the other half of my soul, and I was one of the missing pieces to hers.

And now that I've found her, how am I supposed to walk away when my time in this world is up?

If my mother was right and this *is* fate, then the answer is I won't.

Not by choice.

∾

Don't miss a second this super spicy paranormal reverse harem Pre-order your copy of Possession now!

Also by Meg Anne

Brotherhood of the Guardians/Novasgard Vikings

Undercover Magic *(Nord & Lina)*

A Sexy & Suspenseful Fated Mates PNR

Hint of Danger

Face of Danger

World of Danger

Promise of Danger

Call of Danger

Bound by Danger (Quinn & Finley)

The Mate Games

A Spicy Paranormal Reverse Harem

Co-Written with K. Loraine

Obsession

Rejection

Possession

Temptation

The Chosen Universe

The Chosen Series: The Complete Series

A Fated Mates High Fantasy Romance

Mother Of Shadows

Reign Of Ash

Crown Of Embers

Queen Of Light

The Chosen Boxset #1

The Chosen Boxset #2

The Keepers: The Complete Series

A Guardian/Ward High Fantasy Romance

The Dreamer (A Keeper's Prequel)

The Keepers Legacy

The Keepers Retribution

The Keepers Vow

The Keepers Boxset

Gypsy's Curse: The Complete Trilogy

A Psychic/Detective Star-Crossed Lovers UF Romance

Visions Of Death

Visions Of Vengeance

Visions Of Triumph

The Gypsy's Curse: The Complete Collection

THE GRIMM BROTHERHOOD: THE COMPLETE TRILOGY

A SEXY & HUMOROUS URBAN FANTASY ROMANCE

CO-WRITTEN WITH KEL CARPENTER

REAPERS BLOOD

REAPING HAVOC

REAPER REBORN

THE GRIMM BROTHERHOOD: THE COMPLETE COLLECTION

Also by K. Loraine

REVERSE HAREM STANDALONES

Their Vampire Princess (A Reverse Harem Romance).

All the Queen's Men (A Fae Reverse Harem Romance).

∼

THE MATE GAMES

(CO-WRITTEN WITH MEG ANNE)

Obsession.

Rejection

Possession

Temptation

ABOUT MEG ANNE

USA Today and international bestselling paranormal and fantasy romance author Meg Anne has always had stories running on a loop in her head. They started off as daydreams about how the evil queen (aka Mom) had her slaving away doing chores, and more recently shifted into creating backgrounds about the people stuck beside her during rush hour. The stories have always been there; they were just waiting for her to tell them.

Like any true SoCal native, Meg enjoys staying inside curled up with a good book and her cat, Henry . . . or maybe that's just her. You can convince Meg to buy just about anything if it's covered in glitter or rhinestones, or make her laugh by sharing your favorite bad joke. She also accepts bribes in the form of baked goods and Mexican food.

Meg is best known for her leading men #MenbyMeg, her inevitable cliffhangers, and making her readers laugh out loud, all of which started with the bestselling Chosen series.

ABOUT K. LORAINE

Kim writes steamy contemporary and sexy paranormal romance. **You'll find her paranormal romances written under the name K. Loraine and her contemporaries as Kim Loraine.** Don't worry, you'll get the same level of swoon-worthy heroes, sassy heroines, and an eventual HEA.

When not writing, she's busy herding cats (raising kids), trying to keep her house sort of clean, and dreaming up ways for fictional couples to meet.

Made in the USA
Monee, IL
20 November 2024

70664736R00280